THE HEAVENLY THRONE

The Lord of War

Yuri Ajin

Lit Orange

Copyright © 2023 Yuri Ajin

All rights reserved

The characters and events portrayed in this book are fictitious. Any similarity to real persons, living or dead, is coincidental and not intended by the author.

No part of this book may be reproduced, or stored in a retrieval system, or transmitted in any form or by any means, electronic, mechanical, photocopying, recording, or otherwise, without express written permission of the publisher.

Introduced by Lit Orange
Translated by Nevena Markovich
Edited by Sanja Gajin
Edited by Teodora Pecarski

The Heavenly Throne 11

The Lord of War

Kai's memory has returned, Acilla has been saved, and he has finally been reunited with his friends, allowing him to once again focus on his main goal — leaving the Trial Worlds and returning to his sister. But this will not be as easy as it seemed at first.

The turbulent events have led Insulaii, Ferox, and Bellum to collapse. Old conflicts flared up with renewed vigor, prompting forgotten Masters to emerge from the shadows and begin their final game.

The stakes are sky-high, and a global re-division of all three worlds is just around the corner. The chaos will not bypass Kai and the Eternal Path Temple. And it depends only on them whether they will survive this storm and make history, or whether they will end up in the dust, like many others before them.

Will they be able to survive in a cruel world ruled by strength and skill?

In the world of cultivation, where there are always new heights to reach?

The Path Of Cultivation
A BRIEF GUIDE

Energy

Energy, both *prana* and *ki*, is a special spiritual substance that allows sentient beings to influence and shape reality through weaving techniques. Energy that isn't bound to matter or compressed into crystals is called free energy.

Energy exists inside all living beings, but only those with an awakened warrior layer of the soul or its equivalent can manipulate it.

Energy enters the Ecumene from somewhere beyond its borders, flowing in the form of ley lines. There are millions of them, and they all converge into the Central World. This leaves the Peripheral Worlds with little energy, and the Middle ones with a moderate amount.

When the amount of energy increases, then its particles begin to merge, gaining density. When the amount decreases, the reverse process occurs, and large particles are divided into smaller ones, losing density.

The Will of the Universe

The Will of the Universe permeates all matter, yielding only to that which is subject to someone's *Spark*. The frequency of the Will of the Universe is considered neutral. Only this frequency is capable of attracting *Sparks* from the World of the Dead, which is why the Shadows and Artificial Spirits, whose will comes from a *Spark* that has already left the universe, don't have it.

The presence of the Will of the Universe creates resistance when cultivators try to influence their environment and assert their own *Will*. And since the main carrier of the Will of the Universe is energy, the higher its density, the stronger the Will of the Universe is and the more resistance it can provide. The degree of resistance depends on the degree of influence of external *Will*. In other words, the more power the cultivator uses, the stronger the Will of the Universe resists. This is the reason why the same techniques can have different outcomes on different planets.

Soul

The soul is the fundamental part of any living being. Usually located in the abdominal region, it consists of three main parts: the *Spark*, the soul energy, and the *Soul Shell*.

Souls are formed when a sufficient amount of the Will of the Universe accumulates in one place.

Most often, this happens during the development of the mind, which stimulates the development of the *Will*. Normally, this occurs before the soul forms, so the *Will* vibrates with the neutral frequency of the Will of the Universe.

In rarer instances, an Elemental Spirit is formed due to the accumulation of *Force* particles of a certain element. All the power of the Will of the Universe collected inside them combines to form a developed soul. Such a quantity of the Will of the Universe in one place makes this type of soul stronger than usual. That is why Spirits are born no weaker than the *Exorcist Stage*.

Spark

The *Spark* is the core of any soul. It is an eternal and indestructible object with its own *Will* and empty consciousness (an observer without thoughts, emotions, and memories). It represents the inner "self" of the being, while everything else is just a superstructure over it.

The *Will of the Spark* is an invisible force capable of subjugating and controlling reality.

Unlike other components of the soul, the *Spark* is brought into this reality by the Will of the Universe from the World of the Dead. Once this happens, the frequency of the vessel's *Will* becomes unique. From that moment on, the *Spark* remains in the center of the soul, until the connection between them is severed. That is, until the vessel dies.

The development of the *Spark* is called its evolution, which occurs during key breakthroughs and greatly enhances its *Will*, making it stronger.

When the vessel dies, the *Spark* returns to the World of the Dead, where its cleansed before being sent to reincarnate.

This also applies to Spirits. Even though their souls are born powerful, they remain at the first stage of their evolution. This occurs because the accumulation of particles attracts not one *Spark*, but a multitude of them. Fighting for dominance among themselves, they exert pressure on each other and evolve. The first one to achieve the level of evolution equal to the power of the *Soul Shell* gains the right to inhibit it.

Although the power of the *Will of the Spark* grows as it

develops, it is impossible to control it without understanding its workings. However, there are workarounds. Mainly with the help of the inner instruments of the *Soul Shell* responsible for controlling energy, creating *Force* particles, soul techniques, and so on. Strengthening the *Spark* directly enhances these abilities.

The other way is through *Will* abilities granted by the *System*:

• *Master's Will* — the primary ability to control the *Will*, available to all True Masters. It allows the cultivator to use telekinesis and manipulate minds;

• *Field of Superiority* — expands the telekinetic and mind controlling aspects of the *Master's Will* within a limited area around the cultivator;

• *Desolation of the Weak* — allows the cultivator to draw and steal energy from a being with a weaker *Will*;

• *Complete Submission* — allows the cultivator to move and manipulate objects to increase their defense and strength, modify their bodies, and enhance their weapons and techniques, forcing the atoms of their body to remain in place even when they are under great force. Greater level of mastery allows them to influence other people's techniques and dispel them;

• *Look of the Lord* — one of the rarest *Will* abilities. It greatly enhances the subjugating aspect of the *Master's Will*; and

• *Elemental Will* — the general name for the class of the rarest *Will* abilities. It allows the cultivator to use the elements without energy, *Force* particles, and techniques. By itself, this ability is weaker than other techniques, but it can greatly amplify and improve them.

There are also Advanced versions of these abilities,

which are more powerful and versatile.

The highest level of *Will* control is the *Divine Will*. This is not a *System* ability, but a *Divine* one, available to those who have reached divinity. It allows the cultivator to directly influence reality by reading and rewriting its informational component.

Soul Energy

The soul energy is the soul's primary resource, by default spent on the functioning of the *Soul Shell*. It can also be consciously utilized through techniques that extract it from the soul to strengthen techniques (no more than one-fourth of the general supply per day). A lack of soul energy can lead to death, since one's life span also depends on it.

Spent soul energy can be replenished in three ways: with divine power, *Soul Spirit Fruits*, and the introduction of artificial soul energy, a combination of *Yin* and *Yang*, into the *Spark*. This only applies to that amount of energy taken from the general pool. The volume of one's reserve cannot be expanded beyond its original size by any means other than reaching a new level of development.

The *Soul Shell*

The sphere surrounding the soul that performs all the functions associated with spirit abilities.

It consists of three layers:

• Mental — located closest to the *Spark*, it's responsible for all intellectual abilities. Initially, this layer functions in parallel with the brain, or any of its equivalents, but as it develops, it begins to prevail over the "flesh";

• Emotional — responsible for emotions, as well as the connection of the mental and warrior layers, it is necessary for using *Forces*, which cannot be grasped by an ordinary mind; and

- Warrior — the outer part of the *Soul Shell*, it is responsible for all the basic abilities: *ki* and aura manipulation, control and creation of *Force* particles, spirit perception, and intuition. In the vast majority of cases, this layer is inactive, and must be activated before embarking on the path of development.

The quality and potential of the *Soul Shell* varies depending on origin and lineage. Breakthroughs in the first two stages of development don't influence the *Soul Shell* much. From the third, they do. The conditions for the breakthrough vary, but the initial ones for their initiation are always the same.

First, it is necessary to prepare the *Soul Shell* for the breakthrough. This process is called the "restoration of the soul" and it happens through the prolonged use of *Meditation Techniques* that saturate it with energy and are based on the cultivator's primary element. The faster a cultivator can do this, the better their soul will absorb energy and boost their development. After each breakthrough, the saturation level resets, and the process has to be restarted. With each new level and stage, it takes more and more time.

Secondly, the soul needs to be of certain quality. If its foundation is lacking, then the *Soul Shell* will not be able to reach its full potential, making further breakthroughs impossible.

And lastly, it is necessary to have a desire to become stronger. If the *Will* is not strong enough, then the breakthrough cannot be initiated.

Stages of development

Stages of soul and body development.

Mortal

Refers to all those beings who did not embark on the path of development.

The *Body Endurance Stage*

The first stage of development, the essence of which is the gradual strengthening (tempering) of parts of the physical body. This is often done by inhaling energy (*Breath of Power*), which is then absorbed into the flesh. The larger and stronger the body, the more energy it can absorb.

The tempering process is divided into seven levels:

- *Lung Endurance*
- *Blood Vessel Endurance*
- *Heart Endurance*
- *Internal Organs Endurance*
- *Skin Endurance*
- *Bone Endurance*
- *Muscle Endurance*

Upon reaching the last level, the energy supply will increase, allowing for the preparation for the next stage of development.

The *Mind Endurance Stage*

The second stage of development, the essence of which is to strengthen the parts of the body associated with the central nervous system.

It is divided into three levels:

- *Sensory Organs Endurance*
- *Spinal Cord Endurance*

• *Brain Endurance*

Completing this stage increases the *ki* supply and enhances physical, cognitive, and emotional abilities, such as reaction speed, reflexes, memory, and so on.

The *Soul Endurance Stage*

The third stage of development, during which the cultivator is engaged in creating an internal energy system.

It is divided into three levels:

• *Opening of the Acupuncture Points*

To break through to this level, a cultivator needs to open at least 270 acupuncture points and 45 soul nodes out of the total 360 and 60 respectively. Each soul node equals 6 acupuncture points. There are also 120 hidden acupuncture points that do not have soul nodes. Opening 60 of them grants the *Soul Manifestation* feature (usually reserved for *Exorcists*), and another 60 grants *Complete Aura Concealment* (usually associated with *Elementalists*). After reaching this level, the cultivator gains a *Small Energy Cover*, which increases their parameters by 10% of the total *ki* supply, and the maximum life span increases to 150 years. This can also be achieved through alchemy.

• *Meridian Formation*

These are special spiritual channels connecting the acupuncture points to the soul nodes. The quality of the breakthrough depends on their thickness and length. The number of meridians depends on the number of previously discovered soul nodes. After reaching this level, the cultivator's maximum lifespan increases to 200 years.

• *Source Creation*

A special vessel is formed around the soul, to which

the meridians are attached. After that, the cultivator's energy system is considered complete. Now they can absorb/release energy through acupuncture points, conduct it along the meridians, and store it in the source. They no longer need the *Breath of Power*. The further supply of energy depends on the size of the source. After reaching this level, the cultivator's maximum lifespan increases to 250 years.

Exorcist

The fourth stage of development and the first stage of True Mastery. Those who reach this stage are considered True Masters.

The stage is divided into initial, middle, end, and peak levels.

- Initial (lifespan: 400 years)

- Middle (lifespan: 500 years)

- End (lifespan: 600 years)

- Peak (lifespan: 700 years)

To achieve this stage, the cultivator needs to overload their source and meridians with energy, destroying them, and then form an *Astral Body* from the fragments. This process requires a huge amount of energy, as well as several weeks of isolation to prepare the soul.

After creating the *Astral Body*, the cultivator needs to continue to strengthen it and maintain the energy vortex in the place where the source once was. When the *Astral Body* can no longer be improved, the cultivator can start preparing for the breakthrough to the next stage.

The breakthrough has three stages: *Cracks Creation*, *Shards Stage*, and the *Recovery Stage*.

The quality of the breakthrough is determined by the

quality of the created *Astral Body*.

If one of the stages fails, the cultivator dies. At best, they will remain disabled: they will lose most of their strength and their lifespan will be shortened.

A successful breakthrough results in the following:

1. The *Will* evolves into the *Master's Will*;

2. The first sixty hidden acupuncture points are opened and the cultivator acquires the Master *Soul Manifestation*;

3. The source is transformed into a complete *Astral Body* and the energy pool is increased;

4. The *Small Energy Cover* evolves into the *Medium Energy Cover*, which not only increases their parameters by 10% but provides a layer of invisible armor that can only be penetrated by energies of equal or greater density;

5. Oftentimes, the cultivator may fail to tame the raging energies, resulting in rapid de-aging. This not only changes the appearance but even slightly affects the physical capabilities of the cultivator, since a child's body does not have the same capabilities of an adult one;

6. The cultivator gains access to the inner soul world. Not everyone manages to unlock these gates, but those who do gain the ability to accelerate their progress; and

7. If the *Soul Manifestation* has already been acquired, then a breakthrough will increase it by 1 level.

The most common *Soul Manifestations* are:

• The ability to create parallel streams of consciousness

• Increased *ki* recovery rate

• Increased rate of *ki* release

- Easier control of *Particles*
- Simplified *ki* control
- Increased spirit stamina
- Increased spirit perception
- Better memory
- Better concentration
- Increased amount of soul energy released per day
- Increased soul stability

The rarer *Manifestations* are:

• *Perfect Soul* — increases spirit protection, heals soul injuries, restores soul energy, and allows *Soul Shell* exchange for short-term buffs. The drained *Shell* suffers no consequences, healed by the *Manifestation's* passive powers. Known owners: Kyle.

• *Supreme Simulation* — allows the cultivator to create realistic simulations within their soul world. Known owners: Kyle, Kai.

• *Forced Enlightenment* — allows the cultivator to accumulate various information and consciously trigger Enlightenment based on it. The vaster the knowledge and the more valuable the information, the higher the quality of the Enlightenment. Known owners: Kyle.

• *Spirit Memory* — bestows an almost perfect memory. Known owners: Kyle.

• *Ultimate Focus* — allows the cultivator to increase the level of concentration at will. Known owners: Kyle, Kai, Ryu Araki.

• *Cover Expansion* — allows the cultivator to temporarily strengthen and expand their *Cover* to form a barrier. The cultivator must stand still for the barrier to be maintained. Known owners: Kyle, Elea.

• *Everything and Now* — allows the cultivator to release the entire supply of available *ki* without any consequences. Known owners: Kyle, Ailenx.

• *Untamable Stream* — allows the cultivator to release any amount of soul energy. Known owners: Kyle, Rune'Tan.

• *Renewal* — allows the cultivator to restore their spirit endurance reserves. Known owners: Kyle.

• *Restoration* — allows the cultivator to restore their entire supply of energy. Known owners: Kyle.

• *Surveillance Zone* — enhances and expands the area of spirit perception. Known owners: Kyle.

• *Sudden Suppression* — allows the cultivator to emit their aura and immobilize anyone it touches, preventing them from using their spirit powers. Known owners: Kyle, an unnamed dorgan from Cloud Abode.

Typically, a cultivator can only have one *Soul Manifestation*, but Heavenly Miracles, the greatest geniuses of the Ecumene, along with the Divine Children, are able to acquire them all.

Elementalist

The fifth stage of development and the second stage of True Mastery. The goal of this stage is to create cores inside the *Astral Body* based on one's elements.

To reach this stage, the cultivator must complete *Core Appropriation*, *Separation of the Vortex*, *Core Compression*, and *Strengthening of the Astral Body*.

The quality of the breakthrough is based on the degree of compression of the elemental cores.

Upon becoming an *Elementalist*, the cultivator:

1. Opens another 60 hidden acupuncture points and gains *Complete Aura Concealment* if it has not already been achieved at the time of breaking through the *Opening of Acupuncture Points* level.

2. Uses an elemental *Meditation Technique* and forms the *Elemental Cores*. The cores are divided according to the elements and enhance abilities, with the central core being based on the cultivator's primary element.

3. Acquires a special ability, a core skill (only if their breakthrough was perfect).

4. Gains more energy.

The stage is divided into 4 levels:

• Initial (lifespan: 1,000 years)

• Middle (lifespan: 2,000 years)

• End (lifespan: 3,000 years)

• Peak (lifespan: 4,000 years)

Holy Lord

The sixth stage of development and the third stage of True Mastery. To reach this level, a cultivator needs to experience the *Holy Punishment of Heaven*, and then absorb the remnants of its power.

Holy Punishments of Heaven are divided into different versions. The vast majority of cultivators pass the weakest version, and only a few risk facing the overwhelming power of their full version.

Any peak-level *Elementalist* is capable of bringing down the *Holy Punishment of Heaven* on themselves, but this can only be done in the Distant, Middle, and Near Worlds.

The Peripheral ones do not have enough energy for this.

The quality of the breakthrough is determined by the amount of absorbed *Holy Punishments*, which depends on the amount of damage the cultivator has sustained. The less they suffered, the easier and more efficiently they will be able to absorb the remaining energy.

Failure during breakthrough results in certain death.

If the cultivator manages to withstand the *Holy Punishment*, then its power will flow into their body and soul, strengthening them and raising their level.

This will lead to:

1. A significant increase in the maximum energy reserve and physical parameters depending on the quality of the breakthrough (up to 500 units for a weak *Holy Punishment* and up to 2,000 for a full one);

2. Evolution of the *Average Energy Cover* into the *Full Energy Cover*, which increases their physical parameters by 15-20% of the total *ki* supply (depending on the quality of the breakthrough); and

3. *Soul Manifestations* gaining another level.

The stage is divided into 4 steps (10 levels):

• Initial:

❖ Level 1 (lifespan: 6,000 years)

❖ Level 2 (lifespan: 7,000 years)

❖ Level 3 (lifespan: 8,000 years)

• Middle:

❖ Level 4 (lifespan: 9,000 years)

❖ Level 5 (lifespan: 10,000 years)

- ❖ Level 6 (lifespan: 11,000 years)
- End:
  - ❖ Level 7 (lifespan: 12,000 years)
  - ❖ Level 8 (lifespan: 13,000 years)
  - ❖ Level 9 (lifespan: 14,000 years)
- Peak:
  - ❖ Level 10 (lifespan: 15,000 years)

Divine Stage

The seventh stage of development and the final stage of True Mastery.

Successfully reaching the stage will lead to:

1. A significant increase in the maximum energy reserve;

2. Gaining the ability to fly without techniques and artifacts; and

3. If a cultivator uses the advanced version of the *Meditation Technique* and has an ideal breakthrough, it leads to enhancing their *Core* features and more powerful *Core* skills.

The stage is divided into 5 levels:

- Initial (lifespan: 25,000 years)
- Middle (lifespan: 50,000 years)
- End (lifespan: 75,000 years)
- Peak (lifespan: 100,000 years)
- One Step away from Divinity (lifespan: 125,000 years)

Star Emperor

The eighth stage of development and the first stage of divinity. A stage when a being ceases to be considered a True Master and becomes a deity. The method and conditions for achieving this stage are unknown. The name of the stage is associated with the power of the divine beings, which allows them to create entire interstellar empires.

Star Emperors have *Divine Will* and are able to influence reality itself.

The stage is divided into 4 stages:

- Initial
- Middle
- Final
- Peak

Lifespan: presumably unlimited

Limitless

The ninth stage of development and the second stage of divinity. The method and conditions for achieving it are unknown. Features unknown.

The *Higher One*

The highest, and the last stage of development and the third stage of divinity. Pinnacle of the path of development. The method and conditions for achieving it are unknown. Features unknown. According to official data, there are only two holders of this stage in the Ecumene now: the Heavenly Eye of La'Gert and the Heavenly Night of Tel'Naal.

Beasts and Spirits

The path of development for these beings is slightly different, beginning at the *Exorcist Stage*.

At the *Elementalist Stage*, Beasts become *Tyrants*, while

the Sprits become *Elementals*, the type of which depends on their primary element.

At the *Holy Lord Stage*, Beasts become *Holy Beasts* and Spirits — *Holy Spirits*. At this stage, both gain sentience and the ability to assume a humanoid form.

Corresponding to the *Divine Stage* are *Heavenly Beasts* and *Heavenly Spirits*.

Both Beasts and Spirits can become *Star Emperors*.

Elements, their Paths, and the Stages of their mastery

By observing the natural or artificial manifestations of various elements through contemplative meditation, the cultivator is able to grasp the essence of these elements (information). The more comprehensive the understanding (the more information they obtain), the stronger and better they can use the elements by manipulating the *Force* particles.

A *Force* particle is that part of the cultivator's *Will* imbued with their understanding of a certain element.

In total, six stages of elemental understanding are known so far:

1. The *Hearing Stage* — the level of understanding of the *Forces* of a particular element, that is, embarking on its *Path*. Each of them can be mastered partially, completely, or perfectly, which is called the gradation of understanding. The higher it is, the more powerful the *Force* will be in the hands of a cultivator. The quality of the created techniques depends on their level of this element.

2. The *Seer Stage* — the level of mastering the *Force of Form* of a particular *Path*, which makes this element more

material, and influences the created techniques. The *Force of Form* can also be mastered partially, completely, or perfectly.

3. The *Learner Stage* — the level of mastering the *Force of Fusion* of a particular *Path* by combining all the previous *Forces* of a given element and then gradually merging them with one's soul, body, and mind. The gradation of understanding the *Force of Fusion* depends on the average understanding of all previous *Forces*. A cultivator creates their personal *Force of Fusion* once and for all and can't increase its understanding after that. That's why it's better to perfectly master all the previous *Forces* before moving to this stage. Without very high understanding of the *Force of Fusion*, a cultivator will never be able to expand the knowledge of the elements and form a *Sphere*.

4. The *Walker Stage* — the level of the advanced study of the *Force of Fusion*, analysis of details and awareness of the entire "construction", that leads to the perfectly understood *Force of Fusion*, which allows a cultivator to create their own *Sphere*. *Spheres* have four levels of development: initial, average, full, and peak.

5. *Perfect Understanding* — the level of understanding of the elements, which allows the cultivator to change and improve their *Sphere*. There are four levels of development of the *Advanced Sphere*: initial, average, full, and peak.

6. *Beyond Perfect Understanding* — the sixth level of understanding of the elements. The only thing known about it is that it cannot be reached by a soul that has made a breakthrough or has stayed too long in a space with a distorted flow of time, like ATS of the *Heavenly Complex*. This level is available only to deities.

The *Sphere*

A *Sphere* is an area of space saturated with the cultivator's *Will*, which acts as an active carrier of their element. Inside the *Sphere*, the cultivator's primary element dominates over any other, strengthening their techniques and weakening their enemies. To counter a *Sphere*, the cultivator needs to replace it with their own.

Rank

Denotes the strength of a technique, artifact, or alchemical preparation, based on the level of their creator's knowledge of the elements. Each rank, except for *Low*, *Earth* and *Pseudo-Divine*, is divided into four levels of quality: low, medium, high, and peak.

Currently, only nine ranks are known:

1. *Low* — the simplest energy manipulations;

2. *Earth* — the simplest weaves of energy;

3. *Silver* — complex weaves supplemented by incomplete or at least partial knowledge of at least one fundamental elemental *Force*. Corresponds to the *Hearing Stage*;

4. *Gold* — weavings based on all the *Forces* of a particular *Path*, or even its *Force of Form*. A partial understanding of all the *Forces* will result in low quality, while the complete or perfect one will result in medium. If the *Force of Form* of this *Path* is also present, then partial understanding will lead to a high quality, and the full or perfect understanding to peak quality;

5. *Royal* — weavings based on the *Force of Fusion*;

6. *Imperial* — weavings based on the *Walker Stage* level knowledge of the elements;

7. *Pseudo-Divine* — weavings based on the initial understanding of the elements at the *Perfect Stage*, but

without the full *Advanced Sphere*;

8. *Divine* — weavings based on the understanding of the *Perfect Stage* in the form of an *Advanced Sphere*. Four levels of an *Advanced Sphere* correspond to four levels of rank quality. Only *Divine*-rank attacks or higher can injure a deity; and

9. *Heavenly* — weavings based on the understanding of the elements on the *Beyond Perfect Stage*.

Kai Arnhard's Powers And Abilities

Development stage: *Holy Lord*, initial stage

Level of strength and skill: *Seven Big Stars*

Elements:

• *Path of Sword* — peak *Sphere* (peak quality, *Imperial* rank)

• *Path of Space* — full *Sphere* (high quality, *Imperial* rank)

• *Cold Void* (concept of the *Higher Force of Time Slowdown*) — full *Sphere* (high quality, *Imperial* rank)

• *Yin* (concept of the *Higher Force of Destruction*) — full *Sphere* (high quality, *Imperial* rank)

• *Yang* (concept of the *Higher Force of Creation*) — full *Sphere* (high quality, *Imperial* rank)

• *Heat Void* (concept of the *Higher Force of Time Acceleration*) — full *Sphere* (high quality, *Imperial* rank)

• *Radiant Void* (concept of the *Higher Force of Time Reversal*) — full *Sphere* (high quality, *Imperial* rank)

Special features

Will Abilities: *Master's Will, Field of Superiority, Advanced Complete Submission*

Soul Manifestations: *Ultimate Focus* (3rd level), *Supreme Simulation* (2nd level)

Bloodline

Kai possesses one of the strongest bloodlines in the Ecumene, derived from the power of an ancient monster — the Nine-Headed Heavenly Hydra — that was created by the First Ones themselves. The main strength of this bloodline is its incredible regeneration, able to restore hardened flesh. In addition, this is one of the few bloodlines that are able to evolve as its owner develops, granting them new powers.

Kai currently possesses three bloodline abilities:

• *No Limits* — removes restrictions on the development of physical parameters. The amplification rate increases along with the growth of the owner's level of development. The higher the parameters, the slower their accumulation.

• *Six Body Gates* — permanently increases the owner's initial stats by 250% as long as they have at least 5% of energy in their body.

• *Partial Transformation* — grants the owner partial transformation into the bloodline's carrier and increases their initial parameters by 400%. Allows limited and temporary redistribution of parameters from one characteristic to another. This ability can be used only once per day.

Prior to the *Exorcist Stage*, instead of *Partial*

Transformation, there is its weaker counterpart — *Life Rampage*.

The last stage of the evolution of the Nine-Headed Heavenly Hydra bloodline is the creation of the *Heart of the Hydra*, which will greatly enhance the owner's regeneration and the aforementioned abilities. The *Heart of the Hydra* is physical and located in the body.

Central Core abilities

The *Elemental Core* is a spirit organ that forms during the breakthrough to the *Elementalist Stage*. The cores are divided according to the elements and they enhance their abilities, with the central one being based on the cultivator's primary element.

Kai originally used the *Cold Void Meditation Technique* to break through, basing his core on that concept. However, during the breakthrough, the *Cold Void* core merged with the *Heat Void* core due to the concepts' affinity with the *Higher Path of Time*.

The key feature of any central core is a unique ability, similar to a *Divine Gift*. Acquiring such an ability is only possible by compressing the core during the breakthrough.

Owning two concepts, Kai's central core granted him two abilities at once:

• *Ice Reflection*. Upon activation, the core creates a perfect copy of Kai in a parallel stream of time, splitting his consciousness. Existing in a parallel time stream, the copy is invisible to all but the deities. Provided, however, that their intuition isn't highly developed, in which case, they can feel a slight sense of danger emanating from the copy. As soon as the copy interacts with the other stream or exists more than a few seconds, it is ejected from its timeline into the main one. The copy cannot exist forever, but if the original dies during the ability's activation, its *Spark* will move to the copy's body, which will become the new original and continue to exist.

• *Borrowing Flame*. Upon activation, the core begins to burn the body, speeding up the passage of time, but granting power from the future in return. This ability allows the user to increase their initial parameters by as much as 1,000%. The more active the ability, however, the faster the body is destroyed.

Combined with *Ice Reflection*, this ability allows Kai to unleash its maximum potential without risk to his health.

The *Heavenly Mortal Style*

The *Heavenly Mortal Style* commonly refers to a set of abilities acquired upon reaching the *Divine Stage*. They can also be obtained through certain soul modifications.

This style consists of five levels:

• *Absolute Self-Control*

The cultivator learns to control their soul and body at all times, down to their smallest component. This ability allows them to calculate the required amount of energy, *Will*, and particles for any action, as well as the necessary distance of movement in combat.

• *Technique Compression*

Based on *Absolute Self-Control*, it includes three separate skills:

❖ *Creation of Ideal Particles*

Enhances techniques with higher-quality *Force* particles and concepts. Ideal particles are invisible to the naked eye and much more difficult to capture with spirit perception.

- ❖ *Ki Taming*

    Makes any weaving tighter and technique more compact, increasing its power.

- ❖ *Multiplication*

    The creation of multiple techniques at once now works a little bit differently. Before reaching the *Divine Stage*, a cultivator can summon techniques in different points of space. *Multiplication* makes it possible to disintegrate a single weaving into multiple techniques.

• *Advanced Will Usage*

This ability consists of six skills. The enhanced soul allows the *Divine Stage* cultivator to form a stronger connection with their techniques. Anyone can change the form of their technique if its essence or its trajectory allows it, but only those possessing *Advanced Will Usage* can acquire the following abilities:

- ❖ *Sealing*

    Masks the physical manifestation of a technique, making it even more difficult to spot with spirit perception.

- ❖ *Targeting*

    Makes the technique move after the target on its own.

- ❖ *Embedding*

    Allows the embedding of one weave inside another.

- ❖ *Interruption* and *Resumption*

    Allows the user to disassemble a technique into weaves and then activate it again.

❖ *Return of Power*

Allows the user to return some of the energy and particles into themselves, if the enemy evaded or activated a defense technique.

• *Force Compression*

Allows the user to use *Will* to control the kinetic force created by movement.

• *Foresight*

Allows the user to read other people's intentions and predict the most likely outcome. It's an extremely draining skill, but incredibly useful in combat.

The *Yin-Yang Phantom Tattoo*

The *Yin-Yang Phantom Tattoo* is a special mark created by the Destroyer himself, Or'drok Okka Yashnir. Deities own the *True Tattoo of Destruction and Creation*.

The *Tattoo* grants several abilities:

• *Yang Concentration* is the ability to accumulate and strengthen *Yang* particles, which saves strength and makes techniques based on this concept more powerful;

• *Yin Concentration* is the ability to accumulate and strengthen particles of *Yin*, which saves strength and makes techniques based on this concept more powerful;

• *Primal Flash* is the ability to unleash a burst of concentrated *Yang* power. It can be used as an attack, but it is more useful in creating techniques or strengthening the body;

• *Touch of Nothingness* is the strongest attacking ability, allowing the user to erase an object from reality if its resistance is not too strong;

• *Yang Form* turns the user into an Angel, a powerful being with powers at the cost of their soul, flesh, *Astral Body*; and

• *Yin Form* turns the user into a Demon, a powerful being with powers at the cost of their soul, flesh, and *Astral Body*.

The *Trophy*

The *Trophy* is a mysterious object that replaces Kai's *Spark* and grants him unique abilities.

There are seven unique abilities in total:

• Perfect memory — the ability to remember everything. With a hundred *Trophy* particles, the memory capacity becomes unlimited, the search for information in it becomes instantaneous, and the memories of a past life are unlocked (provided that the past life began with a hundred *Trophy* particles);

• Energy vision — the ability to see energy;

• Soul protection — prevents others from reading the user's soul at the informational level of reality, which allows them to hide the presence of their *Trophy* and its abilities;

• Neutral energy control — the ability to subjugate *prana*, which is usually considered impossible. It also improves the overall quality of energy control; and

• *Soul Shell* protection — unlocked upon receiving the first particle of the *Trophy*. It protects *the Soul Shell* against spirit contracts and spirit attacks. At fifty particles, it provides protection from divine spirit attacks. At five hundred particles, it protects the user from *System* oaths. At this point, the soul no longer needs to be prepared for breakthroughs.

Upon activation, the *Trophy* increases energy control, allowing its owner to:

• Saturate their body and *Cover* with energy without suffering damage;

• Fly by manipulating energy density;

• Enhance techniques with higher amounts of energy;

• Suppress attacks by increasing energy density;

• Form techniques from a great distance;

• Block the activation of artifacts by subordinating the crystallized *prana* within them;

• Limit control of matter through the control of energy particles inside it;

• Summon false *Holy Punishments of Heaven*;

• Suck out energy from matter; and

• Create and maintain more weaves simultaneously.

Other skills and features

The *Favorite of the Forces* — a rare soul feature that accelerates the understanding of elemental *Forces* and allows its owner to master as many as eight elements, instead of the usual five.

Adored by the Forces — an extremely rare soul feature that accelerates the understanding of elemental *Forces* and allows its owner to learn up to thirteen elements.

Cryde — Kai's special technique that allows him to imitate the power and properties of the *Spheres*. This helped him create concept *Spheres*.

Main Factions Of The Trial Worlds And Their Members

INSULAII

Eternal Path Temple

Kai's base of operations on Insulaii. Controls the entire Avlaim region.

Lilith Emerald Flame (Lilith Rising Star) — the matriarch of the Rising Star Sect and one of the Hierarchs of the Eternal Path Temple. She first crossed paths with Kai in the Trial Worlds. *Divine Stage. Master of Seven Average Stars.* Possesses many divine artifacts. Surprisingly similar in appearance to Kai's mother.

Ragnar — the first Templar of the Eternal Path Temple. An aesir who ran into Kai on Insulaii on a Wandering island. *Divine Stage. Master of Seven Small Stars.* Simple and straightforward, likes a good fight.

Nyakonalavius (Nyako) — a feline Dorgan. A master of arrays who also met Kai on a Wandering island. *Divine Stage. Master of Seven Small Stars.* Can be annoying.

Anatos — a four-armed aquatic Beast. Kai's first follower on Insulaii after a failed attempt on his life. *Divine Stage. Master of Five Great Stars.*

Hiro Ando — also met Kai on a Wandering island. Peak-level *Elementalist. Master of Seven Small Stars.* Good-natured.

Ron — former bodyguard of the Ando twins. *Divine Stage. Master of Six Small Stars.* Has green hair.

Raven Shaw — former admiral of the Third Fleet of the Four Mists Cartel. One of the Hierarchs of the Eternal Path Temple. *Divine Stage. Master of Seven Small Stars.* Egomaniac. Witty.

Ryu Araki — student of the Eternal Path Temple. The winner of the Great Insulaii Tournament. *Exorcist. Master of Six Small Stars.* Uses twin spears and resembles someone...

Shan Wu — the head of the Order of the First Elements. *Holy Lord. Master of Seven Small Stars.* Fair and just.

Viola — the Guardian Spirit of Kai's *Twin Blades of Nightmare. Divine Stage. One Step Away from Divinity. Master of Four Small Stars.* Beckoned by the crimson river and the song of steel.

Acilla nor Adria — Kai's mentor, whom he met back in Nikrim. Born on a Central World as a daughter of a goddess and a vampire, she lost her freedom to the head of the Vinari clan. *Divine Stage. Master of Seven Average Stars.*

Shacks Eldivize — one of Kai's oldest acquaintances, whom he met back on Saha. *Holy Lord. Master of Six Small Stars.* Likes to joke and fool around. Always has an ace up in his sleeve.

Malvur di Santos No'Rhythm — a giant Kai met on Nikrim in Udin. *Holy Lord. Master of Five Big Stars.* Not very talkative.

Lily Wayat Stenshet — one of Kai's oldest acquaintances, whom he met back on Saha in the Alkea Empire. *Holy Lord. Master of Five Big Stars.* Ivsim's beloved.

Ivsim — one of Kai's acquaintances, whom he first met in the Caltea region of the Alkea Empire on Saha during a local tournament. *Holy Lord. Master of Four Big Stars.* Blind from birth. Lily's beloved.

An'na Divide — one of Kai's old acquaintances, whom he met in Udin on Nikrim. *Holy Lord. Master of Six Small Stars.* Brilliant swordsman.

Guts — one of Kai's old acquaintances, whom he met during his stay in the Cloud Abode. Their relationship began as that of business partners, but the two soon bonded and became friends. *Holy Lord. Master of Five Small Stars.* Loves money.

Ailenx — one of Kai's followers, whom he met before entering the Cloud Abode. *Holy Lord. Master of Four Big Stars.* Elf. Very devoted to Kai.

The Han Nam Union

The second strongest organization on Insulaii. Controls the Tyr region.

Zhou Han Nam — the head of the Han Nam Clan and Union. *Divine Stage. One Step Away from Divinity. Master of Seven Average Stars.*

The Twin Dragon Union

The third strongest organization on Insulaii. Controls the End region.

Kuro and Shiro — twin brothers. The heads of the Twin Dragon Sect and Union. *Divine Stage. One Step Away* *from Divinity. Masters of Seven Average Stars.*

The Four Mists Cartel

The pirate organization that terrorizes Insulaii. Secretly worked for the Knolak Empire and the Heavenly Exaltation Cult. Had lands in Avlaim until they were captured by the Eternal Path Temple, forcing the Third and Fourth Fleets stationed there to surrender, after which they merged to form the Sea Trading Company and began to work for the Eternal Path Temple.

Sirius Delane — the head of the Four Mists Cartel and admiral of its First Fleet. A Spider *Heavenly Beast. Master of Seven Average Stars.*

The Knolak Empire

The strongest faction on Insulaii, created by the three mysterious Princes of the Abyss.

Green — the emperor of Knolak and the first Prince of the Abyss. In the past, he bore the name Greenrow Yoni but has recently awakened, returning his real memory and name. He has incredible power, incomparable with his level of development, as well as vast knowledge. *Holy Lord.* His Star rating is unknown.

Void — the second Prince of the Abyss. Asura. *Divine Stage. One Step away from Divinity. Master of Seven Great Stars.*

FEROX

The Everstein family

The strongest faction on Ferox and the oldest clan in the Trial Worlds. It mainly consists of sylphs bearing the Eye of the Void bloodline that allows them to manipulate space. The surviving members of the clan that served La'Gert, the past ruler of the Ecumene. Currently in hiding.

Derek von Everstein — the head of the Eighth Division (a subsidiary of the clan located in the Avlaim region on Insulaii). *Divine Stage. Master of Seven Average Stars.* Concluded a profitable trade agreement with the Eternal Path Temple.

Diana von Everstein — Derek's youngest daughter. *Holy Lord*. Was a *Master of Six Small Stars* before she was turned into a puppet.

Victor von Everstein — the patriarch of the Everstein clan. *Divine Stage. One Step Away from Divinity. Master of Seven Great Stars*. Yolana's brother and husband.

Yolana von Everstein — the matriarch of the Everstein clan. *Divine Stage. One Step Away from Divinity. Master of Seven Great Stars*. Victor's sister and wife.

The Vinari family

One of the strongest factions on Ferox. They framed Kai's team in order

to capture Acilla.

Regis Glian Vinari — the head of the Vinari clan. *Divine Stage. One Step Away from Divinity. Master of Seven Big Stars.*

BELLUM

Mountain Sect Alliance

The third most powerful faction on Bellum after the Cult and the Order.

The O'Crime family

Descendants of the ruling branch of the Heavenly

Manticore Clan.

Rosen O'Crime — an unofficial member of the Mountain Sect Alliance, one of the members of the Heavenly Manticore Clan. *Peak-level Elementalist. Master of Seven Great Stars.*

The Hidden Temple

Bellum's fourth strongest organization. A mysterious and rather closed organization whose main goal is to fight the Cult and adepts of the dark arts.

Zarifa Ali — the main talent of the Hidden Temple. She met Kai on the Contender's Road, where she persuaded him to spare Illarion Yen Talos. *Holy Lord. Master of Seven Great Stars.*

The Order of Purity

Contesting with the Heavenly Exaltation Cult for the spot of the most powerful organization on Bellum. Controlled by Higher Ones, it has rather strict views about the races worthy of joining them.

Deus Yen Talos — the third Master of the Order of Purity. In alliance with the head of the House of Blood, Rihanna Bloodclaw. *Divine Stage. One Step Away from Divinity. Master of Seven Great Stars.*

Illarion Yen Talos — the biggest talent of the Order of Purity. Mistook Kai for Kyle, attacking him on the Contender's Road. *Holy Lord. Master of Seven Great Stars.*

The Heavenly Exaltation Cult

Unofficially, it is the strongest organization in the Trial Worlds. Denounced and persecuted in the rest of the Ecumene for its use of the dark arts, it consists of five internal organizations called Houses: the House of Resistance, the House of Dolls, the House of Blood, the House of Famine, and the House of Passion. The Heads of Houses lead the Council of Pillars. Above them all is the mysterious head of the Cult, Sazarek.

Rihanna Bloodclaw — the head of the House of Blood. Works with the third Master of the Order of Purity. *Divine Stage. One Step Away from Divinity. Master of Seven Great Stars.*

Kyle Reinhard — the unofficial head of the House of Resistance. A Faceless Being, bearing his ancestors' Progenitor Bloodline. Bears a strong resemblance to Kai Arnhard. Owns *Trophy* particles. *Holy Lord. Master of Eight Stars.*

Raphael — the head of the House of Famine. A fae. *Divine Stage. One Step Away from Divinity. Master of Seven Great Stars.*

Orion — the head of the House of Passion. *Divine Stage. One Step Away from Divinity. Master of Seven Great Stars.*

The Puppeteer — the head of the House of Dolls. Rumored to be the oldest among the Pillars. *Divine Stage. One Step Away from Divinity. Master of Seven Great Stars.*

The Collisium

A mysterious organization of Beasts and Spirits located in the depths of the Cursed Continent on Bellum.

Yusa Softlight — one of the Guardians of the Collisium. Demigod Butterfly. *Master of Seven Great Stars.*

Other

Chag — an old acquaintance of Kai, whom he met back in Nikrim during the war with Niagala. Chag observed Kai for some time during the expedition to Belteise and then disappeared only to reappear in the Trial Worlds under a disguise. At the moment, he's forced to obey Green. *Divine Stage. Master of Seven Great Stars.*

Sakumi Ando — Hiro Ando's twin. Exceptionally cruel and selfish. She left her brother for dead to join the Four Mists Cartel. User of dark arts. Peak-level *Elementalist. Master of Six Small Stars.*

Or'drok Okka Magnus — the Shadow of an unknown but extremely powerful being. He promised to return Kai's memory if he destroyed the Elder Runes. He taught Kai the *Heavenly Mortal Style* and helped him complete the *Cryde Technique.*

Prologue

Before her lay puddles of whitish liquid left from the dead Formless, part of the wall that had turned into sand together with the passage to the laboratory, mauled bodies, and destroyed equipment.

Having returned from the meeting of the Pillars to Mekhan, the official capital of the House of Blood, Rihanna rushed to her floor. Not much had changed since Acilla was abducted: according to the protocol, the entire area was automatically sealed until Rihanna's arrival to preserve even the faintest trace of the fugitive.

"As you requested, madam." Mekhan's Guardian Spirit appeared near Rihanna in the form of a tall humanoid with many tentacles instead of arms and a crimson ball of fire for a head. *"I summoned all the members of the House to Mekhan you asked for, relocated those loyal to you to the other capital, reduced the number of guards on the floor, turned off the spatial vibrations detector, and let that incapable coward who called himself a mayor to keep quiet about the attack from the House officials. I did the dirty work for him."*

"He died?"

"Yes. Together with twenty-six rank three Junior Apostles and one rank three Senior Apostle. In total, we lost three hundred

and eighteen Divine Stage *cultivators and two dozen* Holy Lords."

"How many of them were conspirators?"

"Eighty percent."

"Great." Rihanna suddenly smiled. "What about the others?"

"Almost everyone has been declared dead. The third department is already interrogating the survivors."

"Have you found out anything yet?"

"Yes, my lady. The analysis of the fragments of the mayor's soul and the minds of some of his associates showed that the conspirators were most likely connected to the House of Resistance. But that is all that we have been able to find out for now. We'll keep looking."

For the first time during the conversation, Rihanna was truly surprised.

I didn't expect that. I thought that the Puppeteer was behind everything, but it seems that Kyle decided to join the game. Rihanna only recently learned that Elroy Reinhard was actually killed and replaced by his son. "What about the culprit?"

"Fled to Ferox. The trail went cold due to the cataclysm that happened on that world."

"I see," Rihanna said surprisingly calmly. "You can stop looking for him."

I hope my hero is happy, she added to herself with a pleased smile.

With this move, Rihanna killed two birds with one stone: getting rid of most of the conspirators who decided to turn against her, and fulfilling her master's request — letting

Kai Arnhard save Acilla and squander all his *Divine* combat artifacts along the way.

Recalling her assignment brought back memories of events that happened three years ago, when the unofficial head of the Four Mists Cartel, Sirius Delane, working for the House of Blood, encountered the rapidly growing underwater empire of Knolak. Investigating its mysterious appearance, he ran into the Princes of Abyss. Through a twist of fate, they found out about his connection with Rihanna and demanded that he convey a message to her.

Rihanna initially thought of ignoring their demand and abandoning her unfortunate subordinate, but she became interested in the Princes and their empire when they fought against the Insulaii Unions. Thinking that a new unknown faction might interfere with her plans, she agreed to meet with them.

Little did she know that this decision would change her life.

Meeting Green turned everything upside down. The only thing more shocking than his power were his plans, in many ways similar to her own. Rihanna was old. Very old. Perhaps the Puppeteer was the only person in these worlds who could be older than her. She had already lived for more than one hundred and twenty thousand years and she was approaching the final stage on her journey: a few more centuries, and the time allotted to her would expire. She understood this very well, and so she wanted to spend the final years of her life in the same fashion as it had begun — fighting. She wanted to bring chaos into all the Trial Worlds. She wanted to start the biggest, most horrifying, and most destructive war in their history.

However, this didn't prompt her to start serving Green.

Rihanna knew perfectly well what awaited her, an

adept of the dark arts, outside the Trial Worlds. That's why she had declined the Exodus and, accordingly, deprived herself of any attempts to become a deity. Green promised not only to revert her soul to its active phase but also to grant her protection from the *System*, thus putting the final weight on the scales and tipping them in his favor.

Ancient and powerful, Rihanna bowed before the emperor of Knolak, agreeing to serve him.

It was on his orders that she arrived at the Rising Star Sect earlier than Lilith had predicted, forcing Zazrimmu to be more proactive, in response to which Kai was also forced to jump the gun. Otherwise, he would have delayed taking over the sect, and then the entire region. Kidnapping Acilla from the Vinari clan was also Green's plan. As was her rescue.

"Did you manage to save the information on the vampire?" Rihanna asked, feeling her blood simmer with anticipation of future events.

"*Of course, madam,*" the spirit answered meekly. "*Everything has been preserved.*"

"Wonderful." Her unsettling smile made the spirit flinch. "It's time for us to pay a visit to the Order of Purity."

***

The consequences of Kai and Kyle's battle were so disastrous for Ferox that the planet's stunned leaders were forced to assemble on the very same day, despite their mutual dislike and disagreements. Representatives of all the major factions — the Eversteins, the Vinaris, the Sevrum Alchemy Guild, the Eastern City-States Coalition, the Liharus Empire, the Blossom Garden Sect, and the Heirs of Kao — assembled in a gathering of unprecedented magnitude, driven by desperate times that called for desperate measures.

When everyone arrived, the strongest of those present,

Victor von Everstein, began the meeting.

"As you already know, a cataclysm struck our world. Massive earthquakes, tsunamis, volcanic eruptions, the Akama Mountains crumbling into the rift, the annihilation of all living creatures in the Akama Desert, the destruction of the Red Heavenly Tree, and, finally, the destruction of the satellite Eof. All this has hurt or will hurt each of us. Therefore, we have gathered here to reduce the consequences of the cataclysm as best as we can, prevent its recurrence, and discover the cause of this plague."

"Do you have any idea who could have done this?" Regis Glian Vinari inquired.

"Do you seriously think that a mortal could have done this?" the Matriarch of the Blossom Garden scoffed. "Somewhere on the periphery of the Ecumene, perhaps, but not in the neighboring worlds. The energy resistance is too high here. No cultivator alone could unleash a cataclysm of this degree."

"The reason may lie in the Trial Worlds themselves," the Emperor of Liharus said. "What if the recent discovery of the Abyss on Insulaii triggered something in the Heavenly Exaltation Pagoda? I heard something shady happened at the very end."

"What difference does it make, if the peak of the cataclysm has already passed?" the head of the Alchemy Guild interjected, preventing Regis from answering. "We must first suppress its echoes, and only then look for the culprits! Do you have any idea how much money I have lost and how much I am losing right now?! Earthquakes, tsunamis, and Eof's fragments are destroying the infrastructure and even entire cities. The ocean Spirits, the planet, and the heavens themselves seem to have gone crazy, attacking everything around! This needs to be stopped immediately!"

"I second that." The chairman of the Eastern City-States Coalition nodded. "We must slow down the movement of the tectonic plates, and divert the largest parts of Eof from their current trajectory if we don't want them to collapse on us."

"Our clan—" Victor began but abruptly fell silent.

The building they were in suddenly shook.

"Ahem..." Victor continued when things calmed down. "Our clan is already dealing with the satellite's largest fragments. We are well aware that if parts of Eof fall on Ferox, the consequences will be devastating."

This news took the burden off everyone's shoulders. All of the attendees represented the largest factions on the planet, but not all of them were able to deal with the impending threat on their own. The fact that the Eversteins — the masters of space and gravity — agreed to do this, made it possible for many to breathe easy. However, they all understood that the Eversteins weren't doing this out of the goodness of their hearts. Deep within the satellite's bowels lay precious deposits of rare materials. Before, it was unprofitable to mine them there and deliver them to the planet, but now the Eversteins had the opportunity to get the most valuable and largest pieces of Eof for themselves.

Next came the discussion of ways to tame the natural disasters that had swept the world, as well as the raging Spirits. Usually, these creatures originated in and inhabited hard-to-reach places. As they were usually in no hurry to leave their habitat, they posed an insignificant threat to the factions unless provoked.

However, the battle between Kai and Kyle greatly affected not only the physical world but also the spiritual one. Due to tectonic shifts and the removal of a huge amount of *prana* from the atmosphere, many spirit geysers disappeared or changed their path, many Clusters and Superclusters of *Force* particles were destroyed, along with the Spirits' native habitats. All this eventually led to many Spirits, particularly the unintelligent ones, going on a rampage. And since Spirits lived in groups and were ready to join forces with others of the same kind in case of an impending disaster, they turned their anger to the cultivators of the Trial Worlds.

The meeting continued through the rest of the day. None of the faction leaders left the building during this time, taking only occasional breaks to make executive decisions in accordance with new data and agreements.

At some point, Victor, distracted from the conversation, suddenly raised his hand, attracting attention. The voices subsided.

"I have just received important information regarding the cause of the cataclysm."

"You what?"

Having pulled out a memory scroll sent to him from the *Storage*, he installed it in a socket connected to the room's main array.

"Take a look."

As he closed his eyes and activated the scroll, everyone got access to the memories stored within it.

The mundane meeting room was replaced by a beautiful garden and a clear, bright sky. Looking at the world through the eyes of an unknown protagonist, they saw an elf woman talking to the owner of the memories. There was no sound, and it was impossible to read lips. The person through whose eyes they observed the scene hid these details, but the conversation wasn't really that important.

Suddenly, they felt like they were suffocating. Only not due to the lack of oxygen, but lack of energy. The amount of *prana* in the area declined rapidly. The majestic plants withered, artifacts broke, and the elf turned pale. She tried to do something, but it was already too late.

A few moments later, a mysterious figure flew over the city. Following it, energy began to burst out of matter, even out of the bodies of True Masters. The elf died instantly, and the man felt excruciating pain as his *Astral Body* shattered. Realizing that he was about to die, he placed his memories into a scroll so that someone might learn what became of him.

The last thing he saw before he perished was another figure flying over the city.

"This is one of the cities in the Akama Desert. As you can guess, the figures flew from the side of the Akama Mountains, the suspected epicenter of the cataclysm, to the Red Heavenly Tree, which was also destroyed," Victor said when everyone finished reviewing the memories.

"Impossible," someone whispered in horror. "What kind of power is this? Are they gods?"

"Have you noticed their clothes?" someone else said. "It's hard to see, but those are the Cult's robes."

Curious, many rushed to re-watch the memories.

"Could this be Sazarek? Does the legendary head of the Heavenly Exaltation Cult really exist?"

"Nonsense!"

"What about the other cultist? I have never seen anything like it."

"Does it strike you as suspicious that they can fly at such a speed on Ferox, where *Divine Stage* cultivators are restricted?"

"*Divine Stage*?! If these are *Divine Stage* cultivators, then I'm the king of the universe!" someone exclaimed in frustration.

"Is there really something going on with the Trial Worlds? Where could they have come from? And, most importantly, what do we do now?"

Chapter 1
THE HIDDEN TEMPLE

Kai woke up. Slowly emerging from the darkness of unconsciousness, he felt a surge of blinding rage cloud his mind. All he wanted was to destroy everything around him. His desire to kill was so potent that his aura and *Spheres* unleashed waves of aggressive energies out of his body. The consequences of his transformation into a demon still tormented him, leaving the emotional layer of his soul in disarray.

In addition to his profound hatred for everything that existed, Kai also experienced nightmarish pain. Something was trying to penetrate his soul, beating against it like a hammer. Kai's *Shell* was unique in that it was impossible to damage it in this way, but that didn't mean that he couldn't feel pain.

A myriad of images flashed before his eyes, out of which two stood out in particular: the decapitation of some old man and the sight of Diamond's corpse sitting propped against the wall. An ocean of information was poured into his mind, but it was immediately pushed back out as if his soul resisted such a volume of data. No mind, not even his, could take in more than fifteen years' worth of incredibly detailed memories at once.

Frozen between unconsciousness and reality, experiencing both pain and rage, Kai couldn't do anything but scream. His body began to convulse as an uncontrollable force surged in all directions. Unaware of his surroundings, he didn't know that he was in a soundproof room deep underground, tightly bound by chains that suppressed his power.

"Hold on," a vaguely familiar female voice said. "The teacher is already here."

But her words never reached Kai. Enraged, he jerked his whole body toward the girl, wanting to tear her apart with his bare hands, but she only smiled. On his own, he couldn't even open his eyes.

Suddenly, there were footsteps, followed by a firm grasp on his head that kept him in place. A powerful force suppressed him, and then someone's palm touched his abdomen. Soul techniques were poured into him, plunging Kai into darkness. As if swept away by an invisible hand, the rage and pain no longer tormented him.

He woke up again a day later. This time, he was unbound.

Grimacing at the unpleasant weakness in his body, Kai sat up and looked around. He was in a small room with stone walls and a bed. There was no other furniture, but there was plenty of energy, making this room a great place for meditation.

"Where am I?" Kai asked listlessly. "Wait... Kyle."

Fragments of their battle flashed through his mind. He vividly remembered their duel in the city, but his memory got hazy after he turned into a demon. And while he couldn't remember the details, he knew that he lost to the cultist, returned to his human form and lost four hundred and forty-five particles of his *Trophy*. He thought that would be his end, but then he was saved by someone.

Closing his eyes, Kai checked the state of his body and soul. He remembered that he digested and used his *Soul Shell*, body, cores, and bloodline as fuel for the *Demon Heart*. And yet, here they were, as if he had never used the *Yin Form*.

Regardless, he still felt the consequences of losing almost half of his *Trophy*, causing his energy-controlling ability to decrease accordingly. Secondly, the artifact that restored his human appearance wasn't able to restore everything. He no longer had the *Demon Heart* — that is, he could no longer turn into a demon until he accumulated many *Yin* particles, which could take years or even decades.

What's going on here? he wondered. *Did someone suppress the emotional layer of my soul with a technique? Possibly. I can undo it, but what's the purpose of all this? And what happened to my memories?*

Other than the battle with Kyle, he also remembered escaping from the cultists, rescuing Acilla, and Green opening the gates of the Heavenly Exaltation Pagoda. But he only had a vague recollection of the Contender's Road, the descent into the Abyss, and the tournament. Even more confusing was the fact that these were his first memories, as if his life was a blank page before that.

All of this led him to believe that a technique capable of blocking most of his memories had been placed on the mental layer of his soul. He understood that this barrier could be removed, but Kai's gut told him not to rush it. He was too weak — Green used Chag's *Complex* to restore everything that had been turned into fuel, but only at the most basic level. In other words, Kai was resurrected completely exhausted both physically and spiritually. During the days that he lay unconscious, some of his strength returned, but it would take weeks before he recovered fully.

To speed up the process, Kai moved to the *Storage*, where he visited Acilla and Viola. Alas, neither of them was awake. Acilla's condition had not changed since Kai found her, and she continued to sleep, while Viola was simply exhausted. She needed time to recover.

Having visited the two, Kai made another discovery: due to the sealed emotional layer, he practically didn't feel Viola's presence, despite the spiritual link connection. The same was true for his swords. He also noticed that it prevented him from creating and using *Force* particles of all elements, except for the *Cold Void*, which seemed to have become a little stronger.

Deciding to postpone healing the minor wounds on Viola's *Astral Body* until she awakened, Kai headed to the alchemy warehouse. After picking up a couple of infusions that would restore the strength of his soul and body, he went to a room labeled "Mind Halls."

Having already lost his memories once, Kai made sure not to step on this rake again. From the very first day he woke up on Kaiser's Ark, he recorded his memories using a special artifact.

Before leaving the *Storage*, he studied the past year's events for about a quarter of an hour. He would have liked to spend more time in the Mind Halls, but he had to return to reality. The owners of his cell must have noticed that their guest woke up. No doubt, they would be eager to have a chat with him.

Returning to the outside world, Kai saw a bald giant clad in monk robes standing near the door. He wore huge black beads around his neck, and in his right hand, he held a large white staff with a decorative sphere that radiated intense heat, while his left hand rested on his chest. If Kai had studied the records of his journey along the Contender's Road in as much detail as he wanted to, he would have remembered that he had already seen this man in Zarifa Ali's group.

"Greetings, Path brother," the monk said. "I have been ordered to take you to my mentor."

"How long have you been standing there?" Kai asked as he reached for the clothes folded beside the bed. A moment later, the weaves embedded in the fabric activated, and the purple robes moved right onto his half-naked body.

"Patience is the first thing that the servants of the Hidden Temple are taught," the giant replied. "A little over ten minutes."

"I see." Kai turned to face him. "Let's go then, shall we?"

The monk nodded and left the room. Kai followed.

They walked along an empty corridor that led them outside the huge cave filled with dozens of stone pillars that served not only as a support for the entire construction, but also as the dwelling place of the Temple's servants. Kai and his guide emerged from one such pillar and headed to the largest of these structures over one of the many connecting stone bridges. All this was illuminated by strange huge mushrooms that covered the walls, floor, and ceiling of the cave.

Gazing at the other monks who were crossing the bridges or standing in the many open areas protruding from the pillars, Kai pondered.

The Hidden Temple is one of the strongest factions of the Trial Worlds, but seems like they don't have that many followers.

There aren't even three hundred thousand people in this cave. On the other hand... Kai concentrated. *Each of them is quite strong. The atmosphere reminds me of my Temple.*

The suppression of the emotional layer of his soul had made Kai unperturbed by the fact that he woke up in an unfamiliar place. If these people wished him harm, he reasoned, they wouldn't have gone through the trouble of giving him a warm, soft bed and mending his clothes. But how did he end up here? And why were these two seals placed on his soul?

Kai knew little about the Hidden Temple. From Shaw's stories, he learned that this was a rather secretive organization, a stronghold in the eternal fight against adepts of the dark arts. According to legend, its founders were survivors from one of the Cult's "farms." Since then, they sought to eradicate the Cult and its heretical practices.

The Temple's followers had little to no contact with the outside world unless it was related to their opposition to the Cult, but they remained one of the most formidable factions of the Trial Worlds. They were led by the First Abbot and the Sage. The former was directly involved in the management and affairs of the organization, and the latter was a recluse who engaged with others very, very rarely. Each Abbot eventually became a Sage, going into seclusion and handing over the affairs to his best student.

After a few minutes, they reached the central pillar of the cave, where the best students lived and trained. The giant's mentor met them in a large training hall. Despite the fact that visitors were infrequent in the Hidden Temple, the hard-working students didn't pay even the slightest attention to Kai, staying completely focused on their training.

Noticing the newcomers, the man nodded somewhere

upstairs and continued his lesson.

"Let's go."

Leaving the hall, the giant led Kai to the top of the pillar, to a place filled with elemental particles and energy. For those seeking power, this place was a paradise in terms of learning the *Forces*.

Sitting on a flat oval stone near a small pond, Zarifa Ali meditated, contemplating the *Forces* of the *Path of Sand*. Fully immersed in this process, she didn't react to their arrival.

Leaving Kai, the giant started to meditate as well. Unsure of what else to do other than follow their example, Kai withdrew into himself and concentrated on restoring his physical and spiritual strength.

Half an hour later, the First Abbot finally honored them with his presence.

He was a short, bald man with a beard and simple red-and-yellow robes. His forehead was decorated with nine black dots. Seven small spheres hovered behind him, and a thin golden staff rested in his hands.

Having greeted Kai with a familiar gesture, the First Abbot sat next to him right on a pile of fallen yellowed leaves.

"You can call me Kal'het, young man," the monk said in a melodious voice. "I apologize for being late. I don't have much free time, and we are not used to having guests."

"Kai Arnhard," Kai introduced himself in response. "What have you done to me, Grand Master Kal'het? I feel your presence in my soul."

"I tried to help you, as Zarifa asked me to. You were tormented by unnatural burning rage and wild pain. Unfortunately, I wasn't able to determine its cause, so I was forced to temporarily seal the emotional and mental layers of your soul. Some of your memories might be missing for I had to tamper with them. Sooner or later, that rage shall pass, and it will be possible to remove the seals. As for your memory, I fear that I can't help. From what I understand, something too strong was trying to get into your mind, destroying it. By partially sealing the memory, I put a halt to this process, but only for a while. If you want to solve this problem, you'll need assistance of a more powerful Soul Master. As far as I know, there are only four of them in the Trial Worlds: the Grand Master of the Order of Purity, the Frost Troll Gabba, the Puppeteer, and Raphael the Devourer."

"You talk so calmly about them, even though the last two are the heads of the Cult Houses. Aren't they your sworn enemies?"

"They are indeed my enemies, but I do not hate them. I pity them. I still recognize their achievements. They are talented masters. It would be foolish to deny it."

"I see... I understand. But I have no desire to get involved with them, and the Frost Troll Gabba is already dead. He was never able to break through to the *Star Emperor Stage*."

"Sad news." Kal'het sighed, not doubting Kai's words for a moment. "In that case, the Grand Master of the Order of Purity is your only option. But if rumors are to be believed, he is already in the process of breaking through to the next stage and becoming a deity. Whether his breakthrough will end successfully or not, no one knows, but it is unlikely that you will be able to get him to help you. However, I don't know everyone and everything, so maybe there are other Soul Masters in the Trial Worlds that are superior to me. In any case, I advise you to carefully study your soul and revisit this matter once you restore your strength. Something tells me that only you can understand the root of the problem."

"Thanks for the advice. I had something like that in mind. If you don't mind me asking, how did I get here?"

"The day before yesterday, a man left you near one of the entrances to our shelter. He had the most peculiar eyes. Do you know him?"

"Hm." Kai drawled. "I guess we can say that."

"I would be lying if I said that your appearance wasn't rather strange and suspicious, but Zarifa recognized you and convinced us to help you. As she told us, she is in no small debt to you."

"Rest assured that it will be decreased after this. But it's hard for me to judge how valuable your help was."

Kai hadn't forgotten... These people used his men during the tournament as bait for the Guardians of the Abyss. They were involved in killing his subordinates.

"Everything is relative, young man." Kal'het smiled slyly. "For some, a loaf of bread is a mere trifle, but it can save others from the painful death of starvation. I think it will be fair if her debt is cut in half."

After some thought, Kai agreed. He remembered the tearing that threatened to destroy his mind perfectly well.

"Did Zarifa tell you who I am?"

Kal'het nodded.

"In that case... How about a trade? I don't know why the Hidden Temple keeps to itself, but I think you might be interested in the alchemy and artifacts the Eternal Path Temple has to offer," Kai said and handed Kal'het a *Spatial Ring*.

To his delight, the First Abbot didn't refuse. He agreed to spend the next day drawing up a trade agreement, as well as paying Kai the remainder of what Zarifa owed him, one billion two hundred and fifty million *Runes*. With that, he left the garden, returning to his business.

***

Kai returned to his room to meditate. He intended to spend the rest of the day recuperating and exploring his soul.

Over the course of the next ten hours, he found out a lot. First, he sorted things out with the *Trophy*, gaining access to its powers after the Confrontation of Sparks with Kyle.

As I expected, the Trophy *is responsible for my energy vision, the ability to subdue neutral energy, perfect memory, and soul protection. But what I didn't expect was that the* Trophy *and the* Spark *are one and the same. I thought they were just close to each other. As it turns out, my* Spark *is not a* Spark *at all, but something artificial. This is consistent with the fact that instead of dying, I was resurrected in a new body. It's rather unpleasant to think of myself as something like a Shadow.* Kai frowned. *I can not only use bonuses from the* Trophy's *passive skill, but I can also activate it, thus increasing my energy control. I'll be able to saturate my flesh and* Cover *with huge amounts of energy, strengthening myself and my defenses, drain or strengthen matter from a distance, block someone's access to energy, create false* Holy Punishments, *block or even destroy artifacts, and manipulate the density of* prana *in the area, increasing the degree of energy resistance. But the active* Trophy *may take years to recharge. By the looks of it, I can now fly by manipulating energy density without activating the* Trophy.

The study of the *Trophy* allowed Kai to better understand his partial amnesia. As it turned out, all his memories were constantly archived in the *Trophy*, since this tool was perfect for that. Neither his brain nor *Shell* could withstand the volume of information that this artificial *Spark* could accommodate. To maintain constant access to it, a special connection formed between the *Shell* and the *Trophy*. The most important information was stored in the mental layer of the soul, while the most detailed information was stored in the *Spark*.

It was almost impossible to delete data from the *Trophy*. In case the brain or the *Shell* were damaged, the missing part would be restored from the "archive", ensuring nothing was truly lost.

Unaware of all this, Magnus had still deprived Kai of his memory. When it kept coming back, he used a technique so strong that he damaged the connection between Kai's artificial *Spark* and the *Shell*, creating a crack in it. Ultimately, only the connection formed in the moment of his rebirth in the body of Kai Arnhard survived. The connection that was responsible for the memories of his life on Earth.

However, by returning Kai's human form, the *Heavenly Complex* mended even that broken bond. The power of the Higher One invested in it turned out to be capable of even such a feat, but the process was far from perfect. For some reason, the *Trophy* transferred the erased memories to the *Shell* not in the usual form, but in the most detailed way, which exceeded the memory capacity of a single soul. Secondly, instead of the gradual transfer of information, as it normally happened, the data was copied quickly and all at once, straining the soul further.

Studying the *Trophy* led Kai to contemplate his duel with Kyle. In light of the recent events, he gained new insights.

Green deliberately gave Lilith my exact location. It was as if he knew that I would run into Rosen on the Road. He also arrived at Kronos just in time to save us from the Formless. Then he gave me Acilla's location and showed up just in time to save me from Kyle on a completely different planet. I'm sure the battle ended near Bellum, even though we started on Ferox, he thought, recalling how the Trial Worlds pulled them back.

Rules allowed both Kai and Kyle to pass through the barriers surrounding all three planets and protected them from the deities and their wrath. However, the two weren't allowed to go beyond the star system. The farther they moved from the Trial Worlds, the more the space around them distorted, pulling them back to Bellum.

Ultimately, it all comes down to the fact that he knew that I would fight Kyle. He purposely allowed him to take half of the Trophy. Now he won't rest until he takes the other half, as well. However, given the current circumstances, I can't match his level. Kyle no longer needs to prepare his soul for breakthroughs. He's a Master of Eight Stars, *while I don't even have* Seven Great *ones. He probably lost to Green and won't dare to go after me in the near future, but how long will this last? I have to become stronger as quickly as possible so that I'll be ready for our next encounter. And there are probably only two people that can help me with that... Magnus and Green. There are no guarantees when it comes to Magnus, especially given Kyle's* Heavenly Mortal Style, *which he could have only gotten from him. So, all that's left is Green, which is what he seemed to want. But why?*

Taking a deep breath, Kai opened his eyes.

On the other hand, I'm grateful to him. I would have spent years looking for Acilla and decades rescuing her if it wasn't for him. I wouldn't have been able to infiltrate Mekhan so easily without his Divine Gift. *Without his help, attacking the House of Blood so brazenly even with a* Trophy *would've been too dangerous...*

As he pondered, his gaze suddenly focused, and his face became serious.

"You're here, aren't you?"

"Yes," Magnus said calmly.

Turning around, Kai stared at him with some displeasure.

"How did you get into my *Storage* without any of the defense arrays going off?"

"Does it really matter?" Magnus answered with a question. "Shouldn't you be more worried about your memory right now?"

"When you deprived me of it, you obviously didn't think it through. Otherwise, you wouldn't have been so careless."

"Yes and no. I really didn't know about your... features, so I went ahead. You have already freed many of my fragments, giving me back more knowledge and strength. Thanks to you, I can now fix your problem. It won't be difficult for me to normalize the connection between your *Shell* and *Spark*, or even recreate it from scratch."

"But I will have to give you something in return, right?"

"Yes," Magnus confirmed, ignoring the venom in Kai's voice. "I didn't expect this to happen so soon, but one of the Ice Gates are about to open. I want you to go through them, find the Elder Rune, and destroy it. Even if you just damage it, it'll be enough. Once that happens, I will let your memories flow into your soul without overwhelming you or putting a strain on you. After that, you're free to ignore the rest of the Elder Runes. I know that the punishment for violating your oath won't hurt you in any way, so there's no need to force you to go after those that remain on Insulaii."

"And then I'll be useless to you. What's stopping you from simply getting rid of someone who could potentially seal you as U'Shor had once done?"

Magnus didn't answer right away.

"Nothing," he finally admitted.

"In that case, swear that you won't harm me or my organization once I've completed your request. I've heard that for beings of your level, words are not just random sounds. Unshakable principles and firm confidence in one's own thoughts, actions, and words are the guarantees of one's integrity at the *Divine* level. If you break your promise you'll put your sanity on the line."

"I swear," Magnus answered without thinking.

"Great." Kai nodded. "Do this and also promise to make me a *Master of Eight Stars*, and I will complete the task."

"You're asking for too much. I will not comply with the second requirement."

"And if I refuse?"

"You will die. As will all your loved ones. I won't let this slide."

"But if you do so, you will lose your only opportunity to become whole again."

"You foolish child. How do you think I escaped the first time? I could and can destroy the Elder Runes. It's just much faster when someone else does it while I tend to... other matters. But you are not irreplaceable."

"Is that so? Very well. What about revealing the secrets of the eight-volume techniques to me and training me for another two years?"

"Your memory and a promise to do no harm is all you will get. There is no point in bargaining anymore. Make a decision."

Chapter 2
CALM

"Don't you think the deal is a bit unfair?" Kai asked. "We used to work differently up to this moment."

Magnus chuckled in response.

"No. It seems to me that you have miscalculated. To teach you the *Heavenly Mortal Style* in a month, I demanded that ten Elder Runes be destroyed at once. Right now, I need you to simply damage just one. Do you think this is a fair price to pay for the secrets of eight-volume techniques, two extra years of training, and helping you become a *Master of Eight Stars*? Don't be greedy."

"Fair enough." Kai nodded. He had made these demands just to understand Magnus better. Judging from his answers, Magnus indeed knew how to make someone into a *Master of Eight Stars*. Only he refused to do so. "Still, I should get at least some kind of compensation for my work in addition to my memories."

"Stop playing dumb. You understand everything very well," Magnus answered coldly. "My promise not to harm you and your organization is your reward. But if you want, I can give you some tips and tricks about the eight-volume techniques. In that case, however, it's either one or the other. Take your pick."

Kai sighed.

"Fine. My memories and the promise in exchange for the Rune."

"Very well."

With that, the two swore an extended oath.

"So... Where are these Ice Gates and when will they open?" Kai went straight to the point. "I only have the Bellum Pass for three days. Is the Rune on Bellum at all?"

"Yes, the Ice Gates are on this world. Don't worry about the Pass, I've already reset the counter."

If Kai's emotional layer hadn't been suppressed, this would've surprised him. Opening the interface, he confirmed Magnus's words that he could stay on Bellum for thirty more days.

"I've put the coordinates here," Magnus continued, placing a memory scroll in front of Kai. "But I don't know the exact opening time. Only that it should happen within the next week."

"Understood. And what can I expect to find there? Where do the Gates lead?"

"I don't know. The only thing that I can tell you is that there will be many other Contenders who will want to open the Gates."

"And you can't help me in case of emergency?"

"That's right. I can't approach or enter the Gate while the Elder Rune stored within is intact."

"That's bad... What about my current condition? While

my soul's emotional layer is suppressed, I can only use the *Cold Void*. In addition, my core, body, and soul are depleted. The same goes for my weapon's Guardian Spirit. Without it, I'm weaker. I won't manage to recover by the time the Gates open. If someone else gets to the Rune before me, it'll be much more difficult for me to get it."

"Don't worry. No one will be able to acquire this Elder Rune. U'Shor's mechanism will kill all intruders, and then use their bodies and souls to reseal the Gate. The only way to avoid this is to destroy the Rune, to which everything is connected. Others will interfere with you, believing that they can take the Rune, but do not fret. They won't be able to do anything. As for your current predicament... I fear that there's nothing that I can do to help you." Magnus shook his head. "I need to save as much power as I can so that when you damage the Rune, I can take advantage of the mechanism's weakness and break through the Gate, and then finish what you started. Otherwise, everything will be meaningless."

Grimacing, Kai took the scroll. After learning the location of the Ice Gates, he thought for a few seconds and then nodded reluctantly.

"I'll move out tomorrow night."

Without answering, Magnus disappeared.

***

Green and Kai had long since disappeared. Kyle still sat in place with his chest pierced, staring into space. A few hours later, he finally got up, picked up the sword that was pushed out of his body by regenerated tissue, and silently wandered into the unknown, as if in a trance.

He never stopped walking. A couple of days later, he reached the border of a northern state that belonged to the Order of Purity. Sensing a town nearby, Kyle decided to head toward it.

Leaving no traces on the snowy road, he approached the settlement's gates. They were closed. Kyle jumped over the wall without any of the guards noticing him. The city's defensive arrays missed him, too, including even the one that was specially designed to detect Adepts of the Dark Arts and surround them with foul-smelling black fog. The power of the Formless made it possible to hide even the *System* mark.

The small town was located in an area with an unusually low energy density for Bellum. On one hand, this made it a fairly safe place, but on the other, cultivators were a rare sight and they usually didn't linger around for too long. The strongest person here was the head of the city — a *Mind Stage* cultivator. As for the guards, they were either at the *Body Stage* or ordinary mortals.

Assuming the appearance of a local wrapped in a thick fur coat, Kyle trudged along the main street, studying the passersby. After a while, he spied an interesting development nearby and instantly teleported there.

A group of five teenagers was beating an older man while laughing and throwing insults his way, hoping to humiliate and make fun of him. They kicked him on the head, tried to push him to his knees, rolled him in the snow, and dragged him in different directions. The man tried to fight back, but he was outnumbered.

However, that wasn't what caught Kyle's attention. He didn't care about the peasants and their games. Instead, he looked at the girl who was calling for help and trying to assist her beaten father. Three slightly older girls held her to the ground. They kicked her in the ribs and tried to shut her mouth but the girl resisted like a wild animal, biting and scratching them.

One of the guys decided to intervene. With a powerful

slap, he hoped to shut up the girl who was screaming at the top of her lungs, but she only began to fight harder, forcing him to use his fists.

All of this was taking place not far from the main street, in broad daylight. Many people had a chance to observe what was happening yet no one rushed to help. The townspeople diligently pretended not to notice anything, and the guards standing around the corner pretended to be deaf.

Having read their minds using the *Master's Will*, Kyle quickly understood what was going on. As it turned out, the teens were the children of influential city entrepreneurs. At a recent major holiday, they got drunk and then raped this very girl. Upon learning this, her father filed a lawsuit in search of justice. He was offered to sweep everything under the rug in exchange for a large sum of money, but he refused. Unfortunately, the corrupted local authorities allowed the boys' parents to get off with a small fine. The teenagers weren't punished in any way, which only made them more arrogant and privileged. Therefore, they decided to take revenge on the man, provoking him into a fight and crippling him.

But the most interesting thing in the whole story was the fact that the girl was awakening — her soul's warrior layer had activated.

There were four ways to embark on the path of development: automatic, alchemical, conscious, and volitional. The first case involved the natural awakening of the warrior layer. This could be a racial characteristic or simply a high innate talent inherited from powerful parents. The second method required the use of expensive drugs to activate the warrior layer. The conscious way of awakening was based on constant physical and mental training, as well as meditation, during which the cultivator had to imagine the flow of *ki* and manipulate it into correct nodes.

As for the volitional method, everything depended on chance. To trigger the warrior layer, the cultivator had to overcome a crisis, often a life-threatening one. This didn't always guarantee success, but chances were high enough for many to deliberately put themselves in danger. More often than not, when faced with the possibility of dying, many awakened their warrior layer despite not having any special bloodline, alchemy, or training.

But the young lady in question wasn't an experienced warrior, which made her awakening much more special. In her, Kyle sensed considerable potential. She wasn't a descendant of someone powerful; it was just that her soul had formed very well. Sometimes, the universe orchestrated such surprises, the apogee of which were those very Heavenly Miracles that could be born even among mere mortals. The girl was a diamond in the rough.

It's a pity that she woke up so late. Had the conditions been more favorable... Alas... Kyle thought. *Fortunately, the dark arts can fix this problem.*

A moment later, the city seemed to freeze, encased in the will of a *Master of Eight Stars*, its power binding the bodies and even the thoughts of all its inhabitants. Only the girl's mind remained active.

A formidable, majestic figure appeared before her. For this occasion, Kyle retained his true appearance and clothes.

"Hanna," he said, "what is it you want the most?"

"I want to kill them all," the girl answered after some hesitation, her voice determined.

"A woman of action. You will make a fine addition to my collection." Kyle smiled. "Eat this."

A small black pea appeared in Kyle's hand — the *Essence of Force* created from the body of a cultivator at the *Mind Stage*.

Hanna swallowed the pea without hesitation. Hundreds of images filled her mind. But, unlike viewing a memory scroll, these memories didn't just slip by. Instead, they were firmly woven into her soul, becoming her own. In just a few moments, Hanna learned about the path of development as well as how to feel and control energy. She even mastered a few techniques and two fighting styles: *Fist* and *Sword*. Creating this *Essence*, Kyle had done a little experimenting so that the *Essence* could obtain his opponent's knowledge and skills, but not parameters or understanding of the elements.

"You know what to do," Kyle said, removing the invisible shackles from everyone around.

Using her newfound knowledge and experience, Hanna easily escaped her captors and killed them one by one. Despite the fact that the *Essence* didn't change her personality, her attacks were determined and devoid of any emotion. It was as if she had been preparing for this moment all her life. Only when the guards came running to the screams of the dying teenagers did Hanna stop. Slightly confused in the face of the armed and trained fighters, she almost let go of her last victim, but then anger prevailed once again. In the end, she finished off the guards, too. She felt no pity for those who never bothered to help her father but came to save those bastards.

Exhausted, Hanna fell to her knees beside her father. By this time, he was no longer breathing — one of the blows broke his skull.

The street was empty. Only Kyle remained where he was. Nodding in satisfaction, he moved Hannah and her father's body to his *Storage* and quickly left the city.

They say that by teaching someone, you can improve your own skills. Well, this is my chance to test this theory...

While wandering aimlessly around the northern part of Bellum, Kyle replayed his fight with Green in his head over and over again. During the skirmish, he was shocked, but after it all ended, he felt intense pleasure, incomparable with anything that he had previously experienced in his life. His boredom had not only subsided but disappeared without a trace.

The defeat didn't break the previously invincible Kyle. On the contrary, it motivated him, helping him see an even higher peak of cultivation. With his actions and words, Green had pointed him toward his next goal.

He would be prepared for his next meeting with Kai and Green.

***

The bowstring creaked. Holding his breath, Shacks was in no hurry to let go of it. Looking out for a target only he could see, he waited patiently. Several hours passed, but he didn't even move. Frozen on a large branch of a huge tree, barely distinguishable from the foliage, he waited for the perfect moment.

As the sun sank behind the horizon, he began to think that nothing would come of his hunt, but he quickly discarded this fear. He had been pursuing his target for several days now. He couldn't back down now. Not when it was finally so close.

In the end, his patience was rewarded. A huge beast, similar to a porcupine made of stone, finished devouring another monster that dared enter its territory, and headed back to its lair.

Squeezing inside, it hid in the underground darkness. Visually, Shacks lost it, but spiritual perception, enhanced by a technique, still allowed him to observe his target. Soon, the porcupine reached the deepest point of the burrow, where it entered a meditative state so that it would digest and assimilate the power of its meal.

Beasts that survived the first *Holy Punishment of Heaven* lost the ability to walk the *Path of Absorption* inherent in them from birth, gaining intelligence instead. However, some of them could still absorb someone else's power through eating by using a technique. To humans and more intelligent beings, this was still considered dark arts, but animals, simple as they were even at this stage of cultivation, didn't care for such rules.

It was already midnight. The porcupine had been meditating for several hours and was almost done absorbing its meal.

It was time.

Shifting on his spot and concentrating even more, Shacks activated the tapestry of weaves embedded in the arrow and saturated it with power. The abilities of the bow and the projectile itself were activated at the same time.

Shacks let go of the string.

Unleashed, the arrow broke the sound barrier through the guise of a sound-concealing technique. As if alive, it bypassed every tree and branch until it pierced the ground and reached the firmament. Drilling through a hundred feet of soil, the arrow hit its target.

Sensing the threat, the beast awoke abruptly, but it was already too late. Breaking through its hide, the arrow dug into the flesh and reached the *Soul Shell*. The porcupine died on the spot.

Shacks didn't rush to his prey. Instead, he listened.

Having detected no signs of life after fifteen minutes, he slowly and carefully approached the lair of the Heavenly Beast.

"I've still got it," he sneered, observing the slain beast.

After cleansing the carcass of the remnants of his technique and the destructive effects of the poison that was in them with a special mixture, Shacks moved it into his pocket dimension.

The following morning, he returned to the Collisium — the home of many intelligent Spirits and animals on Bellum, as well as the only piece of land clear of rune fog on the entire Forgotten Continent. During the months spent here, he managed to get acquainted with most of its sparse population.

Deciding that it'd be best to wrap everything up as quickly as he could, Shacks went to one annoying old woman, to whom, after an hour of bargaining, he sold the carcass of the Heavenly Beast.

With that out of the way, he could finally rest. He was on his way to his cabin when he suddenly noticed a familiar aura nearby. It was moving toward him.

"Missed me, big guy?" Shacks asked with a smile.

Malvur replied with an indifferent shrug.

"We were summoned. The Mountain Sect Alliance will open the Gate soon. Don't go anywhere, we'll move out soon. We'll meet *him* soon."

Outwardly, Shacks didn't change, remaining relaxed and playful as ever, but everything inside him tensed up.

Right. Then the time has come.

Malvur nodded firmly.

Shacks, Malvur, Ailenx, Ivsim, and Lily had long decided that if they failed to convince and stop Kai, then they would betray the Collisium and flee with him.

***

A flying boat soared across the inky sea of the universe beyond the Trial Worlds, fueled by a huge amount of *Runes* and divine particles.

Aboard it was a group of four, at the head of which stood a tall, stately dark-haired man in his forties with a neat beard, perfect posture, and an aristocratic face.

Looking at Bellum, a small distant dot on the horizon, One frowned.

Almost three weeks ago, the Abyss that opened up on Insulaii closed. Lilith and Ryu soon returned to Kaiser's Ark, but the Master never showed up. He was gone, but his clones continued to exist, which meant that he was alive.

Unfortunately, they couldn't contact him through a spirit connection, as the distance between them turned out to be too great. Kai was on some other world. But there was no way to send a group of clones in search of him, because the Four Mists Cartel and the Han Nam and the Twin Dragon Unions had declared war on Avlaim.

By using a special artifact that Rosen received from Yashnir, as well as an unimaginable amount of *Runes*, they cut off Insulaii from Ferox and Bellum for six months. Transfers through the Gates and *Altars* were also blocked.

Fortunately, their opponents had greatly underestimated the power of the Eternal Path Temple. More than eleven thousand clones became an army of nightmares.

The Cartel was rapidly losing its troops in a desperate attempt to flee Avlaim when three days ago, all the clones without the Master's Will fell into a deep sleep. The simultaneous loss of almost ten thousand warriors turned the tide of the battle on all fronts.

Avlaim was losing.

One and Six guessed that something terrible must have happened to their master if he had to put the clones to sleep and take back the Willpower he had allocated to them. Worried as they were, they couldn't just leave the Temple and risk losing Kaiser's legacy.

For a while, they pondered what to do, but when the massive blackout happened, they decided to trust their instinct and do what they thought would be right for both their organization and its members.

From the very beginning, they attempted to break through the barrier their opponents had set up over Insulaii. That day, they finally made a small gap in the dome that would let through only weak mortals and objects that didn't have a *Spark*. Fortunately, that was all they needed.

The clones weren't truly living beings, so they could pass through. But since their connection with Kai weakened and it was no longer possible to find him through it, One had to take with him the only person who had been drawn toward their master from the very beginning.

Igdrasil.

Chapter 3
ICE DIMENSION

The long underground staircase ended in a small dark corridor that led upward. Kai's footsteps echoed in this strange place filled with ripples of spatial distortion.

After negotiating the terms and signing a trade agreement with the Hidden Temple, as well as receiving the promised *Runes*, Kai left the underground city. His next destination was the Ice Gates.

"Here we are," Zarifa said, stopping in front of the stone door. "You're on your own from here."

"Thank you for seeing me to the exit. You really didn't have to."

"Perhaps, but I wanted to. I owe you that much. Say... Is it true that the Mentor didn't allow you to use the *Altar* to move to Insulaii?"

"Not really. He offered it, but I refused. I still have some unfinished business on Bellum."

"I see... In that case, I wish you good luck. I hope our paths will cross again. I'd like to spar with you once more. I don't often see people who can keep up with me. I've learned all I can from my brothers and sisters, so fighting someone from the outside is a nice change of pace."

"I hope so, too." Kai nodded in agreement, a half-smile dancing on his lips. "Take care, Zarifa."

"You, too."

Turning around, he grabbed the handle, but the door didn't budge. With a slight frown, Kai looked over his shoulder to ask her what to do, but Zarifa was nowhere to be found.

"When did she...? What's that?"

The corridor that lead back to the underground city now ended inside a large cave, from the mouth of which he could see the surface. Kai had been moved so easily and quickly that even his perception had failed to notice it. All this indicated that the corridor's array was the work of someone with a high understanding of the *Path of Space*.

The Hidden Temple is living up to its name. I wondered why they didn't take any precaution, but this is much better than simply blindfolding me. The spatial array keeps its true location hidden. How interesting...

Having emerged onto the surface, Kai found himself in the middle of a lush jungle. He took a deep breath and focused on the *Trophy*. Without activating it, he carefully reduced the energy density in a small area around him while simultaneously increasing it in his body. This continued until the difference between the densities reached a value equal to the difference in the *ki* density of an *Elementalist* and a *Soul Stage* cultivator.

As the energy resistance around him decreased, Kai felt an extraordinary lightness, as if a boulder had been removed from his shoulders.

From there, things were easy. Having experienced and practiced levitation before with the *Field of Superiority*, Kai quickly got used to flying.

He had seen many places during his lifetime, but the view that opened up in front of him was still breathtaking. Wherever he looked, there was a green jungle, spreading to the very horizon. Only the ominous silence reminded him of just how dangerous these places were.

For a little while, he allowed himself to have some fun and perform various tricks. After several minutes, he returned to the matter at hand and took out an artifact-map. Despite its *Divine Rank*, it didn't work in the underground city, but whatever barrier had prevented it from working there, it didn't work outside. As the artifact came to life, a giant and extremely detailed projection of Bellum's main continent appeared in front of Kai. Having determined the location of the Ice Gates using Magnus's coordinates, he deactivated the map and adjusted his course.

Under the invisibility of the *Semi-Solid Energy Zone* and a special artifact, he cut through the skies of Bellum, until a large dark spot appeared on the horizon. As he got closer, it became clear that what he was looking at was actually an anomalous storm. Judging by its size and density, it had been raging over the eastern coast for thousands of years.

"Bingo."

Picking up speed, he entered a cloud of acidic rain capable of corroding even the purest of metals. Soon, he was picked up by a gust of wind so strong that it could demolish an entire building in one fell swoop. This place was a death trap, but Kai didn't care. Focused on his goal, he continued to fly as if he wasn't in the middle of the storm.

Conditions got only worse as he drew closer to the eye

of the hurricane. Relying only on his *Energy Cover*, *Complete Submission*, and ability to manipulate energy, he entered it despite how dangerous it was.

For the most part, it consisted of wind and water, since it was located above an ocean, but there were traces of other elements as well: streams of fiery air, rocks, lightning flashes, chunks of icebergs, rivers of blood, and so on.

It was a natural disaster on a planetary scale.

In the historical chronicles of the Trial Worlds, there was no explanation as to where this anomaly came from. However, there was a date — it appeared about eighteen thousand years ago. Coincidentally enough, Magnus was sealed approximately at the same time, and the Ice Gates were located inside the storm. It was believed that this was where U'Shor defeated Magnus, and the storm was the aftermath of their fateful battle.

Despite all his energy control, Kai couldn't break through into the whirlwind. There was so much *prana* in the anomaly that it would take him several weeks to dispel just a hundredth of it. He wasn't going to activate the *Trophy* for this, so he needed an alternative solution.

Teleporting won't work. There are too many spatial distortions.

Revealing *Phobos* and activating the *Tattoo*, he enhanced his attack with a considerable amount of soul energy and unleashed the full power of the *Primordial Flash* at the tornado. But his efforts were in vain. The beam of snow-white energy disappeared into the whirlwind without doing almost any damage.

Cursing under his breath, Kai put away his weapon and flew up. He rose into the upper layers of the atmosphere, and then into the exosphere, where the storm ended. Having bypassed the barrier, he plunged into the center of the tornado.

The situation inside was much calmer than on the outside, but there were still many dangers. As if alive, the anomaly tried to hit Kai with lightning and rocks.

At the point where the ocean met the anomaly, the tornado turned into a huge whirlpool, its pull so strong that it sucked up all the water from the bottom, revealing the Ice Gates.

Having descended, Kai discovered a giant artificial barrier, covering the entire ocean bottom. It was surprisingly stable considering the environment it was in, and so well-hidden that he wouldn't have noticed it if it weren't for his energy vision.

Carefully piercing through the surface layer of the whirlpool, he followed it to the bottom. Once there, he wandered around the barrier, studying it.

Having not yet recovered from his battle with Kyle, Kai felt his energy being draining. However, he didn't let this stop him from completing his mission. It took a while, a little longer than he would have liked, but he eventually found what he had been looking for. Due to its proximity to the anomaly, this section of the barrier was weaker than the rest and even slightly damaged. As expected, there could be no perfect defense in such a place, unless we counted the anomaly itself, which only a madman would risk disturbing.

I hope this works, Kai thought.

By controlling gravity, he pulled a massive stone the size of a hut from the depths of the whirlpool.

Temporarily reducing the weight of the boulder, Kai slammed it into the damaged section of the barrier, restoring its original weight at the last moment. The attempt was partially successful: the barrier withstood, but a few cracks appear on its surface. Nonetheless, this was enough for Kai to manipulate the surrounding space and slip inside.

The atmosphere under the barrier was strikingly different from the one inside the anomaly. The terrifying pressure of elemental energy was gone, allowing Kai to relax a little. The anomaly couldn't harm him anymore, but his instincts still made him tremble before its monstrous natural power. According to stories and legends, just contemplating the storm from a relatively short distance was a good test of willpower.

Having erased even the smallest traces of his presence, such as the space distortions and the echoes of his willpower, Kai hurried to get away from the damaged section of the barrier. Someone would soon be here to check it out, and he had no desire to meet the current owners of these Gates.

Hidden from the outside world by the barrier was a small town, founded by the people of the Collisium, who guarded these Gates until they lost the war to the Mountain Sect Alliance. The small settlement was crowded with True Masters, some of whom seemed to have arrived quite recently.

Looks like the Gates are about to be opened...

Studying the town from the outskirts, Kai realized two things. Firstly, there were about fifteen thousand cultivators here, not a single one of them below the *Elementalist Stage*. New Masters were still arriving through a giant Arch bought at the *Altar*. With the exception of the strongest *Divine* items, only it could form a stable dimensional tunnel with the outside world next to such an anomaly.

Secondly, even though all these people belonged to different organizations, they were a part of the Mountain Sect Alliance.

If one of their leaders shows up, that will greatly complicate my task. They have three Divine Stage *cultivators with* Seven Big Stars, *as well as one* Master *with* Seven Great Stars. *I really don't need them getting in the way right now.* Kai frowned. *Did Magnus know about this when he sent me here? First Magnus, and now Green. Everyone is trying to manipulate me. It's a nasty feeling, but I can't do anything about this for now. The plan is to play along until I'm able to make my move to turn the tide.*

Realizing that staying here any longer would put him at risk of being discovered, Kai moved to the *Storage*. With his tracks being covered, it was almost impossible to detect him there.

I need to restore as much energy as I can. Things are about to get really difficult.

***

The moment had come.

An army of *Elementalists*, *Holy Lords*, and *Divine Stage* cultivators stood in front of the Ice Gates. On one hand, against the true strength of the Mountain Sect Alliance, such an army seemed as big as a colony of ants against a raging tide, but on the other, sending too many people on an expedition this important could prove disastrous.

Necks craned back, they all stared in awe as the Gates began to open. With a rumble and a roar, the doors parted, releasing a wave of insane cold. Kai was also watching, impressed by the echoes of the overwhelming power that escaped from the spatial transition.

As the Gates opened, they revealed an opaque veil of blue-white color. Instead of rushing inside, the Alliance sent several groups ahead to test the waters. Upon returning, they reported their findings to their leaders, after which the entire army moved forward in orderly rows.

Kai found this decision strange. To send all your men into the unknown so quickly was as foolish as it was hasty — unless you knew everything that there was to know about a location, especially one as old as mysterious as this one.

Through his studies, Kai had learned that the new Army of Truth was in some way connected to U'Shor, the creator of this place. And while the O'Crimes, who took control of most of the Mountain Sect Alliance, knew something about the Gates and how to open them, Kai knew nothing about either the family or the mysterious portal.

As the army passed through the veil, leaving only a few hundred servants in the town, Kai followed after them. Reaching the Gates, he lingered in front of them for a bit before stepping into the unknown.

The space around him distorted. A wave of wild cold washed over Kai, penetrating even through his *Cover* and hardened skin. For a moment, he once again felt like an ordinary mortal, who could freeze to death. Even after four days of difficult contemplation, his soul's emotional layer hadn't returned to normal, and so he remained limited by the elements and the techniques he could use. All he could do was rely on the *Cold Void*, artifacts, and his willpower. Viola was still slumbering, so he didn't expect her to come running to his aid anytime soon.

Kai found himself in an endless snow-covered wasteland, frozen in eternal twilight. The place wasn't just a half-open pocket dimension, but a world of its own, somewhere outside the Ecumene.

As soon as he stepped foot into this new world, he was forced to fend for his life.

The unbearable cold wasn't a problem only for Kai.

Many people died in a matter of seconds. Their cores frozen, a strange force began to seize their bodies, transforming them into multi-armed monsters made of ice and snow. Saturated with runic fog and divine particles, these creatures possessed not only great physical strength, but also incredible elemental resistance.

Quickly after the Alliance members were turned into monsters, chaos erupted.

No one was prepared for the massacre that followed.

Initial information about this place indicated something completely different, but the intelligence squads seemed to have been deceived.

Kai was caught in the crossfire of the confusion and chaos that broke out. He managed to dodge most of the techniques and block a few with his blades and willpower.

With the portal gone, he was stranded here. His best bet would be to move away from the Alliance as quickly as possible. Unfortunately, his invisibility didn't work well against the creatures, and he was forced to escape into the air.

Once he was at a safe distance away from the deranged Alliance, Kai looked around the battlefield. The expedition was doing much worse than it seemed at first. The creatures were rapidly evolving, growing smarter with every second, while their numbers continued to increase. On top of that, they worked as one, communicating without words.

But that wasn't the worst thing. No.

In the beginning, Kai thought that they only appeared from the corpses, but he was wrong. Looking closer, he noted that they also formed by themselves, as if growing out of the ground. Curious about this phenomenon, he used his energy vision and learned that this entire dimension was essentially one giant trap.

This is bad, he thought, gritting his teeth as he pondered. *But at least I know that I'm in the right place.*

Catching a glimmer in the periphery of his vision, he raised his head to see a phoenix made of ice and snow appear on the horizon. To his misfortune, however, the bird's brilliant presence seriously decreased the temperature and strengthened the creatures.

Bastard!

Like the creatures, the phoenix wasn't a living being, but a very complex spiritual mechanism. Moreover, it was constantly evolving. Unlike the monsters, however, it wasn't just a part of the trap, but its heart.

It was the very Elder Rune that Kai needed.

"Fuck," Kai cursed. He couldn't sense and rate its power, but he'd say that the phoenix was very powerful, at least close to *One Step away from Divinity* level.

Chapter 4
ICE DIMENSION 2

"What do you think is in there?" the old chief of the settlement asked as she gazed upon the Ice Gates.

"I don't know," her friend and old rival answered with a shrug. "Hopefully something of value, and not some nightmarish creature. What do you think?" Grinning, the elf turned to the woman.

There was no answer. His friend shuddered all over, and then froze.

Surprised, he grabbed her by the shoulder and spun her to face him.

"Are you all right?"

She rose her eyes to meet his. Her figure seemed to blur for a moment, and then the elf's decapitated body sank to the ground. The woman was gone before the head even stopped rolling, having teleported to the Arch installed near the town.

As expected, such an important object wasn't left unguarded. A handful of *Elementalists* and a couple of *Holy Lords* were protecting the passage. They bowed their heads in respect as soon as they saw her. No one thought to ask what she was doing here.

"Chief!"

Approaching the Arch, the woman connected a powerful artifact to it and activated a spatial transition. The portal opened with a hum, but its passage didn't lead to its usual destination, the lands of the Alliance, but somewhere else.

For a few seconds, nothing happened. The guards observed the chieftain and the portal in perplexed silence. The woman remained unperturbed as ripples passed through the veil of the portal, and a short, stocky dwarf in armor emerged from the unknown.

"My lord," the chieftain greeted, bowing deeply. "The task has been completed."

"Well done." The dwarf nodded, smiling softly at the sight of the open Ice Gates.

As soon as he revealed his aura, the town began to fill with corpses. Dozens of people died one after another, unable to withstand the pressure of the Puppeteer's power.

Following their leader, a river of the House of Doll's strongest poured out from the Arch, filling the empty town. The chieftain, having fulfilled her duty, also joined their ranks.

Having collected and "preserved" the Masters' bodies, the Puppeteer gave out an order. Soon, a squad of almost five thousand Adepts, consisting only of *Divine Stage* cultivators, advanced into the ice dimension.

The little town nestled in the center of the anomaly was drowned in silence, broken only by the quiet hum of the portal. Suddenly, something invisible hit the barrier, disrupting the tranquility of the scene. The attacks went on for a while, but there was no one to react to the small gap that soon appeared in the barrier. The veil shattered like broken glass, letting the intruders through.

An invisible flying ship halted in front of the Ice Gates. With Igdrasil's help, the clones found out that their creator was inside the ice dimension. However, they were in no hurry to go after him.

One thought long and hard, but he couldn't find the right solution. He was wasting precious time.

"Twenty-Three, check the other side," he finally said, turning to his brother.

"Right away."

Disembarking the ship, Twenty-Three passed through the shimmering portal and disappeared. With every passing minute, One became gloomier and gloomier. Twenty-Three was alive, but it was impossible to contact him through either the mental link or a communication artifact. Neither seemed to work in that place.

When his brother didn't return, One cursed, looked at the little Ent, and sighed heavily. A decision had to be made.

I can't abandon our Master. I'm sorry, little one, but I have to take the risk, even if it costs us both our lives...

"One-Hundred-and-Six, stay here with the ship," he ordered the youngest of the clones who had gone with him. "If... When we find the Master, your task will be to get him out of here. Hide and await our return."

One-Hundred-and-Six nodded firmly. He knew that their creator could transfer his consciousness into the bodies of clones, so he understood what his brother was getting at.

After that, One transferred Igdrasil to a separate pocket

dimension.

Together with another clone, he approached the Gates.

***

At about the same time, similar Ice Gates were slowly opening on the other side of the planet. In front of them stood thousands of Heavenly Beasts and Spirits, led by the five most powerful demigods, Guardians of the Collisium. One of them was Yusa Softlight, next to whom stood Shacks, Lily, Malvur, Ivsim, and Ailenx.

"Have you figured out how to stop your comrade?" Yusa inquired.

"Yes, but first we need to find him," Lily replied. "Kai is very good at hiding. Even the strongest Masters can't detect him from a distance."

"Hah. He's almost as good as I am," Shacks added with a sneer. "*Almost.*"

"I hope you remember that we will be forced to intervene if he tries to destroy the Elder Rune," Yusa said, opening one eye.

"Of course. However, we'd like to ask you for a favor," Ailenx spoke up. "He will stay in hiding until he gets a chance to get close to the Rune. That's where we want to catch him. Please, don't intervene until the Rune is in danger. Give us a chance to stop him first."

"Hmm."

The five bowed respectfully.

"Please."

"You only get one try," Yusa finally answered. "Not more than a minute. If you fail, I will attack him."

Why are you wasting time with these kids? another Guardian asked Yusa.

Their friend could come in handy in the fight against Magnus. He has the same power as the Founder, Yusa reminded him. *It would be unwise to get rid of him right away. We shouldn't try to control him with threats and force either. Such ways bring nothing but trouble in the end.*

You've become too soft. Those damned two-legged freaks.

Meanwhile, the Ice Gates finally opened, and the Collisium's army set off for the long-awaited battle.

Today would be the day, they thought. Today would be the day they win.

As soon as they found themselves in the ice dimension, the cold and a group of strange creatures attacked them. Not even U'Shor's followers were an exception to the defensive systems of this place.

"It shouldn't be like this," one of the Guardians muttered in confusion as he gazed back at the now closed portal. "The founder created this place differently on purpose. Something changed it..."

"It doesn't matter now," said another. "The Alliance's exit point should be on that side. We need to defeat their army and locate the threat!"

***

Since the ice phoenix appeared, the course of the battle had changed. Though the bird was insanely strong, it lacked skill and experience, much to the relief of the Alliance. Prepared as they were, it didn't take much for them to resist its influence. Their army was led by three *Masters of Seven Great Stars*: the head of the Alliance, as well as the first son and first daughter of the O'Crime family, Varimas and

Valorie. The two used *Divine* artifacts and all their other resources without hesitation.

It seems that the part of Magnus enclosed in the phoenix weakened and influenced its vessel, granting the bird something akin to a Soul Shell *and strengthening the array,* Varimas realized. *How ironic... But now I understand why this place is so different from what U'Shor told Lord Yashnir.*

Suddenly, his intuition warned him of danger. Just when a hail of mighty lightning bolts swept past him, he defended himself with one of the *Divine* artifacts. The attack was aimed at the phoenix, but it hit a dozen Alliance members in passing, killing them right where they stood. The phoenix was unscathed.

The attack meant that the cultists had finally arrived. Like the O'Crimes, the Puppeteer was also interested in the part of Magnus that was imprisoned here. Followed by five thousand *Divine Stage* cultivators, he joined the battle.

A real carnage ensued. Some of the adepts rushed at the Alliance, while some battled the phoenix. As they were surrounded, the number of Alliance leaders rapidly declined, despite all their talent and power of *Divine* artifacts. Even the true descendants of the Heavenly Manticore were on the verge of death.

As for the phoenix, it was shackled with many techniques and bombarded with thousands of attacks. The creature screeched in despair, but it couldn't even move a feather to defend itself.

Watching what was happening from afar, the invisible Kai thought that he wouldn't have to intervene, but then... A third party unexpectedly joined the battle. Thousands of various monsters and Spirits in their true forms appeared out of nowhere, taking by surprise not only the cultists but even him. Up until now, they had been hiding under the influence of some *Divine* artifact.

"PUPPETEER!!!" a roar full of hatred filled the air as something very bright flashed in the sky. For a second, the world lost its colors and the air became warmer.

***

"Oooh, boy," Shacks whistled. Like the other four, he was observing the battlefield from the sidelines for the time being. "We were worried about nothing. Kai's crazy, but not even he is crazy enough to risk his neck here."

"Doesn't matter. We shouldn't lower our guard," Malvur remarked. "We need to find him."

"You go find him!" Shacks snapped, continuing to watch the battle with interest. "Do ya see what's going on down there? They'll turn us into minced meat."

By this time, new ice creatures stopped showing up, and the already-created ones were no longer recovering. Having redirected all of the array's power to itself, the phoenix could no longer support them. At first, this made little difference, but once the Collisium entered the battle, the monster managed to break free from the shackles that bound it. The phoenix compressed all the available power of the array for its most devastating attack yet.

The space shuddered. The phoenix's body emitted an invisible wave that touched almost everyone trapped within the dimension. A moment later, thousands of people fell to the ground. For some unknown reason, they suddenly became victims of Insulaii's restrictions, which temporarily turned them from *Divine Stage* cultivators into peak *Elementalists*.

Those who remained on the ground or were far enough away from the epicenter only felt the faint echoes of the attack.

But the phoenix didn't stop there.

With a loud cry and a flap of its mighty wings, it unleashed a nightmarish spatial storm on the entire dimension. All that were caught within it were tossed from side to side like a leaf caught in the wind, while their bodies were stretched and violently squeezed. This went on for a full minute. By the end of it, almost half of all those who entered the dimension were dead. The rest were thrown into one pile.

Exhausted, the phoenix disappeared, hiding in the depths of the dimension. Its plan was to let the intruders kill each other while it rested. It would reappear later, once things settled down, to pick off any stragglers.

Shacks, Ivsim, Lily, Malvur, and Ailenx were among the survivors. By heavenly grace, they even ended up close to each other. But that was where their luck ended. No sooner did they open their eyes and come to their senses that they were drawn into the battle between the three factions.

Let's go to the edge of the battlefield, Ivsim hissed through a spiritual link. *We need to get out of here or we'll be killed before we manage to find Kai.*

Slowly but surely, they made their way out, stopping only to defend themselves from incoming attacks and clear the path. They had no choice. It was either them or the enemy.

Besides relentless physical attacks, Malvur used the *Path of Earth* to maintain a small-scale earthquake in the area around him. With it, he hindered the movement of their opponents, slowing them down and knocking them off their feet, allowing his friends to finish them off quickly and easily.

All of a sudden, an invisible anomaly hit the earthquake-affected area. Wasting no time, Malvur rushed forward. His spirit perception was silent, but his intuition guided him correctly.

Soon, his glaive collided with someone else's blade, creating a shower of sparks. Malvur's opponent fell to his knee with a grunt, his invisibility torn off. He shouted something to someone, but Malvur didn't even think of stopping. He wouldn't get a chance like this again. His opponent was weakened by the recent spatial storm, making him an easy target.

The second attack broke through the man's defenses, cutting off his head in one swift strike.

The spatial wave Malvur released destroyed the man's body and *Storage*. Two spheres of dark matter burst open, throwing out various artifacts, vials, scrolls, and something small and wooden.

Finding himself in an icy dimension filled with deadly cold, Igdrasil managed to emit only a short, silent cry that was quickly drowned out by the storm and the sound of the battle raging around him.

Malvur froze as if rooted to the spot. The fog that had covered his mind suddenly lifted, allowing him to realize what he had just done.

The only people he knew that were invisible to spirit perception were Kai and his clones.

Malvur's legs buckled. He fell to his knees, dropping his weapon.

A moment later, a wave of insane bloodlust swept through the area.

Chapter 5
FRIENDS

Continuing to secretly observe the battle from the side, Kai was overwhelmed by a sudden feeling of pain, fear, and despair all at once. The sensations were so strong that they made him tremble all over and lose control of his invisibility. A child's cry fell on his mind like thunder. Breathless, he gripped his chest that burned with hatred.

After the flames of rage came a profound emptiness, as if he had lost something extremely close to his heart. Kai unconsciously broke Kal'het's seal, freeing the emotional layer of his soul. Together with his emotions, remnants of his demonic nature gushed out. His fury intensified, almost blinding him, manifesting in the whites of his eyes turning red.

A moment later, he was already somewhere else. Standing before the remains of One and Igdrasil, Kai froze them with the *Indestructible Cube Technique* and moved them to his *Storage*. This was the last thing his conscious mind managed to do before he was completely consumed by his fury.

In his hands, his swords burned with dark green flames. The *Nightmare World* swallowed up the entire area.

Those stricken by Kai's bloodlust fell to their knees, staining their robes with blood and snow. Shouting madly, they grabbed their heads, gouged out their eyes, and bit off their tongues, their souls sinking into the abyss of fear and horror.

Only Malvur remained conscious, his mind protected by an amulet acquired on Belteise. Still on his knees, he looked at his friend's back with disbelief and deep remorse. Kai whirled around, and their eyes met for a moment. But even if rage hadn't overshadowed his mind, he still wouldn't have remembered the giant.

Malvur didn't even have time to blink when Kai appeared next to him, quick as a bolt of lightning. A sharp stab of pain jolted the giant, and then his right arm flew into the air, where it disintegrated in the *Flame of Death*. Both his physical and *Astral Bodies* were damaged around the wounded area. Kai was about to deprive him of the rest of his limbs when a strong shockwave knocked him down and threw him back several feet.

Tumbling in the air, Kai came to an abrupt halt. His hair was disheveled and his robes torn, but he seemed otherwise unharmed. Panting with anger, he raised his gaze to look at the man who dared prevent him from delivering justice.

"Kai! What are you doing?!" Ivsim shouted in disbelief. "Malvur is your friend! Stop!"

But Kai only bared his teeth in response and flung himself at the young cultivator in front of him. Caught by surprise, Ivsim failed to react in time. He could only watch as *Phobos* sank into his stomach and filled his body with *Force* particles. Heavily wounded, he was thrown back without the hope of getting up.

Immediately forgetting about him, Kai turned back to Malvur. But before he could even raise his swords, strong currents of water enveloped his body, binding him. Ailenx spared no effort, using both his soul energy and the rare *Soul Manifestation Everything and Now*, coupled with the additional energy of special *Vessels*, to support his *Water Body* and grant him incredible strength.

But he couldn't hold Kai back for a long time. The *Cold Void* gradually froze his watery body. The only reason why Ailenx was able to keep him put was Kai's anger. Blinded by it, he didn't think of using any techniques, only killing.

Seizing the moment, Lily appeared behind Kai, her blade imbued with power, while Shacks stopped to his right, aiming an arrow straight at his head.

"Ya need to calm down, my friend. I don't know what's going on here, but I'll plant this arrow between your eyes if you so much as breathe too loudly," he said, his words firm and heavy even without being enhanced by the *Master's Will*.

Unfortunately, Kai didn't hear him. Like a trapped beast, he thrashed and growled, trying to break free of Ailenx's shackles.

"You fucking idiot," Shacks muttered under his breath and turned to Lily and Ailenx. "Take those two and get out of here!"

Overflowing with power, the arrow shone brightly and rushed forward. But it didn't hit Kai. Unconsciously turning his head into a black mist and protecting his *Astral Body* with *Spheres*, he dodged it at the last moment. But Shacks didn't need to wound him, only to distract him. Taking advantage of the moment, he threw himself forward and grabbed his friend by the arm. A moment later, they both disappeared, hiding inside the dark dome of the *Duel Zone*. In all three Trial Worlds, Shacks's rating was lower than Kai's, so he could challenge him just by touching him.

Finally free, Kai leaped at Shacks, but he simply went through him, as if the archer was just an illusion. It was impossible to start a duel without discussing its conditions and placing a bet.

After several failed attempts at attacking Shacks, Kai gave up. The anger continued to rage in him, not subsiding for a second. Frozen in a fighting stance, he never took his bloodshot eyes from his opponent.

"You're clearly out of your mind. Well, more than you usually are," Shacks remarked as he crossed his arms over his chest and cocked his head to the side. "I don't know where you've been all this time, but something tells me that chopping off limbs isn't a proper way to greet your friends anywhere in the universe. How about we have a drink instead? It's been a while, hasn't it? And here I thought you'd be happy to see me... Honestly, I'm a little hurt."

Alas, there was no answer. Kai was clearly not in the mood for dialogue.

"No? Shame. I have some good wine. Seems I'll have to beat the shit out of you after all." Shacks sighed. As the smile faded from his face, his personality and aura shifted. His gaze turned cold and blank, and his expression became impassive. The change was so sudden that it left Kai feeling on edge despite the rage clouding his mind. In an instant, a threat materialized before him, one so dangerous that he'd rather avoid getting involved with it. "You know, I've been thinking about this moment for a long time. Our only real fight was sixteen years ago when we first met. Alkea... What a nice place that was. Shame I had to kill Lily's grandfather. You were a force to be reckoned with then. And look at you now... Foaming at the mouth, like some rabid dog..."

Shacks was silent for a few minutes, lost in distant memories. The Great Tournament of the Celestial Plateau, the new adventures on Earth, the battle with Liu, the search and pursuit of Jiang Dao, the slavery ring in Udin, the Fist Fight, the Cloud Abode, rescuing Kai, the fight for the giants' capital, the journey to Belteise, the war with Niagala, almost three centuries of training on the planet where time flew faster, and, finally, the Trial Worlds. It was a journey of a lifetime.

"You know, I have a dream... I always wanted to have a place where someone was waiting for me, and people were always glad to see me. A home and a family. Not the Bright Moon Clan, where I was just another tool, but a real home. And you gave me that. You, Acilla, Malvur, An'na, Ivsim, Ailenx, Guts, and even Lily. For the sake of that dream, I'm ready to remove any obstacle. Including you, important as you are to me. Unfortunately, in a fair fight, I'm no match for you. My abilities are negligible within the Ecumene. I'm not the best even in our group. My energy control and sensitivity are worse than Lily's. I'm not developing as fast as An'na. I'm not as devoted to training as Ailenx. And I'm not as strong in spirit as Malvur. But that's fine. I don't have to be any of those things. I have a little something of my own... Something that makes me stand out from the rest of the crowd." He tapped his head with his finger. "I haven't told anyone about this, but at the middle of the *Elementalist Stage*, I managed to gain perfect understanding of all the layers of the soul's mental layer, so now my intelligence reaches the upper bar of *Seven Big Stars*," he explained without a drop of arrogance. "I'm aware that that won't be enough to defeat you, so I came prepared. Long ago, I came up with a plan to eliminate each of you in case you went rogue. To be honest, I'd love nothing more than to never have to use it, but I'd be lying if I said that this doesn't make me happy to some extent. I don't think I'll get the chance to fight you like this ever again."

Unfolding his arms, Shacks cracked his neck and closed his eyes. The smile returned to his face, as mischievous as ever. Those more perceptive would perhaps see a trace of malice in it, the only reminder of the killer that lurked deep within the archer's soul.

"Fortunately, Malvur is still alive, so I suppose I can go easy on you. I'll still give you a good ass-whopping, though. Heavens know you've deserved it," he said with a grin. "Gotta beat this bullshit out of you, don't I?"

The five minutes allotted for discussing the terms of the duel ended. As if aware of this, Kai attacked with a short but very swift and violent blow. Shacks didn't even lift a finger in response, continuing to smile. The *Blades of Nightmare* pierced through his flesh, and...

Suddenly, Kai's body was cut into four pieces, which was what should have happened to the unharmed Shacks. The reason for this was Shacks's *Divine Gift* — the *Power of the Bright Moon*. More specifically, it was thanks to the *Seventh Order: The Armor of Lies*. Using this ability, Shacks covered his body with an invisible film of energy that reflected all the inflicted damage back to his opponent.

The wound even touched Kai's *Astral Body*, disorienting him for a second. The pain was so sudden and strong that he failed to sense Shacks's double even with his energy vision. Hidden in the shadows, it released the bowstring, firing an arrow that it had been imbuing with various techniques for the past five minutes.

The projectile pierced his stomach, tearing his barely fused body apart again. Blood and tissue scattered in all directions, but Kai didn't die. Having protected his head and *Astral Body* in time with the *Cover*, he reflexively activated *Partial Transformation*, enhancing his regenerative abilities. Encased in black scales, a new body began to materialize at astonishing speed.

But Shacks wasn't going to sit and wait for his friend

to recover. At the moment the first projectile was fired, he took out three arrows, which he now released into Kai's half-regenerated form.

"Are you curious about the plan I had for you?"

"Argh!"

"No? Well, I'll tell you anyway. Step one: disorientate the target. Hurts like a bitch, don't it?" he sneered. "Step two: suppress its main ability. Your bloodline."

The anatomy of the three fired arrows and the three that remained in his *Storage* consisted not only of rare spiritual materials based on the *Paths* of *Death*, *Blood*, *Poison*, and *Fog*, but also of the special venom that coated them, specifically created to counter the abilities of the Hydra bloodline. To make it, Shacks had been secretly collecting samples of Kai's blood and flesh every chance he got.

"Remember all those fights in the Cloud Abode? You left enough of yourself behind to make another you," Shacks remarked.

As soon as the arrowheads touched Kai's flesh, they turned into long, very thin worms made of fog that slithered into his body, wreaking havoc within.

As the scales started peeling off, the power bestowed upon him by *Partial Transformation* declined, and his regeneration weakened. The poison and the parasites generated by the arrows were sucking all the life out of Kai. He tried to destroy them, but Shacks left nothing to chance.

Using the *Third* and *Fourth Orders* of the *Divine Gift* — the *Blackfathom World* and the *Mist Army* — he filled the *Duel Zone* with thick fog, reducing the visibility to zero, and suppressing Kai's spiritual perception to no more than three feet. However, this didn't prevent him from observing Shacks through energy vision. But only until the moment when

Shacks activated the *Seventh Order's* invisibility.

Kai swung his swords at the fog warriors, disregarding any semblance of tactic and finesse in swordsmanship. He looked more and more like a mindless beast backed into a corner and less like a trained cultivator with a plan.

But his parameters were still high. Even though the arrows had weakened him, *Partial Transformation* and *Cover* helped him maintain some of his former strength, mostly physical. In such a state, he continued to pose a considerable threat.

"Step three: wear down the target and weaken its defenses," Shacks muttered, unleashing several attacks along with his clones.

Kai managed to repel and block some of the arrows. Those that hit him, he failed to see with his energy vision because they struck from rather unexpected places. He struggled against it for a while, but he finally caved in when Shacks and the clones fired another volley, breaking through his defense.

Soon after, the fog warriors, like the fog itself, disappeared. Shacks squatted in front of Kai, staring into his eyes as they slowly returned to their normal violet color.

"Had enough yet?" he asked.

Despite his victory, Shacks didn't look good. Attacking, supporting clones, as well as the prolonged use of three *Orders* took a lot out of him, forcing him to resort to drinking a couple of expensive potions to recover.

Slowly coming to his senses, Kai tried to focus on the person before him. Fragmented images broke through the fog surrounding his mind, and broken memories of recent events flashed in front of him like through a kaleidoscope: a large-scale battle in the ice dimension, a sudden outburst of rage, Igdrasil and One, or rather, their frozen bodies, an attempt to kill the culprit, and a fight with some archer. Anger flared up in Kai's soul again, but this time it was his own, and not that of the demon whose essence still remained in his soul.

The *Primordial Flash* and the *Inevitable Healing Technique* surged into his body in a wave, washing away the fatigue and restoring strength to Kai's body and soul. Invigorated, he weaved several other abilities, including *Borrowing Flame*, and filled himself with power.

Sharply opening his eyes, he teleported straight into the air, avoiding several arrows and appeared right in front of Shacks, decapitating him. Just like the first time, the *Armor of Lies* reflected all the damage, except that Kai flashed with the golden light of the *Radiant Void*, trying to do the same. The techniques clashed violently. The confrontation dragged on for a while, until both duelists froze, fully focused on each other.

"So, the game's still on?" Shacks grinned. "Good. Good... I didn't like the other guy. You ain't yourself when you're pissed."

Ultimately, the *Radiant Void* lost to the *Power of the Bright Moon*, and a straight crimson line appeared on Kai's neck for a brief second before being healed by the Hydra's powers. Kai's intuition told him that the invisible film of Shacks's *Armor of Lies* was gone.

Couldn't handle the load? Kai thought. *Good.*

Ignoring the arrow that stood frozen at his neck, Kai went around Shacks, who was moving as if in slow motion. The archer's parameters were inferior to his. On top of that, he also had better movement techniques and reinforced *Spheres* (especially of *Cold Void* and *Space*), so he moved almost ten times faster than Shacks did.

Stepping behind his opponent, Kai activated the *Burning Ice Curse Technique* and plunged his blade into Shacks. No sooner did the steel enter the supple flesh than his intuition warned him of incoming danger. Something powerful gripped his wrist, after which Shacks's image blurred into a misty haze and exploded into a shower of sparks.

Without a hand, Kai barely managed to jump back. Poisonous fumes entered his system, and his body shuddered every now and again, struck by discharges of lightning. But worst of all was the powerful gravitational blow that hit him square in the chest, greatly slowing him down.

A clone trap? he wondered. *But I saw his* Astral Body, *cores, and even soul. Is it all an illusion?*

Having predicted Kai's attacks, Shacks had been using a clone from the very beginning. Aware of the power of his opponent's energy vision, he had wrapped the clone up in the *Sixth Order: Soul-Intoxicating Mist*, which, other than making the user invisible, influenced the perception of others.

With all this, Shacks lured Kai into a trap and won himself the last few seconds he needed to finish the installation of a huge combat array that summoned and activated dozens of *pseudo-Divine* artifacts. Weapons resembling ballistas surrounded Kai, pointing their sights at him. At the same time, a strong barrier rose, locking him inside the array.

With a grin on his face, Shacks saluted his dumbfounded friend and rose his hand. As if on his command, the installations opened fire. However, instead of arrows, they sent forth waves of tiny projectiles. The barrier wasn't an obstacle for them.

After several minutes of relentless creaking and

whistling, the ballistas fell silent. A figure emerged from the plume of smoke and dust. Exhausted but alive, Kai broke out of captivity.

And then froze.

What... Why am I here? he found himself wondering. *Why am I inside the Duel Zone? I vaguely remember that I fought someone, but... There's no one here...*

Shacks had disappeared with the help of the *First Order: Reality-Cutting Mist*, erasing the very fact of his existence. Everyone, except for Sawan who still remembered him, or rather, knew something about him, instantly forgot about him.

Stricken by such a strong feeling of cognitive dissonance, Kai didn't immediately become aware of the object that entered the area of his perception after leaving the array. Turning his head to the right, he saw a strange item that radiated the power of *pseudo-Divine* rank, *Runes*, and *Divine* particles. To a certain extent, it looked like some kind of mechanism. But the weirdest thing about it wasn't its appearance or power, but the inscription engraved on its surface.

With love, Shacks ♥

Three things happened at once.

Firstly, Kai froze in place, halted by his intuition that was all but begging him to turn around and run as fast as he could.

Secondly, the ballistas were gone.

And thirdly, a large explosion struck the planet.

"A little gift from my pals back on Earth." Shacks smiled to himself. "Pretty neat, huh?"

***

Falling to one knee, nauseated and weak, Kai tried to catch his breath. He had survived only due to the combination of the central core's abilities and a huge amount of energy, but even so, he was greatly injured. Being so close to the epicenter of the explosion, he was exposed to an unimaginable amount of radiation filled with energy and *Forces*, which had taken a toll on his body. Its power was so great that Kai was rotting alive until his regeneration and healing techniques kicked in. It took a little while, but they eventually caught up and overcame the hostile energy, expelling it from his system, and mending what could be mended.

After drinking a healing potion, Kai stood up and focused. Slowly, ever so slowly, the one he forgot, but who should have been here, appeared.

"There you are," Kai spat, revealing his blades.

In one quick jump, he was near his opponent. As *Phobos* approached Shacks's face, he flung forward an unusual contraption made of silvery metal. In its shape, it resembled a crossbow, but there was no arrow, no cocking mechanism. Instead, there was a hole, glowing bright yellow. There was a flash, followed by a blinding beam, in which Kai felt more than ten elements at once, woven into the enormous power of a *pseudo-Divine* technique.

Kai distanced himself from the archer that transformed in front of his eyes.

His hair turned white, and his eyes now reflected the bewitching expanse of the starry cosmos, constantly moving and shimmering. *Supreme Order: Ancestral Breathing Mist* allowed its user to absorb the experience, knowledge, skill, and even physical strength of several ancestors at once. Right now, Shacks was at least a *Master of Seven Big Stars*.

The second major change was his weapons. Instead of a bow, he held two of those strange contraptions, both of which were medium-quality of the *Divine* rank, naturally imbued with Sawan's divine power. Their main feature was a complex net of symbols and weaves, designed for the simultaneous use of at least ten elements. For almost any True Master, even if they were the *Favorite of the Forces*, such a weapon was useless, but in the hands of the holder of the *Divine Gift* of the Bright Moon clan, they revealed their true potential.

Sawan agreed to create these weapons for Shacks in exchange for insights into the Bright Moon clan. He knew that with so many abilities and such functionality, this *Divine Gift* could only be the creation of a Higher being.

"Shall we continue this dance?" Shacks chuckled, beckoning and provoking Kai.

A moment later, both duelists faded into invisibility.

Chapter 6
AWAKENING

As the fog dissipated, the *Duel Zone* filled with ice pillars was revealed. The monstrous monuments radiated cold and spatial fluctuations even though the fight had already ended.

Shacks sat motionless, back leaned against a broken pillar. He had lost. The borrowed power was leaving his body and soul, never to return. He wouldn't be able to use the power of these particular ancestors anymore. Being a one-time resource, the *Supreme Order* was to be used only as the last resort. So, he did just that. And yet, here he sat, broken and empty.

If nothing else, he thought to himself with a smile, *it was one hell of a show.*

"I knew… you'd be… stronger than… before," he panted, "but I… never thought… that it'd… be this much… It was… a good fight… I have no regrets… If this is… how I go… then… so be it…"

"Your plan… was stupid… and risky… Don't… you think… you've put… too much… at risk?" Kai asked. Holding onto a pillar for support, he stood a couple of feet away.

"You... could... have died..."

"Ain't... that the... point? Nah... I'm glad... I went... all out," Shacks croaked and then laughed. "But I... won't... let you... win! Ha! I... give up!"

The *Duel Zone* generated a strange wave of power. Bypassing Kai, it fell on Shacks. In an instant, his skin and hair turned gray and his body was covered with ash. A series of *System* messages appeared in front of Kai, confirming his victory.

"You... win..."

The space around him solidified and shattered, returning him to the ice dimension. Hidden under the veil of invisibility once more, he looked around and listened to his intuition. The archer's friends were gone. He had bought them enough time to escape.

I'll deal with them later, Kai told himself and looked up at the sky.

During his battle with Shacks, many things changed on the outside. A handful of people remained fighting on the ground, and even they looked close to giving up and scattering in different directions. In the sky, the battle was drawing to a close.

Up above were two cultivators from the Heavenly Manticore Clan. In addition to them, there were two Guardians of the Collisium: Yusa Softlight and the Water Spirit, Bao Mountain Stream. Of all the members of their organization, these two were the strongest. The other three Guardians, as well as the head of the Mountain Sect Alliance, had already fallen.

As for the cultists, only the Puppeteer remained. Sitting on a levitating throne, he controlled dozens of marionettes with the invisible threads of some technique.

Having dealt with both representatives of the Collisium and the descendants of the Heavenly Manticore, he was the main contender for victory. Aware that he was avoiding getting involved in the fight, relying on his puppets to preserve his strength, the Guardians and the Manticores decided to set aside their differences and join forces for the time being. They didn't help each other out, but they stopped exchanging attacks, focusing their resources on the common enemy instead.

The fourth side of the conflict was the phoenix. Having absorbed the power of all those Masters who died in its domain, the bird returned much stronger. With the combined knowledge of the Masters, it increased not only its power but gained new skills as well. And while the process of "digestion" was not yet over, it could no longer remain in hiding, lest it risked its dominion being destroyed while it slumbered.

All participants of the final battle were, in their own right, worth an entire army of *Divine Stage* cultivators. To be around them right now was to court death. Something not even Kai was willing to entertain. Not after he had just felt its icy breath on his neck.

Is there really no other way? he thought to himself, squinting at the distant figures. *Will I have to use the* Trophy *after all?*

On one hand, he didn't want to waste a resource that would take several years to restore, but on the other, he didn't have a choice. In order to complete Magnus's task and regain his memory, he had to get close to the phoenix and attack it with the *Tattoo's* ability. And without the power of the *Trophy*, doing this was impossible under the current circumstances.

Having made up his mind, Kai unleashed the power of

one-hundredth of his *Spark,* that is, five *Trophy* particles out of five hundred. Doing this made him feel extremely light, making him realize that the *Trophy* not only enhanced his energy control but also simplified the impact of his *Will* on *prana.*

Holding back for a little while longer, Kai filled as much of the ice dimension as he could with his *Will*, pushing it all the way to the borders of the spatial array. There was some resistance at first, but he soon managed to seep his power through the barrier and capture more and more energy. Slowly and unobtrusively. He was like the Will of the Universe: everywhere, but unnoticeable. He hoped that this way, he'd remain hidden until the moment was right.

His *Will* was at its limit, prompting him to drink a couple of potions to recover. Assuming the lotus position, he watched the battle and waited.

The sky was alit with the power of various skills and techniques as the finale grew closer. Clashing again, the two Demigods sustained severe injuries, Valorie was dead, the puppets lay broken, and the Puppeteer was struck by the Manticore's *Death Poison*. He reacted in time and managed to stop it from spreading through his body, albeit at the cost of many resources.

As for the phoenix, it was bound. Having seen the scope of its incredible strength, the other three parties trapped it until they dealt with one another. Whoever remained would have the honor of fighting the phoenix and claiming its corpse as their trophy.

It's now or never.

At that moment, all the energy Kai had subjugated to his will surged through his body. In a matter of seconds, all of his physical parameters exceeded three hundred thousand units. As their value continued to grow, his *Energy Cover* became impenetrable to the attacks of any initial *Divine Stage* cultivators.

The remaining *prana* was used to form *Radiant Cold, Flame of Doom, Eternal Flame, Indestructible Cube,* and many other techniques. Combined, their power rained down on the fighters, seeking to kill them. Kai, still invisible, teleported himself to the phoenix. Having filled the *Tattoo* with a lot of compressed energy, he activated the *Touch of Nothingness*.

The phoenix cried out, but remained flying. Despite all his strength, all Kai managed to do was leave several cracks the size of a finger on its body.

"YOU!!!" Yusa's angry cry rang out, and it felt as if a mountain fell on Kai's shoulders. Their *Field of Superiority* almost shackled him to the spot and nearly knocked him unconscious.

Despite Kai's current strength and his best efforts, his attacks only scratched the ancient *Divine* Masters and killed the few weakest ones. He didn't activate his *Spheres* to enhance his techniques, fearing that this would give out his location. The only reason his attacks had any effect at all was their number and the super-dense energy created with the help of the *Trophy*.

Unfortunately, even with the *Semi-Solid Energy Zone*, Kai was unable to hide. His opponents didn't see, hear, or feel him with their spiritual perception, but they still sensed an unfamiliar will beside the phoenix. Had it not been for the preemptive strikes that had bought him some time, Kai wouldn't have been able to use the *Touch of Nothingness*.

As he suspected, even with the *Trophy*, he was no match for the strongest Masters of the Trial Worlds.

"YOU BASTARD! HOW DARE YOU TOUCH THE FOUNDER'S CREATION?!" Yusa shouted, seething with rage and power.

A giant beam of *Light* and *Fire* rushed toward Kai, burning both the air and space in its way. Crude and primitive, but extremely powerful, the attack would have incinerated him had he not created a huge ice shield in front of him. Reinforcing it with super-dense *ki* and *Primordial Flash*, Kai hoped to hold back the attack long enough to think of a way out. Unfortunately, he underestimated Yusa.

Having delayed the beam for a fraction of a second, the ice barrier exploded with a loud bang. Fortunately, Kai managed to redirect all the energy his body had absorbed to strengthen the *Energy Cover* and increase his resistance. Once again, he was alive, but seriously injured. Not only was he so burned that his regeneration was struggling to keep up, but more than thirty percent of his *Astral Body* was also destroyed. Even some of his cores were damaged.

Cursing under his breath, he activated another ten particles of the *Trophy*. The greatly simplified control over *ki* allowed him to form and infuse energy into the *Spark* without much effort.

Kai tried his best to fly as far away from the battlefield as possible. He didn't manage to get far when someone's powerful grip tightened around his neck.

"What an interesting specimen," the Puppeteer drawled.

Kai's fist flew at him like a meteor, unleashing the power of hundreds of false *Holy Punishments*.

Like a father playing with his child, the Puppeteer intercepted Kai's fist with his palm. His hand creaked and clicked, like a mechanism falling into place. Kai was stunned. He couldn't have imagined that anyone could stop his attack so easily.

"He is mine!!!" Yusa cried out. "I will not forgive his transgression. To damage the founder's most precious creation... Prepare to die!"

Reflexively looking in the direction of their overwhelming voice, Kai suddenly realized that it was difficult for him to move. Only a moment later did it dawn on him that the Puppeteer's *Will* was holding him in place, seeping into him, trying to take control of his mind and soul.

Seizing the opportunity, Varimas flew toward the phoenix.

The vessel is damaged. This is my chance to get the Rune. Mother will be very unhappy if I return empty-handed. And without Valorie... Poor Valorie. But where did the descendant of the Hydra come from? Moreover, one with the Destroyer's tattoo? Wait... Hold on... Observing Kai, Varimas identified the frequency of his will from the memory scroll Rosen left him. *Didn't Rosen say that he killed him with* Death Poison? *How did he survive? Judging by his strength, he seems to have regained some of his past memories. This is bad. Very bad... He could destroy all our plans. Since he came here and attacked the phoenix, he must be connected to Magnus in some way. U'Shor warned us that a part of him escaped. I bet he is using the Hydra to free himself, the bastard. Under no circumstances should this be allowed. We must collect all the parts first!*

Having crossed several miles in an instant, Varimas was a step away from his goal, when time itself seemed to have stopped. Everyone in the dimension was conscious yet immobile.

The figure of a tall young man with thick, long white hair and a light blue eye without a pupil appeared next to the phoenix. Everyone saw him, but no one could feel either his energy or his *Will*. He was like an illusion that only existed in their minds.

It's him... Varimas shuddered, swallowing hard.

With a lazy glance across the dimension, Magnus touched the damaged phoenix. At first, nothing happened, but then there was a loud crack. The giant bird exploded, shattering into a myriad of ice fragments and leaving behind a small ball of light. All was quiet for a moment, and then the dimension was bathed in divine power.

Pulling the ball toward him, Magnus took it in his hand, observed it for a while, and then inserted it into his empty right eye socket. At last, he got back the first part of his body.

With the sphere gone, the overwhelming divine power subsided, hiding inside the Shadow.

"What a reunion," Magnus said, grinning into the Puppeteer's face. "Did a child's toy mistake itself for a great warrior? Pathetic. You wanted to get some of my power? Wanted to use your creator? Or was it Sazarek's order?"

"My lord, I don't—" the Puppeteer began in a panic as Magnus's *Will* loosened its hold on him.

"Save it," Magnus interjected. "You took the side of a traitor. Nothing can justify you. You can hide and use my body parts for protection as much as you like, but I will find you. Your days are already numbered. As well as Sazarek's."

With that, Magnus touched the Puppeteer's forehead with his finger. The touch, light as a feather, held more strength than any of the previous attacks combined, turning the cultist into dust.

Through the gust of ash, Magnus turned to look at Kai.

"Consider this a parting gift," he said and snapped his fingers.

The space shuddered and the dimension began to collapse. Huge spatial rifts appeared all over the place, leading to various parts of Bellum. Unable to resist Magnus's power, the Guardians and Varimas were thrown out of the dimension. The portals through which they passed closed behind them, preventing them from coming back.

Ungluing his gaze from the rifts, Kai turned back to Magnus, but there was no one around. Staring dumbfounded into the empty space, he suddenly realized that there were no more gaps in his memory. There were no flashes of pain, no visions tormenting the mind, no fragmented images... There was nothing. His memories had truly returned.

Realizing this, Kai laughed aloud.

Finally, it was all over.

Finally, he was back.

Kai Arnhard. The real him.

***

Having deactivated the *Trophy*, he descended to the ground. The snow crunched under his feet as he concentrated on his spiritual perception. Something unsettling was stirring in his gut. The reunion with his friends hadn't gone well. Frankly, it had gone the opposite of well.

"Fortunately, Igdrasil wasn't hurt," he muttered. "An artifact protected him from the cold. But whose was it? Lilith's? It feels like her... The situation is worse with One, but he managed to freeze his soul before dying. Even though it's a little damaged, I can restore both it and the body. Which only leaves Malvur and Ivsim. I should have no problem reattaching Malvur's arm and fixing their *Astral Bodies*."

Sighing, Kai gathered himself and took off. He hadn't

yet sensed his friends, but he detected one half-dead clone that managed to save his artificial soul and hold out.

"M... Master?"

"You'll be all right. Hang on."

Having placed the clone into stasis and put him in *Storage*, Kai continued his search.

He didn't know how long he flew over the endless snow-covered wasteland before he finally felt a familiar aura. Hoping that his friends weren't preparing to leave, he picked up speed so that he wouldn't lose them once again.

Ailenx, Lily, Ivsim, and Malvur had settled down near a small crack that led to the lands controlled by the Order of Purity. Deciding to wait there for Shacks, they suddenly sensed a powerful yet familiar aura. Jumping up, they revealed their weapons and prepared for a fight.

Lily and Ailenx stepped forward, shielding the wounded Ivsim and Malvur.

Not wishing to startle them, Kai landed a little bit further away.

"I'm not here to fight you," he said as calmly as he could and raised his hands in front of him. "I'm unarmed."

"Hold on."

"Malvur? What's going on?"

"It's him."

"What?"

"It's Kai."

"He tried to kill you a moment ago!"

"No. Listen."

Malvur explained what had happened. The Kai that stood before them now wasn't the same one who tried to kill him. His aura was calm and serene, nothing like the turbulent sea of the angered demon.

"Is... Is it true?" Ailenx asked cautiously.

Kai gave a sad smile.

"It is. I'm so sorry about this whole mess."

"What happened to you? And where... Where is Shacks?"

"Long story short, at the whim of a powerful being, I ended up on Insulaii and lost my memory. He was holding my memories hostage until I fulfilled our agreement."

"So, you didn't know who we were when you attacked?" Ivsim asked.

"I didn't. Still, I'd like to apologize. To make matters worse, the emotional layer of my soul was also affected. At that moment, I was completely out of my mind."

"You don't say," Lily snapped, but her gaze softened despite her harsh words.

"You have nothing to apologize for." Malvur staggered toward Kai. "It's all my fault. I'll do whatever I can to make it right."

"Malvur, you don't—" Kai began, but the giant interrupted him.

"I do. I don't know what came over me. But that's not an excuse. I'm ready to give my life for his."

"Malvur. It's fine," Kai tried again, putting his hand on his friend's shoulder, but the giant was adamant.

"That child! His aura was almost like yours!"

"A child?!" Lily, Ivsim, and Ailenx looked at each other in surprise. "What child? What happened while we were apart?"

"Another long story," Kai told them before turning back to Malvur. "You're right, our auras are the same, but he's not dead. A divine artifact protected him."

"It... It did?" Malvur breathed out a sigh of relief. "Thank the Heavens."

"But what about Shacks?" Ailenx returned to this question.

Kai frowned and retrieved the unusual weapons from his *Storage*.

"I don't remember, but I can only assume that we couldn't have discussed the conditions due to, well, me being out of my mind. The battle must've started by default. After buying you enough time, he gave up and... He was killed by the *Zone*."

His words struck like thunder from a clear sky. Everyone froze with disbelief on their faces, their hearts in turmoil. Malvur gritted his teeth, Ailenx and Ivsim stared blankly at Kai, and Lily lowered her head and shuddered.

There was silence. Until...

"Are you kidding me?!" Lily suddenly exclaimed and raised her head to look at Kai. "How dare he?! I was supposed to be the one to kill him! I'll bring him back and kill him again!"

***

A deathly silence hung over the table.

After leaving the ice dimension, shocked by Shacks's death, the group found itself in a city ruled by the Order of

Purity. They all needed to rest and recover, so the first thing they did was find a tavern.

They spent the night meditating and contemplating, and gathered on the lower floor the next morning. They sat there for several hours, mourning in silence and drinking.

"Woah! Oops! Pardon me!"

A staggering man almost ran into Ailenx. He was wrapped in a dark, dirty cloak, and he reeked of alcohol.

Pushing the man away, Ailenx glanced at the innkeeper. Soon, the man was taken away by the guards. No one was willing to face the wrath of an entire group of *Holy Lords*.

A few minutes later, Ivsim tried to start a conversation, but his attempt fell on deaf ears. Everyone was preoccupied with their thoughts.

"Oops!" A hairy man's hand fell on Lily's shoulder. Brazenly embracing the girl, he made her cry out in surprise. For some reason, she didn't feel him approach. No one had time to react when the same man grabbed the bottle from the table and hiccupped loudly. "Hey, pretty girl, how about you tell me your name?"

Before Lily could tell him where he could shove that bottle, Ivsim found himself behind the drunkard and twisted his arm, forcing him to howl in pain. But the cry quickly turned into a chuckle.

"C'mon, lad, my grandmother has a better grip!"

"You?!" Having caught a glimpse of the face hidden under the hood, Lily jumped up from her chair. "You!"

"Why the long faces, eh? Who died?" Releasing Ivsim, Shacks smiled from ear to ear and started laughing. "Ah, man... If you could see yourselves right now. Hilarious."

Taking a deep breath, Kai rubbed the bridge of his nose.

"Of course, you have to put up a show..." Kai rolled his eyes and then took a second to reflect on how their recent fight ended.

Just as he was about to finish off Shacks, the archer suddenly pierced his mind and reached his consciousness with facts about Earth, Diamond Evans, the planet's technological advancement, as well as many other things, including their friendship and past. All this made Kai freeze, calm down and think.

Before the duel was over, Shacks asked Kai to tell the others that he had died and proceeded to use the *Fifth Order: Deception of Death* on himself. Like the Trial Worlds, the *Power of the Bright Moon* was created by the Higher Ones, allowing it to deceive even the Rules, thus making it possible to leave the *Duel Zone* alive.

"You owe me one, buddy," Shacks answered, hearing Kai's muttering. "I saved your friends... True, I saved them from you, but a deal is a deal! Now where's that booze?!"

Chapter 7
THE END OF A CHAPTER, AND THE BEGINNING OF A NEW ONE

While the battle between Spirits, beasts, cultists, and cultivators raged on in the ice dimension, peace and tranquility reigned in the Collisium the way they always did. This little piece of paradise in the center of the Cursed Continent had existed for millions of years, having managed to shelter countless animals and Spirits of the Trial Worlds. No matter how much time passed, and no matter what was going on in the world, the Collisium remained unchanged. Over the course of its long existence, the ever-blossoming forest had faced many threats: adepts of the dark arts, hordes of fog-like beings, and even "wandering" super-anomalies. But no matter how many times it was in danger, the Collisium had never before failed its inhabitants.

Until today.

With the Guardians and the sentinels gone, the Collisium was left with its many animals and Spirits. The residents' daily routine was interrupted when an unfamiliar presence of terrifying power emerged in the forest, its arrival heralded by a creeping mist of thick milky-white fog that filled the air.

The guest was a tall, broad-shouldered man in white armor made out either of wood or bone, adorned with skulls and unusual designs. His face was as pale as the fog that followed him, his hair long and gold, flowing around his face as if tousled by a breeze, and his eyes orange, devoid of pupils and irises.

Finding himself in Collisium, he walked toward the heart of the forest. Wherever he stepped, white, dead trees burst out of the ground. Falling down, their many scarlet, pink, and orange leaves destroyed all life around them.

Born from a divine tree formed by the *Forces* of *Death* instead of *Life*, the undead High Ent had a unique and extremely powerful ability that allowed him to combine these two *Forces*. This made his techniques especially destructive for all living things.

Feeling that it was in danger, the forest whipped the intruder with its roots and branches, while the remaining inhabitants of the Collisium rained their techniques at him. But none of the attacks reached the trespasser. A cloud of leaves, neither dead nor alive, whirled around him, blocking every blow. The Ent didn't even blink. Ignoring everything that was going on around him, he strode forward with confidence.

After several futile attempts, the flow of techniques began to slow down. The forest became filled with invisible spores of death. They were microscopic, but their number and power were devastating. The bodies of the animals decomposed, rotted from the inside, and mutated. Spirits became overgrown with flesh, which clung to their *Astral Bodies* and souls, making them look like living beings. This was accompanied by excruciating pain and the inevitable destruction of their spiritual essence.

But even if the inhabitants of the Collisium died, their *Shells* continued to live. Obeying the Ent, the newly-created monsters pounced on those who managed to protect themselves from the spores and survive. However, in the end, no one escaped death. The carnage was quick lived, but it was very effective.

"Greetings, Master Abaddon," Qi said with a bow.

Qi was a bi-elemental spirit of *Wood* and *Cold* that had helped rescue Kai's friends and that Kai saw in the Spirit Dimension. He was also the one who, acting as a beacon, revealed the location of the previously unreachable and impregnable Collisium to Abbadon, the Third Prince of the Abyss.

"Well done. The Lord will be pleased," the Ent said with a faint smile and patted the Spirit's shoulder.

After that, he looked at the thick trunk of the oak towering before him. Next to the giant trees of the Collisium, it seemed nondescript. But looks could be very deceiving. Abbadon knew better than to judge anything by its looks. In the very center of this oak lay the heart of the forest.

Having lived through several lifetimes, the ancient spirit of the forest was nearing the end of its current existence. But it persisted. While the Spirits and the animals defended the forest and attacked Abaddon, it focused on what would probably be its last act of resistance. And now it stood, cracked and rotted, defeated, naked before its assailant. With the tree dead, its Guardian Spirit could no longer do anything.

Destroying the oak, Abaddon exposed a column hidden inside it, a mysterious object left by the last members of the civilization that had once lived in the Collisium.

[Dreamer's Seal]

Rank: ???

Class: gamma

Come forth and lift the veil.

Mesmerized by the sight of an artifact capable of granting him a glimpse into the future, Abaddon stood frozen in awe for several minutes. Studying the column with his perception, he tried to unravel the secrets of its strength. In the end, the enigma of divine power turned out to be too complex for him. Nevertheless, he gained some insight into its workings, which gave him enough clues to figure out how to break through to the *Star Emperor Stage*.

With a sigh, he transferred the *Dreamer's Seal* to a special *Storage* and walked away.

"The task has been completed. The 'seer' is dead. No one will interfere with the Lord's plans," Abaddon said to Qi.

"And the mission?"

"All in its due time."

***

"There. That should do it." Kai exhaled with a smile of relief.

Looking at Igdrasil stretching his arms toward him, he couldn't believe that the Ent survived the cold of the ice dimension and the collected power of so many cultivators.

Seeing his caretaker, Igdrasil smiled, forgetting all about the gripping fear it had experienced in that strange place.

"I'll have to thank Lilith if this was her doing..."

Taking Igdrasil in his arms, Kai fed him a mixture based on Spirit Herbs and his blood. Alfred had done a great job with it. He'd have to thank him later too.

"Aw, look at you. So, what tree did you bang to get that?"

Suppressing the urge to roll his eyes, Kai squinted at Shacks.

"Did they not teach you manners back home? Learn to knock."

"Ah, forgive me, the holiest of *Holy Lords*!" Shacks exclaimed in feigned devotion, not removing the smile from his face. "Seriously though... Do I want to know what happened? Like, did you really bang a tree or...?"

"By the Heavens, Shacks! Did your parents drop you on your head when you were little?" Lily winced.

"No. Well... Okay, once, but—"

"Ents are born from *Spirit Plants*. Honestly, couldn't you read a book once in a while?"

"So, do the two plants, like, do they... or...?"

"You... You can't be serious..."

"What? I'm just asking!"

Dropping the conversation, Lily approached Kai and Igdrasil. She had long learned to ignore Shacks and his desperate attempts at acquiring the attention he had never been given by his parents.

"What's his name?"

"Igdrasil. Ig for short."

"Interesting name. May I hold him?"

Looking thoughtfully at her, Kai handed her the little Ent.

"Looks good on you, if I may add. You should consider getting one too."

"You—"

Barely restraining herself from punching Shacks, Lily sighed and took Igdrasil in her arms. To her pleasant surprise, he didn't protest being taken away from his caretaker. On the contrary, he settled down in her hands and stared at her with curiosity.

"Ah, he's so cute... Ow!"

Giggling, or at least making a sound that resembled a giggle, Igdrasil reached for her beautiful golden hair, clearly intending to have a taste.

"I think he likes you," Kai remarked.

"I want to hold him, too!" Shacks exclaimed.

"He's not a toy," Lily snapped, stepping back from him, and smiled at Igdrasil. "Right, little one?"

"Why do you refer to it as he? As far as I know, Ents are sexless," Malvur asked.

"I'm just following Kai's example," Lily replied.

"I just felt weird calling him it," Kai explained with a shrug.

"Do you plan to train him when he grows up?" Ailenx asked, curious.

"I thought about it. He has almost the same

predispositions as me, the same bloodline, and there is a strong spiritual connection between us. I probably couldn't find a more suitable student even if I tried."

"So... Where did he come from?"

"Well, ya see, Ivsim, when mommy Ent and daddy Ent love each other very much..."

"Oh, shut up!"

Kai shook his head.

"Shacks. Malvur. You remember the tree that grew on the floating island? Where you and An'na fought Lightus?"

"Oh, yeah, I remember that," Shacks muttered, nodding. Looking at Ailenx, Lily, and Ivsim, he added: "Ya know, I was *this* close to finishing off that prick of an elf when Kai appeared. He just won't let me have any fun."

"Anyway," Kai said, interrupting him. "I received that tree as a reward and cultivated it using my blood and soul energy, among other things."

"I see... By the way, now that you mentioned An'na... Do you know what happened with her?"

"I do." Kai returned Igdrasil to his arms. "She and Guts should be somewhere in my region of Insulaii by now."

"In *your* region?" Lily asked, raising an eyebrow.

"Exactly. Ah, right. I didn't tell you... Another long story short, I managed to establish my own organization. I also made almost all of Avlaim's factions into my vassals. A branch of the Everstein clan still refuses to join me. Other than that, I'm basically the ruler of the entire region."

"Of course you are," Shacks mumbled under his breath.

Everyone else looked, if not shocked, then at least

surprised.

"What did you call it?" Malvur asked.

"The Eternal Path Temple."

"I like it!" Ailenx commented, supporting Kai as always.

"Of course you do." Lily sighed. "Why a temple and not a sect?"

"I think I can guess," Ivsim said thoughtfully. "I believe the teachings of his organization are based not on a particular fighting style, element, or set of techniques, but on a certain philosophy. Most likely, the Eternal Path is the designation of the Warrior Path, and the Temple is, in this case, an organization in which warriors are brought up. Am I close?"

Smiling, Kai nodded.

"You are absolutely right. Initially, I just needed an organization to get resources and influence, to return my memories and find you, but then I realized that if I wanted to rely on it in the future, the foundation of such an organization should be much stronger than it is the case with ordinary sects. It goes without saying that I'd like for you to join it."

"My desire to follow you remains unchanged, older brother," Ailenx was the first to answer. "I would be happy to join the Eternal Path Temple."

Malvur only nodded.

Lily and Ivsim looked at each other.

"I don't mind. After all, we already followed you to the Trial Worlds," Lily answered for both of them.

There was silence as everyone turned their heads to Shacks. As if unaware of their presence, he continued to pick his ear with his finger and stare at the ceiling.

"I don't know," he muttered after a while, examining a piece of ear wax. "I'm a free bird! I'll need to think, weigh all the pros and cons, find out more about your business, pray to the Heavens, do some betting, read the stars, do a ritual dance, toss a coin, see a soothsayer..."

"What I'm hearing is that you want the benefits without the effort."

"Ah, you know me so well."

"You're as complex as a piece of white paper," Lily mumbled.

"In any case, enough about me." Kai put the sleeping Igdrasil into the cradle. "I'd like to hear what kept you guys busy in the meantime."

"Compared to you, nothing..." Ivsim muttered sourly and then sighed. "We were either running from the Vinari clan or waiting for the Ice Gates to open so that we could meet you."

At this, the conversation turned to Kai's friends and their adventures.

At some point, everyone got tired and returned to their rooms. Kai was left alone. Sent to the *Storage*, Igdrasil was still asleep, so after sobering up with a healing technique, Kai decided to take care of his clones. It would take a lot of time and effort to fix One, so he first helped the other clone he had found in the ice dimension. He regenerated his flesh, strengthening it, and improved the artificial soul, adding to it a new level of understanding of the elements.

When Twenty-Three came to his senses and told his master about the war that broke out on Insulaii, Kai's good mood turned grim.

Come dawn, their group left Bellum on the same flying ship the clones arrived. With the seal gone, One-Hundred-and-Six could feel his creator again, so he sailed the vessel straight to him the moment he left the icy hell of the anomalous hurricane.

Chapter 8
THE UPRISING

About a month ago...

Despite the storm of runic mist caused by the opening of the Heavenly Exaltation Pagoda, the mechanisms of the Contenders Road and the Garden continued to operate, thus saving the lives of dozens of various faction members. Lilith included. After sitting out the catastrophe in a sheltered meditation area, she returned to contemplating the Pagoda and absorbing the air that hastened the soul's preparation for a breakthrough.

Waking up from meditation, she suddenly found herself in a completely different place. In an instant, the gloomy and quiet coniferous forest was replaced by a bright blue sky and a jungle full of life. Kai's *Group Ticket Home* had sent her to the Ark.

Having found herself in a familiar place, Lilith looked around and listened to her intuition.

"Strange," she drawled. "It's like the tear wasn't even there. The protective barrier seems intact. Did the transfer leave no traces at all? Or am I just so tired that I can't detect them?"

After a moment's pondering, she shook her head, pushed her thoughts aside, and focused her attention on the approaching duo.

"Ah, Lilith, my dearest! My heart trembles at the sight of you!" Shaw exclaimed and spread his arms as he walked over to her. "Fall into my embrace, my beloved! Let us celebrate our reunion!"

"Put those arms down before I cut them off," Lilith hissed. "I suddenly miss the silence of the Abyss..."

"Cold as ever." Shaw sniffled sadly, shoving his hands into his pockets. "Ah, my heart..."

"Welcome back," Nyako said. "But where is Kai? And where is Le'Gut?"

"What?" Lilith was confused. "I thought he was back already. And what does Le'Gut have to do with anything?"

Seeing her reaction, Nyako frowned. Even Shaw turned a little serious.

"Ulu only reported one mark — yours," Nyako explained. "No one else has appeared on the island. Le'Gut followed you into the Abyss. Didn't you meet him there?"

"He followed me? What a fool..." Lilith sighed, clenched her fists, and lowered her head. "Why didn't he listen?"

"Looks like he never found you," Shaw muttered to himself. "Although I never particularly liked him, you have my condolences, dear... Still, we should be more concerned about Kai's fate now. What happened in the Abyss? Did you see him there?"

"Yes." Lilith looked up. "We went through the Contender's Road together, and then we split up. He said that he would buy an item that would return us both to the Ark."

"But only you came back," Nyako noted.

Lilith nodded.

"Are his clones alive?" she suddenly asked.

"They looked fine when we last saw them," Shaw replied.

"Clones are spiritually connected to their creator. They should feel him regardless of the distance. Theoretically..." Lilith pondered for a little bit, after which she jumped onto the platform Nyako and Shaw had used to get here. "I need to get to the city!"

"I see you're in a hurry. In that case..." Shaw smiled smugly, turning into a giant raven. "Hop on! I'm much faster than those things!"

Without arguing, Lilith and Nyako jumped on his back. With a flap of his mighty wings, Shaw pushed off the ground and soared into the air, carried far by *Wind* and *Sound*.

What even happened there? What did that guy want from Kai? he asked, switching to the spiritual link. He could have tried shouting, but the wind was so strong that the two probably wouldn't have heard him.

I don't know. I met Kai after he left, Lilith lied, deciding not to talk about her meeting with Green. *Shortly before we were thrown out of the Abyss, a strange rune storm broke out in the dimension. Maybe something happened to Kai then.*

Back in the city, the clones were alive and well, which meant that Kai was all right. Unfortunately, when asked about their maker and his whereabouts, they couldn't provide any useful information. They were just as clueless as the trio.

Having sorted through their options, they decided to

stop by Accelerated Time-Space. The clones in it had the *Master's Will* so they could probably tell them more. This would take some time, since halting Accelerated Time-Space wasn't instantaneous, so they returned to the temple and settled there to continue their conversation over a cup of fragrant wine.

"What's everyone else up to?" Lilith asked at some point. "And why did you meet me and not Ulu?"

"She's meditating," Shaw replied curtly, putting his feet up on the table.

"The purified pill gave her the boost she needed," Nyako explained in more detail. "She's almost done preparing for her breakthrough to the *One Step away from Divinity* level. As for the rest, Hiro and Ragnar have devoted all their time to training."

"Having their asses handed to them by Rosen hit them hard," Shaw added with a grin. "They haven't left the Hall of Fame since, fighting his copies day in and day out."

"Wipe that grin off your face, or I'll do it for you," Lilith told him, glaring at him over the edge of her cup.

"Darling, you misunderstand me. I recognize their strength and respect their perseverance, but you need to be aware of your limits, which they are not. And given your story… If Kai couldn't defeat him, what hope do those two have? No matter how much they train, they will never reach his level. Ragnar is already approaching his peak. I think his maximum is *Seven Average Stars*. Being younger, Hiro has more potential, but Rosen is still only an *Elementalist*. The only thing those two are doing is wearing themselves out."

"And what would you do if you were in their shoes?"

"Me?" Shaw smiled. "Well, first I'd have fun with some pretty ladies to mend my broken heart and pride. Then, I'd analyze the fight, figure out my mistakes and my opponent's weaknesses. After that, having become wiser, I'd return to my normal life. Well, that's not entirely true. Maybe I'd prepare some kind of plan for the future, just in case." He shrugged. "I already spend every free moment I have working on myself. I don't see why I'd have to break my bones training just because I was defeated by someone stronger. Even True Masters need rest; otherwise, there will be no benefit from all that hard work. The problem with Hiro and Ragnar is that not only were they sure of their victory, but they also assumed a certain responsibility toward Kai, whom they respect deeply. They feel like they let him down, and now they're trying to make up for it. But in our world, there is always someone stronger. And there is nothing shameful in being defeated by them. Of course, I'm not saying that Hiro and Ragnar should give up, but they should manage their expectations."

"I wonder how you'd feel if you had been defeated by Rosen," Lilith murmured, tucking her hair behind her ear.

"So, if you defended our leader's honor instead of Ragnar and lost, you wouldn't care?" Nyako asked.

"First of all, I wouldn't fall for such an obvious provocation. Why should the words of some charlatan bother me? He offended Kai's honor? Who cares? Kai certainly doesn't. And, secondly, even if I found myself in such a situation, I wouldn't care. If I know that I have done everything that is in my power to defend something I believe in, then what is there to be ashamed of? Of being too weak? That's stupid. I can't always be the strongest."

"My, my, who would have thought? There's an ounce of intelligence in that thick skull of yours after all," Lilith sneered. "Still. Is your oath worth anything at all? Or are you here just for your own benefit? Are you going to leave the moment you get everything you can from the Temple? This organization isn't a port whore, Shaw, so that you can just come in and get what you want and then leave."

"No need for slander, dear Lilith." Shaw shook his index finger in front of her. "In exchange for patronage, I swore to follow, protect, and assist our dear friend. And I am a man of my word. As long as Kai walks the Warrior's Path, I will follow him. I see his potential. If you ask me, one day, he will become a *Star Emperor*. That's how much I believe in him." Shaw smiled. "But just because I'm his follower doesn't mean that I have to gravel before him and do whatever he says. He's a grown man; he can defend his own honor if he wants to."

"Alfred, just in time," Nyako said, interrupting him.

"I hate to interrupt your conversation, but the deactivation of Accelerated Time-Space is almost complete. Another minute and the clones will be here," the assistant reported.

Exchanging glances, the trio rose from their chairs. A moment later, they were in a completely different part of the Complex, where the transfer array connected to Accelerated Time-Space was located.

As soon as they arrived, two men appeared on the transfer platform — One and Six. While the time inside was under acceleration, communication with the outside world was unavailable. However, having noticed that the workings of Accelerated Time-Space were being halted, they abandoned what they were doing and prepared for departure.

Without wasting time on explanations, Lilith demanded that they determine Kai's whereabouts. Unlike regular clones, these two had the *Master's Will* strong enough to realize that Kai was not only somewhere far away, but also in the same space as them. Somewhere within the Heavenly Exaltation Pagoda.

Hearing this, Lilith felt relieved.

"Then where exactly is he?" she inquired. "Did he end up somewhere on Insulaii?"

"I'm afraid we can't determine his exact coordinates." Six shook his head, then looked at One. "We need to invite the rest of our brothers to help us. If we unite, then perhaps we will be able to strengthen our spirit connection and learn more."

Confirming his words, One nodded.

"In that case, what are you waiting for?" Nyako asked. "Go back there and gather the others. This is an emergency, so reactivating Accelerated Time-Space will have to wait. It's too expensive to stop it twice a day anyway."

"How much time will you need?" Lilith asked before the clones teleported away.

"A few hours, I suppose," One said.

"Fine. Go."

"Ladies, I suggest we take a walk around the island," Shaw proposed.

"Have you lost your mind?" Lilith frowned. "You want to go for a walk now?"

"I have a bad feeling about this. Kai is gone, and everyone in Avlaim knows about his reign. I suggest we check the island's defense systems just in case."

Lilith squinted at him.

"You're up to something."

"Surprisingly, no. Not this time. I'm used to trusting my intuition. There is no such thing as too much caution."

"He's right," Nyako said.

"In that case, I will check the state of the army and read the intelligence reports. I've been lost in the Abyss for a whole month, it's time to get back to business," Lilith agreed.

"By the way, two *Holy Lords* showed up in your sect looking for Kai Arnhard," Nyako recalled.

"Who are they?"

"They said their names were An'na and Guts. I sent a request to the Avlaim factions under Kai's rule to find out more about them. But no one had heard of them before."

"As it turned out, they're not from Insulaii. They came from Ferox, where they seemed to have worked as mercenaries."

"But how do they know Kai's real name and where to look for him?"

"That's the interesting bit. They said they are his friends, Apparently, the Second Prince of the Abyss told them that Kai captured Avlaim."

So, he's Green's subordinate. Lilith grimaced. *Didn't he tell Kai that he knew where his friends are? And the names are the same. Is that really them?*

"Thanks. I'll talk to them in person," she said. "I just don't understand why you, the head of the technology center, are doing this, and not Shaw?"

"Not my responsibility," he retorted with a shrug. "Also, there's my reputation of being a pirate. There was no one better suited for the task. We don't send regular Temple followers to solve such matters."

"I suppose you're right."

With that, the trio went their separate ways. They all had a lot to do.

About half an hour later, they felt that something was very, very wrong. As they hurriedly left the Complex, they saw the sky turn red.

A powerful barrier enveloped the entire planet.

***

Unfortunately, Ryu didn't know the Ark's coordinates, so he was transferred somewhere deep into Nogatta, the main island of the Rising Star Sect.

After spending some time orienting himself in the unfamiliar wilderness, he set off. It took him half a day to reach the capital, where he turned to the sect's representatives for help. He was still listed as one of its disciples sent to the Eternal Path Temple for training, so he wasn't politely but firmly asked to leave the premises.

Entering the main building, he went to the pavilion with a transfer array, stepped on one of the platforms, chose Moon Haven as his destination, placed his wrist with the sect's tattoo to the designated device, and... remained exactly where he was.

"What do you think you're doing, boy?" The junior elder who was assigned to watch, manage, and repair the platforms jumped up to him. "Why did you choose Moon Haven if you don't have the necessary permission? C'mon, son, this isn't a toy."

I don't have permission? Ryu was surprised. *Did they erase me from the system after I started serving the Eternal Path Temple? But I'm still listed here, they couldn't have...*

"I need to go there and find a representative of the Eternal Path Temple, or, even better, get transferred to their branch," he began to explain. "I'm not only a disciple of the Rising Star Sect but also a member of the Eternal Path

Temple. I need to get back."

"I didn't get a word of what you just said, son. Still, I can't help you. I'm just here to observe. If you really need to get there, you should talk the head of the pavilion. Perhaps he can be of some help."

Having thanked him, Ryu did just that.

Upon finding the right office, he knocked on the door. There was no answer, but since he felt an aura behind the door, he still entered. Inside, a short, fat man with a crooked nose and deep-set eyes was intently studying some scrolls and papers.

"As a member and disciple of the Eternal Path Temple, I wish to request assistance from the Rising Star Sect. I need to contact a representative of the Temple, which is located in Moon Haven, or just get access to their offices," Ryu explained and fell silent, waiting for an answer. When after half a minute he didn't get a response, he raised his voice. "Hello? Sir? Did you not hear me? Hey!"

Twitching his cheek and grimacing, the man put the documents aside, raised a displeased glance at the visitor, and examined him from head to toe.

"Do you have an appointment?" he asked in an unpleasant voice. "Master Dong accepts visitors only if they have an appointment."

"You don't understand, I have an important matter—"

"Young man," the man interrupted Ryu. "Everyone has important matters here, but rules are rules. Go to the registration office and make an appointment. The commission will review it and give you an answer within two weeks. And now I must ask you not to disturb me, I am very busy. You know where the doors are."

Ryu stopped to think for a moment.

Well, if you're going to be an asshole to me...

"Sir."

"Young man, I think I've made myself clear."

"Crystal clear. But I'm also very busy, so here is what we are going to do. You will help me get what I need, or I will cut you into pieces so small, they'll need a magnifying glass and a miracle to put you back together," Ryu said as calmly as he could, imbuing his voice with the *Master's Will*. The man before him was a senior elder, but as a cultivator, he was very weak, so he didn't need much to get his point across. "Do I make myself clear?"

Deathly pale and shuddering, the man tried to call the guards through an artifact, but he couldn't even control his energy, let alone limbs. A few moments later, unable to take the pressure, he fainted.

"What's going on here?!" At the same moment, the manager of the pavilion flew out of his office. "Who are you?! How dare you attack my assistant?!"

He tried to suppress the trespasser with his will and aura when he realized that he couldn't break through his defense.

"Guards!"

Soon, Ryu found himself surrounded. The *Elementalists* tried to capture him as soon as they entered through the door, but he dodged all of their attacks surprisingly easily and deftly. Annoyed, the manager decided to stop holding back.

Ryu dealt with the guards so easily that he saw no reasons to hesitate now. Without taking out his weapon, he unleashed a flash of bright light and disintegrated into a myriad of shimmering particles, activating *Light Bringer's Attire*, the technique that fit the best in his arsenal.

One, two, three… five… seven… ten… twelve… Fourteen heavy blows hit the guards almost simultaneously. Ryu had become so good with this technique through honing it on the Contender's Road that he now knew how to appear in several places at once, evenly distributing particles of light and forming clones of himself from them.

Aware of just how devastating this technique could be, Ryu didn't use its full power. He didn't want to kill the guards, only to incapacitate1 them. They grunted and yelped as they fell but none of them suffered serious injuries.

Suddenly, an unfamiliar young man appeared in front of Ryu, smiling broadly.

Ryu's eyes widened, but he didn't have time to do anything. The young man raised his hand and… smacked Ryu on the forehead.

The impact knocked the young *Exorcist* back a couple of feet, nearly leaving him unconscious. His will and aura were instantly suppressed.

"Would you calm down already?" the young man asked, continuing to smile.

Grimacing and focusing his eyes with difficulty, Ryu stared at the blond. He was an initial-level *Holy Lord* and *Master of Five Small Stars*. Along with him, five more *Elementalists* appeared. However, unlike those who attacked Ryu, these were the elite guards.

"You sure made a lot of noise here, Young Master Ryu," the blond said, folding his hands behind his back. "Why is that?"

"Your assistant was very rude. I wanted to teach him a lesson by intimidating him, but his goons attacked me, and I had to defend myself," Ryu explained.

"Master Dong? Is that true?" the blond asked.

"No! He's lying!" Dong shouted angrily, holding on to his aching chest.

"Are you sure? Can you confirm that with an oath?"

"Um... Well... I... To be honest, I can't say for sure..." he stumbled. "I was in my office at that moment but my intuition tells me that he's lying! In any case, attacking a senior member of the sect is unacceptable behavior!"

"You are right, of course, Master Dong. It is unacceptable. Only, we still need to figure out who attacked whom first."

"What difference does it make, Master Leo? I'm an elder of the Rising Star Sect, and he's a brazen outsider! How did he even get here? Even if what he said is true, what right did he have to touch my subordinate?"

"Master Dong, it seems that you suffered a concussion. An *Exorcist* capable of dealing with a group of *Elementalists* is more than a brazen outsider, as you called him. A person with such strength and talent must be treated with the respect he deserves."

Startled, Dong finally realized his mistake. As genuine fear reflected on his face, he fell to his knees and touched the floor with his forehead.

"Young Master!" he exclaimed, turning to Ryu. "Please, forgive me. I shouldn't have attacked you. Please, forgive this old fool. Hearing my assistant, I thought that an intruder had infiltrated the sect. Rest assured, I will do everything I can to avoid repeating such a foolish mistake. I truly thought we were threatened. I am sorry for offending you."

Ryu looked up at the grinning Leo as Dong kept apologizing and making excuses.

"It's fine. You acted according to the rules."

"Thank you. Thank you, young master."

"Young Master Ryu, if you would... Let's continue this conversation in my office," Leo suggested as he headed for the door. "I'm sure we have a lot to talk about."

Once they were alone in the corridor, he turned to Ryu.

"What's all this about? And don't tell me it was because he was being rude. You've been in this sect long enough to know how little it takes to get someone exiled. So why put on a show?"

"You are quite perceptive, Master Leo." Ryu smiled. "Truth be told, I didn't want to waste time. Making a scene was sure to get the attention of a higher official. Of an official who knows about the Eternal Path Temple."

"So that's what it was..." Leo nodded. "But what would you have done had I not known your identity? Had I not seen your fight in the Grand Tournament finals? Congratulations on your victory, by the way."

"Thank you. If we are being honest, I don't know what I would have done. I hoped I'd get lucky, and I did. Perhaps I would have resisted a little and then surrendered. Even if the guards imprisoned me, the information about a member of the Temple would have quickly reached those who know about it."

"A plan that is as bold as it is reckless." Leo laughed. "Here we are. Come in."

He opened the door to his office. It was a small

room, spacious enough to fit its owner and his clients, and decorated modestly, containing only whatever the minister needed to conduct his work.

Once they were seated, Leo nodded and beckoned the young *Exorcist* to tell him his story. In as few words as possible, Ryu explained to him what happened and why he needed to return to Kaiser's Ark as soon as possible.

"I can contact Moon Haven and ask them to convey your message to a Temple representative. They are sure to send someone for you."

Ryu bowed his head.

"I'd be very grateful."

"Wait here a bit." Leo nodded and left the office.

He returned a few minutes later with the good news.

"An envoy will be here in fifteen minutes. While we wait, why don't we talk about the Temple? I understand that you are bound by oaths and spiritual contracts, but I won't probe too deep. I'm very interested to hear about this mysterious organization."

"Of course."

Ryu didn't give him specific details, sharing general information about the Temple instead. He spoke about the hierarchy, the Temple's philosophy, the strict selection process of members, the possibility of not leaving one's previous organization, and the prohibition of other factions from preventing their members from entering the Temple. None of this was secret, but those who knew about it were still few and far in between.

"Is your leader really the sole ruler of Avlaim?"

"As far as I know, he is. Among our most prominent

members are Lady Lilith, Master Shaw, and Master Shan Wu. Several leaders of powerful factions publicly expressed their desire to become his followers after he demonstrated his skill in a fight with one of the strongest members of the Temple. I don't know whether you believe me or not. I'll understand if you don't. Much of this sounds too good to be true."

Leo closed his eyes and thought for a while.

"Understood," he finally said. "Thank you for telling me all this. Now... I have... a silly request, so to say. Could you give me your autograph?"

Ryu stared at him in bewilderment.

"Sorry, what?"

Leo chuckled.

"My sons are big fans. As soon as they found out that you were a member of our sect, they begged me to find you and get an autograph."

"I... Yeah, of course. I'd be honored."

Having sealed his image and signature in a memory scroll, Ryu thanked Leo for all his help and left his office.

For a while, the *Holy Lord* sat in silence, observing the wooden doors.

"I remember you, Ryu Araki," he thought aloud, tapping his finger on the table. "Although all information about you is classified, you scored the highest in the Sect's entrance exam four years ago. How did you do it, I wonder... Four years ago, you were only eleven, taking your first steps on the path of cultivation. I'm not mistaken, it was definitely you — same aura, same face. And now, you are the strongest *Exorcist* on Insulaii. What have they done to you? You were a child when you left us, and you returned a grown man... But how? Should I take the risk and jump on board, or is it better to wait? Interesting..."

Leo wasn't alone in his pondering. Little by little, more and more Masters of Avlaim toyed with the idea of joining the Eternal Path Temple.

***

It was evening by the time he arrived. Exiting the teleportation room, Ryu reported first to Samson and then to Ragnar, whom he found in the company of Nyako and Shaw. The two were very pleased with Ryu's return. Up until recently, they considered him dead. Congratulating him on his victory once again, they listened to his story about the Abyss and the Contender's Road, talked about his new status as a Special Disciple, and offered him to join one of their departments instead of the army.

By the time he was done giving his reports, it was around midnight. Eager to see his friends, Ryu sought them out. Oberon, Gradz, and Inna were shocked by the news of his return. They were so happy that they decided to have a party that lasted until sunrise.

Ryu spent the entire morning meditating to recover, after which he left the city and went to his favorite place — a secluded cape located at the south of the island. For a while, he observed the ocean in silence. He needed to clear his mind and find some tranquility. The last couple of weeks were truly hectic.

Taking a deep breath, he extended his hand in front of him and imagined an exquisite black scroll appearing in his palm. He felt a slight heaviness in his hand and the emanations of a mysterious force in his soul.

The scroll held the technique that he got in the Heavenly Exaltation Pagoda. Its cost exceeded the value of entire treasuries, not only of the Trial Worlds but also of the entire Ecumene. Unfolding the scroll, Ryu observed its golden surface. Engraved upon it were several lines of magnificent black letters.

Infinite Potential Technique

The last and greatest creation of the Trials Worlds' creator. One of the five eight-volume techniques of the One Path set. With it, you can overcome any obstacle, but only if you are willing to put everything on the line. With it, you...

Unfortunately, Ryu couldn't unfold the scroll any further. No matter how hard he tried, the golden parchment didn't budge. The most interesting thing was that no one but him could see or feel the scroll. It was as if it were a mere illusion. A product of his wild imagination. When he tried to talk about it, he found himself unable to do so. His mouth wouldn't open, his lips wouldn't move, and his tongue refused to form a coherent sentence.

After half an hour of struggling to fully open the scroll, he threw it into the ocean. He knew that he was a fool to throw away something so valuable, but he didn't care. He couldn't get rid of it anyway. Heavens knew he tried.

The scroll whizzed through the air but as soon as it got close to the surface of the azure waters, it disappeared, and Ryu again felt the presence of something powerful inside him. The damned thing was firmly attached to him.

The waves never stopped crashing into the rocks, breaking against them in myriads of drops. Mesmerized by this sight, Ryu began to meditate. He came out of this state only after a couple of hours, when the skies turned scarlet, and the Temple tattoo burned his wrist.

The war was about to start.

***

Somewhere very, very far...

He was a true prodigy. A representative of the elder race of aesirs, endowed with the Progenitor bloodline, the child of deities, and the heir to a powerful sect in the Central World. He had the highest potential and seemingly boundless possibilities.

He became the best swordsman of the Ecumene. No one was a match for him. His talent was recognized not only by Or'drok, Tel'Naal and La'Gert but even by their teacher, Atrazoth, the previous Ruler of the Ecumene.

Administrators repeatedly came to him with various tempting offers, and the *System* had bestowed him with the title of the Heavenly Sword.

He was half a step away from becoming a Higher One.

Did Ulrich regret what happened? Did he regret losing it all? Probably not.

Having once met Yashnir and heard him out on his offer to join his Army of Truth, Ulrich demanded only one thing in return — a fight in which his blade could demonstrate its full potential. By the end of the Great War, Yashnir fulfilled this request. Ulrich got a chance to fight against the main defender and the strongest *Administrator* of the *System* — Three-Faced. Even now, Ulrich didn't remember exactly how the fight went down, but he would never forget the euphoria he felt then. How his sword sang. How beautiful his dance was.

That fight was the pinnacle of his life as a swordsman.

Alas, his happiness was short-lived. Feeling that his

mistress was in danger, Three-Faced fled, leaving a few *Administrators* behind to finish the fight. Among them was Ulrich's former student. Thanks to the support of the Heavenly Throne, the *Administrators* were extremely strong, but they weren't as good as their master. Ulrich was ready to die, but only in an exciting duel, not in a meaningless fight one against the world. He tried to escape somewhere to the periphery of the Ecumene, creating a nightmarish spatial storm in the process, but he was overtaken at the last moment. His former student, that treacherous beast, put a deadly Curse on him.

Ulrich suppressed it, but he was too weak to deal with the consequences.

Not wanting to accept such an inglorious death, Ulrich clung to life with the desperation of a drowning man holding onto a piece of driftwood. Over and over again, he recalled his duel with Three-Faced, wanting to once again feel that euphoria and to remember how his blade's thirst was quenched. Refusing to die, he wandered aimlessly through the distant worlds of the Ecumene for hundreds of years. Following the will of his Master Yashnir, he found the First One's Cycle of Life and long after that, the *Azure Cube* created by his brothers.

Despite the Army's sacrifice, the artifact they created was practically useless. The *Azure Cube* had the ability to attract the souls of Yashnir's warriors, but only their fragments. Broken, they had no *Spark*. Ulrich spent a lot of time experimenting with the artifact. At some point, he came up with an idea of putting the Cycle of Life in the *Cube's* center. This not only increased its power but also gave it the ability to capture *Sparks* and revive them in new *Shells*. Thus, Ulrich successfully implemented his master's plan to reincarnate the Army's seventh hundred Legion.

But it would have to wait its turn. If anyone was being

reincarnated, it was Ulrich. He still had a fight to finish, after all.

Having spent the last of his strength to unite the two artifacts, he placed his things inside the *Cube*, implanted the power of the *Tattoo of Destruction and Creation* into Yashnir's statue, and then died. But his *Shell* didn't disintegrate, and the *Spark* didn't go to the World of the Dead for complete purification. The *Cube* captured it, and then the long process of rebirth began.

For hundreds of millions of years, the Cycle of Life held Ulrich's *Spark* within itself. Reincarnation could begin once the purification process was completed, when his soul reached a mortal level. Choosing the ideal vessel, the *Cube* infused Ulrich's *Spark* with it. Soon, the young Jiang Dao was born. One day, he would become one of the strongest Masters on Saha.

"What an old dream," Ulrich muttered as he opened his eyes. "But what a pleasant feeling that another part of me has finally merged with the new soul. How wonderful…"

Having gotten up, he looked into his inner world. A huge purple sphere surrounded by golden shards appeared before him. The former was his current *Shell* while the latter were particles of his divine one, which contained his memory, power, knowledge, and skills. The *Cube* preserved everything, leaving the reincarnated soul the opportunity to become its former self.

The merging of his old and new souls had barely begun. However, with his armor, shield, and sword, as well as the *Cube* and the *Tattoo*, which he could control with the fragments of his old *Shell*, Ulrich was no weaker than most *Star Emperors*.

"It seems that I became an *Exorcist* and reclaimed the *Will of Sword*. As I suspected, this not only transfers memory and knowledge to me but also saturates the new *Shell* with strength, changing it and forcing it to develop rapidly. At this rate, I'll be a deity again in twenty years, even if I don't spend a single day training or meditating. My new soul will develop on its own thanks to the strength of the old one. How convenient." Ulrich smiled.

Although he was abandoned somewhere far beyond the Ecumene, there were reasonable beings here, too. And what was most interesting, one extremely powerful Spirit ruled this galaxy.

A Spirit that had become a deity a long time ago and had become a Higher One.

A Spirit that lived during the era of the First Ones.

A Spirit that once fought them.

Ulrich was dying to talk to him.

Chapter 9
THE FIRST GENERAL

A gigantic dark room with a high ceiling filled with glass cylinders. Inside them, encased in bluish liquid, were dozens of slumbering children. This was Ulrich's first memory after rebirth, from the time when he didn't know his name yet.

He spent most of that period of his life sleeping. In rare moments of awareness, he was able to observe his surroundings. The people changed, but every time he opened his eyes, there was someone standing by some of the vats. Sometimes, they'd inject the liquid with other chemicals, sometimes they'd perform what seemed to be rituals, and sometimes they'd take the children out for testing.

The number of children, or subjects, as the people called them, kept changing. Waking up, Ulrich would notice that some of them, having grown, were replaced by younger specimens. Rarely anyone stayed for more than a few years. In the end, he was the only one left in the room.

"Jiang Dao. It's time to wake up."

That was where the experiment ended. As he later learned, the Seven Blades Clan was trying to create a child with the potential of a *Holy Lord*. To do this, they took the newborn children of True Masters and placed them in an artificial environment that was supposed to contribute to the formation of a *Soul Shell* of the highest quality. Alas, this process depended on so many factors that it took the clan's researchers a lot of time and resources to perfect it.

The second stage of the project involved strengthening the souls and bodies of children with increased talent. The methods used were often severe, acquired through trial and error, so the mortality rate was high in the beginning. The alchemists' concerns were dismissed by the clan's leaders, and the research continued. Methods were changed and improved, but they didn't give significant results. Everything came down to the poor conditions for cultivation in Saha and the lack of strong Masters and high-quality resources.

But the clan's leaders persisted and the alchemists retorted to artificially enhancing the bloodline by crossing it with that of beasts and other powerful creatures. Eventually, they managed to isolate the necessary bloodline and implement it, increasing the body's and soul's stamina in the first century of life, but that was nowhere near enough.

After this breakthrough, things went better, and in the next couple of years, they finally managed to create the perfect specimen.

After leaving the laboratory, Jiang Dao, whose mind had already been implanted with all the knowledge he would ever need, became the Old Man of the Gray Mountain's personal student. With his patronage, he gained access to the clan's best techniques, resources, and training facilities. At the age of ten, he awakened the warrior layer of his soul, strengthened with the *Key Part: Soul*, which allowed him to become a peak *Elementalist* at the age of ninety — an achievement never before seen on Saha.

But even after that, Jiang Dao didn't get his freedom, remaining only a tool in the hands of the Old Man. Always under someone's supervision, he was forbidden to leave the Celestial Plateau.

Until one day.

That faithful day, the Old Man unexpectedly ordered his student to go to Alkea and find the third *Key Part* of the Gates of Ecumene. Little did he know that this was the place where Jiang Dao was drawn to from the very first moment of his new life.

Guided by his sixth sense, Jiang Dao entered the *Azure Cube* and so, he returned the fragments of a *Divine Shell*. As they merged with the ancient artifact and the Cycle of Life inside of it, Ulrich's memory slowly began to return.

It turned out he wasn't the only one who experienced rebirth. Although the *Cube* was created to attract souls for this exact reason, the chance to catch a rapidly weakening one somewhere in the vast expanse of the Ecumene was about the same as the chance to randomly dig up a *Divine* artifact in one's garden.

And yet it happened. Four times, including Ulrich himself.

First was U'Shor, a lucky low-rank soldier of the Legions who lived up to his name even in his afterlife. Second was someone who was reborn with the help of the *Azure Cube* in an unknown place and at an unknown time. The remnants of his *Divine Shell* had never been stored inside the artifact nor had he received the *Yin-Yang Phantom Tattoo*. To make matters more confusing, the very mention of his rebirth was erased from the *Cube's* records. Something that, in theory, should have been impossible, since Ulrich had placed his spiritual mark on it before his death. The only reason why he even knew about their rebirth was through historical record that the Cycle's energy supply was almost completely depleted at some point.

The third anomaly was Kai Arnhard. His *Divine Shell* was also never stored in the *Cube*. Only his *Spark* was reborn. This, too, should have been impossible. Without a *Shell*, the *Spark* was supposed to end up in the World of the Dead. And yet, the *Cube* still brought him back and bestowed him with the *Yin-Yang Phantom Tattoo*.

Unable to understand how and why that happened, Ulrich decided to meet the boy in the Belteise Endless Labyrinth once he had regained the entirety of his memories and checked the *Cube's* chronicles. Attacking Kai, he searched his soul for the presence of *Divine Shell* fragments, or at least traces of merging with it, but he found nothing. Disappointed, he left Kai alone, warning him about Nomen, who had once tried to break into the *Cube* and capture it. If it weren't for the protective measures Ulrich had left in it before his death, Nomen would have succeeded in this endeavor. The *Cube's* chronicles were damaged by his attempt at breaking in, but what little Ulrich did manage to learn about that day was enough to make him vary of Nomen. And seeing his image in Kai's memory made Ulrich wonder which side the boy was on.

In the end, Ulrich decided to leave him be and observe. By that time, his soul and body were on the verge of disintegration. The consequences of the Blades' experiments and the use of the *Key Parts* had left their mark. He had to complete his plan as soon as possible.

His original intention was to sever the connection with his crippled body by using his old *Divine Shell*, but he quickly changed his mind after learning about Elize's plans and the

Bright Doom Tattoo she received. Taking advantage of her blinding hatred, Ulrich liberated his soul from the rotting flesh and finally started the process of rebirth through the *Cube*. Only this time, his new vessel was chosen not by the artifact, but by himself.

His choice was Jiang Suin, his student and one of the prodigies of the Seven Blades Clan, who had been cultivating the *Soul Seed* within himself. The essence of this technique was the destruction of the old *Shell* and the formation of a new one. Save for the tempered body and mind, the entirety of the development process was reset.

It took only a year and a half for the Cycle to produce a *Spark*. Raising the new *Shell's* foundation to ten points with an *Elixir*, Ulrich visited Belteise's imperial palace already in a new body. He blackmailed Sawan into revealing Kai's whereabouts and used the palace's portal to go after him. For a little while, things were going his way, but then he ran into several unpleasant surprises.

Firstly, he was denied entry into the Trial Worlds, which disrupted the transfer. Ulrich soon realized that the problem lay in his soul. Surrounded by fragments of the *Divine Shell* from the life before last, it was too powerful. He didn't know if this restriction had always been in effect, but a few things hinted that it had appeared relatively recently. Quite possibly because of U'Shor, who got reincarnated and whose power got firmly imprinted on the informational level of the Trial Worlds' star system. Something he had done caused the Heavenly Exaltation Pagoda to track his soul, study it, and block the passage of all reincarnated souls of that high power.

Secondly, fate had played a cruel joke on Ulrich, crossing his path with that of his former student, a traitor turned *System Administrator*. But the surprise wasn't the meeting itself, but the fact that the latter was now guarding the Trial Worlds.

Why would the *System* decide to put a guard at the Trial Worlds, Ulrich wondered. Especially given the identity of their creator? The Trial Worlds had never been plundered by deities from the Central and Nearby Worlds before. Their barriers had withstood the onslaught of so many gods for so long. But now, the *System* started to care and wasn't only protecting this place but also preserving it, although it could have destroyed it on its own. It wanted to use it somehow. But why? Was it waiting for something?

Ulrich didn't know, and he hadn't come here seeking answers. After the fight with his former student, he was stranded in a distant system of worlds far away from the Ecumene, and his current goal was to return, but first he'd meet with the ancient Higher One that ruled this galaxy.

Ulrich had gone through the High Council of his servants, consisting of twenty-three *Star Emperors* and one *Limitless*, before his request was even considered. It took a lot of convincing and arguing, sometimes even violence, before the Council finally approved his request.

At last, he'd meet the elusive Higher One.

***

Ulrich walked toward a small archway. Having made sure that it wouldn't spit him out into some unknown part of the universe, he stepped into the flickering portal.

Pressure, blinding light, and unbearable temperature — he felt them all at once. Yet there was no hostile presence, and the sensations were too weak to be a trap.

Using spiritual perception, he realized that he was in outer space, close to a giant star thousands of times larger than the suns that illuminated the inhabited worlds of the Ecumene. It was its light and heat that he felt upon his arrival.

Having expanded his perception to its limit, Ulrich discovered a colossal spatial rift. Next to it, the star seemed no more impressive than an ordinary lantern.

He had heard of such rifts before, but this was the first time he had seen anything like it. They were called Great Wounds — open injuries on the body of the universe, left over from the warring times of the Spirits and the First Ones. Their conflicts had dragged on for many centuries, causing the loss of a colossal amount of energy. It was from the countless Great Wounds that the *System* pulled the power for the Heavenly Throne, simultaneously saturating with strength the only piece of the universe that hadn't suffered in those wars — the Ecumene.

"HAVE YOU SEEN ENOUGH?" a powerful voice sounded in Ulrich's head, making him tremble like a small child.

All of Ulrich's consciousness was focused on the awakened ancient being. He was paralyzed before it. The presence wasn't a manifestation of divine power nor the pressure of an aura or will. No. It was the power of an entity capable of destroying this entire galaxy. He felt something similar when he first met Yashnir.

"DID YOU COME TO OFFER ME TO PARTICIPATE IN THE WAR AGAINST THE HEAVENLY THRONE?" it asked.

"How do you know that?" Ulrich asked, surprised, once he finally pulled himself together.

"WHO DO YOU THINK I AM? I DO NOT NEED TO REACH YOUR THOUGHTS TO READ THEM. YOU HAVE THE MARK OF THE ONE THAT MANAGED TO COMBINE CREATION AND DESTRUCTION. I KNOW WHO YOU ARE."

"You know Master Yashnir?"

"HE HAS TRIED TO CONVINCE ME TO DO THE SAME MORE THAN ONCE. ONLY IT CANNOT BE DONE. DO YOU THINK THAT WE CAN DO ANYTHING TO THE HEAVENLY THRONE? DO YOU THINK THAT WE ARE STRONG ENOUGH TO DESTROY THAT WHICH HAS ABSORBED THE POWER OF EVERY FIRST ONE BEFORE THEY LEFT?" A painful blow fell on Ulrich's soul. *"YOU WASTED YOUR TIME COMING HERE. YOUR MASTER TRIED TO DESTROY THEIR CREATION. AND WHERE IS HE NOW? DEAD, LIKE ALL THOSE THAT CAME BEFORE HIM."*

Covered in blood and sweat, Ulrich groaned as he straightened his back. His voice was strained, summoned with difficulty.

"You are wrong…"

"ABOUT?"

"Master Yashnir… is alive!" Ulrich grinned through the pain. "He didn't… die… He managed… to seal himself before… Before Tel'Naal and La'Gert… wounded him… Before that… Before that, he… brought his sword down… on the Heavenly Throne and… left a crack on it! I saw it! Do you hear me?! Their creation… is not perfect! It can be destroyed! There is… always a chance!"

Hearing no answer, he continued.

"The war… is not over! Even after all this time… Even after his apparent death… Even under such conditions… His plan still continues!" Ulrich growled. "With or without you, sooner or later… He will achieve his goal! Do you hear me?!"

Chapter 10
WAR PREPARATIONS

The sound of footsteps echoed down the long, lavishly decorated corridor. The guests walked quickly, paying no attention to the precious jewelry, fine ornaments, and rare works of art, as if everything around them was nothing more than dust in their eyes.

The leader of the group was a tall black-haired man with an imperturbable and at the same time, arrogant expression on his face. A beautiful girl was clinging to his left arm, almost purring with pleasure. It seemed that she didn't care about anything in this world when she was next to him.

They were followed by two identical women with fox ears. Oi and Mia O'Crime were formidable *Holy Lords* and *Masters of Seven Big Stars*, although their innocent appearance would tell you otherwise.

"How was it in the Abyss?" Oi asked. "Did you find what you were looking for, little brother?"

"I was one of the first to reach the finish line of the Contender's Road. After gaining access to the Great Altar, I used Lord Yashnir's artifact on it as instructed. They were right. The treasure is indeed in the Pagoda. Now all that remains is to get it. With it, victory in the upcoming war with La'Gert and the *System* will be as good as ours," Rosen said, pleased with his work.

"Tina told us," Mia spoke, nodding at the girl clinging to her brother, "that some kind of runic storm had begun there. Was that your doing?"

"No. Why would you think that?" Rosen snorted in annoyance. "What's next? Are you gonna ask if I was the one who opened the Pagoda's gates?"

"Why do you think the storm has anything to do with that?"

"Do you have another explanation? U'Shor sealed the Pagoda so that it would stop absorbing the fog. All that time, the mist was piling up around it, and since now everything has disappeared, it's logical to assume that the Gates have opened. It has nowhere else to go. I don't know why now though... Perhaps U'Shor's seal couldn't keep them closed any longer, or the Pagoda has some kind of defense mechanism. Who knows?"

"You don't think it's weird that it happened right when a bunch of people entered the dimension through the Abyss?" Oi inquired.

"Are you implying that someone is behind this?" Rosen raised an eyebrow. "Are you really that foolish?"

"You're such a brat!" Mia scowled at him, standing up for her twin. "Don't talk to your sister like that!"

"She needs to think before she opens her mouth! Even if the Pagoda opened, it means nothing to us. You can get to the treasure only with the whole key."

The conversation fell silent for a moment. Turning once again, the group approached a large staircase. They were nearing their destination.

"And what are you planning to do next?" Mia asked.

A wide smile suddenly appeared on Rosen's face.

"I killed Kaiser on the Road. In the Tournament's finals, he called himself the sole ruler of Avlaim. I see no reason to delay our plan any longer. In fact, it's time to pick up the pace and take over Insulaii. First, we're going to meet with the Unions and persuade them to join us. After that, I'll start a war with Avlaim. We'll deal with their leaders one by one. Some of their vassals are ready to come over to my side. In the end, the whole planet will become mine. It'll be a resource base for completing our task."

Rosen wasn't afraid to talk about his plans aloud, since they were all covered by a soundproof barrier.

"Look at you, a proper evil genius." Chuckling in response to her brother's pompous speech, Oi patted him on the head.

"Stop that!" Frowning, Rosen pushed her hand away.

"Though, now I understand why mother sent us here. Having learned about Kaiser's true identity from the reports, she figured out what you would do and decided to send us as a safety net," Oi continued as if nothing had happened.

"That's kind of unfair," Mia muttered. "When we took our exam, we had no safety net at all. And she sent the two of us to help you right away!"

"Not my fault that she loves me more than all of you combined." Rosen grinned smugly and shrugged.

"You won't be the youngest one forever," Oi teased him.

That was the end of their conversation. From there on, they walked in silence, lost in their thoughts, and only Tina — the crown jewel of Rosen's harem — was still smiling, rejoicing at the return of her beloved from the Abyss.

The doors opened automatically, letting them into a small but luxurious guest room. On the left side were three representatives of the Han Nam Union and on the right were two members of the Twin Dragons.

They all looked gloomy and not particularly chatty.

"What's this supposed to mean?" Aash'Tsiron, the Dragon matriarch, snarled, her heavy gaze whipping Rosen before it turned to Zhou Han Ham. "You old bastard. You said that an important representative from Bellum wants to meet with us. What is this brat doing here?"

"Watch your mouth, you hag," Rosen casually replied and sat himself on a chair. Tina and his sisters were left behind. "I am that important representative."

"You son of a bitch!" Shiro jumped up from his seat after hearing the words addressed to his mother. His aura seeped out of him, pushing down on Rosen's shoulders.

"Calm down." Rosen rolled his eyes in annoyance. At the same time, Shiro's aura disappeared, and he was pushed back into his seat. "Have you forgotten that your stage means absolutely nothing in this world? I am a *Master of Seven Big Stars* with one of the strongest bloodlines in the universe, and you are a pitiful *Master of Seven Average Stars*, who got his title only due to Insulaii's limitation on the soul's layers. Yes, I'm aware of this little secret of yours," he added with a grin, noticing the surprised looks of the representatives of both Unions.

Folding his arms over his chest and frowning, Shiro swallowed back the rest of his objection.

"Anyway, my name is Rosen O'Crime, in case anyone has forgotten. I am the son of the unofficial matriarch of the Mountain Sect Alliance. Zhou Han Nam knew about all of this from the very moment of my arrival on Insulaii. So far, our cooperation has been quite fruitful."

The Dragons and even Zhou Han Nam's subordinates turned their gazes to the old man.

"That's right." He nodded, confirming Rosen's words. "He is important. I just don't understand why you brought us here, Young Master Rosen. Didn't we agree that only my Union will work with you?"

"There has been a change of plans," Rosen explained. "But don't worry, our contract will not be violated."

"Let's get down to business. What are you offering us?" Aash'Tsiron asked.

"Something rather interesting. I'm sure you'll like it," Rosen replied, smiling. "You see, I met Kaiser in the Abyss..."

As soon as they heard the name, Zhou Han Nam, Aash'Tsiron, and Shiro became even gloomier.

"...and killed him. Avlaim has no ruler at the moment, so I suggest a joint war against it. I'll participate as well. I don't have huge armies, but I have plenty of power and artifacts. I don't believe any of you would like to face Lilith on your own."

As Rosen had anticipated, the leaders of both Unions agreed to his proposition almost immediately. But their desire to conquer this wayward region wasn't the only reason they decided to make a deal with the devil.

Thank you so much, Kaiser. Thank you for killing Zhou's granddaughter and one of the Dragons during that chaos on Kronos. I didn't even have to work hard to persuade them. Thank you again, wherever your Spark is!

Having discussed the main points of the joint military campaign with the Unions' representatives, Rosen went straight to Avlaim. Unfortunately, his meeting with Derek didn't bear any fruit. Having learned about Rosen's intentions, the Eversteins refused to provide him with mercenaries, which led Rosen to the conclusion that they were allies of the Eternal Path Temple.

But Rosen wasn't upset. His second meeting, which began the next morning, ended successfully. The Four Mists Cartel, or rather, the remaining two fleets led by Sirius Delane, agreed to join the war on his side.

As for Knolak, the empire never responded to his proposal to meet. It didn't want to get involved in any confrontations above the water surface, and even his connection with the pirates didn't help Rosen arrange a meeting with the Princes.

Fine, I'll manage without them.

Having finished with all the meetings, Rosen ordered the servants to activate the *Divine* artifact his mother had received from Yashnir and place an indestructible barrier over the entire planet.

***

The leaders of Avlaim's factions arrived at Nogatta one by one and went straight to the Temple's headquarters. Lilith, who temporarily took over the organization, didn't dare to invite them to Kaiser's Ark again.

The information she had received made her suspicious of almost everyone around her.

Within a few minutes, the spacious meeting room was filled with dozens of the most powerful cultivators in the region. When all the guests were finally seated, Lilith climbed the podium and greeted them.

"First of all, thank you all for coming. I think you are all aware of the red barrier that enveloped Insulaii the day before yesterday and cut off communication with other worlds. If the reports I received are correct, this was the doing of the Han Nam Union. If nothing else, we know that their region is the source of the barrier's energy supply. This was done to prevent the Eversteins from helping us. I'm sure you already understand why I've gathered you here. The Twin Dragons and the Han Nam Union intend to invade and capture Avlaim. In other words, ladies and gentlemen, they want war."

The news shocked some of the younger clan leaders but most kept a straight face. The Unions' openly hostile actions in the finals of the Grand Tournament and Kai's disclosure of his status as the ruler of Avlaim made many think about the possible consequences even then.

"They are preparing for war as we speak," Lilith continued. "We have already prevented several sabotage attempts and killed more than a handful of usurpers and spies. And while we are keeping a close eye on any suspicious activity, we are sure that there are many lying in wait. I advise you to be vigilant and tighten security around your borders."

"Why are *you* the one meeting with us, Lady Lilith?" The leader of the Northern Isles Union raised his piercing gaze. "Where is Kaiser?"

"He is not on Insulaii at the moment," Lilith answered. "After leaving the Abyss, he got transferred to another world. Most likely, he's on Bellum."

Before the meeting began, the clones had completed their ritual, informing Lilith of their master's fate.

"What does that mean?" One of the leaders was indignant. "Kaiser brought war on Avlaim, and left us to fight it on our own?"

"How is that fair?!"

"I advise you to choose your words carefully," Lilith snarled. Her warning imbued with her *Will* instantly cooled the ardor of the faction leaders that had almost turned to shouting. "Cease your squabbling. With or without Kaiser, the Unions would have eventually tried to capture Avlaim. We shouldn't waste time arguing. What's done is done, and the fact that you're all united under Kaiser's banner can only benefit you. Or do you think the Unions will take pity on you? Even if you surrender, they'll rather kill you and appoint their own member as the new head than waste time and effort to remove the spirit contracts. All of those thinking about deserting or changing sides, speak right away. I'll execute you myself to save us time. No one? Good. In that case, let me remind you that, according to wartime laws, any attempt at sabotage is punishable by death. I'm well aware that there are loopholes in Kaiser's contract, but don't think that you can exploit them without consequence. Either you are with us, or you are against us. There is no in-between."

"I agree with Lady Lilith," Shan Wu said. "Now is not the time to fight amongst ourselves. The Han Nam Union and the Twin Dragons tried to capture Avlaim more than once, but our ancestors fought back, driving the invaders away from their lands. As their descendants, we'd be spitting on their sacrifice if we succumbed to fear and doubt."

"That's all nice and well, but how will we do it?" the old man who raised the question of Kai's whereabouts spoke again. "*Can* we do it? They have never before united to try to take over Avlaim. We have always fought against one army… How many warriors do we have?" He looked at Lilith.

"About two and a half thousand peak level *Elementalists* with *Three Small Stars*, fifty-two *Masters of Six Stars*, and six *Masters of Seven Stars*."

"Is that so...? If my memory serves me right, the Unions should have more than thirteen and a half thousand combat-ready cultivators, about three hundred and fifty *Masters of Six Stars*, and eight *Masters of Seven Stars*."

"That is correct." Lilith nodded. "We are outnumbered and our chances of holding out are rather slim, I will admit. But don't forget that they have to fight on our territory, which is riddled with many deadly traps. This is where we have an advantage, especially considering the Temple's defensive and combat systems, which we'll share with you. By the end of the day, all your combat-ready cultivators should arrive in Nogatta. You'll be allowed to use the Temple's portals for their transfer. The Temple will take over the supply of our troops with high-quality potions and artifacts. Make sure that your soldiers have all the necessary materials. Spare neither money nor manpower. Now is not the time to be stingy. In addition, as the temporary head of the Temple, I also order you to send to the Ark all your people who are at least peak *Exorcists*. The minimum threshold is *Three Big Stars*."

"Yes, Lady Lilith!"

"The meeting is adjourned! Dismissed! May the Heavens be in our favor."

***

A few days later, when an entire military town had formed around the Temple, inhabited by thousands of True Masters, Lilith finished finalizing the battle plan with the faction leaders. She still had many tasks to take care of, but first she wanted to deal with one interesting case that wasn't related to war preparations.

Reaching one of the guest rooms, she politely used the bell to announce her presence, although she could have entered without it, as the lock would automatically open in front of a Hierarch. The door opened to reveal a charming blonde with a few blue curls and a steely, unyielding look.

"Good evening, my lady," she greeted and bowed.

"Good evening." Lilith nodded, entering the room. "An'na Divide, right?"

"That's right. And you are?"

"My name is Lilith. I am the Matriarch of the Rising Star Sect, a Hierarch of the Eternal Path Temple, and Kaiser's follower. Although, he's probably better known to you as Kai Arnhard."

An'na's eyebrows rose in genuine surprise.

"And where is your companion?" Lilith inquired, looking around.

"He is meditating. I'd rather not disturb him unless it's absolutely necessary. He should be out soon enough. Would you like some tea?"

After thinking for a second, Lilith nodded.

"Chamomile, if you would."

"Of course."

The two were drinking tea in awkward silence when Guts entered the room. Seeing that they had a guest, he bowed politely and inquired about the reason for her visit.

"I'm Lilith, the temporary head of the Temple. I'm here to talk to you about your friend, Kai Arnhard. Please, join us for a cup of tea."

The three of them had a long conversation about Kai. Lilith confirmed her connection with him through a *System* oath and listened to An'na's and Guts's story about how they got to the Trial Worlds and got separated from their friend. She kept asking questions about Kai and cross-referencing the information with what she already knew. In the end, she used the *Runes of Truth* on the two so that she was convinced that they were indeed who they claimed to be.

And then she made them an offer.

"I understand that you don't owe us anything, but how do you feel about helping your friend's organization in the war? Or even better… How do you feel about joining the Eternal Path Temple?"

An'na and Guts looked at each other, smiling.

"We didn't just decide to blindly follow Kai to the Trial Worlds. In fact, we are one of his first followers. We will be more than glad to become a part of his organization."

***

Twenty days flew by in the blink of an eye. The army was equipped with the best armor, weapons, and alchemy available, multiple lines of defense were formed, plans and backup plans were developed, and numerous traps were prepared. Thanks to the Temple's strict but sensible control, the entire region had been ready to meet the invaders for a week now.

Avlaim's army was divided into three parts: two groups of seven hundred and fifty combat-ready Masters, and one group of a thousand regular soldiers. Having supplemented them with thousands of *Three Small Star Elementalists* and *Exorcists*, who would act as "batteries" controlling the huge defense and combat arrays, the General Staff formed three fronts.

Western, led by Ragnar and Nyako.

Eastern, which Shaw and Hiro had to defend.

And the northern one, where the largest number of both ordinary warriors and elite *Seven Star Masters* went.

Fortunately, there was no threat of invasion from the south, since there was a huge anomaly in the icy ocean.

The Unions worked slower than expected, so they failed to surprise their opponents. But they were still too intimidating of a force to be underestimated.

As soon as the information that the enemy troops had finally moved toward Avlaim came, everyone was seized with excitement.

Tension grew on all three fronts.

Only a few hours remained before the official start of a new world war.

Chapter 11
BATTLEFIELD — WEST

"Brings back memories," Nyako said, joining Ragnar on the balcony, from which they had a great view of the vast city.

"What are you talking about?" he asked, surprised.

"It's from here, from the heart of the Land of Wind, that my journey to the Rising Star Sect once began. Kaiser... Or rather, Six, sailed out of here, too."

"Ah, I see. It's been almost a year since we met on the ship that took us all to the Wandering Islands."

"Yeah. More precisely, for him only a year of the standard time has passed, but for us it's been more than a hundred." Nyako chuckled.

"That explains the pain in my joints." Ragnar laughed.

For a while, they observed the rows of True Masters milling below like ants. The whole island was enveloped in an extremely oppressive atmosphere. A few believed that Avlaim would be able to withstand the onslaught of two

Unions at once. Many had faith in the ideas and words of their faction and squad leaders. But for some it wasn't enough, and only spiritual contracts and *System* oaths stopped the weak-willed fighters from deserting.

Standing next to each other, Ragnar and Nyako were in high spirits, despite the upcoming massacre. They had done their best, and while they didn't doubt their success, they didn't think for a second that winning would be easy. The combined army of the two Unions outnumbered Avlaim. Defending hundreds of small border islands simultaneously was impossible for their small forces. Because of the vast number of waterways between the isles, the General Staff decided to establish a line of defense a little further from the border, building it along the twenty-seven largest western islands, including Monsoon, the main island of the Land of Wind.

It was also the first node of the Great Western Frontier — a colossal array that covered all twenty-seven islands. It united dozens of large cities and hundreds of fortresses, turning them into a single defensive structure. At the same time, it could be used for combat as well. Nyako had made sure that it was powerful enough to maintain a continuous spatial connection between all these points, allowing not only the quick transfer of information, people, and resources but also energy, which greatly strengthened each defensive point.

But the array's most important property was its ability to generate waves of spatial interference that prevented the enemy army from penetrating deeper into the region using teleports and bypassing the defense line. And even if they managed to swim past and defend themselves from the artillery, the Great Western Frontier could generate a catastrophically strong spatial storm at any point. However, since such an attack required an unthinkable amount of resources, it was feasible only in a few places. Thus, it was to be used as the last resort.

"Master Ragnar. Lady Nyakonalavius." One of the Temple followers came up to them. "They are here."

***

Fifty-three warships were rapidly approaching Avlaim's western borders. The third fleet of the Han Nam Union, numbering about eighty thousand cultivators, was about to launch an invasion. The armada was led by an experienced *Divine Stage* cultivator *One Step away from Divinity*. Sitting on the prow of the flagship, the *Master of Seven Small Stars* watched the approaching patches of land with a smile on his face.

"This day will go down in history."

"Master Felgan." One of the Union leaders approached him. "The preliminary intelligence report is ready."

Felgan nodded without turning around.

"Speak."

"More than a hundred of Avlaim's border islands are empty. The entire populace was evacuated. All the important infostructure was either dismantled or destroyed. They retreated a little deeper into the region, forming a line of defense along the largest western islands. That makes it more difficult for us to break through since the number of waterways in that area is much smaller and easier to control. There is also information about the existence of a largescale array that covers the entire line of defense."

"They are well prepared," Felgan commented. "But it won't help them."

We have known about all this for a long time, as well as about the number and location of their troops. They don't stand a chance!

The fleet entered Avlaim's waters, where it split into three groups, following Felgan's decision to attack several points at once. By doing this, he hoped to break the array's connection with the islands and gain access to more convenient routes, along which they'd sail deeper into the region.

In the beginning, the path through the abandoned territories was relatively unhindered. Despite the occasional underwater mine, the Han Nam Union didn't need to slow down. Most of the artifacts were detected in advance and destroyed, and those that managed to go unnoticed could only leave a small crack in the ships' protective barriers.

However, halfway through, they encountered a far more formidable challenge than mines.

Felgan was thinking of returning to the captain's cabin when suddenly there was a violent explosion that shook the entire deck. Similar blows erupted a moment later, knocking out many of the weak *Elementalists*, who were unfortunate enough to be on deck at that moment.

When the dust settled, the crew noticed that all the barriers were covered with a web of cracks.

"Everyone inside!" one of the officers on the deck shouted. "Wave two inbound!"

The new attack landed just as the *Elementalists* and energy suppliers were sent to support the barriers. The activated array united the ships' defenses, forming a single dome above them. As a result, instead of nightmarish explosions, only small pops were heard, and the vessels didn't even sway.

"Observation post spotted! Man the cannons!" the admiral reported.

The guns of three long-range cruisers turned in the right direction.

Without any sound, several dozen fireballs flew into the distance and flared up brightly somewhere on the horizon.

"Observation post destroyed!"

Immediately after this, the third salvo hit the single dome.

"Idiots!" Felgan hissed, rolling his eyes. "How could you miss a whole observation post? What are the sensors for? If Avlaim's long-range artillery weren't so useless we would have already suffered our first losses!"

The ships progressed further with little resistance. They were attacked a few more times, but they discovered the enemy's observation posts in time to get away from artillery attacks.

After an hour and a half, the first squadron of the Han Nam Union's third fleet was approaching its goal — the Monsoon Island.

"We'll dock north. At El'Kart," Felgan ordered. "That's the shortest route to the capital."

***

"Master Xi Wou..." A pale man turned to the commander after receiving the report. Swallowing hard, he continued, "The north and northwest strongholds have been destroyed. The enemy is heading straight for the city."

Everyone at the command post fell silent in horror. The commander's eyes widened sharply.

"So quickly?!" Xi Wou couldn't believe his ears. "We couldn't even hold them for a few minutes..."

But before he got a more detailed report, a powerful explosion shook the whole city.

"The port barrier has been breached! The enemy is launching an attack! I'm getting the visuals now!"

A large hologram appeared in the middle of the command post, broadcasting events directly from the port. Numerous small boats were quickly heading toward the shore while the menacing silhouettes of enemy cruisers loomed in the distance. Thousands of attacks had already fallen on the enemy, but they had little to no success. The enemy sent forward their strongest fighters — *Masters* of *Six, Five,* and *Four Stars*, led by Felgan.

"How soon can you close the gap in the dome?"

"We need at least three more minutes!" the assistant reported in a panic.

"Shit!" Xi Wou yelled out and clenched his fists until they crunched. "We don't have that kind of time!"

The enemy landing force had crossed more than half of the way when it was engulfed by a bright fiery flash. The hologram shook and disappeared, and the people at the command center felt a slight tremor under their feet.

"What was that?!" someone shouted.

"It looks like a strike from the capital's long-range artillery array."

One by one, the devices flickered back to life, having previously shut off due to strong energy fluctuations.

"Successful strike confirmed. Restoring surveillance."

The hologram hummed and revealed the aftermath of the catastrophic attack. Or rather, that was what the officers had hoped for, only their expectations weren't destined to come true. The restored picture showed intact cruisers. Under the cover of a huge blue barrier filled with what seemed to be runic fog, they were approaching the destroyed port.

This was followed by footage of enemy Masters landing on the shore. Soon, the Union came into direct conflict with the defenders of Avlaim. Within just a couple of minutes, the first line of city defense fell. Teleportation-blocking artifacts were disabled along with it. Immediately after this, a full-scale landing of enemy troops began. The space bent and distorted, and more and more Masters appeared with loud pops.

Before the observation post was destroyed, the officers had time to see how the enemy troops set up hundreds of high-quality defensive and combat arrays.

Xi Wou felt his insides go cold.

"Why?!" He gritted his teeth under the confused stares of the silent officers. "Why is no one responding to our signal?! What are they doing? Where are the reinforcements?! What's taking them so long? How are we supposed to hold the city?! Are they out of their goddamn minds?! Idiots! Do they not understand that this is the most important battle in this entire war?! If we let the enemy land and gain a foothold on the island, we'll need a miracle to defend it!"

His angry speech was interrupted by another ground-shaking explosion. Spitting profanities, Xi Wou went to the window that overlooked the huge underground pavilion. Five thousand meditating *Exorcists* were supporting the southern node of the city's defensive array by participating in a massive ritual.

He frowned. About a thousand *Exorcists* had collapsed due to overvoltage after the barrier was attacked again.

About half of them were dead.

"Master Xi Wou... The eastern node has been destroyed. Without it and the port, the city barrier will soon collapse."

Grimacing, Xi Wou turned to his subordinates.

"Split the energy supply and switch to protecting key areas. Prepare transfer arrays. We are retreating to the capital!"

Then he went downstairs. Being a *Master of Six Small Stars*, he was going to join the ritual to strengthen the barrier and give the others time to retreat.

Avlaim's troops left the coastal city in a few minutes. Immediately after that, the remaining nodes were blown up.

***

"Looks like El'Kart has been captured," Nyako absentmindedly said as she sipped her tea.

"Not even an hour has passed," Ragnar grunted, looking at the interactive map of the western front. "So many deaths... I think he'll be here soon."

A few minutes later, a noise came from the hallway.

"Let me through!" Xi Wou shouted and slammed the door open. Behind him, the unconscious guards were lying on the floor.

Entering the room, he stared at Ragnar and Nyako's unbothered expressions.

"You!" he began, and then choked. He knew he should show humility before his seniors but he was too enraged to care about etiquette right now. "W-Why... Why didn't you send reinforcements?! Why didn't you help us?! We lost El'Kart! Now they have a free pass for further invasion of Monsoon! Why aren't you doing anything?! Hey! Are you even listening to me!?"

Ragnar chuckled.

"What do you mean, we're not doing anything? We're having a tea party. Would you like to join? It's delicious."

Xi Wou stared at him, dumbfounded.

"Is this some kind of a prank...?" He was confused. This couldn't be real. There was no way they were this relaxed while people were dying outside. "Why did you let them in?"

"What did you want us to do? Send all the troops to El'Kart? For what? So that you can turn off the barrier at the right moment and leave us defenseless against the enemy armada?"

"What...?" Xi Wou was taken aback and indignant. "What are you talking about?! Why would I do that?!"

"You can stop pretending," Ragnar sneered. "The jig is up."

"He's not pretending right now," Nyako remarked.

"Yes, you are right about that. Having had his memories altered, he can't even begin to fathom what we are talking about. But that doesn't change anything. Betrayal is betrayal."

"I agree." Nyako nodded, and Xi Wou found himself bound by the water chains of the room's built-in array.

Having lost the ability to move, the shocked man tried to use his spirit power, but the array blocked it using the *Force of Soul*.

Approaching Xi Wou, Nyako took off his *Spatial Ring*, removed the mark, and rummaged through its contents. Somewhere in the back of it, stashed away, she found a large golden egg — a *Divine* artifact capable of destroying almost any barrier provided it was close enough to its source.

"What is that?! How did that end up in my *Ring*?!"

A terrible pain pierced his mind. One of the mental marks activated, and, without hesitation, he tried to destroy his own soul.

Fortunately, Nyako anticipated that he might try to commit suicide, so she made sure that he couldn't. Right now, Xi Wou's warrior layer was almost completely blocked, making him an ordinary mortal.

"How did he circumvent Kaiser's spiritual contract?" Ragnar asked, rising from his chair and approaching Nyako.

"Looks like Lilith was right. They didn't break the spirit bonds, only suppressed them. His name is still in the scroll, but breaching the contract can no longer harm him. Suppressing someone's mind isn't easy. It can take a while until the counterparty dies and you're risking your life if something goes wrong. But apparently, someone believed that the reward is worth it."

"The Unions are too generous with *Divine* artifacts for someone who has an advantage... Or at least thinks they do."

"They aren't leaving anything to chance, it seems. Perhaps this is the same person who installed the barrier over Insulaii."

"I think you're giving him too much credit."

"Whatever the case, he's too dangerous to have around." The array knocked out Xi Wou. "We'll delve into his soul later. He has fulfilled his role as a traitor anyway. The Han Nam Union will launch their attack from the exact place we wanted them to do it."

"Good." Ragnar grinned and cracked his knuckles. "We'll start the second phase soon and avenge our fallen brothers."

***

After capturing the coastal city of El'Kart, the Union set about deploying a variety of defensive, offensive, and transport arrays, to carefully search for and neutralize traps along the way. After a few hours, they formed a proper base on the island. Once they reached the land, they no longer needed constant support from the ships.

With the headquarters set up, Felgan ordered them to launch an attack.

The first squadron of the Third Fleet was divided into ten divisions, each of which consisted of a hundred powerful cultivators and two thousand low-level artifactors. The former could do much better with the proper cover of the latter. One was left behind to defend the base, while the other nine divisions moved deeper into the island under the support of artillery. Using mobile arrays, they occupied an advantageous position, fired at the enemy, broke through their barriers, and destroyed their equipment. Then they entered direct combat, suppressing Avlaim's forces with sheer numbers.

Thus, within five hours, the Han Nam Union captured about a third of the island on its way to the capital. Outnumbered and overpowered, the defenders couldn't do much, but they kept attacking, unwilling to give up. They managed to destroy some of the troops and decimate the entire Third Division, but none of that prevented the opposing force from advancing.

The Union's main goal was the capital. To reach it, they needed to get to the Great Western Frontier, besiege it, and then break through the barrier with specialized equipment that could only be used close to the already weakened dome.

So far, the Sixth Division had gone the farthest. At some point, it had to slow down its advance so as not to break away from the others. Taking up a convenient position in a small town, hastily abandoned by Avlaim's citizens, the Unions' troops settled down and waited for new orders. Intoxicated by their dizzying success, the soldiers were already rejoicing at the prospect of victory and greedily rubbing their hands at the sight of other people's resources.

"In a couple of days, there'll be nothing left of their defense!"

"Give it a week or two and Avlaim will be ours!" one of them exclaimed. "Our sect has been promised several islands near Nogatta. I can't wait for their resources to flow into our pockets!"

"Just don't cry too hard when you reach their empty treasuries. Do you really think that they left anything behind? They're stupid, but they're not *that* stupid."

The man froze for a moment, and a whole range of emotions flashed across his face. He experienced every sensation from bewilderment to sadness in the span of a second as his hopes and dreams were crushed right in front of him.

Loud laughter followed his cry of frustration.

"Damn it!"

"What's going on here?!" their officer snapped. He was a tall, bulky Dorgan with *Six Average Stars*. The soldiers stiffened at the sight of him. "Have you forgotten where you are?!"

"No, sir!"

"Officer Bor!"

"What are you doing then, huh? Why did you leave your posts? Who will defend the array if we are attacked?" Bor pointed to a tall pillar emitting tremendous power. In its spatial pocket were three hundred meditating *Elementalists*. "What do we pay you for?!"

The pillar was the central defensive array of the Sixth Division. Four more were located in the north, south, west, and east parts of the town each. Together with the central one, they formed a dome over the entire settlement. A total of one and a half thousand people were engaged in supporting the barrier, and another thousand were distributed among twenty artillery arrays. As with defensive arrays, they had spatial pockets inside them to accommodate array operators.

"But Officer Bor!" one of the men tried to object. "Who would attack us now anyway? We already dominate the battlefield. Avlaim's soldiers can't harm us."

"Are you sure?" Bor said menacingly. "Have you forgotten about the Third Division?"

"With all due respect to the fallen, it was entirely their fault."

"Do you think you're doing better than them now? Get back to your positions!" Bor's voice exploded. "If I see you like this again, you'll only be guarding and cleaning the lavatories until the very end of the war!"

Frightened by such a prospect, the soldiers began to disperse when suddenly there was a distant bang. Jerking to the side, they saw a brief flash in the south side of the town, followed by a loud, unpleasant sound that spread through the air.

"The emergency signal... To your positions! Quickly!" Bor barked, snapping the soldiers back to their senses.

"Protect the array! And you two," he pointed to the strongest of them, "follow me!"

Without waiting for their answer, he rushed south. But before he even had the time to leave the town's central square, explosions sounded in several more places.

"We are under attack! The enemy has penetrated the barrier!" Bor shouted so loudly that everyone bound by the *Spiritual Link* shivered. "The southern defensive array is damaged! Northern, eastern, and western are under siege! The enemy is—"

The voice died down abruptly in the heads of his subordinates, and the whole Sixth Division shivered this time from the horror of the realization that the aura of their commander had gone out. At the same time, the auras of many Masters were rapidly disappearing. Echoes of battles came from every direction. Explosions, flashes, screams, reports, and death cries came down on the small town all at once.

"Speed up!" Bor shouted at the duo as he jumped up onto the buildings to get a better view of the scene ahead.

What's going on? Where are the enemies?! Why can't I sense unfamiliar auras? It feels like we're fighting against our own men! How did they get close to the dome without us noticing them?! How did they break through it?! What the hell is going on?!

Sensing a group of allies in a nearby three-story building, Bor leaped down from the roof and walked straight toward them.

The barrier that covered the building parted in front of the Union mark, letting him through, and he went to the three officers who were standing in the garden next to a couple of artillery arrays.

"Bor! You are alive!" one of them exclaimed happily.

"What's happening? Where is the enemy?" Bor asked anxiously.

"We have no idea," one of them grunted. "Everything happened so fast! The southern defensive array has been destroyed. I don't even know if the rest of them are functional."

"Our soldiers fell dead although there was no one next to them!" added the third, the youngest, and the least experienced among them.

"Safron, calm down. It must be—"

"THEY ARE HERE!!!"

A heartbreaking cry came from the outside, and another aura went missing.

The invisible enemy stopped holding back.

"AAAAAH!"

"NO! STOP! ENOUGH!"

"HELP!"

"HERE!"

Sensing danger to his right, Bor swung his blade, creating a powerful gust of wind. His excellent reaction time, vast combat experience, and considerable strength allowed him to effortlessly repel the imperceptible attack. But his relief was short-lived. Immediately after, he sensed even greater danger, from all sides at once.

Bound by the pressure, Bor fell to one knee and stuck his sword into the ground, unleashing the maximum amount of soul energy. A wall of scarlet wind shot up into the sky, forming an impenetrable ring around him and blocking the incoming attack.

Watching the battle unfolding before his eyes, Bor knew that he couldn't do much to help the others. The least he could do was scan the enemy, use a one-time artifact and send the information about them to the rest. After that, he'd stay with his soldiers until the bitter end. Suddenly, a figure without an aura appeared in front of him. It was a woman wearing the emblematic purple robes of the Eternal Path Temple army. Her face was hidden by a white mask with a large "IX" written on it.

One look at her was enough for Bor's entire body to freeze. Gazing into her purple eyes, he somehow understood that she was smiling under the mask.

A blade flashed through the air.

Both Bor's body and his *Wind* shield were cut in two.

***

Eleven thousand of Kai's clones finally came into play. Sharing knowledge and memories with their creator, almost all of them were *Masters of Five Small Stars*.

From the very beginning, Lilith suspected that there were traitors in the ranks of Avlaim's defenders — moreover, they were at the very top of the social pyramid. The Unions had decided to enter this war way too quickly and confidently, although invasions weren't on their agenda. From what she knew, they had originally intended to push their interests through economic and political methods.

She assumed that they had caught wind of Gabba's death. However, the only way anyone could have learned this was if they had been at the reception hosted by the Eversteins. They had signed an alliance with Temple, so only those who became Kai's vassals after that event remained under suspicion. Lilith was even more convinced of her suspicions after she told the faction leaders about the upcoming war.

Out of this fear, she withheld information about the clones, as well as about Nyako and Shaw, who became *Masters of Seven Small Stars*. The traitors had already disclosed the position of Avlaim's troops, their number and power. They probably also knew the commanders' development levels and most of their plans. But this only benefitted Lilith's little scheme, because it allowed her not only to uncover the moles but also to feed them false information.

In the end, everything turned out exactly the way she wanted.

The Unions were confident in their advantage. Blinded by their arrogance, they didn't even entertain the idea that the Temple could have such a formidable weapon in its possession. Each clone wasn't only a powerful Master in itself, but it could, just like its creator, become invisible, and fighting that which you could neither see nor sense was simply impossible. Retreating wasn't an option anymore either — the invading troops had gone deep into the territory, surrounding them.

Barriers and arrays turned out to be useless against such an army. The Temple's technology was far above anything that the Unions owned, so the clones had no issue breaking through the defense of Han Nam's divisions and suppressing their arrays. The strongest of the clones, the first six, remained on the Ark to support the connection between doubles and make sure they were working in unison.

Ultimately, the situation on the battlefield dramatically shifted. The combined army of the two Unions and the Cartel numbered about sixteen thousand, but they could hardly oppose an invisible and perfectly coordinated threat. The invaders began to lose their hold on all three fronts. Dozens of soldiers died every minute.

Felgan, stationed at the base set up in El'Kart, listened in horror to the numerous reports on death and destroyed equipment. There seemed to be no end to them. The Sixth and First Divisions were almost completely destroyed, while the rest retreated to the coast, leaving many of their soldiers and equipment behind.

"By the Heavens..." Felgan sighed in shock. "How is this even possible?"

A moment later, the world was drowned in a nightmarish roar, and everything around was flooded with blinding light. A simultaneous barrage of multiple long-range artillery arrays struck El'Kart, wiping the First Division and the entire base from the face of the planet. The previously impervious barriers were quickly swept away.

The space above the city distorted, opening a portal.

"Amazing!" Ragnar grinned and patted Nyako's shoulder. "You did an excellent job!"

Paying no attention to his gesture, she focused on her spirit perception, while using her multifunctional staff.

"About thirty Masters survived," she said without opening her eyes. "But their leader seems to have escaped. Some weak *Divine* artifact had transferred him onto a ship."

Ragnar grimaced. He had been dying to vent his anger on someone after losing to Rosen. This would have been the perfect opportunity to get a load off his shoulders.

"Let it go, Ragnar. We wouldn't have let you do it anyway," Eleven added. "Our main task is to eliminate their commanders as quickly as possible."

Twenty-Six nodded in agreement.

"Fine. But that doesn't change the fact that he got away." Ragnar sighed. "Will the artillery reach the ships?"

"It will, but the arrays are recharging. It'll take them at least an hour, and by then they'll be long gone from the island's vicinity," Nyako explained.

Up to this moment, Avlaim's artillery arrays couldn't harm the enemy troops and structures in any way, but as soon as Lilith's issued the order to attack, Nyako raised their power level from fifteen to a hundred percent.

It no longer made sense to hide the Temple's true strength.

**

Meanwhile, on the eastern front, there was an ongoing confrontation right in the middle of the ocean. The Sea Trading Company's fleet, led by Shaw, and the Four Mists Cartel's fleet, led by Sirius Delane, clashed at the borders of the region in a massive battle. When a part of the Dragons' fleet joined the skirmish, the Company had to retreat, but when the enemies found themselves deep enough in the Temple's waters, the clones hiding in its depths launched a surprise attack.

And then the real battle began.

Soaring into the sky, Shaw settled the score with his old friend.

And Hiro...

"We meet again." Standing right on the water, Sakumi smiled. Like Hiro, she was a *Master of Seven Small Stars* now. However, unlike him, she reeked of dark arts. "Honestly, I was surprised to hear that you survived. I suppose I should be thankful to the Heavens for bringing you back to me. A loyal dog always returns home, doesn't it? It'll be nice to have you serve me again."

Sakumi was speaking in all seriousness. There wasn't a drop of sarcasm in her voice, only dissatisfaction with the fact that Hiro had ceased to be her servant. To her, he had never been a brother, but someone who would fulfill her every whim and desire.

"I'll kill you," Hiro said with all the calm and cold he could muster. He seemed not to be threatening her, but rather convincing himself of the deed that he was about to commit.

In response, Sakumi laughed.

"You don't have the guts to do it! I know you well, brother."

Hiro didn't answer.

Gathering all his determination and ordering the others not to interfere, he rushed at his sister.

***

"That's it?" Lilith sneered. Covered in golden flames, she glared at her opponent hiding behind a *Divine* barrier. "*You* supposedly managed to defeat *Kai*?"

Bloody and mutilated, Rosen tried to get up, but his legs gave way, and he fell again. All his strength wasn't enough to defeat a Phoenix. Even if her bloodline was just temporary.

"I really hate that we have to do this." Oi came out of invisibility. She was the one who activated the artifact that saved her brother. "Unfortunately, you leave us no choice."

"Oh, two more. The Manticores have decided to stop hiding. Commendable. Come on, both of you at once. I don't have time to waste."

"Bold words for someone who is about to die," Mia

taunted.

The twins activated *Partial Transformation* at the same time. Their *Manticore Hearts* raced to the top.

"Bring it on." Lilith grinned.

Chapter 12
BATTLEFIELD — EAST

An hour earlier

The Union's and the Dragons' forces successfully invaded the northern part of Avlaim. They were led by Zhou Han Nam, Shiro, and Aash'Tsiron.

Opposite them stood an army controlled by three leaders of the Northern Islands Union, including Shan Wu and Lilith.

"Looks like it's about to start," Rosen commented with a pleased smile as he watched the projection showing the movement of the Unions' troops.

He was in no hurry to participate in the battles, remaining on his ship. Just in case, he had sent Tina to the battlefield. She was a *Master of Seven Big Stars*, so their troops would be able to handle just about anything with her support. He wanted to demonstrate that he could capture Insulaii not by using his strength but by relying on his intelligence, so he chose to stay back and watch his plan unfold.

"What is this?" a child's voice rang out.

Turning around, Rosen saw a girl with pinkish skin, red hair, and small horns on her forehead, who was curiously studying the projection of the northern part of Avlaim. She was only seven years old, but she was already an initial-level *Exorcist*. Having stepped on the path of development at the age of four, she was unaware of her strength and potential. Despite possessing intellect higher than that of any mortal, as well as extensive knowledge, she was still a naive and curious child.

"This is a map of enemy territory, and these dots," Rosen pointed with his finger, "are our warriors."

"What about those squares?"

"These are supposed enemy positions."

"Why are they dimmer than our circles?"

"Because we have more warriors. The brighter the dot, the more of them are in that place."

"Wow! Will we win?"

"Of course! Don't even doubt it for a moment." He picked up the girl and put her on his lap. "Bored already?"

"Yeah. Those guys are not fun. They only talk about cultivation... I don't know why they bother when they are so weak."

Rosen laughed.

"Do you want to observe the battlefield for a while?"

"Yes!"

Ten minutes later, she got bored with this activity, too, and she went to play catchup with Rosen's sisters, leaving him to observe the battle that had just begun to unfold.

As expected, the Unions' forces pushed through Avlaim's defenses on all three fronts. Everything had gone according to plan. Rosen was looking forward to a quick victory, but his optimism was shattered when reports about sudden enemy attacks began to arrive in rapid succession. Numerous points on the projection dimmed, and some even disappeared from the map.

Rosen jumped up from his chair.

"What the hell?!"

He tried to contact the commanders and officers, but there was no answer. The tension grew with every passing second. Minutes stretched like hours, and he had no idea what was going on.

Returning to the projection, Rosen carefully analyzed the recent events and tried to assess the situation. He was so engrossed in his thoughts that he didn't immediately notice the activation of one of the communication artifacts.

"Rosen! Rosen, damn you! Answer me!" came Zhou Han Nam's panicked voice.

"What's going on there?!"

"We were wrong! They have a lot more troops! Thousands of *Five Star* and dozens of *Seven Star Masters* surrounded us! And they are all invisible! Neither our eyes nor spirit perception can detect them! It's a trap! Shiro is dead! I almost got killed, too! You've sent us to our deaths, Rosen! Do you hear me?!"

"Calm down! Retreat your men! I'm on my way!"

Breaking the connection, Rosen gritted his teeth.

What the hell is he talking about? Invisible to perception? Like Kaiser? But there are thousands of them... Are they really his clones? Can they live after the death of their creator? Or could he still be alive? But how?

Suddenly, another transmitter was activated. It was Tina's.

"Hey, Manticore," a familiar female voice taunted. "I have your girlfriend. She's in a lot of pain, y'know? If you don't come quickly, she may not be able to endure the torture that we've prepared for her."

Startled, Rosen rushed to the artifact, but the connection was already interrupted.

He turned to the projection and found Tina's mark on the map. He matched her location with the source of the incoming message, and everything inside him shriveled up. The hope that Lilith — and he was sure that it was her voice he heard — simply took Tina's communication artifact was shattered.

It's definitely Tina's mark. They couldn't have just caught her... Not with the artifacts she had on her. They came prepared, the bastards. They knew about her from the beginning. I only ever told Kaiser about her. That fucker must be alive! But why was Lilith the one to get in touch with me? Something's not right here. My **Poison** *was too strong... There's no way that he survived unscathed. He must be half-dead by now, with only enough strength left to work from the shadows. What are they hoping to achieve? Do they really think that Lilith can handle me? I don't know. But they will pay for every moment of Tina's suffering!*

Ordering the crew to return the ship to Tyr, Rosen grew a pair of huge wings and quickly headed south. His twin sisters followed, staying invisible. After all, they had promised mother to keep him safe.

***

Somewhere on the eastern front

Hiro charged forward along the water surface at full speed. Four *Spheres* unleashed all their power on his sister, almost knocking her off her feet. Sakumi revealed her *Spheres* in response and even strengthened them with the *Field of Superiority*, but she couldn't completely get rid of the invading pressure. Her brother's will was one stage stronger than hers.

To Sakumi, who was genuinely shocked by her brother's attack, Hiro's silhouette turned into a blur. Thanks to his elements, he surpassed her both in speed and power. She, on the other hand, was a more versatile warrior. The *Paths* of *Sword*, *Water*, and *Lava* gave her durable defense, strong attacks, mobility, and the ability to heal. She was a Jack of all Trades, but truly a master of none in specific.

As soon as they were close to each other, Hiro pulled his sword from its scabbard. The blade gleamed in the light, and then extended.

Sakumi's arm was cut off at the very shoulder.

He can use the first level of the Divine Gift *at such a distance?!*

A moment later, Hiro was by her side. Having spent a lot of energy on the *Infinite Strike*, he returned the katana to its sheath and prepared to attack again. Whistling through the air, his sword was already breaking free again. Moving from the bottom up, it was on his way to cut Hiro's sister in two, when Sakumi suddenly bared her teeth. Bloody tourniquets erupted from her wounded shoulder, instantly regrowing her severed arm. Taking out her blade from the *Spatial Ring*, she grabbed it with both hands and brought it down abruptly, blocking her brother's deadly attack at the very last moment.

Empowered by the same *Divine Gift*, the swords

collided, generating a powerful shock wave and turbulent ocean waves. Sakumi's blade cracked, while Hiro's katana was met with colossal pushback. Unable to stand on its surface, he dove under the water.

Hiro was shocked by the speed of his sister's regeneration, her physical strength, and reaction time, all of which were granted to her by the House of Blood's forbidden alchemy. He quickly found himself captured by Sakumi's main element. She no longer needed to create water from scratch, only subdue the existing one with techniques, which saved her a lot of effort.

Dozens of invisible water kites were heading toward Hiro from all sides at once. Without having time to weave a defensive technique, he was forced to manually deflect all attacks. Turning into a whirlwind, he wielded his katana at insane speed, cutting through and destroying his sister's techniques. After a couple of seconds, the pressure around him dramatically increased. The water squeezed his body more and more, slowing him down and making it more difficult to defend himself. Soon, the azure waves turned scarlet.

Sakumi was hiding in the water. Aware of her brother's combat specializations, she'd much rather prefer to keep her distance and avoid close combat.

But she couldn't keep him at bay forever.

Fighting back, Hiro bought himself enough time to form a single weave.

Roaring Gap Technique!

The magnificent blade drew a perfect circle, and the sea split in two. A nightmarish spatial storm roared into existence. Volumes of water were lifted into the air, but most were thrown aside.

The storm continued to repel the water and block Sakumi's attacks.

Rising into the air, Hiro bent his knees and pulled the katana back while still holding it with both hands. A moment later, a small black dot appeared at the tip of the blade and slowly grew. The larger it became, the more distinctly its eerie buzz was heard, generated by the huge speed of its rotation.

At the same moment, a blade burst out from somewhere in the depths of the sea Sakumi was hiding in. Breaking through the wind, the *Infinite Strike* reached Hiro but ended up only piercing the edge of his stomach instead of his head.

Hiro didn't defend or dodge. Concentrating on his technique, he ignored the incoming threat. The space continued to distort and shrink while his air cocoon grew, sucking everything into itself with the force of a tornado.

Gotcha! he thought, locating Sakumi's energy in the water.

His technique flared up with even greater force, all of which was directed in one single point.

There was nowhere to hide.

Sakumi was yanked out of the sea and pulled straight toward Hiro's blade with incredible speed. She spared no effort to protect herself, but the difference in the quality of their techniques was too big. She continued to use the *Ando Clan Legacy*, while Hiro had long ago switched to the peak seven-volume techniques Kai made for him.

As a result, the mouth of the water monster only partially pierced Hiro's air cocoon and *Cover*, leaving a huge burn on his back and exposing his muscles, ribs, and even lungs. Sakumi's elemental particles entered his body, crashing into his flesh and *Astral Body*. Someone else would have faltered or even lost consciousness, but Hiro didn't even flinch.

A moment later, the cocoon and the black sphere disappeared. They were sucked in by Hiro's katana. Sakumi was now within range. Clad in armor made of lava and shocked by her brother's power, she released a wave of soul energy and drank an elixir. With her entire body swelling unnaturally, she brought her sword down on Hiro.

Their blades clashed again, but this time Sakumi's physical strength was useless. Her bones began to crack and crumble, and blood gushed from her eyes, nose, and mouth. Ignoring the nightmarish pain from the drops of magma that fell on him from Sakumi's armor, Hiro continued to push forward.

It seemed that their confrontation had been going on forever. Ultimately, Sakumi broke down. The *Divine Gift* was taking too much strength from her, so she had to deactivate it. The power of the *Perfect Weapon* left her sword, and Hiro's katana shattered it. His blade moved toward her throat, when a wall of lava appeared in its path, escaping from his sister's mouth.

Lava wasn't as good when it came to defense as *Earth* or *Metal* were, but on the other hand, it was more mobile and had a higher damage output due to its heat and spray.

As soon as Hiro's sword collided with the wall, thousands of lava droplets flew into the steel. The wind swirled around the blade, drawing in and destroying most of them, but some still fell on his flesh, leaving burns and depriving him of his right eye. Even though Sakumi's technique looked unassuming, the power invested in it was enough to overcome his *Cover*.

However, Sakumi wasn't done yet.

Magma started turning into the strongest rubber. Hiro's imperturbability, which had been preserved until now, wavered. Sakumi surprised him with this technique, but he quickly realized that her strength was enough to hold back his blade for just a moment or two and buy her some time to counterattack.

Shouting furiously, he released all his accumulated power.

His katana shone like a star, the rubber wall was torn apart, and the lava armor was blown off Sakumi. She had leaned back a little, so Hiro's sword only nicked her just below the neck, but the released power of the technique swept her high into the sky.

Sakumi cried out in pain but didn't lose consciousness. Finally completing the last of the many identical weaves, she activated her technique. A large flow of magma escaped from her palm, taking the form of a giant dragon that headed in Hiro's direction.

But he was no longer there.

Bastard! Sakumi felt the scalding heat of mortal danger behind her back.

While he had been in the water, Hiro didn't want to risk with this technique. But now there was nothing stopping him. Having left the mark with his very first blow, he could finally use the *Eternal Pursuit Technique* and automatically transport himself to Sakumi.

The world darkened, turning day into night.

Seeing her brother behind her, Sakumi couldn't believe her eyes.

"You—"

Hiro's body was clad in long robes woven from *Darkness* itself, his eye sockets exuded black fog, his white hair had acquired the color of night and lengthened, and the katana's blade turned into a thin, dense stream of dark wind.

At the first glance, there was nothing special about Hiro's aura, but upon a closer look, one could feel an invisible blade at their throat.

The vast battlefield suddenly fell silent.

The weaving of *Midnight Dominance* was so complex, largescale, and energy-intensive that Hiro could maintain it for a couple of seconds at most. After a grueling battle, he had to invest the remaining half of his soul energy to activate it.

Using the last of her power, Sakumi activated her clan's most powerful *Divine* artifact. Hopefully, it'd be strong enough to protect her.

But alas.

One wave of Hiro's sword and the two halves of the screaming Sakumi fell into the water. The lower part of her body began to sink, but the upper part remained floating on the surface.

Despite the crushing power of her brother's attack, Sakumi regenerated little by little. The upper part of her *Astral Body* was mutilated, but she managed to prevent it from being cut in half as well. At the very least, its lower half was still connected to the upper one, so her core and soul were protected.

I don't have enough strength... I'm going to lose...

Descending to the surface of the sea and dispelling

Midnight Dominance, Hiro went to his sister.

It was time to end this battle.

"Hiro, don't!" Sakumi pleaded through tears. "Please, stop! Are you really going to kill me? Do you really want to kill your sister? We don't have anyone but each other! Or do you only see me as a monster? You made me like this! Or have you forgotten what you did as a child? You are the one who created the demons in me! Defeat them, not me! Take pity on your stupid sister... Help me! I don't want to be like this! Save me! Please..."

The sudden change in his sister's demeanor made Hiro falter. Her face, tears, and pleading voice rooted him to the spot.

The remnants of the barely defeated inner demon stirred.

It's happening again... What am I doing?

Hiro looked at his blood-soaked hands, remembering the horror that he had once experienced. The sight of Sakumi reminded him of what he had done as a child. About the pain that was brought upon his sister. About the oath that he kept for more than a hundred years.

Hiro's determination faltered, but he wasn't alone in this fight against his sister.

Something green flashed in front of him. Ron rushed at Sakumi and tried to finish off the girl with his most powerful technique, but... Glancing up, Hiro saw his friend with a knife sticking out of his chest. The *Divine* artifact pierced all his defensive barriers, destroyed the sword, deprived him of a limb, and mortally wounded his *Shell*. All the *ki* and the soul energy was drained out of him.

"Keep your promise, master!" he croaked, bulging his

eyes. "Kill her... Agh!"

"Ron!"

Sakumi laughed hysterically at the sight of the dying guard. She was surrounded by yet another *Divine* barrier.

"What an idiot you are, Hiro! I told you that you would never have the guts to kill me! Ahahahaha! You really bought the story about my inner demons? I'm not as weak as you! The Cartel checked my soul. I don't have them! Do you hear me?! Not a single inner demon! Not a single one! Ahhahahaha! Now you'll get what you deserve, weakling! Ahaha!"

A moment later, the barrier that surrounded Sakumi contracted into a beam of light.

Hiro's *Astral Body* cracked, and his *Shell* thinned. His eyes were filled with blood, and pain tormented every cell of his body. But he felt none of it. Unbridled rage drowned out all other feelings and senses.

The last, third level of the Ando *Divine Gift* was usually unlocked only upon reaching the *Star Emperor Stage*. It couldn't be achieved through any training, and in True Masters, it could only be awakened by accident. During the entire existence of this *Gift*, less than a hundred Masters have reached its third level. Even the deity who created this power didn't understand the peculiarity of the souls of these warriors.

And today, one more name was added to the list.

Perfect Weapon: Execution.

Hiro swung his katana. Right in front of him, like an illusion, appeared Sakumi. The edge of the blade sliced through her neck. Physical and *Astral* flesh gave way without resistance, but when the sword was almost halfway through,

Sakumi disappeared. Hiro flinched and began to roll over onto his back.

Ultimately, he didn't have the strength to keep the *Execution* going until the end.

His consciousness was fading away.

I failed once again, Ron…

Chapter 13
BATTLEFIELD — NORTH

Hitting the water surface like it was concrete, the six-limbed Heavenly Beast shuddered and assumed a humanoid form. A moment later, a gigantic crow landed next to it and changed its shape.

"Well, well, well… Would you look at that? Sirius Delane, beaten and humiliated. Ha! I told you I'm the best cultivator there is!" Shaw gloated. "Quiet, are we? Cat got your tongue?"

"If it weren't for us, you'd be the one lying on the ground right now," Forty-Three said, landing next to Sixty-Nine.

"Yes, yes, well done," Sirius sneered. He was crippled and shackled but he was all but beaten. "Now the score stands at twenty-one to eighteen. I'm still beating the shit out of you."

"Let's not get into details." Shaw waved him off. "You just can't admit that I, Raven Shaw, am the best there is! You should've listened, Sirius. I told you to join me, but you thought you knew better. And look at you now…"

"Perhaps..." Sirius tried to shrug, but he had no shoulders. "And now what? Will you kill me?"

"Where's the fun in that? I need to even the score first! No matter how amazing I am, I still recognize your experience and knowledge. You'll be useful to the Eternal Path Temple."

"The Temple..." Sirius scoffed. "Look at you, following that Kaiser around... I have to admit, I was very surprised to learn that our freedom-loving Raven decided to serve someone."

"Not to serve, but to follow," Shaw corrected him. "He's... quite an unusual person. Though I doubt he'd be willing to work with you."

"I take it the problem is the dark arts?" Sirius grinned. "Ah, you freedom lovers... Always blind to the bigger picture..."

"How do you know?"

"How wouldn't I know? It's as clear as day. It's ironic, you know? Your precious Kai Arnhard will kill millions and decimate entire cities without so much as blinking an eye, but when it comes to dark arts, he's suddenly too good to get his hands dirty. What a hypocrite," Sirius spat. "And none of you are any better."

The clones behind Shaw tensed up.

"How do you know his real name?" Shaw asked, astonished.

"How? Shaw, it's like you don't know me. I did a little research back when the first mention of the Eternal Path Temple slipped through."

Shaw's face crooked. He had forgotten just how good

Sirius was at gathering intel. Or rather, he had hoped that he had gotten worse at it over the years.

"In any case, you're right," Shaw remarked dryly. "It's because of the dark arts."

"Then there should be no issues. While I don't deny my cooperation with the House of Blood, I never used anything they gave me. You can think me a fool all you want, but I'm not stupid enough to willingly exile myself from the society of *honorable* Masters. Adepts don't care, they work with anyone. Unlike the 'righteous' Masters, they don't have such prejudices."

Surprise flashed over Shaw's face.

"Your life, I guess," the Raven hissed. "But wipe that smirk off your face or I'll do it for you. I know that you don't feel anything, you don't have to pretend in front of me. I hate this feature of yours."

Emotions were an integral part of any creature's soul, man-made or otherwise, and they played a key role in a cultivator's development, connecting the mental layer of their soul with the warrior layer, thereby allowing the manipulations of the universal laws. And while there were those whose emotions were obstructed for one reason or another, the blockage of the emotional layer always had negative consequences.

However, there were also those who were simply unable to experience anything. In one being in a trillion, a *Soul Shell* whose layers were connected in a slightly different way than usual was formed. Such individuals didn't have emotions, but they still had a firm grip on their minds. The result was a rather rational being, bearing no negative consequences. This phenomenon was a mystery even to the deities.

Sirius Delane was one in a trillion.

"If it's all the same to you," Sirius said. The last speck of emotion disappeared from his face, replaced by boundless indifference. He didn't even seem to care about his own death.

***

Somewhere on a deserted northern island

Despite all his strength, Rosen failed to so much as scratch Lilith. With the Phoenix Progenitor bloodline coursing through her veins, she was too powerful for him to handle her on his own, so Mia and Oi had to intervene. Having moved their wounded brother to a pocket dimension where he could tend to his injuries and recuperate, they activated *Full Transformation,* a much more powerful version than the partial one. Among all the descendants of the Star Beasts, only those with the blood of the Heavenly Manticore possessed it.

Full Transformation required a large amount of energy and *Will*, so the sisters temporarily traded the ability to weave techniques for incredible physical strength and powerful abilities. They increased in size, turning into lionesses with scorpion tails and large membranous wings.

As soon as this happened, they were enveloped by golden flames. The temperature increased so much that even the surrounding stones began to melt. The starfire that surrounded Lilith took on the form of two massive folded wings, and she gained an aura of flames. The intensity of the heat it generated had long since exceeded any normal limit.

But the golden inferno didn't do anything to discourage Mia and Oi from fulfilling their duty. The Manticore had endowed them with *Instant Primary Adaptation* that acclimatized their bodies to block at least half of the damage as soon as they faced any threat.

Being a slightly faster than her sister, Oi was the first to approach Lilith. Her razor-sharp claws flashed like a *Divine* weapon and collided with Lilith's blade. Empowered by the *Will of Fire*, the latter incinerated a part of the former's paw, damaging the *Astral Body* in the process. With a cry, Lilith flew back, knocked down by Oi's physical strength that broke several bones in her hands.

A scorpion tail rushed toward the descending figure. Lilith was about to cut it in two, but then the other sister intervened.

Mia's furious roar shook the air and ground and made Lilith's body and soul turn numb. Seeing an opening, Oi rushed forward and closed her giant mouth with a deafening click. Having managed to move aside in time to lose her arm instead of half of her body, Lilith used *Phoenix's Flight* and teleported herself several feet up.

The acid saliva had already begun to dissolve the limb when it suddenly turned into a golden flame. Mia's insides shuddered and her mouth was ripped apart, and then a torrent of hellfire engulfed both her and her sister.

Having healed her arm and *Astral Body* with the *Phoenix's Healing Flame*, Lilith continued to shower the twins with *Battle Fire*. Despite the Manticores' ability to adapt and regenerate at an incredible speed, the Phoenix Progenitor bloodline was still more powerful. Lilith's attack lasted about three seconds before the sisters finally broke free.

After drinking a *Manticore Extract Infusion* and using the blood of their *Manticore Hearts*, Mia and Oi eventually managed to adapt to Lilith's golden flame and regenerate their physical and spirit flesh. Their bodies began to radiate cold, and their skin became covered with thick ice armor. Maintaining such a complex defense quickly used up their energy reserve, but it helped them escape from the overwhelming stream of monstrous flames.

Sensing the twins flying toward her from different directions, Lilith soared into the sky. Her speed and power were incredible, but she was inferior in every other aspect, so she preferred to keep her distance.

Just how many resources do they have?! They are only peak Holy Lords! Their Hearts *had just formed, so where did they get so much* Blood *from? It should have been depleted a long time ago!*

But no matter how much time passed, the sisters didn't show a hint of fatigue. On the contrary, they became faster and resisted Lilith's attacks even better. They even managed to corner her, sticking her with viscous saliva to the barrier that covered Insulaii.

I'm so stupid! I should have hit them with my strongest abilities right away so that they don't have time to adapt! I should have known better! she lamented. *But how was I supposed to know that they have so much* Blood*?!*

Sensing that she was on the verge of losing, Lilith decided to use her blade again. However, this time she didn't just draw blood, but pierced her heart with *Force*. As much as she didn't want to do this, she had no choice.

Sacrificing ten thousand years of her life, Lilith unlocked the full power of the bloodline.

Mia and Oi were about to finish her off when they were blinded by a sudden flash of bright light. The shock wave that followed knocked them back.

Before they had time to recover, they were captured by a huge phoenix. A golden column descended from the sky with lightning speed and nailed them to the ground, which was melting and evaporating under them with a loud sizzle.

No trace remained of the cold they had emanated earlier. Their armors were riddled with cracks.

Clutching the two Manticores in her mighty talons, the fully transformed Lilith prepared to unleash one of her strongest attacks by directing more and more power to her beak. Desperately resisting, the twins kept stinging her with their tails, but to no avail. Their poison was weaker than the flames, evaporating before it had enough time to adapt.

Soon, the preparations were completed.

A piercing cry shook the air, and a dazzling beam of light descended on the sisters. The fire engulfed the entire rocky island, turning it into a bright star on the ocean surface for a few seconds.

They're still alive? Lilith noted with a mixture of displeasure and anger. She could not only feel their auras, but also traces of *Divine* artifacts. *Automatic protection? And one this strong... That's a rare find.*

Unfolding her wings, Lilith filled the space around her with a flurry of fiery feathers just in time to defend herself. Had she hesitated even for a fraction of a second, the twins would have torn her apart.

There were dozens of them. A whole swarm of Manticores rushed into the fiery storm, causing the feathers to combust. A cascade of deafening explosions swept over the area, killing only half of the horde.

Rapid Division was another key ability of the *Manticore Heart* after *Full Transformation*. By spending many drops of *Blood*, the twins created their own miniature army. Each of the clones was outwardly indistinguishable from the original, but it had only forty percent of its strength.

Realizing that it wouldn't be easy to get rid of the horde, Lilith turned into a falling star using *Flight*. The twins and their copies chased after her. By this point, they had already adapted to her speed, so they could keep up while also attacking her with frosty spit from a distance.

After a few long seconds, Lilith started losing speed.

She's tired! Don't stop now! We've got her! the sisters thought at the same time.

They continued the pursuit when the phoenix soared sharply.

"Where's she going? That's where the barrier is! Idiot! She'll never break through it! The artifact was created by Lord Yashnir himself!"

But Lilith continued to rise higher and higher. When she was only a few miles away from the planetary barrier, she suddenly folded her wings, turned around, and rushed back. The twins, who didn't expect such a maneuver, didn't have time to scatter in different directions, which cost them seven copies. However, Lilith's move worked in their favor.

"She's out of her mind! We've invested so many drops of *Blood* into adapting to her flames that even that beam can't kill us!" Mia smiled. "She doesn't even know where the originals are!"

The Manticores were ready to attack when their bodies burst into flames. Gold turned blue, transforming into *Frost Flame*. Having saved this rare power for the very end, Lilith changed the nature of her strike and took the twins by surprise. Such an attack was available only to the carriers of the Phoenix Progenitor bloodline, and Lilith made sure the Manticores couldn't defend themselves from it.

Mia and Oi were encased in ice, slowly fighting against it, but their *Primary Adaptation* failed to help them. They were shackled long enough for Lilith to summon a wave of nightmarish heat and pass it through the sisters' bodies.

A miniature sun shone in the skies of Insulaii so brightly that it was seen throughout the north of Avlaim and in some of the southern lands.

Despite Lilith's best attempt at unleashing the power of the *Phoenix Combustion* as high in the air as possible, Insulaii's surface still suffered damage. The temperature on the nearest islands rose, and the entire territory turned into a giant sauna. Many weaker beings lost consciousness or even died from a sudden heat stroke and trees and other plants were rapidly drying up.

***

Lilith slowly landed on the ocean's surface. Having spent the last of her strength on *Combustion*, she returned to her *Partial Transformation* form — more precisely, to what was left of it. Only tatters remained of her once beautiful robes, and she had only one of her magnificent wings. The strength of the Phoenix bloodline was almost depleted, and even if she tried to get more, nothing would come of it: her soul and body could no longer withstand such power.

Trying to catch her breath and recover from the intense fight, she stood hunched over, with her hands on her knees.

She was surrounded by nothing but water.

Where am I? she thought and reached for an artifact. *I'm exhausted... My life is now shorter by thirteen thousand years. Not even the gods can give me that back. What a mess...*

Her intuition interrupted her train of thought, warning her of danger. A strange pink beam pierced her head, and she suddenly disappeared, dispelled like a mirage.

The artifact had moved her several miles to the side. Looking toward the horizon, Lilith realized that the threat was all but gone. Wasting no time, she revealed her entire arsenal of *Divine* items.

A cascade of explosions, multi-colored beams, bloodthirsty creatures, strange giant objects, invisible waves of power, and much more filled the open sea. To summon such a storm, Lilith used all of her *Divine* artifacts that didn't require the investment of a large amount of strength.

Left unarmed, shackled by unusual, thick purple cords, she hung limply one foot above the water.

A scorched, hunched creature with three arms, two heads, and Mia's aura materialized before her.

For at least one of them to survive the *Combustion*, Oi sacrificed herself — she gave away her flesh and *Astral Body* and merged with her sister.

"Don't worry," the creature croaked or grunted. "I won't kill you... For now... A true descendant of the Phoenix Progenitor is a valuable trophy... But you will pay for my sister's death. You'll regret the day you were born... More than once."

Lilith laughed right in her face.

"Keep dreaming!"

Smiling wide and overstepping her physical and astral bounds, she activated what little remained of her bloodline's power and wrapped her body in a fiery tornado. The heat was so scalding that it made Mia jump back in fright. She was still covered by a *Divine* barrier, so she didn't suffer any damage, but she could feel the rising temperature just the same.

When the flames died down, Lilith was nowhere to be found. There was no trace left of her body and soul.

"She killed herself?! That bitch!" Mia shouted furiously.

She had spent a lot of strength on capturing Lilith, but that was no reason to lose her patience now. She had to clear her mind and think.

"No, it can't be that simple. Something's wrong here... Ah, but of course... The damn bitch!" Her whole body shook with rage. "If what the legends say is true, I'll start hating Phoenixes even more...!"

Chapter 14
THE CRUCIAL MOMENT

Blood, entrails, charred corpses, pained screams, fire, death… War was ugly, but for cultivators, it was an inevitable part of their chosen path.

"I give up! I give up!" a wounded Union soldier shouted. Hiding his weakened aura, he tried to pretend to be dead, but it was impossible to trick the clones. "Please, have mercy! I'm begging you!"

By this point, the clones were no longer hiding. There were no more enemies nearby anyway. So far, the Temple soldiers had killed almost half of the Union troops.

Approaching the surrendered man, Nine threw him a scroll.

"Sign it."

The man nodded nervously. Picking up the spirit contract, he ran his eyes over its text and turned pale.

"I… I can't…" He swallowed hard, looking at the strict terms with fear in his eyes. "To be a POW under these rules…"

"Your faction's contract doesn't allow it?" Nine guessed.

Startled, the man nodded hesitantly.

"I see..." Nine sighed. With a slight movement of her hand, she cut off his head. No one was going to spend money on releasing prisoners from their contracts. Especially if they were weak.

The spirit contract was the most effective way to control someone. It was also the cheapest, since one scroll was enough for as many as several thousand *Elementalists*, unlike slave collars.

Six-Hundred-and-Thirty, dragging another prisoner, picked up and handed a scroll to Nine. She gratefully accepted it, but then suddenly frowned.

"What?" she asked, noticing his gaze. "Do you need something?"

Shaking his head, he silently left.

For Nine, this wasn't unusual. Some of her brothers had been looking at her like that for a long time, but hardly any of them dared to say anything.

When Kai made the clones, he told each of them to choose an appearance for themselves, believing it would contribute to the development their unique personalities. Most of them retained a likeness of their creator with subtle variations. Nine was among the more daring ones, who went in the complete opposite direction, altering her gender.

At one time, she was sent to infiltrate one of Insulaii's many sects in order to find the Elder Rune located on their territory. As the sect only accepted women, Nine assumed a different body. At first, it was only a disguise, but over time, the new appearance became an integral part of the clone's personality. The sudden change caused some of the older and more adult counterparts to criticize her, saying that their creator's clone couldn't be a woman since he was a man himself, but Kai had no objections. If anything, he encouraged it. But that didn't stop the criticism and tasteless comments, to which Nine put an end by beating the shit out of anyone who was audacious enough to tell any of it to her face. It was their own fault for picking a fight with one of the strongest clones, she told herself.

The battlefield was quickly cleaned up: bodies were thrown in a ditch and burned, and loot safely stored inside the common *Storage*. With everything taken care of and reported, Nine's squad headed further north. Less than half an hour later, they caught up with another enemy division. Using invisibility, the Ninth Squad approached the barrier.

Standing before the shimmering veil, they had a choice: they could either deplete the operators' strength by pelting the barrier with attacks or hit point-blank as hard as possible. The Ninth Squad consisted of ninety-something clones. By joining their energy and channeling it through an artifact designed specifically for breaking through barriers, they unleashed an attack that punctured a hole in the dome big enough for all of them to get through. Catching enemies by surprise, they attacked with the speed and might of a hurricane. Within seconds, the ground was littered with corpses.

Numerous as they were, the Union soldiers weren't strong enough to deal with the clones.

Having trained in the *Complex*, more than fifty clones had managed to acquire not only the *Master's Will* but also *Complete Submission* and the *Field of Superiority*. Unfortunately, they couldn't teach these techniques to the rest of their brethren, since the ability to control one's *Will* lay deeper than the mind and memory. They could exchange only vague images, simple thoughts, and sensations.

The main disadvantage, however, was still their fragility. The clones needed months to re-accumulate their *Will*.

All this influenced the Temple's defense strategy. Avlaim needed to win as soon as possible, because the longer the war lasted, the weaker its defenders would become. To combat this, the clones were given better resources and told not to skimp on them.

Breaking through the enemy formation, the clones used a variety of rare artifacts and alchemy. With them, their effectiveness on the battlefield increased many times over, allowing them to decimate entire crowds in one fell swoop.

Nine moved from one target to another like an invisible chain of lightning. Rare were those who remained standing after her first blow. The destruction of the enemy forces was in full swing when the barrier above them suddenly disappeared.

What? Nine looked up, surprised. *But we haven't destroyed the arrays yet. Why...?*

Her thoughts were interrupted by a deafening roar. The ground trembled, a ball of bright light blazed in the distance, and a powerful wave swept through the forest, causing Nine to instinctively duck.

Are they attacking their own people to get rid of us? she wondered, sensing the death of four of her brothers.

No sooner did the tremors die down than the clones scattered, activating additional defensive artifacts. The entire detachment retreated, narrowly avoiding being hit by a massive attack that struck their previous position. Those who didn't make it far enough died right where they stood. In total, about a hundred clones fell on the western front. It was the first time that the enemy forces, albeit at the cost of their own soldiers, managed to demonstrate at least some resistance.

The Ninth Squad needed to regroup and come up with a new tactic, but new orders never came. All of a sudden, the clones began to fall unconscious. The dumbfounded Nine fell to her knees, experiencing a strong spirit pain. For a moment, it seemed to her that someone was trying to empty the mark where her *Will* had been accumulated, but the pain receded as fast as it came. Her master was in trouble... Kai had failed to draw the strength he needed to fight Kyle from his most powerful clones, the distance between them was too big for him to do so. But he did manage to extract the energy and *Will* from the ordinary clones.

With her soul trembling like a hummingbird, Nine struggled to get up. For a few seconds, she stared in disbelief at the sight around her, and then she opened her *Sphere of Space*. As one of the first clones, she had created her own *Crydes* in Accelerated Time-Space long ago. So far, she only had two, *Sword* and *Space*, but it was enough. The concept *Spheres* weren't available to her or the other clones — they didn't have the kind of soul protection that would allow them to withstand such a load.

Having come to her senses and moved her brothers to the *Storage*, Nine hastened to retreat. Anxiety and powerlessness grew stronger and stronger as she learned that not all squads had been as lucky as hers. Hundreds and thousands of clones were dying en masse.

***

One and Six opened their eyes. Nearly unconscious, they were forced to cut off contact with the others. Despite having the strongest *Wills* among all the clones, they couldn't ignore the mystical call. Pale and visibly shaken, they struggled for breath.

"What happened?" came a worried voice in their minds.

Slowly turning his head, Six cast his gaze at the huge egg that stood before him. It was the *Golden Phoenix Egg*, inside which Lilith's new physical and *Astral* bodies were being formed. She had left it on the Ark before the war started, and her soul was transferred into it after her fight with the O'Crime twins.

Phoenixes had always been famous for their ability to resurrect. Usually, they could have only one egg at a time, and it took them a thousand years to create it, but the carriers of their Progenitor bloodline had special abilities and could have up to three eggs at once in different parts of the Ecumene. As long as at least one of her eggs remained intact, Lilith's soul could only be destroyed by the First, or at least the Higher Ones.

"Thousands of our brothers have lost consciousness. Master has deprived them of the support of his *Spark*," One explained in a listless voice, trying to calm his soul and restore the unification of minds. "Many of them are already dead."

The news shocked Lilith.

"Why?! How could that happen?!"

"Something must have happened to him," Six suggested. "He tried to draw the *Will* out of us, older clones, but he couldn't. The distance must've been too great. We need to do something."

"I agree. I have insisted on a search mission before. We must use the full power of the *Complex* and hit the barrier to create a breach in it and leave Insulaii."

"But we can't allocate that much power to the *Complex*

when we need it to save our lives. We have to be smart about how we spend the *Divine Particles*. And our numbers have significantly decreased."

"Survivors can be awakened. We, the elders, can saturate their marks with our *Will* and support them until Master restores contact with them. But you're right. We suffered great losses. We may lose, but that doesn't matter if the Master dies. He is more important than Avlaim and even the Temple. As long as he is alive, we'll be able to reclaim everything. Without him, the war loses its purpose," One explained, holding back his emotions. "I'll lead the search party while Six continues to maintain the connection. Considering how many of us remain conscious, this shouldn't be difficult."

"Why do you get to decide who will go?" Six frowned.

"Do you want to argue about it now?" One asked, disgruntled. "Don't forget that even though we are equal in strength, I'm still the main among the clones. As per Master's orders."

There was nothing more for Six to say.

Wasting no more time, One went to the *Complex*. He informed Alfred about everything, but to his bewilderment, his request was declined. Alfred couldn't move the artifact from the Ark without a direct order. One tried to appeal to his sense of reason, but to no avail. Being an artificial Spirit, Alfred couldn't disobey even though One was almost a carbon copy of his master.

As a result, preparations for the rescue mission were delayed. But when, a day later, the clones' connection with Kai weakened due to the blockage of his emotional layer, One didn't hold back anymore. Taking away a large portion of the resources intended for the region's defenders, he and a few clones under his command eventually managed to create a small hole in the barrier.

***

"Where I am?" Rosen groaned. "Why am I covered in bandages?"

"You're awake!" exclaimed a hoarse, barely familiar voice.

"Who are you?" Rosen asked the cloaked hunchback figure looming over him. Recognizing his sister's aura, he jumped up but fell back, groaning in pain. "Mia? What... What happened to you? Did Lilith do this to you?"

"Yes." The figure nodded. "But I'll recover, don't worry."

"Did you defeat her?"

"Yes, but she's alive. At least I think so... I didn't feel the remnants of her soul. If legends are to be believed, the power of the Phoenix can revive her."

Rosen cursed. He had underestimated Lilith. Way too much.

"What about Tina? Did you save her?"

Mia shook her head.

"I'm sorry. It was too late. And..." She bit her lip, "Oi sacrificed herself to save me."

Hearing such terrifying news all at once, Rosen went limp. All emotion disappeared from his face. His eyes turned empty.

"How...?" His hands trembled. "Why...?"

Despite the way they interacted, the siblings actually loved each other deeply, and so the loss of Oi and on top of that his lover, Tina, hit Rosen hard. For the next ten minutes, while Mia talked about the events that took place over the previous three days, Rosen continued to stare into empty space.

Once she was done, he extended his hand to her and revealed a blood-red pebble.

"I assume you spent both your drops of *Blood* as well as the ones mother gave you? You can have mine. Create copies of yourself and send them to the battlefield. We must end the war before Lilith returns!" he shouted furiously.

"Are you sure? Mom won't be able to accumulate so many drops soon."

"I don't care! I'll delay my breakthrough if that's what it takes. Let's spill their blood and capture Avlaim's resources. Kaiser and Lilith are alive, but unable to join their army. We need to take advantage of this opportunity while it lasts!"

***

After disabling most of the clones, the stampede of Union and Cartel soldiers gave way to a new offensive. Despite their recent losses, they still outnumbered Avlaim's army and posed a serious threat.

On the fifth day, the situation on the fronts changed dramatically with the arrival of three hundred copies of Mia. Even though they were half as powerful as the original, they were clones of a *Master of Seven Big Stars* and able to adapt to almost anything. An army of invisible clones wasn't much of a problem for them either.

From that moment, things went south for Avlaim's forces.

On the seventh day, the northern line of defense, the longest and most problematic, fell.

On the ninth day, Avlaim's eastern fleet, having lost two-thirds of its vessels, was forced to retreat.

On the tenth day, the western front was broken through.

"Master, we might not finish all the preparations in time," a man said with a predicament of doom in his voice, monitoring the state of the transfer array. "They've taken over the entire capital. The source of spatial interference is getting closer. The chances of a successful escape are low…"

Half-listening, Ragnar turned around and looked at the several hundred wounded and exhausted soldiers who were still waiting for an opportunity to evacuate. Enemies broke through the barrier a day ago and had already established control over more than seventy percent of the city.

Suddenly, someone grabbed Ragnar by the hand.

"Tell me you're not thinking what I think you're thinking!" Nyako hissed at him. She was seriously injured, but that didn't stop her from performing her duty.

"Don't worry, I won't meet the same fate as Shan Wu," Ragnar said sternly. "It's too early for me to die."

"Don't even think about it!" Nyako was now shouting. "You can't take that kind of risk!"

"Hey, hey, calm down. All right? Everything will be fine!" Ragnar laughed, and then patted Nyako's fluffy ears. "For good luck! Where's the space blocker?" He turned to his assistant.

"Are you seriously—"

"Where?" Ragnar repeated sternly.

"O-Over there!" The man pointed north. "Seven miles away from us."

"Awesome!" Ragnar patted him on the shoulder, nearly knocking him off his feet.

"No! Stop! Ragnar!" Nyako screamed. "Don't forget, I'm still your senior! You must obey—"

A sudden click made her pass out.

"Take care of her. I'll destroy or at least disable the blocker, and distract them for about fifteen minutes. Use that time wisely."

"Yes, sir!"

Ragnar swallowed several rare and dangerous elixirs, felt them rush through his veins in a burning stream, and left.

After all, who, if not me, knows how to endure?

The Han Nam soldiers, who were besieging the center of the capital, weren't expecting serious resistance at this point so they were caught by surprise when Ragnar appeared on the battlefield. Upon the sight of him, their triumph turned into fear. Invulnerable to regular attacks, Ragnar arranged for a massacre. Not even Mia's doubles could get to him. Avlaim's defenders watched the aesir's uncontrollable rampage with both horror and awe. He ripped and tore, turning everything around him into a bloody mess. One mutilated body at a time, he moved toward the spatial interference generator. Six of Mia's clones tried to kill him and even fired from artillery arrays several times, but he was unstoppable.

Through a shower of blood and entrails, the Temple soldiers made an escape.

Chapter 15
POWERLESS

Far in the mountains, a city stood ablaze.

The barrier had long since yielded under the onslaught of enemy attacks. The defenders desperately fought for the freedom of their homeland, but in the end, they, too, fell.

The once beautiful and flourishing city was turned into ruins. Atop the palace, looking at how everything that his ancestors had built was being destroyed, Shan Wu couldn't stop squeezing his weapon and trembling with rage. There was nothing he could do other than powerlessly observe from the sidelines. If master Gabba was still alive, he wouldn't be pleased with his student's weakness…

"Enemies are close!" came a shout from behind him.

Shan Wu felt the invading auras drawing nearer. The palace's defensive arrays had successfully eliminated most of the attackers, but there were still too many of them. Their goal was the central array's core, located at the top of the building.

Their last line of defense.

Slowly getting up from his chair, Shan Wu turned

around. Fifty of the Order's strongest members bowed their heads before him. Wounded and tired, they were preparing to take their final stand.

"Master Shan Wu," they addressed him, "leave the city while there is still time. Use your parents' *Divine* artifact and head south. If you die here, it'll all be in vain."

"He's right, young master. Leave everything to us!"

"Master Shan Wu! Please, listen to us."

Despite being so young, Shan Wu was loved and respected by all the elders. He was a worthy leader of the Order of the Primordial Elements.

"Quiet." Shan Wu raised his hand. "I'm not going anywhere. This is my home. This palace was built by my ancestors. Do you think I would just abandon it? Run away? Who do you take me for? If I am destined to die, then I would rather face death in my own home, protecting it, than anywhere else. What kind of master abandons his men and his land? I will stand with you until the very end! We will either win or die together! Do you hear me?!"

For a few seconds there was silence, interrupted only by occasional explosions, and then the elders threw up their weapons and fists and shouted in one voice.

"YES, YOUNG MASTER!"

"Now get ready!" Shan Wu smiled. "The enemy is close."

Preparing various artifacts and drinking expensive potions, the Order's last defenders were ready to meet their enemies. A quarter of an hour later, the last barriers were destroyed, and a crowd of invaders poured onto the upper terrace.

A fierce battle ensued.

There were several times more opponents, but the unbridled rage and desperate determination of the Order were a force to be reckoned with. The defenders fought to the last drop of blood. At one point, seeing their opponents' backs, the Order almost started celebrating, thinking that they had won, when two figures in long dark robes appeared on the battlefield.

Noticing the guests, Shan Wu decided to take care of them on his own. Using every resource and technique available to him, he swirled in a frantic whirlwind. His opponents turned out to be extremely strong, but he managed to defeat the weaker of the two after some struggle.

The other one put up a difficult fight. A ray of light fell on Shan Wu from the darkened skies and hid him behind a thick yellowish barrier. His opponent, who was approaching him at that exact moment, barely had time to react. They jumped back just as the beam fell, but they lost their arm in the process.

Looking up, Shan Wu saw an elongated steel cylinder hovering in the air — the central array's core.

Smiling, he transferred Hundred-and-One from his *Spatial Ring* onto the battlefield. He was one of the few senior clones on the northern front who managed to survive after losing communication with Kai.

After awakening Hundred-and-One, Shan Wu took out a scroll, put today's memories into it, and handed it over to the clone. Immediately after that, Hundred-and-One was encased in a translucent green sphere — the effect of the *Divine* artifact that Shan Wu had inherited from his parents.

"I'm sorry we had to meet under such circumstances, but I'm glad that I met all of you and became a member of the Eternal Path Temple," Shan Wu added his voice to the scroll.

"I'm sorry that I'm breaking my oath and that I won't be able to continue to protect the Temple, but I have no other choice. This is my home. This is where I'm needed the most. I hope you'll forgive my selfishness. I hope to meet you again in the next life."

Clenching his fists, Shan Wu turned around. The barrier around him was covered with cracks. It was about to fall apart.

"For the Order of the Primordial Elements!" he shouted furiously as he slammed the green sphere surrounding Hundred and One with his sword.

"For the Order of the Primordial Elements!" his comrades echoed in response.

Before disappearing, Hundred-and-One saw Shan Wu jump up to the core of the central array and plunge his hands into a hole in it. Energy vision allowed the clone to see the huge amount of power that had been stored within it. It was Shan Wu's *ki*, *Will*, *Soul Shell*, soul energy, *Astral Body*, and nuclei all at once.

The entire time his enemies were fighting their way to the top of the palace, Shan Wu was preparing for his ultimate act of defense. He knew that he wouldn't be able to win and get out of this alive. At the cost of his life, he activated the self-destruction protocol of all city arrays.

A moment later, Hundred-and-One was tens of miles away from the palace. Turning around sharply, he saw a bright flash somewhere on the horizon. Before the shockwave could catch up with him, a translucent green sphere carried him south at great speed — toward the territories of the Rising Star Sect.

That was the end of the memories. The two scrolls turned black and crumbled to dust.

Hiro opened his eyes.

"So that's how he died," he muttered to no one in particular and smiled wryly. "A man of honor. Amazing determination…"

"Indeed," Nyako agreed. She had returned from the western front a little while ago. "He's always been like that. Even when we first met, he didn't want to let us enter Gabba's cave. He was ready to fight us to the death for it. I don't think he broke his oath."

Lilith nodded grimly. Having recently hatched from the *Golden Phoenix Egg*, she assumed a much younger appearance. It would take a while for her to regain her former shape and restore her powers.

"He did well, putting his memories into a scroll. It helped us a lot. If it weren't for him, we wouldn't have known about the twins and their abilities. His sacrifice allowed us to prepare the eastern and western fronts for their arrival. He saved so many lives."

"Many lives, yes," Nyako whispered under her breath, remembering her helplessness. "But the losses are still great."

"Don't bury Ragnar just yet," Lilith said sternly, rising from her chair. "We can't feel his mark, yes, but his death hasn't been confirmed. For all we know, he may still be alive."

"You're right…"

***

That was the end.

Fifteen days into the war, Avlaim was on the verge of defeat. The northern part of the region was taken over. The remnants of Shaw's fleet were still trying in the east, but their chance of winning was slim. As for the west… By now, the Union, having joined forces with the Dragons, was laying siege to the capital of Nogatta. This was the penultimate line of defense — behind it were only Moon and Sunshine Havens.

The situation was bleak to say the least, but the defenders had no intention of surrendering. Despite the fallen allies and lost territories, they didn't lose their fighting spirit or hope. Their morale was lifted when reinforcement had come. Avlaim's best young cultivators returned from Accelerated Time-Space. By this time, they had become peak *Elementalists*.

Ryu and the rest of the Sixth Team were among the reinforcements. This was their opportunity to help and prove themselves.

Eager as they were, they weren't allowed to rush straight into battle. They were strong but they lacked combat experience. For now, they would defend one of the capital's largest artillery arrays.

Climbing to the roof of one of the tallest buildings in the area, Ryu looked around. There were several defensive groups at the top. He walked toward the one with the most familiar faces.

"What did they say?" Oberon looked at his friend. Inna and Gradz, who were positioned next to him, also turned their heads. "Anything good?"

They watched the flashes flickering in the distance. By this moment, the enemy forces had broken through several sectors of the main barrier and entered the city. The infantry went ahead, clearing the way. Behind it, under the protection of the arrays, the artillery was slowly advancing.

"Nothing new." Ryu shrugged. "We are to remain here and protect the array until new orders come in."

"Understood," Oberon nodded.

"I don't fucking understand! I don't understand it at all! So many years of training to get us ready for this day and they put us on guard duty!" Gradz snarled angrily, tail held high. "I wanna be there! If only you knew how much I want to tear these Union bastards apart! It's their fault that my entire clan had to abandon their home of thousands of years!"

"We most likely won't be allowed to fight today. The command thinks that'd be a waste of manpower. It's foolish to hope for victory in a direct clash when we're this outnumbered."

"I think so, too," Oberon added. "If I were in charge, I'd prefer to surrender the city bit by bit, forcing the enemy to spend as much strength and resources as possible on it."

"Surrender?!" Gradz exclaimed, bewildered.

"Think about it. There's no way we can keep them at bay, but if we surrender slowly, more people will have a chance to escape. Or do you prefer dying?"

"But... But this is the capital!"

"But not the last frontier," Inna reminded him condescendingly. "Behind us is the heart of the Rising Star Sect, which should be protected even more valiantly than the city. In addition, the Havens are located in the mountains, which will aid us during the defense."

"I doubt we'd get some action even there," Ryu jumped in, glancing around at his friends.

"I don't understand..." Gradz frowned, lowering his tail.

"You don't understand or you just don't want to admit it?" Inna forced a smile. "We have already lost. The clones were our main weapon, and now they are gone. With the current forces, we will never win the war. Sooner or later, we will be backed into a corner. Sooner or later, the Company's fleet will be destroyed and enemies from the east will join the siege of the Havens. We will no longer be able to maintain barriers and artillery. Unless a miracle happens, nothing will change."

"Inna is right," Oberon said. "We need to know when to admit defeat and prepare for it. Our current goal is to force them to spend as many resources and manpower as possible to capture the region. After that, we'll go to the Ark and start planning a counterattack. We should wait for the Sovereign to return, recuperate, form a new, stronger army, accumulate resources, and hit them after they think they've won. Understand?"

"I... think I do! Long story short, let's kill them all!" Gradz's eyes blazed again.

"Would you like a drink?" Inna suddenly said, a bottle in her hand. Judging by the label, its contents were rather expensive. "I found several boxes in the cellar. Whoever owned this place was in such a hurry to leave Avlaim that they forgot to take it with them. Well, as they say, one man's trash..."

"Leave Avlaim?" Gradz asked, accepting the bottle. "Where? I thought it was impossible to leave Insulaii?"

"It's not a secret that many wealthy families and strong individuals without ties to the key factions escaped through the south or the Great Sea Belt. Pirates who know routes through the anomalies do well during the war."

"Pirates? The Cartel?"

"Of course not. I'm talking about vagabonds and mercenaries, who are normally afraid to stick their nose out of their comfort zone. They prefer to rob small boats and raid border towns. But now they've grown bolder, flocking like vultures after the Union, picking up everything that their soldiers left behind and making money off refugees. War profiteers, that's what they are."

"And we're not doing anything about it?" Ryu was outraged. "I mean, the fugitives are taking away valuable resources that could go to the war effort. Hell, they're basically sponsoring our enemies by carrying their wealth to their lands!"

"Of course we are," Oberon said. As a member of the Temple's Administration Department, he was privy to these things. "But we can't keep track of everyone. This place was saved, wasn't it? We found several thousand *Runes* in the treasury, and we didn't even begin to count the *Azure Crystals*. We filled lots of spatial chests with them."

"Then why did you leave the wine?"

"We took what we could. There wasn't room for everything. And the Temple has no need for it, anyway. So go ahead, it's my treat."

For a while, they sipped the wine in silence, immersed in their thoughts. Looking at the burgundy liquid swirling in his glass, Ryu remembered his home, a small town not far from here. Having lived in Accelerated Time-Space for more than a hundred years, he really missed it. Fortunately, his family was evacuated to the Ark before the town was seized, so he didn't have to worry about their safety.

"By the way," Oberon said thoughtfully. "Does anyone have any news about Renata?"

"She is in a special squad with the other *Masters of Seven Stars*. That's all I know," Ryu replied dryly.

"I see. That's all right, we have our own *Master of Seven Stars*! Don't we?" Grabbing his friend by the shoulder, Oberon grinned. "While you're with us, we have nothing to worry about!"

"Unless we run into Union leaders or Manticore clones," Gradz grumbled.

"You know, I'm a *Master of Six Stars*, same as you," Ryu mumbled, slightly embarrassed.

"Oh, don't be so modest!" Oberon slapped him on the back. "We are *Masters of Small Stars*, and you — of *Great* ones! You can practically snatch the seventh one, that's how close you are!"

"Yeah," Inna said. "Ryu, remember what Lady Nyakonalavius said? That you're just a little short of her level! Now you are our secret weapon!"

Oberon laughed.

"To our secret weapon!" he toasted.

Gradz also raised his glass.

"Our secret weapon?" Ryu chuckled. "You're forgetting about Renata. She's way stronger than me."

"Let it go, will you?" Inna hissed. "Come on, drink!"

"Okay... Okay..."

Raising his glass, Ryu couldn't help but smile. After so many trials and extensive training, he was confident in his ability to protect his loved ones. Once upon a time, he dreamed of becoming a True Master. He wanted to have the power to do anything and to control others. Now, remembering his old self, Ryu could only chuckle. The Temple had taught him what strength was for. It showed him how important it was to be able to protect what was precious to him. Himself, his sister, his family, his friends, and his beliefs.

Finishing his wine, Ryu closed his eyes, pleased.

When he opened them again everything around him was on fire. Not feeling his hands and hearing only a ringing in his ears, he struggled to get to his feet. His body was in unbearable pain, but he didn't have time to feel it. The world was spinning before his eyes, and his mind was foggy. The remains of the *Wood* armor, which he had subconsciously created, fell to the ground in charred pieces.

Finally getting to his feet, Ryu looked around. Not a trace remained of the building in which, just a second ago, he and his friends were drinking wine.

Dozens of corpses lay everywhere, devoured by flames. There were only a few survivors.

Suddenly, his eyes caught on a familiar detail. Gray fur.

Gradz's tail.

He found the rest of his body, but it was missing a head.

Ryu's eyes widened and he finally began to realize what had happened. Looking around in all directions like a madman, he searched the debris for Inna.

Buried under a piece of the roof, she held out her hand to him. Her face was contorted in a grimace of pain, but she smiled through her tears when she met his gaze.

"Don't forget me," she whispered as her eyes went dim.

As if lost, Ryu took a few clumsy steps toward her and, stumbling on something, fell to the ground.

He hadn't stumbled over a corpse. Yes, it was a body, but it was still alive. Oberon miraculously managed to avoid mortal wounds, but this didn't save him from disability. His entire *Astral Body* was dotted with small holes.

"Ha... Haha... Hahaha... Hahahaha..."

A quiet, hysterical laugh filled the air. Only after a few moments did Ryu realize that it was coming from him.

He had killed and shed so much blood and sweat for the sake of strength. He was ready to face any opponent, even a Manticore clone, just to protect his friends. He was so confident in his abilities that he would've fought a deity if he had to.

For almost a hundred years, he had been preparing for the fight of his life. He never would've imagined that his chance would be taken away from him. There was no way he could have stopped the long-range artillery array reinforced with a *Divine*-rank artifact.

He felt so powerless he wanted to scream, but only croaking laughter escaped his throat. Nothing made any sense anymore. He was consumed by a profound feeling of inadequacy.

He was still too weak.

He still lacked so much more power.

Feeling his body weakening and his mind cracking, Ryu felt something in his hand. The hand that seemed to have been torn off. Looking down, he saw the unfolded scroll of the *Infinite Potential Technique,* his ultimate prize from the Heavenly Pagoda. Turning into golden dust, the parchment, along with knowledge and memories, flowed into his soul.

His mind started to blur again. Before losing consciousness, Ryu heard three heavy blows that reverberated over the entire island. Moments later, a huge column of light descended from behind the clouds, hitting the Union troops. The last thing Ryu saw was a figure hanging in the sky. The power it emanated was almost suffocating.

"Get some rest now," he heard, "I'll finish this on my own."

Chapter 16
DOMINANCE OF THE STRONGEST

As much as Kai wanted to return to Insulaii as soon as possible, he couldn't force the flying vessel to move faster than it could.

The journey back took six days. Kai and his crew returned just in time for the Union forces to lay siege to the capital city of Nogatta. Having in mind the gap the clones had created in the planetary barrier, Kai planned to get back the same way. However, by that moment, almost nothing remained of it. Aware of the severity of the damage, Rosen had poured even more energy, runic fog, and *Divine Particles* into it so that neither Kai nor his clones deprived of the *Spark* could pass through. Even fusing with Viola and attacking with all the might of the *Touch of Nothingness* didn't help. After several failed attempts, he had no choice but to use the same ten particles of the *Trophy* he had activated in the ice dimension.

Kai went all in, but even with an increased power in manipulating energy it took some time. He saturated both himself and the space around with huge amounts of energy to put the pressure on the planetary barrier, and in the end, a part of the scarlet film became thin enough to first be crushed and then absorbed.

As soon as a passage was opened, Kai expanded his spirit perception and focused it on the planet's surface. Quickly locating Nogatta's capital and enemy troops, he unleashed some of the power he had absorbed from the barrier. Several *False Holy Punishments of Heaven* converged into a giant column of light.

They're still standing? Kai wondered, surprised, as he saw the Union's *Divine* barriers covered with huge cracks.

Closing his eyes, he concentrated on the auras of Avlaim's defenders.

"Get some rest now," he said to them through the spirit link. "*I'll finish this on my own.*"

At the same moment, large crystals appeared near the defenders. With a loud shatter, warriors made of ice emerged from the crystalline cocoons and rushed at the Union soldiers. Sturdy barriers shot out of the ground in many places, covering entire groups of the defenders. The wounded were enveloped in techniques and pulled out of the clutches of death.

Having subdued all the neutral energy in the capital, Kai did all he could to remotely help his allies on the battlefield, weaving techniques right next to them.

Suddenly, a streak of bright light split the sky and flashed over the city.

"Is that the best you've got?" Kai snorted as he held out the spinning *Divine* projectile fired at him.

Crushing the metal with his fingers and drawing all the strength out of it, Kai threw away the useless little thing.

A moment later, he was gone.

The shocked Union soldiers continued to stare at the sky, not realizing that their opponent was already near.

"And where is Rosen? Where are the Twin Dragons?" Zhou Han Nam suddenly heard.

His eyes widened in horror and he tried to jump away, but he fell to the ground. Two stumps covered with dark green flames were now where his legs should've been.

Zhou Han Nam screamed in agony.

"I asked you a question!" Kai hissed, stepping on his throat and making him wheeze.

Snapping out of their stupor, the guards realized what had happened and rushed to help their master. But none of them had time to even take a step. Kai's right hand moved at such a speed that it became a blur and *Phobos* turned into a kind of whip.

There was a crackle and a shower of flesh and blood rained upon the battlefield.

"As I understand, my men killed the Twin Dragons," Kai said, nodding to himself. He was rather pleased with what the clones had to report. "What about Rosen and his sisters?"

Removing his foot from Zhou Han Nam's throat, Kai heard a stream of curses.

"Not gonna talk? Very well."

With a swift flick of his wrist, he cut off Zhou Han Nam's hand. This time there was no shouting. Instead, Zhou Han Nam pulled a *Divine* artifact from his *Storage* and tried to activate it.

"Doesn't work?" Kai chuckled.

Thanks to the *Trophy*, all the energy in the area belonged to him — this also applied to the *prana* crystallized in artifacts.

"The time has come! Let us bathe in his blood!" Viola exclaimed, anticipating the delicious carnage. She woke up during their journey to Insulaii, rested and healthy.

"Patience, Viola. We need to interrogate him first."

"How long are you going to stay silent, old man?"

"Go to hell!" Zhou Han Nam spat. "You won't hear a word from me! But you will die! You *will* die! You will pay for the death of my granddaughter!"

"What are you talking about?" With a frown, he cut off the remaining hand. "Still won't talk? Very well."

The methodical butchering went on for about half a minute, until Zhou Han Nam, overwhelmed with spirit pain, began to lose consciousness.

"Manticores," he rasped, half-delirious, as his eyes rolled back, "they... will... kill... you..."

Kai let out a chuckle.

"They are welcome to try. Don't think I'll let you die so easily!"

Having healed the biggest physical and astral wounds with the *Inevitable Healing Technique*, Kai placed the *Burning Ice Curse* in the old man's soul, yanking him out of the darkness of oblivion.

"Since you wanted war so much, I will show it to you in all its glory!"

With that, he took off into the air with Zhou Han Nam.

Hanging high above the capital, he brought the old man back to his senses with another healing technique.

"Are you awake? Wonderful! Then observe! Don't blink. I'd hate it if you missed something," Kai snarled and surrounded Zhou Han Nam with condensed energy, trapping him in the sky. In his current state, the old man was unable to resist, and even if he tried, the *Curse* would tear him apart from the inside. "You can see your army in all its glory! Look closely, O Great Patriarch of the Han Nam Union!"

In the next second, Kai vanished.

Breaking through the weakened barrier again, he appeared near one of Union's defensive arrays. The soldiers surrounding him fell to the ground upon his arrival, turning into withered mummies. Energy left their bodies as soon as Kai's aura materialized itself.

Kai put his palm on the array's smooth surface. Simultaneously blocking a large number of artifacts wasn't easy, so he decided to disable them instead. This required him to touch them.

As his skin made contact with the metal, the energy in the array's material vibrated and fell apart, becoming moldable like putty. With a little bit of effort, Kai managed to untangle the weaves inside the crystallized *prana*, rendering them useless. The array turned off with a dull, throbbing noise.

Without wasting a moment, Kai moved on to the next one.

"*No, no, no!*" Viola shouted as she watched hundreds of soldiers fall dead. "*You did not kill them with steel! What good is a blade if it does not taste blood?!*"

"*Don't worry,* Kai tried to calm her down. *There will be carnage, I promise you. Just wait a bit.*"

No one was able to stop Kai. He destroyed one defensive array after another, until there wasn't a single barrier left over the Union army. After that, he wove a technique that he invented back in the days of training with Sawan. This would be the first time he would use it in a real battle. Until this day, he hadn't participated in such a large-scale confrontation, and the technique was better suited for groups of enemies rather than single targets.

Two balls of green flames lit up in his palm. Hurling them into the distance, he watched as they expanded and turned into a pair of gigantic Emerald Phoenixes. Consisting of all five concepts, as well as the *Paths* of *Sword* and *Space*, and containing not just a memory crystal, but a piece of his soul, they were the pinnacle of his *Creation Technique* with their own weaving.

Spreading their wings, the Phoenixes unleashed a hail of hellfire on the enemy army, aiming at the artillery arrays.

The fiery storm spread everywhere due to the chaos that ensued. The Union soldiers tried to destroy them, but the birds possessed tremendous strength and could, on top of that, also regenerate using the concepts of *Yang* and *Radiant Void*. Without their massive barriers, the invaders were powerless against them. Kai had killed their *Masters of Six Stars* at the very beginning of the confrontation, and only the Union leaders had powerful *Divine* items.

Watching the horror unfold, Kai smiled and unsheathed *Phobos*.

"*You can come out, Viola.*"

The invitation was accepted eagerly, and the demoness materialized before him in a cloud of black and scarlet mist.

He handed her his sword.

"Have fun."

Viola looked at him with her eyebrows raised in surprise.

"Just don't go too far. If anything happens, use the *Nightmare World*," he warned her. "You've learned a lot, so this will be good practice."

Nodding, the demoness accepted the sword.

"Thank you, master."

"Give them hell."

"At once!" she exclaimed and flew off into the distance together with *Phobos*.

Cackling manically, Viola bathed in blood and entrails. She hadn't felt this free in a very, very long time. Her innate power level could be compared to that of a *Master of Five Great Stars* so she didn't need to put much effort into dominating her opponents. To this day, Kai remained amazed by how powerful she was. How did the Heavenly Exaltation Pagoda manage to create a formidable being like her?

Ungluing his gaze from her, he looked at the sky.

"Come to me!"

Focusing on the clones' spirit marks, Kai used a bit of the *Trophy's* power to move the remaining doubles closer to him. All except for Six, who stayed on the Ark. In total, a little more than half a thousand of them survived.

Appearing before him, they knelt and bowed their heads. The *Exclusion Zone Generator* formed above them and Kai spread his arms in greeting.

"It's time for you to become stronger."

Thin tentacles of flesh sprouted from Kai's fingertips. Dividing and multiplying, they moved toward the clones and dug into their bodies. Thickening like roots, they supplied them with energy, making their bodies deform and distort.

After a couple of minutes, Kai opened his eyes and exhaled.

With the renewal of the clones' bodies and souls completed, their initial parameters now exceeded fourteen thousand units. Their artificial souls weren't accepted by the *Rules*, so the peak of their mastery was the third level of the *Holy Lord Stage*.

In addition, Kai replenished their reserves of *Force* particles, saturated their bodies with energy and power of his bloodline, and filled their souls with *Will*. Each clone received only as much willpower as it could hold, so only a few of them were able to wield the *Master's Will*.

"Destroy the Union army!" Kai exclaimed and pointed at the fiery hell that was spreading behind him. "After that, split up into squads and sweep through all of Avlaim! Kill or capture all enemies! Free our homeland!"

"Yes, master!" the clones shouted in unison and activated invisibility.

Removing the *Exclusion Zone*, Kai soared into the air. Zhou Han Nam was still where he had left him, observing with undisguised horror the collapse of the Union's supposedly invincible army.

"Quite the sight, isn't it?" Kai sneered. "Will you tell me where Rosen and his sisters are? Or should I show you more?"

But Zhou Han Nam remained silent, as if he had not heard the question at all. His wide, unblinking eyes were focused on the battlefield. In them, Kai could see the reflection of the dying soldiers and the flames that were hurling toward the border regions.

"In that case, I propose we make a deal," he said after a pause. The old man was too stubborn, and he'd get nothing if he killed him too quickly. "You tell me where they are, and I will spare the Han Nam Clan if its members swear allegiance to me."

This time the old man reacted. Turning his head, he twisted his lips into a nasty grin.

"Burn in hell! I can't stand Rosen, but I hate you more than anyone in this world! You! Damn! Bastard! You will pay for everything! I won't say a word! Die, you— Aghhhhh!!!"

Bending under the *Curse*, Zhou Han Nam choked on his words.

Kai shook his head.

We'll see how long you'll last...

***

Leaving the burning city, a dark figure rushed through the forest.

With Kai's arrival and the fall of Union's armies, Mia ordered her clones to drop everything and retreat in order to preserve the drops of *Blood* embedded in their bodies. The order came a tad too late, as most of them had already entered the capital at that time and were on the front line. Locked in combat with *Masters* of *Six* and *Seven Stars* they had little to no chance of escaping.

However, one particular clone got lucky, having been ordered to stay in the back. Being so far away from the epicenter of the fight, she managed to make her way toward the north shore, where the Unions' vessels were anchored. The fleet should have learned about the defeat of the main troops by now, but she hoped to reach the shore before the ships left.

Her heart sored when she spotted the tall masts in the distance. She picked up the pace and then stumbled, her head blown clean off her shoulders. Her body rolled across the rocky ground for a little while and came to abrupt halt when it hit a boulder. For a couple of seconds, there was silence, and then the corpse twitched and stirred and began to grow a new head.

The clone almost managed to rise to her feet when a part of its torso suddenly exploded. The right hand flew off to the side, and the body, having taking a few clumsy steps forward, almost fell again. Regaining some composure, she turned and held out her hand. A thick, multi-layered barrier erupted from the ground to surround her but was pierced through before it managed to form completely.

The third blow hit her in the stomach, destroying not only her *Astral Body* but also damaging her soul. Unable to withstand such damage, she disintegrated, turning into a puddle of viscous black liquid.

"Man, those things do NOT want to die," Shacks grumbled to himself.

"I know you couldn't have done it better, but this seems like a waste of arrows and energy," Ivsim commented, leaning over the side.

Not wanting to stay in the *Storage*, the group remained on the flying ship, which was now cruising high above the island. They were in no hurry to go down because they could be mistaken for enemies. All they could do was provide long-range support.

"I wouldn't call it a waste," Shacks said. "I'm testing a prototype. If you ask me, this is the perfect opportunity for a fun little experiment."

"For once, I agree with you," Malvur said, observing something in the distance.

"See? The big guy agrees with me!"

"Don't get used to it."

"I need to put this on my calendar!"

Malvur sighed. He should have stayed quiet.

Ailenx sighed as well, but for a different reason.

"He's gone too far again," he said, his eyes fixed on the blazing battlefield.

***

About half an hour later, it was all over. The remnants of the Union army surrendered, valuing their lives over victory. Their ships couldn't leave Nogatta's waters since Kai moved a batch of clones to the northern coast just before they managed to set sail.

Instead of destroying the vessels and the defensive and artillery arrays, Kai had simply disabled them. The Temple could use such high-quality artifacts.

After that, all that was little left to do was help Shaw in the east and clear the region of invaders. Both tasks were completed rather quickly with the clones' help.

Landing in the ruins of the city, Kai was met by a swinging blade. The invisible sickle of the *Will of Sword* sliced through the air and shattered against Kai's palm.

A man sitting nearby jumped to his feet, while the attacker stared at him in shock, squeezing her sword tighter. In a few short moments, her facial expression changed.

"You scared the shit out of me!" An'na yelled, waving

her hands. "What was that? How did you defend yourself?"

"This?" Kai looked at his hand in surprise and shrugged. "Years of training."

"Really now?" An'na mumbled, squinting at Kai. Walking around him slowly, she examined him thoroughly. "Not a whiff of danger from you... It's as if we are on completely different levels... You're insane, you know that?"

"I believe something like a 'hello' or 'long time no see' would be a more appropriate greeting." Kai laughed, approaching her.

Looking into his eyes, An'na relaxed, put away her sword, and hugged her old friend.

"I haven't seen you in ages," she said softly.

"I'm glad that you're all right," Kai said, returning the hug.

"I can't help but notice that shit's always going down when you are around," Guts commented, looking around at the ruins surrounding them. "First in Nikrim, now in the Trial Worlds... With how things are going, we'll have to fight in the Heavenly World, too."

Kai shrugged in response.

"It's not like I chose any of this, mind you."

"I guess it doesn't matter as long as we're on the winning side. After all, war's a profitable business. Unless you are the losing side, that is."

"You haven't changed a bit."

"Business, as usual. By the way, do you happen to need a treasurer or something in that Temple of yours?"

"As much as I'd like to discuss business with you, Guts,

we seem to have company," Kai changed the subject, sensing someone's presence.

A group of twelve *Masters of Seven Small Stars* came closer to them. A special squad that included Renata was led by a *Master of Seven Average Stars* — a young draconoid named Yor.

They had fought at the forefront together with the older clones, colliding head-on with Mia's doubles and the strongest Union soldiers. They were all painfully aware of the fact that they were outnumbered and that they would fail to defend the city. Morale was dangerously low when Kai's sudden appearance changed everything. His power made an indelible impression on them, and the rapid destruction of enemy troops would be forever imprinted in their memory.

Having respectfully greeted him, all of them, except Renata, expressed their desire to serve the Temple and follow its teachings.

"Not everyone can become my follower," he told them. "But the doors of the Eternal Path Temple are open to everyone. Once the war is over, talk to Lilith or any other Hierarch. They will arrange for you to take the test."

Rising, the soldiers bowed respectfully, and Renata approached Kai.

"My lord," she spoke. "We have captured Aash'Tsiron, the mother of the Twin Dragons and the de facto ruler of their lands. Lady Nyakonalavius returned to HQ with her. Aash'Tsiron's condition is pretty bad, so it was decided to put her in a healing array."

Great news. Kai nodded contently. *Zhou Han Nam choses to remain silent, but hopefully, I'll get some information from the Dragon.*

"Lead the way."

Despite her position and status, Aash'Tsiron had long retired and hadn't been practicing cultivation and martial arts in quite a while. She rushed to the front line only out of rage, fueled by the desire to avenge her beloved sons. But when Mia's clones began to retreat, she found herself surrounded. Unwilling to give up, she fought until she couldn't stand anymore.

Renata wasn't exaggerating when she said that the mother of the Dragons was in a terrible state. Even Nyako's healing array couldn't deal with such serious injuries. Luckily, Kai arrived at the headquarters in time and used his healing abilities to pull Aash'Tsiron from the brink of death. After that, bringing her to her senses was just the matter of time.

Fortunately, she didn't turn out to be as tough of a nut to crack as Zhou Han Nam. She didn't need much convincing to tell Kai that Rosen and Mia should be in the Forbidden City — the home of the Han Nam Clan.

But Aash'Tsiron didn't stop there. All the while, she showered Kai with curses and accused him of Kuro's death.

"What makes you think I killed him? You and Zhou Han Nam seemed to have an agreement. I didn't kill anyone on Kronos, save for the Formless."

"Liar! Murderer!" Aash'Tsiron shouted. "Your aura seeped into Kuro's mark at the moment of his death! You can make excuses all you want, but I know what you did! It was the same with Zhou! You are a killer! That's who you are!"

Kai frowned and left the room.

"Pick apart their brains and dwell as deep into their memories as you can. Take a look in their pocket dimensions, too. Find the death scrolls of Kuro and Zhou's granddaughter."

Renata bowed.

"At once."

What the hell is going on...?

***

Few people knew about the existence of the Forbidden City in Tyr, and even fewer knew its exact location. Aash'Tsiron was no exception, but she had certain assumptions, having tried to locate it more than once over the course of her rather long life.

Since Kai didn't have other information, he decided to believe her for the time being.

Using the *Complex*, he quickly moved to Tyr and began the search. Checking all the places Aash'Tsiron indicated took him a lot of time, but he eventually located the Forbidden City in the center of a large anomaly called the Misty Mountains. Due to many spatial distortions, thousands of young Masters went missing in this area annually, eager to test their strength and find ancient treasures.

In the midst of the mountains was a beautiful fertile valley, hidden from the world on all sides, above included. Only those who knew the secret paths in this maze of distorted space could get here. As well as those who possessed energy vision.

Having found the valley, Kai walked right into it.

As the sun rose, signaling the beginning of a new day, the young Masters of the Han Nam Clan scurried through the streets, while the elders went about their business in the palace. The ongoing war didn't seem bother them at all. Perhaps they were unaware of it, or perhaps they chose to ignore it. Kai didn't know. Frankly, he didn't care.

"The level of serenity," he whispered, raising his merged blades.

The power of the *Trophy's* deactivated particles bubbled up inside them again. Dense streams of energy flowed toward Kai from all sides, pouring into his blade. With a low buzz, miniature black holes began to form around the weapon. Expanding gradually, they absorbed more and more energy from their surroundings.

It was another technique Kai had created on Belteise — *True Cataclysm*.

As the upgraded version of *Gravity Collapse*, it absorbed

and combined all of Kai's elements. The deadly mixture of *Yin* and *Yang* remained its key property, making its destructive potential so potent that it threatened even its creator. With an equal amount of energy, it was even more dangerous than the *False Holy Punishment of Heaven*. And given the time and effort necessary to weave it, it was clear why Kai used it only now for the first time outside of the training grounds.

"You wanted war. I'll give you war." He came for revenge, and there was no place for mercy in the worlds of cultivation.

The blade rose and then fell with a sharp whistle.

The black holes rushed toward the barrier surrounding the palace. Kai didn't want to give Rosen a chance to escape, so he used his strongest attack.

A giant fireball fell upon the valley, wiping the entire Forbidden City off the face of the planet. A bright flash lit up the whole island. The ground quaked and the nearby mountains collapsed, reduced to a pile of rubble.

When the temperature dropped by a couple of hundred degrees, Kai landed on the devastated terrain.

He detected at least three auras of survivors. The giant Manticore that jumped out of the dust cloud didn't come as a surprise to him.

Having recovered from her fight with Lilith, Mia was so eager to tear Kai to pieces that she used the *Manticore Extract Infusion* and the remaining drops of *Blood*.

The razor-sharp claws were less than two feet from Kai, who seemed no faster than a snail next to her, when he turned his head to face Mia. The violet gems seemed to stare directly into her soul, making her shudder.

Ultimate Focus was activated at full power.

Black scales covered Kai's body as it was filled with the *Borrowing Flame*. *Advanced Complete Submission* and the *Cover* additionally enhanced his flesh, bringing Kai to the peak of his power. He could only become stronger with Viola or active use of the *Heat Void* core.

Slowly raising his hand, Kai snapped his fingers in front of the monster's muzzle.

Time resumed its flow, and the Manticore was swept away by an invisible wave of *Compressed Force*.

This isn't enough. Kai tilted his head and took out one of the swords from the scabbard.

One swing and Mia's body was split into two equal halves. Reconnective tissues emerged from the flesh, seeking to reconnect the pieces.

Kai nodded resolutely.

This time he pierced her stomach.

The blade sunk deep, reaching the soul.

Mia died on the spot.

As she fell, she resumed her humanoid form. Ripping the *Manticore Heart* from her chest, Kai placed it in an artifact and sent it to his *Storage*. He also teleported her body, having previously frozen it.

There were two auras left.

Despite the dust rising into the air and eclipsing the sun, Kai saw Rosen. Like Mia, he was in the most protected part of the palace. However, he was in a lousy state, with one foot already in the grave.

He wasn't alone. Bent over his wounded body, a little

girl inconsolably wept.

Kai looked at the scene in wonder.

She's as strong as an initial-level Exorcist... A Master of Seven Big Stars *at her age? That's rather unusual...*

"Don't you dare!" the girl shrieked and pointed her sword at Kai. Her hands were trembling and her eyes were teary, but they glittered with steely resolve. "Don't you dare go near my daddy! Don't touch him! He didn't deserve this! Daddy is good! He protected me with his body! You... You are a bad man!"

She tried to use some kind of artifact, but the *Trophy* particles disabled it.

"Leave! Don't touch him!" Her grief quickly transformed into anger.

Kai stopped, unsure what to do.

Such power at such a young age. What did they do to her? She's too dangerous to be spared. She would never accept to join me. She saw my face, so she will hunt me down to avenge her father. Perhaps if I erased her memory with artifacts...? I could try. With such a talent, she will one day become a deity. And while she might be a useful asset, it's just a matter of time before she remembers everything and tries to kill me. I don't need a god on my list of enemies. If I take her with me, the O'Crimes and the entire Heavenly Manticore clan will know where the Ark is.... He took a deep breath. *However you look at it, it's not worth it. Someday, she will grow up and seek revenge. I don't know where I'll be then, but I'd be putting the Temple at risk.*

Kai took a deep breath and stepped toward the girl. The least he could do was make it painless.

"No!" Rosen shouted, finally awake enough to tell what was happening. "Stop! Stay away from her, I'm begging you!"

Kai froze. But only for a moment. In an instant, darkness engulfed both Rosen and his daughter.

The last two auras went out.

He took their bodies as well the artifact that created the barrier over Insulaii. Rosen had launched its deactivation upon learning of the Union's defeat, but it would take at least several days to complete the process due to its immense power.

After some thinking, Kai reversed the shutdown and poured even more power into the artifact. After all, it was an excellent tool for controlling Insulaii, a planet whose dry land was practically under his control.

A few hours later, he returned to the Ark. He went straight to the *Complex*, sat on the *Eternal Throne*, and sent out a planet-wide mental message.

"The leaders of the Han Nam and the Twin Dragon Unions are dead. Their armies have been destroyed. As the winner, I have every right to take everything they owned. From this day on, their lands will be subject to the Eternal Path Temple. Any resistance will be punished by death."

Chapter 17
HOMECOMING

It was finally over.

Sighing wearily, Kai leaned back against the *Eternal Throne* and rubbed his temples.

"There's still a lot of work to be done."

Alfred appeared in the hall, as silent as a shadow.

"Welcome back, master."

"Alfred." Kai glanced at him through his fingers. "I'm glad to see you."

"Please forgive me for allowing Master One to take young Igdrasil on such a perilous journey. I fear you didn't give me clear instructions about the baby, as you did for the *Complex*, so I put his life at risk for the sake of yours." The Spirit bowed. "Your life is of paramount importance to me, second only to your orders."

Kai waved his hand dismissively.

"You did what you thought was best, I can't fault you for it."

"Thank you for your understanding. I hope the young

Igdrasil is all right?"

"He's intact."

"In that case, should I return him to his room?"

Kai summoned the ent from his pocket dimension into his arms. Igdrasil blinked his eyes open, waking up, and Kai brought a bottle with the infusion to his face. Even before leaving Insulaii, One usually took care of the baby, but for the last six days that they traveled through space, Kai was in charge of the ent's meals. Soon, he found himself becoming rather attached to Igdrasil.

He had learned that Lilith was the one who insisted on One and Six setting out to find him, but he couldn't shake off the feeling that they would've failed to do so had Igdrasil not been with them. Without the ent, they never would've found him, and he never would've learned about the war, and would thus not been able to assist.

Looking at the ent, he remembered Rosen's daughter. Being so young, her bloodline hadn't gone through the second evolution, so she couldn't be reborn with *Second Chance*. On one hand, the loss of such a talented cultivator was tragic, but on the other, Kai was glad that he'd never have to worry about her coming after him. Thinking about it, he couldn't help but feel like Igdrasil could potentially find himself in a similar situation one day.

Something stirred in his chest, making it hurt, and his fists clenched on their own.

"I'll make a very strong warrior out of you," he said, looking Igdrasil straight in the eyes. "Someone who can protect both himself and everything dear to him."

In response, Igdrasil looked up from his bottle, smiled, and reached for Kai's face.

"Let him stay with me for now," Kai finally answered Alfred.

"As you wish, Master."

With that, Kai went to Earth Haven with Igdrasil in his arms, straight to the central array's core. There, he met up with Ulu and gave her Rosen's *Divine* artifact.

"Integrate it into the central array," he ordered. "As long as we keep it active, we'll have full control over every entry and exit point from this world. I'll send clones to help you develop transfer arrays compatible with this artifact. From now on, the Temple will decide who will enter or exit Insulaii and when."

"Your wish is my command, master. However, I am afraid we may not have enough resources to further support the barrier," she remarked after examining the artifact.

"Don't worry. The necessary resources will be here soon," Kai assured her. "I'll give you enough *Runes*, *Divine Particles*, and *Azure Crystals*. Several hundred clones will constantly maintain its energy level. I want to make the barrier even stronger."

Ulu bowed again and went about her business, while Kai decided to check up on Six.

He was still maintaining the connection between the clones, so he didn't notice Kai's approach. Without distracting him, Kai healed his body and soul and left the tower. His next destination was the deepest point of the giant dungeon that sprawled under the Ark. There was one more important thing left for him to do.

Once in the underground maze, he used all the acquired knowledge, as well as a few particles of the *Trophy* to increase his control over the *prana*, and directed all of the accumulated energy he owned into the planet's bowels. Putting his hands on the ground, he closed his eyes and steadied his breathing. After a while, beads of sweat started rolling down his body and blood gushed from his nose.

The level of energy density on the Ark began to rise. The Great Spirit Geyser threatened to erupt, approaching the Higher level. These could only be found in the Central Worlds and the Heavenly World, where most of the Ecumene's *prana* was concentrated.

As of today, Kaiser's Ark was the most powerful place in the Trial Worlds in the terms of energy density.

***

A magnificent city floated under them as the ship sailed towards a huge tower with a giant sword hanging above it.

"Is it just me or does the energy level seem higher?" Lily asked, looking up. "And all those training arrays and resources you mentioned... Neither the Three Styles Sect, nor the Cloud Abode, nor even Belteise make such an excellent place to develop. This is truly something else."

Ivsim laughed heartily.

"Remember the Thunder Serpent Clan and the Seven Blades Clan on Saha? Remember how we thought them to be the pinnacle of cultivation? We dreamed of becoming *Elementalists* back then, and now the path to the *Divine Stage* is open to us..."

Lily smiled, reminiscing about the Fallen Star Sect, the strongest organization in Alkea, her homeland.

"Yes... If it wasn't for Kai and all these events, we would have continued to serve the Seven Blades. Or even the Thunder Serpent. We would've been *Exorcists* and would have probably been fighting for resources with the elders, having our own faction within the clan."

"Probably," Ivsim agreed with a chuckle.

"Imagine... To the clan — We would've been gods to the whole of Saha. Even the Old Man and Jiang Dao couldn't oppose us."

"Jiang Dao went to Niagala. And while he did become stronger there, it didn't help him much."

Lily's smile faded. She missed Elize. She was so blinded by revenge that she was willing to sacrifice her own life for it. Thanks to Sawan, Lily and the others knew that Jiang Dao had been killed by Elize, who then also died from the power she had used.

The rest of the journey was spent in silence.

They arrived at the Ark the next day. Agreeing to Ulu's proposal, they went on a tour of the island while Kai was busy with other matters. Shacks was the first to sneak away, as per usual, followed by Lily and Ivsim. Ulu could be in several places at once using parallel streams of consciousness, so she had no problem keeping an eye on all of them.

The group explored different parts of the Ark and learned about the Temple's philosophy, rules, structure, and much more. The tour made an impression on all of them, but especially on Lily.

Back when she found out that Kai had founded his organization on Insulaii, she didn't expect to see a sect that controlled an entire region of the planet. More precisely, all three regions as of today.

Eventually, they regrouped and went to the *Complex* together to meet up with Kai.

After all that she had seen, Lily thought that nothing could surprise her anymore, but as soon as she entered the throne room, she was left speechless. In sensitivity to energy and control over it, she was second only to Kai, so she immediately realized the complexity and power of the magnificent scarlet throne that hovered ahead. It was the center of the island's strength.

Feeling her stagger, Ivsim reached out to support her.

"What's wrong?" he asked.

Instead of replying, Lily peered deeper into the *Throne's* structure, but it turned out to be too complicated for her to comprehend. The thousands of different weaves made the world spin before her eyes.

"Lily?"

The worry in Ivsim's voice made everyone turn around and look at Lily in surprise.

"I'm all right." She shook her head, coming to her senses. "I just... overdid it a little. I'm fine."

"You'll tell me what happened later, okay?"

Lily looked at him and smiled.

"Welcome to the *Heavenly Complex*," an unfamiliar old man said, appearing in front of them. "I am its host, Alfred. The master will be here soon."

At that moment, the door opened, letting in four people. A Dorgan woman in luxurious burgundy robes, a man with black feathers on his hands, a white-haired young man with a downcast look, and a dark-haired teenage girl. Each of them held huge power, forcing the sensitive Lily to shiver from the cold of danger. This feeling became especially acute when she looked at the teenage girl, whose strength seemed incomplete.

Masters of Seven Stars... Lily realized. *Our entire team combined is nowhere near close to them...*

Having greeted Kai's comrades with nods, the Hierarchs and Hiro stood to the right of the *Throne*.

All of a sudden, there was silence, interrupted only by soft, but at the same time heavy footsteps. The Temple members remained unperturbed, but Kai's friends turned around.

A figure emerged from the darkness of the passage and walked over to the *Throne*, where it assumed its rightful place.

Watching Kai, Lily remembered their first meeting, the journey to the imperial capital, the Wildlands, the Stone Wolves attack, the desperate struggle of her guards, Ash's selfless act and his fight against the monsters, the appearance of the berserker and, the arrival of a strong young man at the *Muscle Tempering* level.

He's no longer just a wanderer. Lily smiled. *I'm glad we've met him.*

The rest of Kai's friends had similar thoughts. All but one.

"Too pompous, if you ask me." Shacks laughed, shattering the magic of the moment. "We're not frail little maidens to impress us." He glanced at Lilith. "Well, most of us aren't."

Surprised at such impudence, Lilith turned to him and raised one eyebrow.

"What exactly are you implying?" she asked in a steely voice, focusing her murderous intent on him in an attempt to teach him a lesson.

"I'm just wondering where all the children came from," Shacks remarked with a sly smile, unbothered by Lilith's attempts at intimidation.

"And who is this clown?" Lilith demanded to know.

"Allow me introduce myself!" Shacks bowed ostentatiously. "Shacks the Magnificent, the best archer of the Trial Worlds, the most brilliant tactician and strategist to ever grace this earth, the greatest of poker players, the perfect lover, Kai's best friend, and just a great guy in general."

"Ha! I like him!" Shaw exclaimed but then he turned gloomy. "But if you touch my dear Lilith, you will be adding 'dead' to your long list of achievements."

"Aw, teenage romance, how cute." Shacks grinned and looked at Nyako. "But now this... This is a woman."

"Wow, you have eyes, well done," Nyako remarked dully.

"Please, ignore him," An'na said. "He's an idiot."

"All right, all right... That's enough." Kai sighed, putting his hand to his face. "Some things never change... I believe some introductions are in order."

***

"So you finally got your memory back?" Lilith asked.

"Correct," Kai replied.

"And what is our goal now, since you've remembered everything?"

"The Heavenly World," Kai said confidently. "I want to get to it as quickly as possible, and then use it to return to the Peripheral World from which my journey began. I promised someone I'd go back there."

"Wait a minute... Did you say Peripheral World?" Shaw butted in. "But how?!"

"It's a long story. Lily, Shacks, Ivsim, and I began our journey in the same world. If they're feeling up for it, maybe they could explain. I'm not that good with words, I'm afraid."

"I'd like to explain something to Shacks. In a duel," Lilith added under her breath.

"As you wish, madam." Shacks spread his arms and smiled crookedly. "But don't forget that all is fair in love and war."

"By all means, go ahead. But I strongly advise you not to underestimate each other. Whatever you feel now, it's far from what awaits you."

Lilith stared suspiciously at Shacks, who in her opinion wasn't stronger than a *Master of Six Small Stars*. Shacks smiled even wider, taking Kai's words for a compliment.

With that, the catching up was over and Kai formally invited his friends to join the Temple. To no one's surprise, the first to accept was Ailenx. Devoted to Kai to the level of fanaticism, he fell to one knee and pledged his unwavering loyalty to him.

Malvur was next. Simple as always, he just bowed and nodded.

Lily and Ivsim accepted the invitation, too. Even Shacks didn't make a scene and accepted Kai's offer with seriousness that befitted a young gentleman.

"I'm glad you've joined me. Now, I'll hand you over to Alfred." Kai nodded at the old man who appeared in the hall again. "Register them in the *Complex*, give them personal dimensions, tattoos, and have Ulu list them as Temple members. As of today, we have five more Senior Acolytes and potential Templars," he added contentedly, clapping his hands.

As his comrades left the throne room, Kai discussed the current military situation with the Hierarchs, as well as Avlaim's total losses.

After the destruction of the main enemy army in Nogatta, the small groups of Union soldiers that remained in control of the captured islands stood no chance against Kai's clones. By now, they had liberated more than half of the region, finishing off the enemy fleet along the way.

As for the losses, they were significant. Out of more than eleven thousand clones, about five hundred remained, and out of two and a half thousand Masters, less than seven hundred survived. Shan Wu and two other heads of the Northern Islands Union died. In total, out of the forty-two vassals, only twenty-six remained. Almost all the heads of independent factions in the west defended their lands to the last breath, refusing to retreat.

"Unfortunately, some areas remain occupied. Among them is the Order of the Primordial Elements," Lilith added. "We need to decide what to do with these lands and the survivors."

"Inform the vassals and new faction leaders that I'd like to see them on the Ark. Invite the heads of Tyr's largest organizations, too. They must come to Avlam within a week."

"I will."

"And Ragnar?"

"The search is still ongoing, but so far we had no luck. Hardly any trace can be found in all this mess. But we will comb through everything."

"Good." Kai nodded and turned his gaze to Nyako, who

seemed to be beside herself with worry. "Did you want to say something?"

"I wanted to ask you to remove me from the post of Hierarch." Nyako bowed her head. There was a certain heaviness and at the same time self-hatred in her voice. "After all that has happened, I feel unworthy of this title. I'm too weak to claim it. The Eternal Path Temple cannot have such weak support. I'm ready to continue acting as the head of the Technology Center until someone more suitable for this role shows up."

"Are you sure?"

"Absolutely."

Kai observed her in silence for a little while and nodded.

"I will put your request under consideration."

***

After the meeting, Kai went to the Medicine Hall to check Acilla's condition once again. There were no improvements or any changes whatsoever. Whatever happened to her soul had exceeded the capacity of the *Complex's* healing arrays.

With a heavy heart, Kai went to the *Storage*.

After the war, the top places on Insulai's ranking board quickly freed up. It didn't take Kai long to claim the title of the Legend of the first rank. Now he could buy a few very unique items from the *Altar*: an *Elemental Body Particle*, an *Elemental Soul Particle*, and one-third of the *Exodus Right*.

The former two cost a billion each while the latter cost a symbolic one *Rune*. At the moment, Kai could afford to buy just one *Particle*, and this was only possible thanks to Zarifa's debt, which Kal'het had recently paid off.

As for the treasury, after the war, it was almost empty. Kai was supposed to collect trophies and indemnities from the losing regions, but he planned to use the resources to restore the Temple and Avlaim.

Kai spent almost an hour contemplating his decision. In the end, he decided to get the *Elemental Soul Particle* and one third of the *Exodus Right* from the *Altar* shop. The latter looked like a simple paper amulet with incomprehensible symbols. To his surprise, it wasn't displayed in the energy spectrum, like it was the most ordinary item. Still, there was some strange power emanating from it, so Kai spent another quarter of an hour peering into it. Eventually, he noticed faint energy reflections inside.

"So this is an artifact without a rank. How interesting... It seems that the *System* can't identify it..."

The *Soul Particle* had a rather interesting appearance. When he purchased it, Kai didn't expect to receive something similar to a jet black acorn. Its description was also not displayed in the *System* interface. It was so saturated with power that it was almost blinding to look at through the energy spectrum.

It looks like a Spirit Berry, he remarked. *But no two are the same, so it has to be something artificial if it's sold in bulk.*

Having studied the *Soul Particle* for some time and realized that it ignored any other matter except the buyer's body, and therefore couldn't be transferred to anyone, Kai swallowed it.

First, a pleasant wave of power passed through his *Astral Body*, after which his *Soul Shell* began to change at the informational level of reality. In order not to interfere with the process, he removed the soul protection granted by the *Trophy*.

Attention!

Structural effect detected on the Soul Shell.

Initiating the formation of the artificial elemental layer of the Soul Shell.

...

Attention!

A damaged innate elemental layer of the Soul Shell has been detected.

Merging forces...

Initiating the process of restoring the innate elemental layer of the Soul Shell.

...

Attention!

The innate elemental layer of the soul shell has been restored.

Your status of a [Heavenly Miracle] has been restored.

[Favorite of the Forces] title has been detected.

Initiating the upgrade process of the [Favorite of the Forces] title into [Adored by the Forces].

Time remaining: [62] days [1] hour [23] minutes [16] seconds

Soul's influence on the body has been recorded.

Fundamental physical changes have been recorded.

The elemental body's peak potential has been reached.

Current level of development: [Holy Lord]

Initiating the process of restoring the innate elemental body.

Process accelerated.

Time remaining: [185] days [23] hours [0] minutes [54] seconds

To avoid disrupting the process, continue saturating the body with dense energy until all processes have been completed.

Chapter 18
THE POWER BESTOWED BY THE FORCE

The Heavenly Miracles were the greatest geniuses of the Ecumene, along with the Divine Children. They were rightly called the most brilliant cultivators that originated from mortals. What made them different from ordinary beings was the elemental layer of their *Soul Shell*.

In general, *Soul Shells* were formed when a sufficient amount of *Will* accumulated in one place. It could be the will generated by an infant's mind, or the will of the universe, which manifested as particles.

In the first case, an ordinary soul was born, imbued with the *Forces* of either the *Path* of *Mind* or *Animal*. In the second case, the *Shell* was imbued with the *Forces* of the elements of its own accumulated particles, forming an elemental instead of the warrior layer, resulting in a being known as a Spirit.

However, there were souls that, during formation,

were saturated not only with the *Forces of Mind* but also with those of the elements. Such cases were incredibly rare and usually only occurred in the most energy-dense places, such as the Core and the Heavenly Worlds.

The more elements were in the *Shell*, the stronger they influenced it. In most cases, this simply led to its collapse, but if the child survived the grueling process, their talent would increase significantly. Usually, this was manifested as higher levels of mastery, or as the *Favorite of the Forces* blessing. But the most powerful manifestation was the formation of the fourth layer of the soul — the elemental one. It wasn't an actual additional layer, but a sort of binding force that was evenly distributed between the other three and seemed to hold them together. This was how Heavenly Miracles were created.

Children born with such souls were even rarer than those of deities and were considered an anomaly. Their souls could be called defective, but it was precisely this "defect" that made them stronger than ordinary ones.

All this information flashed through Kai's mind as soon as he read the lines of the *System* messages that appeared before his eyes.

I am... a Heavenly Miracle? He frowned in disbelief. *As usual, the* System *isn't saying much. But the elemental layer... As soon as I absorbed the* Elemental Soul Particle, *the former one began to recover. It even became stronger. I was born a Heavenly Miracle, but then I ceased to be one. Why? Was it me, or was it the previous owner of this body?*

To sort out this matter, Kai returned to the *Complex*. He'd have more chances of studying this process while it was taking place in his soul, so he devoted the next few hours to meditation.

The *Spark* he had occupied belonged to a Heavenly

Miracle. The same way as it happened with La'Gert's five-eyed mark when the original Kai was dying in a ditch in Caltea, his soul began to disintegrate. The "new" *Spark*, the one belonging to Kai from Earth, stopped this process, but the elemental layer of the soul had already been damaged and he lost his status of a Heavenly Miracle.

However, the elements that once lived in his soul still manifested themselves. Upon breaking through to the *Soul Stage*, Kai became the *Favorite of the Forces*, and despite losing his memory in the Trial Worlds, the crack in the *Shell* healed spontaneously, and then, during his training with Magnus, Kai discovered *Supreme Simulation*. His soul, unlike the ordinary ones, had two manifestations.

But why was this body mortal when I first got it? Being a Heavenly Miracle, the original Kai's talent should have awakened in infancy, and by the age of fourteen, he should have become at least an initial-level Elementalist, *despite the low energy density on Saha. Even without resources, he should have had enough talent to comprehend the process of breakthroughs. He had the potential to be the ruler of the entire empire, so what happened? Hmm... Something must have suppressed his warrior layer, preventing it from activating.*

As soon as this thought crossed his mind, he got an idea.

The Eversteins! The five-eyed mark curse! What if that prevented him from awakening? It would also explain the strange vision that I had upon occupying his body. Why were the guards protecting him so weak? And the scarlet lions... They weren't even Holy Beasts... But if the whole clan suffered because of the mark, then that would explain everything... There must've been some kind of a rift between the Hydras and La'Gert, just like with the Eversteins' ancestors...

Concluding that such a version of the story was the

most plausible one, Kai decided to contemplate the *Forces* involved in the creation of the elemental soul layer.

Typically, a soul could hold a bit more than five elements, but concepts took almost a third more space than they did. Being a *Favorite of the Forces* meant that the *Shell* compressed information more compactly, making room for eight elements, or for two elements and five concepts. And if you were *Adored by the Forces*, you could own almost thirteen elements in their entirety. So, when Kai became *Adored* in two months, he would be able to fully master four more *Paths*.

Another bonus of the elemental layer was the ability to master all of the soul's manifestations, including the rarest — the *Perfect Soul*. However, to do that, Kai needed time and special training.

And there was one more pleasant consequence of the elemental layer of the soul, it influenced the flesh and formed the *Elemental Body*. A unique construction that was able to affect the physical body even at this level. It increased the cultivator's reflexes, granted a certain level of resistance to all elements, and strengthened the body, fundamentally changing it in the process.

***

Continuing to squeeze him from all sides, the darkness slowly seeped into the man's mind, aiming to invade it. There was nothing around. No energy, no sounds, no air. It wasn't even possible to determine which side was up and which was down. There was only immense weakness caused by a tight strip of metal constricting his throat. But he didn't feel that either. He didn't even feel his own body.

Centuries might have passed and he wouldn't have been the wiser, but the System confirmed that it had been less than a month.

In one moment, everything changed. First, the man felt weakness, then the force of gravity, and then he saw a flash cut through the darkness.

Sirius found himself inside a large transparent cube, hanging in an endless space filled with hundreds of similar dungeons. A man stood before him.

"I suppose I should congratulate you on your victory, Kaiser?" he asked in a hoarse voice. "Or should I call you Kai Arnhard?"

"I see you've got it all figured out."

"Since you're standing there and admiring me, I assume the war is over. I don't get the news here. Bad reception and all that."

"Shaw's been rubbing off on you, I see."

Sirius sighed.

"He told me a lot about you. You really didn't use dark alchemy. Also, your skills and knowledge could prove quite useful, it's just…" Kai measured him with a cold look. "Your loyalty is questionable. Moreover, there's nothing for you to do in the Temple. Your strength and *Will* deserve respect, but you will not pass the Morality Test. However, if you insist, I'll let you take it. I just think you'd be wasting your time."

"I never wanted to join your circus," Sirius retorted. "I find it funny how you pride yourself in training virtuous cultivators. Virtuous… You don't know the first thing about virtues. You are holding them back. You are holding yourself back. Me — I am only loyal to my goal. As long as I achieve it, everything else is unimportant. Clans, families, friends, foes, you name it, they are all nothing more than tools."

"And what is your goal exactly?"

"To become a God and... feel," Sirius answered rather seriously.

"An unusual, but quite an ambitious goal. You do understand that your chances of achieving this are slim to none?" Kai asked, nodding at the suppressive collar. "I advise you to prove yourself useful to me. Otherwise, I see no reason to keep you alive."

Sirius tilted his head and, without hesitation, listed the thirty-six minor factions of Avlaim that didn't report directly to Kai, but served his vassals. Twenty-seven of them were secretly collaborating with the Unions before the attack. The remaining nine immediately crossed over to their side and aided the fight against Avlaim's defenders.

After that, he named eight organizations from other regions that shared their goal.

"I assume you want to take control of the Unions. These factions will refuse to serve the Temple even under threat of destruction. And then there are the Scarlet Ax Sect and the Meuzim Clan. They will agree to serve you, but I doubt that you need such vassals. Both are known for being extremely violent and overly aggressive, much to their neighbors' demise. Even the Union leaders failed to rein them in because of their strength and numbers. Also, they use the dark arts, though their ties with the Cult haven't been confirmed yet."

"Interesting." Kai nodded. "However, we would've eventually figured all that on our own."

"I don't doubt that you would have. But who knows what problems they would have caused you in the meantime? Efficiency is of extreme importance here. I already have all the information you need. I can also tell you that, despite their name, the Twin Dragon Sect is actually a clan. Almost all members of its ruling elite are related in one way or another. They come from an old Bellum family that was once part of the Mountain Alliance. Fighting for power within the organization, they contacted the Cult for help. When word got out, the family was hunted down and wiped out. However, no one knew that one girl and a handful of their loyal servants survived. Hiding on Insulaii, she cultivated and eventually gave birth to the Dragons who established their own sect. The surviving servants were given high positions among its ranks. Being High Draconians, they have a strong sense of loyalty and filial piety. In case anything happened to Aash'Tsiron or the Dragons, they would take over the sect. Prove to them that you have their leaders, and they will aid you. If you've already killed them, then… Well, they will pretend to play along for a while before stabbing you in the back. I wouldn't advise killing the servants because you will get several fragmented internal factions in return. If you ask me, it's better to keep one powerful faction under control through deception than to have no faction at all."

This information was valuable. Incredibly valuable. But Sirius didn't stop there. He continued to reveal the inner workings of most of Insulaii's factions and even suggested ways to sabotage each and every one of them. He also talked about the relations between Bellum and Ferox and the Unions: who worked with whom, who was actually a part of their strongest factions, whom it was better to put pressure on, where to give in, and so on.

"I'm impressed," Kai said in genuine amazement. "But don't you think you're being too reckless, giving out so much information at once?"

"I want you to know that I am a useful asset and that I deserve to be treated accordingly. This is only a small part of what I know. I am more than an information broker. I am a skilled fighter as well. The Dragons' plan was originally mine. However, becoming a God requires a lot of resources and I'm not strong enough to take what I need by force. For centuries, I have studied the Trial Worlds, looking for different ways to achieve my goal. Using the Dragons seemed most promising path. To that end, I created the Four Mists Cartel and several minor factions, gathered resources, and weaved a web of intrigue. If it weren't for you and this war, a large-scale redistribution of power would have taken place ten years from now. Many would have turned against the Twins and I would have eventually disposed of them and imprisoned their mother. Then I would have aided the Unions in their resistance and, having restored stability in the region, ruled it through Aash'Tsiron. It wouldn't be the first time I operated from the shadows..."

Sirius fell silent, letting Kai think.

"I suggest you keep doing what you're doing," Kai said after a while. "Use your skills to influence the factions and strengthen the Temple's influence in the region, as well as counter any threats and enemies. The conquering of Tyr and Land is still in process, but it's a matter of time before problems begin to arise. Do everything in your power to ensure that the unification under the Temple's rule goes as smoothly and quickly as possible. This will be your first task. In return, I will heal your *Astral Body* and give you limited freedom and high-quality resources. Naturally, you will have to take an oath and sign several contracts. You'll serve me for two hundred years. After that, you will be free if you swear never to oppose the Temple. What do you say?"

"I thought it'd be much longer. Very well. I agree."

"Shaw will come to you with everything you need. From today on, he's your superior. Also, you will be under constant supervision. You won't blink without us knowing. Be warned that you won't get a second chance. One wrong move, and that'll be the end for you."

***

"No... No. No! No!!! NO!!!" Luberg O'Crime cried out, suddenly jumping up from his chair and spilling his tea. "I refuse to believe it! It just can't be!" He slammed his fist on the table, breaking it, and then proceeded to punch the wall. "That bastard!"

"Calm down," Varimas said coldly, casting a disapproving glance at the pile of broken wood and porcelain.

"Calm down?!" Luberg glared at his older brother, now even more furious. "How can I possibly calm down after something like this?! Don't you care at all?!"

However, as soon as Luberg looked into Varimas's eyes, he swallowed his next words. The fury he saw in them made him stop throwing a tantrum.

"Have you forgotten what mother taught us? Restrain your emotions," Varimas ordered in an icy tone.

"I remember her words very well," Luberg said through clenched teeth. "It's just... It's too... Too..." Unable to find the words, he sank into his chair, exhausted. "First, Oi's mark goes out, then Mia's, and now Rosen and his daughter are gone, too. How could that happen? Who could have killed them? They are the strongest cultivators in our family. Three... Three of our siblings are dead. Only three of us remain. Do you know what will happen when mother finds out about this?"

"We're not allowed to disturb her meditation."

"But we can't just sit and wait! We must do something! We must take revenge! We should bring their heads to mother! She'll be done cracking the Elder Rune that contains

Magnus's skull by then."

"Whoever killed them must've been very strong. Do you think we can deal with them on our own? Especially on Insulaii. Do you want us to put our lives at risk, too?"

"Then what do you suggest? Should we just *calm down* and ignore it all?! We still have the family servants, as well as the entire Mountain Sect Alliance! After their leader died, mother seized control of the remaining opposition. With such force, no one can threaten us!"

I wish that was true. Varimas frowned, remembering the power Kaiser demonstrated in the ice dimension. *It had to have been him. A reborn God who regained his memory and part of his powers. U'Shor wasn't the only one... What should I do now? I can't ignore their deaths, but I can't put the others at risk. What is the right choice?*

***

Nine people sat at a large oval table. At its head was Kai, and clockwise from him were Derek von Everstein, the head of the Eighth Division, Laya Karst Iglosiaz, the branch leader of the Order of Purity, the heads of the five strongest factions of the Mountain Sect Alliance, Maron Akl, the head of Insulaii's branch of the Sevrum Alchemy Guild and the patriarch of the Cursed Sword Sect. The latter had been created relatively recently but it had already become famous for the fact that Rosen O'Crime was allegedly its native.

The only one missing was the head of the Vinari Clan, whom Kai planned to visit in the near future.

Despite all their power and high status, the guests were nervous, casting occasional glances in Kai's direction. Particularly tense were those with ties to the O'Crime family, namely the heads of the Mountain Sect Alliance and Maron.

However, they all looked askance at Kai not only

because of his strength but also for one more reason: his *Astral Body* looked quite strange.

A few years ago, Kai would have bowed deeply to any of the cultivators sitting at this table and graveled before them, but now the roles have switched. Now they feared him. Kai loved that feeling. He finally reaped the fruits of many years of hard training and deadly trials. That was why he always strove for power. For only power could give him such freedom. Despite all the pain and loss, he still believed that this was the right decision.

He was no longer a pawn, not just a small figure on the board of a big game, but someone who could come up with the rules.

"Lord Kaiser, as I understand it, we're all here to discuss the end of the war and the barrier that's still hanging over Insulaii?"

"That is correct, Lord Everstein," Kai replied. "The barrier is now under my control, but I certainly don't intend to keep it over Insulaii forever. My subordinates are working on the development of transfer arrays, the activation of which will temporarily enable travel through the *Altars* and Arches."

The guests exchanged glances and hushed whispers.

"However, they will remain under the Temple's jurisdiction," Kai continued, watching their faces darken. "In six months, the construction of the Temple's side branches will be completed. Three in each region. We will place these transfer arrays in them."

"Doesn't the Temple already have offices throughout Avlaim?" someone asked.

"It does. However, they are only used for communication purposes. The plan is to establish nine Small

Warrior Temples, each with its own color and insignia. This will not only promote the Temple but also help strengthen its presence on Insulaii. The standards for entering the Small Temples will be lower, allowing for the recruitment of a large number of cultivators."

"Looking for diamonds in the rough, are you?"

"So to speak. Establishing new branches will allow more efficient management of all three regions. We have already chosen several energy-rich locations. One of them is in the mountain valley, where the Forbidden City was located. Another will be placed in the Order of the First Elements' former capital. Shan Wu's younger brother has already agreed to join the future Purple Temple. Unfortunately, restoring the Order is impossible as it doesn't have enough strong Masters and resources left. The third branch would be located on Monsoon Island, in the destroyed Land of Wind."

"And the other six?"

"We are still surveying the area for suitable locations. The arrays will operate according to a strict schedule. Any travel from or to Insulaii will be controlled by members of the Temple. It goes without saying that using them won't be free. However, I am ready to make certain concessions and even install individual arches inside the branches if you agree to establish close trade relations with the Eternal Path Temple."

Previously, people could move freely between worlds. Now they wouldn't only have to obey the Temple, but also pay for the right to pass through the barrier. The unification of almost the entire planet under the control of one faction was perhaps the worst news for the cultivators from other planets.

New conditions were rather unpleasant, but the

representatives didn't have a choice. After spending almost an hour discussing various issues on this topic, they came to an agreement.

"In that case, we can end the meeting here," Kai announced, standing up. "Once communication with other worlds has been restored, I hope I will finally be able to talk with your leaders."

The representatives bowed respectfully to Kai and exited the hall one by one. Only Derek stayed in his seat, as Kai had requested.

"Maron, Laya." Kai suddenly turned to two who had not yet left the hall. "Don't go too far. I'd like to talk to you a little later."

Maron Akl, the patriarch of the Cursed Sword Sect, almost turned pale at the request, and Laya tensed up.

"As you wish," they replied in unison and exited the hall, leaving Derek and Kai to discuss the conditions under which the Everstein family would operate. Afterward, Kai informed him about Diana's fate. He told Derek how she attacked him on the Contender's Road and died at the hands of Lilith, turning out to be a puppet. He confirmed his story with a Rune of Truth, leaving no room for doubt.

Derek staggered out of the hall shaken by the information he had just received. Kai didn't enjoy being the one to tell him all this, but he had no choice. Hiding the truth could lead to an unnecessary conflict.

Kai didn't forget the message for a second.

Beware of the people who have the five-eyed tattoo...

***

Shortly after Derek left, Laya and Maron returned to the hall at Kai's request.

"You wished to talk to us?"

"I won't beat around the bush," he said. "I want to arrange a meeting with the de facto ruler of the Mountain Sect Alliance, the O'Crime family, and ask the Order of Purity to mediate these negotiations."

Chapter 19
THE ETERNAL PATH EMPIRE

"What happened? Where am I?" he asked weakly upon awakening. "A... collar? Brother? What's happening?"

Rising, he tried to destroy the collar, but nothing happened.

"You don't remember?" his brother asked, standing at the door.

But the man ignored his brother's response.

"Get this thing off me right now! How dare you shackle me?!"

Furious, he tried to jump out of the bed only to fall to the floor, overwhelmed by a wave of unbearable pain that washed over his body. Noticing his bandaged arms and chest along with small cracks all over his *Astral Body*, he finally remembered the fight with his brother. And, consequentially, his defeat.

"And how should I understand this?" he asked gloomily, now a little calmer. "Are you going to hold me here like some kind of slave? Will you keep this collar on me forever?"

"No. Only until I come back. Forgive me, but I have no choice. I won't let you get in my way," his brother said firmly.

"So you decided to betray us? To backstab your own clan? To bow before the freak that spilled our blood?! What for?!"

"How can you be so stupid?" Finally, the mask of detachment fell off. "I'm doing this *for* the clan! For us! You've said it yourself — we have lost too much. Do you want to lose the others, too? There are so few of us left... Look at you and me! If our neighbors weren't in the same position, they would have torn us apart like a pack of hungry wolves! There's nothing else we can do!"

"And your solution is to become his slave? Gods know what he can demand from you! Have you thought about it? No? Think about the elderly! Think about our young! What kind of future will you sentence them to? Aren't you afraid that your decision will destroy our clan instead?! That you will undo everything that our ancestors have done?!"

"I won't agree to just anything. If need be, I'll be the first to draw my sword. But we are better off trying to negotiate and somehow save the clan than perishing."

"Don't be ridiculous! Do you really believe the rumors? He can't be that strong. Listen. It's not too late to join the resistance. These are our lands. Our arrays. Our cities. We hold far greater advantage here than there. If we unite, he won't be able to harm us!"

"We have lost almost all combat-capable cultivators."

"So has Avlaim!"

"We don't have any elite fighters. To speak nothing of

Masters above *Five Stars*."

"So what? We can still fight. Why don't you believe me?!"

"I'm used to trusting my instincts."

"Your instincts!" he snorted, returning to the bed. "And you're willing to put everything on the line just because of some rumors?"

"I've already made up my mind," his brother answered, turning to the door. "You have tried to challenge my decision, but I came out stronger."

"You can't make these decisions alone! You can't decide for the whole clan!"

"I can! You may be the oldest, but I am the patriarch. The elders are gone. I'm the one who decides everything now."

"You will destroy us! Your actions will doom us all! Do you hear me?! All of us!"

His brother just silently left the room.

"Don't let him out of the palace until I return," he told the guards.

"Understood."

***

Ravaged lands, lingering pockets of wild energy threatening to soon become anomalies, barren earth, numerous ruins, mountains of corpses... The deeper he went into Avlaim, the more horrors he witnessed and the more his doubts grew.

Maybe my brother was right after all? What if the rumors are nothing more than blatant lies? But how did all our men die then? A powerful artifact? Help from the allies? Knolak's intervention? He rubbed his forehead. *And where did the entire Han Nam Clan go? Licking their wounds after their defeat, perhaps? What happened to their leader? Do they even have one? Is it worth turning around now? Nogatta is still far away. No one will notice if a small ship suddenly changed its course... No! No, no, no. I've made my decision. I'll trust my instincts.*

The young lord didn't want to admit it to himself, but he was afraid. Not of the upcoming meeting, but of the future. Of the unknown that lay ahead. Alas, there was nothing he could do about it.

The next day, he arrived at Nogatta. Before the ship had even moored, an unfamiliar figure appeared on its deck out of nowhere, wearing purple robes and a white mask with the number eighteen painted on it.

"Welcome to Avlaim. If I understand correctly, this vessel belongs to the Hyōgoku Clan?"

Taken by surprise, the ship's crew revealed their weapons and unleashed their power. Despite the young master's attempt at stopping them, several people rushed at the figure, but the stranger didn't even dodge or defend himself. The steel harmlessly bounced off him and their techniques dissipated before even reaching him.

As the startled crew slowly retreated, the masked man nonchalantly brushed off the dust from his shoulder and straightened his sleeves.

Complete Submission? the young master guessed, clenching his fists. *How strong is his* Will *if he stopped three Masters of Two Stars so easily?*

"I apologize. The journey has been long and my men are tired," he said, stepping forward. "We didn't expect anyone. Yes, this vessel belongs to the Hyōgoku Clan. I am its patriarch."

"Very well." Eighteen nodded. "I will take you to see my master. Let the ship stay here. They won't allow it into the port."

Before the stunned crew had time to realize what happened, Eighteen moved to their patriarch and put his hand on his shoulder. A moment later, both of them were gone.

"We are in the island's capital," Eighteen said as they materialized inside a huge room. He then nodded toward the corridor. "That way, if you would be so kind."

The young master turned around to ask his guide a couple of things but Eighteen had already disappeared. Confused, he hung around for a while before proceeding in the indicated direction. The corridor led him to a large room, where many leaders of the Tyr and Land factions had already gathered.

He was immediately noticed by his acquaintances, who also recently became the leaders of their sects and clans. Distracted by his thoughts, he wasn't in a hurry to start a conversation with anyone. Doubts about the correctness of his decision still weighed heavily on his soul.

After a couple hours of waiting, the door on the opposite side of the room opened to let in two people: a man and a woman. Both radiated great power.

"You may enter," said Lilith. By now, she had fully recovered.

"Unless you're afraid," Shaw sneered.

The guests uncertainly stepped forward.

The adjacent hall was much more spacious and majestic, but the guests didn't pay the décor almost any attention, their gazes fixated on the man sitting on the throne.

Is that Kaiser? The young master frowned. *He seems so... ordinary, but at the same time, there is something frightening about him. I can't feel his aura or his level.*

"I'm glad to see you all." The man smiled once everyone was settled. "I won't take up too much of your time. As you may have guessed, I am Kaiser, the leader of the Eternal Path Temple and the ruler of Avlaim. My conditions are simple. As members of the losing party, you will have to pay an indemnity within three months. The amount will depend on the size of your faction and its participation in the war. We went ahead and did the math. You can see it on the list over there."

Hyōgoku Clan: 86,000,000 Runes

Seeing the figure, the young master froze and turned pale. His clan was an independent faction, not a petty vassal, but still relatively small. A hundred million Runes was a considerable amount in general, let alone after a costly war.

That's almost two-thirds of what's left in the treasury, he thought. *We'll be on the verge of bankruptcy. Moreover, we don't have so many Runes in their pure form. I'll have to sell a lot of artifacts, rare resources, and maybe even some heirlooms... Not to mention that I'll have to lay off half of the staff...*

Looking around, he saw that the other guests were in a similar state. Another look at the table showed that almost everyone present would have to pay exorbitant amounts to Kaiser. Some major factions, such as the Twin Dragons, were billions of Runes in debt.

"From now on, Tyr and Land belong to me. Or rather, to the newly formed Eternal Path Empire. With this change, you will forfeit all rights to any territories you called your own, save for family homes. However, you will have the right to buy some of it back. You will also be required to pay taxes and obey the laws of the empire. As soon as you sign the necessary contracts by which you will become my imperial subjects, you can consider yourselves semi-autonomous organizations."

The more Kai spoke, the angrier and more surprised his guests became. They had been ready to accept the gigantic debts, but the loss of sovereignty and their lands was the straw that broke the camel's back.

"We will not give up our territories!" someone shouted.

"Neither will we!"

"I second that! You are asking for too much!"

"Do you hear yourself?!"

"This is tyranny!"

"We refuse!"

"Your conditions are outrageous and absurd!"

"Conditions?" Kai chuckled. The pressure of his *Will* forced everyone to be silent. "You don't understand... This is an ultimatum."

Those who had expressed their dissent suddenly fell to their knees, wheezing and trembling. Under the horrified gazes of the other guests, they tried to resist the invisible force. But to no avail. After a few seconds of torment, their bodies crumpled, staining the floor crimson.

"Those who don't agree will be eliminated," Kai continued, unperturbed. "I will then extend my offer to your successors. If they refuse, I will continue to kill until someone agrees. Or until your factions are no more."

"YOU BASTARD!" one of the guests shouted and rushed at him in desperation, but his body fell apart into a myriad of bloody pieces without making it even halfway to the throne.

A deathly silence hung in the hall. No one dared to even move.

"No one? No? Wonderful. In that case, before you're handed the scrolls, allow me to show you what happened to those who dared to oppose me."

A projection emerged from the table and expanded, occupying half of the hall. It flickered for a moment and then settled to show what could only be described as the aftermath of ruthless carnage.

The young master of the Hyōgoku Clan clenched his fists, swallowed hard, and smiled nervously.

There were no more doubts. His intuition hadn't failed him. His brother was wrong.

But what's with Kaiser's Astral Body? he wondered as he accepted the scroll.

***

"What do you think?" Kai asked, turning away from the mirror.

"Are those my grandma's robes?" Shacks squinted.

"Wonderful," Lily added.

"Mhm." Malvur and An'na nodded.

"That's a great outfit, big brother," Ailenx said.

"And expensive," Guts mumbled.

"I'm still way more handsome," Shaw interjected.

Lilith approached Kai, adjusted the robes in a couple of places, and nodded.

"Now it's perfect."

"No pressure, but our reputation depends on this," Nyako told him.

"No pressure at all." Kai smiled in response and disappeared, teleporting into the air above the central square where tens of thousands of people had gathered, having arrived from different parts of Avlaim.

As soon as he appeared, the audience exploded with cheers and praises. By now, they all knew that they had him to thank for the victory in the war.

Kai raised his hand in greeting, signaling to the crowd to quiet down.

"We won," he said curtly, prompting the audience to erupt into cheers again. "The price we paid for victory was great, but it wasn't in vain. You have done the impossible, having stood against two Unions on your own long enough for me to return to Insulaii. Your courage, heroism, and perseverance will not be forgotten. Today is a day of mourning, but at the same time, a day of celebration. Today is the day when all three regions will finally be united into the Eternal Path Empire! Today marks the beginning of a new era in Insulaii's history! There will be no more squabbles, conflicts, or factional wars."

Kai's vassals were given the right to retain more land than just their family homes, the cost of buying out their private property was much lower, they could take a loan for restoration, and they had access to exclusive goods and trade agreements with the Temple. Most importantly, they didn't have to accept an ultimatum. In case they didn't want to join the empire, they had the right to leave its lands. Kai wouldn't threaten to take away their lands, but he wouldn't be obliged to protect them either. Only the Rising Star Sect, which still held part of Nogatta by the time Kai arrived, had the right to object. But Lilith didn't protest. She and her sect were fine as they were.

"So let's celebrate our victory! Let's celebrate the founding of an empire! Welcome to the Eternal City! Welcome to your new home, the Eternal Path Empire!"

With that, Kai finished his speech. The square fell silent for a moment before being filled with noise once again.

"GLORY TO THE EMPIRE!"

"I won't hold you any longer. Drink and merry to your heart's content."

As Kai disappeared, various dishes and drinks were brought to the square. Music filled the air, signaling the beginning of the festivities.

***

While the people were celebrating in the city, Kai, together with the Temple's highest officials and representatives of the largest factions of Avlaim, celebrated in the banquet hall.

Standing in one of the corners, three men were discussing something but their conversation suddenly ended.

"Your Imperial Majesty." Ryu bowed.

Next to him stood Six and Anatos. The two of them had aided the war from the Ark, helping Ulu prepare the island for defense.

"The Temple stands above the empire." Kai raised his glass. "For you, I'm not the emperor, but the master mentor."

"Of course." Ryu nodded. "Thank you again for healing Oberon."

"You have nothing to thank me for. I wouldn't leave one of our own hanging."

Having exchanged a couple of short words with Six and Anatos, Kai asked the two to leave him and Ryu alone.

"At once, sir," they said, bowed, and left.

"I was very surprised when I saw your name in the finals on the Road. I read your report. You did great. I remember you demonstrating that Light technique before. To be honest, I thought that it was impossible to pull off such a transformation with this element. I haven't even congratulated you on your victory yet, have I? So much has happened since then." Kai smiled. "I would like you to become my personal student. Granted, there is only one level of difference between us, but I believe that I can teach you a lot."

The offer was shocking, but Ryu kept a calm face. Once upon a time, he wouldn't have been able to contain his emotions, but now, he was cold as ice. The loss of his best friend and girlfriend hit him hard.

"It would be an honor, sir," Ryu replied, trying to smile. "But am I good enough for that? There are more suitable candidates in the Temple, like Renata Vin'Thar. She is capable of reaching greater heights than me. I would hate to disappoint you."

"Who is good enough and who isn't is up to me," Kai replied sternly. "I didn't choose you only because of your strength. Power is undoubtedly important, but one's personality is no less valuable." He poked Ryu's chest with his finger, surprising him. "Perseverance, willpower, stubbornness, and luck play significant roles, too. You still have a lot to learn. The road ahead is long. You know, you remind me of myself when I was younger. The circumstances I had found myself in were... not the best, to put it mildly. I could only dream of things I have today," Kai said with a faint smile, remembering his first years in Saha. "I fought tooth and nail for everything I have today. So, what do you say? Would you like to become my personal student?"

Dumbfounded, Ryu couldn't say anything for several seconds.

"Y-Yes! Yes, sir!" he almost shouted once he snapped out of it.

"Wonderful." Kai smiled, putting a hand on his shoulder. "We will work on your techniques, as well as your strengths and weaknesses. But that's something to think about later. For now, enjoy the party."

"I-I will."

Kai had turned around to leave when Ryu spoke again.

"Sir... Can... Can I ask you something?"

"Yes?" Kai asked, looking over his shoulder.

"I would like to join the retaliatory squad."

"I see... Very well. But be warned that the path of vengeance can easily lead you into the abyss. Keep your wits about you."

"Thank you, sir." Ryu bowed. "I'll keep that in mind."

Abyss or not, this is bigger than petty vengeance.

***

"So? How was it?" Kai asked as he entered a small room. From here, he could observe the audience and the guests.

"Pretty bold move with the *Astral Body*," Sirius said.

"They bought it. The seed of doubt has been sown. Now we have something to work with."

"Do we?"

"As per your request, I disguised myself and mingled. Here is a list of unreliable parties and those who should be watched more closely for the time being." Sirius offered him two sealed scrolls.

"Good." Kai took both scrolls. "What's next?"

"Everything is there. All I need is your permission."

"Patience, Sirius," Kai said as he left the room. "Patience."

***

"So, do we have a deal?" a man asked with a smile as he rose from his chair.

The First Master of the Order of Purity, Kagan Yen Talos, father of Illarion and Deus's elder brother, turned out to be a very simple and pleasant man. For the leader of perhaps the strongest faction of the Trial Worlds, this was an extremely unusual behavior, but to some extent, quite effective. Even Kai couldn't remain indifferent next to him, so the two came to an understanding relatively quickly.

Kai got up to answer Kagan's firm handshake.

"We do."

"Deus will draw up the contract." Kagan nodded at his younger brother, thus ending the negotiations that had lasted for over two days.

A little over a month had passed since the end of the war. The clones had not yet completed a transfer array compatible with the planetary barrier, so Kai had to create a new portal to travel to Bellum.

First of all, he took up debt collection. Illarion's two months had passed and it was time for him to pay what he owed: two billion in Runes and the remaining five in the form of six *Passes*. He was going to give them to Shacks, Ivsim, Malvur, Ailenx, Lily, and Acilla so that they could stay on Insulaii.

Along the way, he discussed trade relations with the Order of Purity. He already had an exclusive contract with the Eversteins, but it only concerned the distribution of goods. It didn't forbid selling the product to specific factions, provided that they didn't resell it, or buying goods from other organizations. The only thing he couldn't do was sell the *Exaltation Elixir* to anyone other than the Eversteins.

The second thing was the upcoming negotiations with the Manticores, who agreed to meet with him on neutral territory in the Order of Purity.

"The Manticores won't be here in another couple of hours. How about some tea while we wait? I have quite the collection."

"Tea?" The mention of the beverage reminded him of Jongo and his love for herbs. How far those days seemed now... "I would love to."

"Wonderful!"

The next two hours went by pretty quickly. Kai was so impressed by Kagan's tea collection that he even bought a few rare varieties.

After a while, the O'Crimes arrived. Their diplomatic mission was led by Rosen's brothers — Varimas, Luberg, and Gotrid, in the company of ten elite guards and family servants.

Having introduced both parties to each other, Kagan let

Kai speak first.

"Since we are unlikely to come to an understanding, I won't even try to resolve the conflict. However, I want to propose a two-year-long truce."

"And why do you think that we need it?" Varimas inquired.

"If you agree, I'll let you bury your dead and heal Tina. I will also return Mia's *Manticore Heart*."

The trio exchanged glances.

"Will you?" Varimas seemed doubtful.

"Absolutely."

"What about Oi's *Heart* and her body?"

"Unfortunately, her body couldn't be recovered. As for her *Heart*, Mia consumed it to gain power. You can check this once you get her *Heart*."

Varimas frowned. He was silent for several long minutes, buried deep in thought.

"One year plus all the artifacts," he proposed.

Kai clenched his fists and frowned. Nevertheless, he agreed.

"Very well. With one exception."

"Yes?"

"The artifact that created the barrier over Insulaii will stay with me."

"No. Either you return everything, or you can forget about the truce."

"Is it that valuable to you? More valuable than their bodies and the *Heart*?"

"We'll get them back one way or another," Luberg grumbled from the side.

Varimas glared at his younger brother.

"I doubt it." Kai shook his head. "Even if you do manage, they will have been used up by then. I don't plan on keeping them for long."

"The artifact," Varimas reminded.

"What if I make up for it?"

"How much?"

"Two billion runes."

"Not enough."

"Five."

"Eight."

"Eight?" Kai pursed his lips. "Very well. Eight."

After that, they discussed possible trade relations. Here, Kai eventually also had to give up profits.

A day later, the negotiations ended. Kai got the desired truce and returned the artifacts and the O'Crimes' bodies.

"He's afraid of us." Luberg smiled. "Did you see how hesitant he was the entire time? He kept playing hard to get, but he conceded in the end."

"It could all be a trick," Varimas said, frowning.

"Are you kidding? Did you notice how weak his *Astral Body* is? Or do you think that's a trick, too? I think he's trying to buy himself some time, fearing revenge... I don't understand how he is still alive with such wounds. Even a *Limitless* wouldn't be able to help him now! I checked it several times during the meeting. Even his soul is damaged."

"I am aware. However, it's all very strange. Don't forget that we are dealing with a reborn deity. This could all be a clever trap."

"Deity my left foot. He's a clown. Do you think he's not looking for revenge? Should we wait to see if he'll try to kill us, huh? What's the point of all this if he's just pulling our leg?"

"You are probably right. Still, we must be careful," Varimas concluded. "We can use an oath-breaking artifact. We won't give him a year. We'll attack much, much sooner."

While the O'Crimes discussed their future plans, Kai returned to Insulaii. Stopping shortly at the Ark, he went deeper into the island's territory.

An old friend was waiting for him there.

It was time to see Green.

Chapter 20
THE WILL

Cutting through the Avlaim skies, Kai couldn't stop thinking about the recent events. Numerous islands and inland seas rushed past him as he replayed everything in his head.

He was behind everything all this time. He turned Kyle against me so that he could save me at the last minute. Kyle will come back for the remaining particles of the Trophy, *I have no doubts about it. I need to do something, fast. Now that Magnus is out of the picture, I can only turn to Green to train me for my next encounter with Kyle,* he thought, looking at the settlements flickering below. *Green knew that I would get my memory back. That was why he said I might not want to contact him. He knew that I would remember Greenrow taking Julie away and trying to kidnap Rune'Tan. He may be a different person now, but I can't just forget everything, can I?* He sighed. *I don't really have a choice, do I? If I hadn't run into Kyle, I probably would have turned down the offer and If I didn't know that there was a* Trophy *owner, I would have sent Green to hell... Though, without his help, I wouldn't have been able to save Acilla so soon. Even with the* Trophy, *infiltrating the House of Blood was risky. Rihanna is no less dangerous than the Puppeteer.*

Having spotted the island he needed near the Great Belt — a giant anomaly separating the north and south of Avlaim — Kai began to slow down and descend.

But why is Green doing this? Why would he help me take the Trophy? *Just what is he planning?*

After landing in the center of the small village below, Kai went to the largest building. He had learned about this place only after returning to Insulaii, when Lilith reported about Void's visit to Nogatta. The powerful Asur, the Second Prince of Abyss, came at the beginning of the war and handed the letter. Disclosed in it were a bunch of coordinates.

"Hey! Who are you?!" a boy of about eight years shouted. The house behind him was strikingly different from the ones surrounding it, sticking out like a sore thumb.

"Get out of here before Uncle Green shows up and turns you into dust!" the boy added.

Kai smiled, slowing down a little.

"Turn me into dust?"

"I saw him do it with my own eyes! There was a whole ship of very strong pirates near the shore! True Masters who destroyed mountains with one stroke! They were causing us a lot of trouble, but then Uncle Green showed up and they crumbled into dust along with their ship! So get out of here! Strangers have no place here!"

"I'm not a stranger," Kai said, approaching the gate and staring at the boy who had retreated further away. "Isn't that right, Green?"

"That's right," Green replied as he stepped out on the threshold.

Startled by his sudden appearance, the boy turned

around.

"Is he your friend, Uncle Green?"

"He is. One of my oldest friends, actually." He looked down at the boy. "And why are you here? I thought I had given you a task."

"I've already finished it!" he reported proudly and held out a *Spatial Ring*. "I've covered the whole area! Everything I found is in the *Ring*. Can I go play now?"

Checking its contents, Green nodded in satisfaction.

"Wonderful."

A moment later, the smiling boy disappeared.

"I don't remember us being friends. Or are you talking about our brief acquaintance in the Fallen Star Sect?" Kai asked coldly. "And what did you do with the boy?"

"I see you've remembered everything." Green smiled. "Don't worry, I've done him no harm. He's in my pocket dimension, connected to the Higher Simulation, where he can play a game I invented for him. That is his reward."

"Reward for what?"

"A job well done. At first glance, there is nothing special about this island, but it's, in fact, a real treasure trove. I have never seen such flora and fauna before. The plants have some semblance of intelligence, and they are all connected through a vast neural network. The same goes for animals. They have a special organ that allows them to connect to the island's network. It's marvelous. And yet, a Guardian Spirit has never appeared in this place. I am trying to find out why by examining samples that the children of this village kindly help me collect. Unlike toward adults, the island is friendly to them."

"I didn't think you were interested in academic stuff."

"I have always been more of a scientist than anything else."

"Really?" Kai raised his eyebrow in surprise. "You certainly don't leave such an impression…"

"I like to keep my enemies on their toes." Green smiled. "I suppose you decided to accept my offer?"

"I gave it some thought."

"Let's talk inside, shall we?"

Opening the door, Green invited Kai into the house and led him to a large office. Inside, four more people were waiting for them.

"You already know Void." Green nodded at the Asur. "That's Abaddon. And those are—"

"Chag and Qi," Kai interrupted Green and froze in the hallway.

"Hi," Chag waved at him, momentarily taking his eyes off his game of cards with Void.

"Hello," Qi greeted politely but listlessly.

"Do they work for you?"

"They've started recently," Green confirmed. "Chag placed you in the House of Blood Apostle's body, and Qi was a spy in the Collisium."

"How interesting… And what about before that? Merais Kwaton — was that you back then in the Rising Star, Chag?" Kai guessed, remembering the strange Elder in Lilith's sect. "What are you even doing in the Trial Worlds? And where is your friend Izao? I still have questions for him from my time on Belteise."

"Merais who? Never heard of him," Chag replied with a grin. "I've only arrived here recently. As for Izao... We parted ways a long time ago. I'd like to see him, though. I have a couple of questions for him, too."

Realizing that Chag wouldn't tell him the truth, Kai decided to switch the topic for now. After all, this wasn't what he had come here for.

Sitting down at his desk filled with various research instruments and samples, Green nodded to an empty chair.

"Have a seat."

Glancing at Chag and Void playing cards, at Qi reading some scroll, and at Abaddon, who, like a statue, watched him attentively from the corner, Kai slowly took a seat. For a few seconds, he and Green stared at each other in silence, until he finally gave in and revealed the reason behind his visit.

"You said that you would help me learn the *Will* skills from the *Tablets*."

"I did." Green nodded. "Interested?"

"Actually, I would like to ask you for one more thing."

"I'm listening."

"I need help healing a friend. Something strange happened to her soul, causing her to fall into a deep sleep."

Even after all this time, the *Soul Masters* Kai found were powerless, and the *Complex's* arrays couldn't help Acilla in any way. Moreover, no one could figure out the cause of her illness.

"Is that all?"

"No." Kai sighed, gathering his strength. "Can you tell me the secret of the eight-volume techniques and how to become a *Master of Eight Stars*?"

"What makes you think that I know that?"

"I see no other way to explain your power. Void must also be one such *Master*, even if his title suggests otherwise. I studied his encounter with the Formless. The *Will* he demonstrated then was beyond the reach of a *Master of Seven Great Stars*.

"Wasn't your strength when you destroyed the Unions' armies beyond the limits of what was possible?" Green smiled. "I felt echoes of your power all the way here."

"Fair enough… So, can you help me?"

"Perhaps."

"Yes or no, Green?"

"Even if I reveal this knowledge to you, it won't give you anything. Until you master your *Will*, you won't be able to use them. I could teach you how to reach perfect mastery, but would you agree to it?"

"Perfect mastery? Of willpower?" Kai frowned. "Neither Kyle nor Void have that. They used the *Tablets*."

"Correct. But you are a human, not an Asur or a lover of the dark arts. Unless…?"

"No. No dark arts."

"In this case, perfect mastery of willpower is the only way." Green spread his arms. "What do you say?"

Taking a deep breath, Kai looked into his eyes.

"I agree."

"Wonderful. Now, it goes without saying that I will not do this for free."

"Name your price."

"You will let us join the Eternal Path Temple."

Kai was genuinely surprised by Green's response. And to a lesser extent, alarmed.

"Why?"

"Does it matter? Now, I'm not asking you to make us Hierarchs. Letting us be your humble followers will be enough. We don't need any privileges or even access to the Ark. Just enlist us and give us the tattoos. Think of us as temporary members."

"Temporary?"

"Yes. I think twenty years is enough. After that, you can either let us stay or expel us."

"And what's the catch?"

"There's no catch."

"Did I hear you right? In exchange for all that, the only thing you want is to join the Temple? Don't you find that suspicious?"

"There is no guarantee that I will be able to help your friend. There is also no guarantee that you will manage to master your willpower or comprehend the techniques. Asking for more would be greedy."

Grimacing, Kai gave it a thought.

"Why are you doing this? Why would you even help me? You sent Kyle after me so that you could save the day at the last moment. And you didn't even try to hide it. You orchestrated everything so that now I have no choice but to turn to you for help. Why would you offer to make me stronger? So I can take the *Trophy* from Kyle? What's next? What game are you playing? What are you hoping to achieve?"

"I don't see how any of that concerns you," Green replied calmly.

"Then how do I know I can trust you?"

"You don't. But you can choose to."

Kai laughed bitterly.

Choose... I hadn't been able to choose from the very beginning.

"Fine. I will accept you into the Temple, but only after you fulfill your part of the deal."

***

"I see..." Green muttered to himself as he opened his eyes and took a step back from the sleeping vampiress. The examination lasted a whole day, but he got all the answers he needed.

"What's wrong with her?" Kai asked.

"Have you ever wondered why she is so weak?"

"Weak? Acilla?"

"Think. A child of a deity, but still a *Master of Seven Average Stars*. You're not even at the *Divine Stage* yet, but you've already surpassed her."

Kai frowned.

In Nikrim, she seemed invincible, but since then I've met stronger cultivators. Illarion and Zarifa, Kyle, Rosen... Next to them, Acilla's talent seems minuscule. But even if her parents were very weak deities, she should be stronger than this...

"Why?"

"Usually, the child absorbs energy while in the womb, but she seems to have received only a part of her parents' power. The rest was sealed inside her. Most likely by her mother."

"But why?"

"The only plausible explanation lies in the structural changes within Acilla's soul."

"Changes?" Kai tensed. "What changes?"

"Look for yourself," Green said and handed him an eyepiece.

Putting it on, Kai saw the world in a completely different light. Almost everything around him lost its color, save for the halos around Acilla's and Green's bodies, as well as the small purple spheres shining inside them. These were their *Astral Bodies* and souls, with minor details highlighted by the artifact.

"Take a good look at her *Shell*," Green instructed. "Ideally, all souls should be the same at birth, but after that, they are shaped by their environment. The more energy there is in one's surroundings, the higher the chance that a certain amount will flow into the *Shell*, strengthening it. The proximity of the three layers to each other can tell a lot about its development. The smaller the distance between them, the more actively they interact and the more talented the warrior will be. This is one of the main reasons why, on worlds with higher energy density, the average talent of the population is higher than that of people from more distant worlds."

As Green talked, Kai continued to peer into Acilla's soul, trying to figure out what was happening to her. Unlike his energy vision, Green's artifact made it possible to see much more and in greater detail.

"Divine Children can't have an elemental layer, since the mother's divine essence protects the child from the elements penetrating its soul. But nothing prevents them from strengthening the child's *Shell* with their power. Because of this, the children of *Star Emperors* are comparable to Heavenly Miracles. But when it comes to children of more powerful deities like the *Limitless*, then..."

"They don't have layers," Kai finally realized.

"Exactly. Their *Shells* don't consist of layers. They are solid, and the functions of the layers are evenly distributed along the entire surface. Such a close structure endows them with great power, surpassing the Heavenly Miracles. This is how she should have been born if hers hadn't been sealed. Her soul was whole but defective. Like an unfinished sculpture."

"And now the sealed power is seeping out?" Kai asked as he removed the eyepiece and turned to Green.

"It seems so. Her divine powers awoke when she found herself in mortal peril and now her soul is struggling to remain whole. It's a lot to take in."

"But why was it all sealed up?"

"I don't know." Green shrugged. "But I assume that this was her mother's attempt at protecting her. There are only about a thousand *Limitless* in the Ecumene, so their children are very important. And very valuable. Especially considering that they are most likely to become *Higher Ones* and claim the Heavenly Throne. It goes without saying that every *Limitless* has plenty of enemies."

"I see... How long until her powers are unsealed?"

"Usually, anywhere from a day up to a week."

"What?" Kai grimaced. "So why...?"

"Why hasn't she woken up yet? My best guess is that someone intervened, trying to influence her soul. Whatever they did, it interrupted the process, putting her in a coma."

"Regis! That bastard!" Kai hissed, clenching his fists. "Can this be fixed?"

"I can restart the process, but the chance of her waking up after that is low."

"Do what you need to do," Kai said without missing a heartbeat. "Whatever it takes."

***

The operation took two days, and all they could do was wait. If Acilla didn't wake up within a year, she most likely never would. In such case, only a *Higher One* could help her, but Kai didn't even know where to start looking for one. Even if he reached this stage someday, Acilla would be beyond saving by then. Her soul would disintegrate as the connection between it and the *Spark* would deteriorate much faster than expected.

"Here." Green stopped not far from a rocky island hidden in the midst of a nightmarish storm. The heavens raged above them, bringing down thousands of lightning bolts. "It will do just fine."

Without hesitation, Kai went down after him into the very center of the Great Sea Belt. It was an ancient anomaly where only madmen usually ventured. Therefore, it was the perfect place for Green to train Kai.

"And now what?"

"First, some theory."

"You sure know how to pick a place for a lecture."

"Time is of the essence. Now. Let's start with the basics. To control your *Will*, you must first understand what it is." Green folded his arms behind his back.

"It's the combined power of the mind and the *Spark*, one that allows you to influence reality."

"Close, but not exactly. I'm talking about a more precise definition. You know what the gravitational field is? Yes? Good. Willpower is like that, too. A field created by a special vibration of the strings. The more of them there are and the more they fluctuate, the stronger the *Will* is."

"Strings?" Kai frowned. "What are you talking about?"

Green chuckled.

"Strings are the basic elements of all things. Everything in the universe is made up of these tiny threads. You are made of cells, cells are made of molecules, molecules are made of atoms, atoms are made of electrons, neutrons, and protons, and the last two are consist of even more fundamental particles, but at the deepest level, it's all made of strings. They weave through everything. And they fluctuate all the time. This fluctuation is how the universe moves, it's what we call information. And information determines the nature of a particular matter, phenomenon, process, and so on. Everything that exists is composed of vibrations of countless strings."

"Wait..." Kai rubbed the bridge of his nose. "What about the three levels of reality? Informational, spiritual, and physical?"

"This is how lower deities understand and describe the world around them. Unaware of the bigger picture, they can only stumble around in the dark, like blind kittens. It all comes down to three types of vibrations: rest, visible matter, and invisible matter. By default, all strings have the first type of vibrations. In this form, you know them as energy. Strings usually don't exist in isolation but accumulate and form something like knots. These are energy particles. And the more knots they have, the higher the energy density is. If a very large number of particles gather in one place, they can form matter. Something visible. This is commonly referred to as the physical world. The invisible vibrations form a substance, but it consists of fundamentally different particles that don't interact with ordinary matter and are invisible to the naked eye. *Soul Shells*, *Astral Bodies*, spiritual techniques, and so on. That's the spiritual level of reality. Contrary to popular belief, it doesn't connect the physical and informational levels, but it is a product of string vibrations. Just like ordinary matter."

"But what about the universe? If strings form everything around us, then what forms the laws of physics, development paths, and so on?"

"Strings, of course!" Green was now amused. "Only not microscopic, but gigantic. Basically infinitely long. They coil together tightly, touch every point of the universe. The universe is many, many coils of these hyperstrings folded into each other. One hyperstring creates three-dimensional space, the other describes the interactions of elementary particles, the third regulates the formation of souls and their development, and so on."

"Development... The one the Creator rewrote?"

"The same one. Ordinary strings always interact with hyperstrings. By exchanging vibrations — that is, information — they receive 'instructions.' For example, the hyperstring of gravitational force is communicating to our bodies, telling us that we are standing on the ground, which is just another accumulation of strings that we call the planet Insulaii. This is how the mechanism of the universe works."

"So when spiritual material is saturated with energy, new strings are added to the already existing ones?"

"Yes. Over time, they copy the vibration of the main strings and amplify it. I see you have many questions, but we are short on time. If you want to go into details, there are a few good scientists in this field in the Core and Heavenly Worlds. Do your best and find their works. Then read and try to understand them. Their knowledge will not only satisfy your curiosity, but it will also pay off in the long run. Eventually, you will learn to perceive the strings and their vibrations and sort of understand the structure of the world. It will help if you have a good theoretical basis."

"And when will that be?"

"When you become a God," Green replied matter-of-factly. "Now let's get back to the matter at hand — *Will*. As I said, it's a field created by a specific vibration of strings. You see, inside each string is the core that creates the so-called Will of the Universe. If the matter suddenly acquires a structure that has a mind — the brain or the mental layer of the *Soul Shell* — then the core's oscillation changes accordingly to synchronize with the *Spark*. This is how our *Will* forms, and it consists of two parts: *Spark* and *Reason*. As the name suggests, the source of the first is the *Spark*, while the latter comes from the core inside the strings that form an intelligent object."

"It's like a unique code… Is that how the *System* identifies the dark arts?"

"Correct. If you destroy someone else's 'code' to put it into your own, the *System* will be aware of it. You can extract the *Will* from dead flesh, but the core won't disappear. It will remain whole for a long time. There are probably only two ways to get rid of it. A plant could digest it, after which it becomes neutral, or a Higher One could remove it. Only deities of this level have the strength and skill to do so. But we've gone off topic."

"Let's not waste time then."

"By manipulating this 'field,' you can influence other strings. Simply put, *Will* allows you to pluck the strings, so to say. How you control them depends on your internal power, but the *Will of Reason* is weak. Only upon reaching the peak of the *Soul Stage* does it become capable of influencing its surroundings."

Kai nodded, remembering how he first manifested his *Will* at the Cloud Abode's entrance exam, for which the System awarded him with the *Master's Will* and the *Field of Superiority* — skills that were installed directly into his soul like software.

"Then there is also the *Spark*, which comes with its own *Will*. Usually, it doesn't stand out until it undergoes the preliminary evolution when its power increases. This is the *Will* that controls *Complete Submission* and other '*System*' skills."

"The *Spark* consists of a huge number of strings that fluctuate extremely strongly? Am I getting this right?"

"Correct," Green confirmed. "To some extent, it's similar to your clones' souls. Do you know why they can raise their *Will* to such a level?"

"Their artificial souls can store the additional energy, unlike the real... The additional strings in their souls receive the corresponding 'code' and become the source of the same *Will*?"

"Exactly."

"But why is their *Will* consumed when they use it?"

"It's simple. When we strain the *Will*, the vibrations begin to fade. Rest allows them to recover, and then you can do it all over again. The additional energy in your clones doesn't copy the entire code, but only a part of it, and therefore doesn't recover on its own. To regain it, they have to use the *Will of Reason* on these strings, so that they become the source of the same power yet again."

"Makes sense."

"Unfortunately, the *Will of the Spark* is much more difficult to control. It doesn't have a mind, only a consciousness. The empty inner self. Imagine that you have been deprived of all feelings and the ability to think. That's the *Spark*. Only when it acquires the *Shell's* mental layer does it fully come to life. Without it, it's just a presence with only one desire — to live. That's what makes the *Sparks* leave the World of the Dead in search of a *Shell*."

"Extremely difficult, but not impossible," Kai muttered. "We can already do that with systemic skills and the 'tools' built into the *Shell*. Creating *Force* particles, controlling energy, forming techniques... The *Will of Reason* is too weak to be sufficient for all of this. But other than that, we have nothing."

"You're right." Green smiled. "We can't directly control the *Will of the Spark*, but we can try to do it through that of *Reason*. It remains only to understand how. Which brings us to the main topic and the reason for our arrival."

With that, Green waved his hand. An invisible force spread out in all directions, making Kai stagger. It seemed that something fundamental had changed around them, but he couldn't understand what it was.

"What did you do?"

"I prepared the site for training," Green said. "Usually, to learn perfect mastery of willpower, you need to be as close to divinity as possible. Only Masters with very strong *Wills of Reason* and *Spark* who have spent thousands of years in contemplation are able to learn how to get in touch with the *Spark*. And only those who manage become deities. Fortunately, you have me to help you achieve the same result much faster."

"So all the Gods have perfect mastery of *Will*?"

"Yes. The *Divine Will* can manipulate the strings and influence their vibrations. This is the ability to manage Information. And it's not a systemic ability, but one's own."

"But if energy is also made of strings, then why can't everyone control it with the *Master's Will*?"

"You are finally asking the right questions. I was beginning to think that you would never realize it on your own." Green laughed. "I'm sorry to burst your bubble, but you're not as unique as you think you are. In theory, everyone can control *prana*, but in practice, this is often not the case. Due to the *System's* meddling with the Laws of the Universe, souls are now born with a reduced ability to control energy. They can subdue *ki*, but not *prana*. *Will of the Spark* simply refuses to work with it. *Master's Will*, *Field of Superiority*, and *Complete Submission* can't be used to subdue neutral energy either. There's an issue with the *Will of Reason*, too. The *System* installs its code into each soul, blocking any, even subconscious attempts to subjugate *prana*, as well as any thoughts about it."

"But why?"

"The Heavenly Throne requires many strings to function, for which it directs the universal energy flows to itself through the entire Ecumene. Now imagine if millions of creatures lived on each planet inside these flows, and they could all subdue *prana*. It would be impossible to maintain the flow. To ensure its survival, the Throne took this ability away from everyone."

Belteise... Kai remembered. *It was destroyed due to serious interference with the universal energy flow.*

"What about the Gods? They can control *prana*."

"Indeed. But there are so few of them that their influence on the streams is negligible."

"And what about you and me?"

"I have my ways, and you have what we call a *Trophy*. It allows you to subdue *prana* despite the ban."

"Do you know what it is?"

"The *Trophy*? Adamantite. The strongest material in the universe. Lilith has a few adamantite dust particles in her sword, but they have lost their former strength. You have saturated adamantite. Its main property is the ability to copy the owner's 'code' and reproduce their *Will*. Simply put, it enhances it. However, your adamantite has certain limitations. Furthermore, it strengthens your *Will* only to subdue *prana*."

"You know so much about this..." Kai couldn't help being amazed. "You say it strengthens the *Will*? Do you have adamantite, too? And where did it come from?"

"Who knows?" Green chuckled. "Either way, it's still too early for you to know. Now let's get back to training."

Kai wanted to bombard him with questions about his existence and many other things, but he knew that he wouldn't get any answers now.

"Before we begin, you must get rid of the soul modification," Green suddenly said.

"What? Why? It let me learn The *Heavenly Mortal Style* from Magnus. I'm not going to get rid of it just like that."

"It might prevent me from helping you. Also, it negatively influences your emotional layer. It causes apathy, and this thing is as dangerous as madness."

Kai froze. Lately, he had been overcome by boredom, which occasionally even affected his actions. Didn't Kyle mention something about his apathy and boredom, too?

"Can it do that?"

"Normally, it shouldn't be able to. However, as far as I can tell, it's incomplete. It's actually a part of another, larger modification. Most likely, its inferiority affects the emotional layer. I doubt that this was done on purpose. No one would install such a flaw into something so precious."

"If I find the full version, can I completely modify my soul?"

"Perhaps." Green shrugged. "As things are now, it will only get in the way. Also, be warned that modifications can't always be undone. I advise you to get rid of it while you still can."

"You don't know anything about the complete version?"

"No."

"Can I replace it with something else?"

"That depends on what you have in mind."

Nodding, Kai spent a few minutes describing the *Heavenly Mortal Style* in detail.

"I see... Very interesting..." Green drawled. "I can only say that if you become a *Master of Eight Stars*, then you won't need it. That's all I have."

"Damn Magnus," Kai muttered under his breath.

Following Green's suggestion, he got rid of the soul modification and lost all the abilities of the *Heavenly Mortal Style*. Immediately upon letting them go, he felt a little weaker. He was too accustomed to relying on their power.

"Great. Now, meditation. First of all, you must shed your mortal coil and see yourself as a *Spark*. Usually, this is done gradually, by disconnecting the body and soul to the point of disintegration. By repeating this process over the years, a Master experiences himself as a *Spark* and feels his desire for life. Only by realizing it, he will be able to develop a way to 'communicate' with the *Spark* in order to use its *Will*. Unfortunately, as this is a long process, I will artificially induce this state for you. Dive into yourself as much as possible, detach yourself from your body, and slowly release yourself from the world."

Looking suspiciously at Green, Kai assumed the lotus position. After a while, his mind cleared. Slowly, thoughts gave way to darkness, until there was nothing left but the void. Within moments, more drastic changes began to occur.

First, Kai let go of the *Forces*, then of his emotions, and then his mind began to dissolve into nothingness. It was like he was erasing himself bit by bit, until there was nothing left of him but the perception of time. But this, too, eventually disappeared. There was absolutely nothing. Just one endless void. Endless hunger.

He lost absolutely everything.

Forever.

Live.

Live. Live.

Live! Live! Live! Live!

LIVE! LIVE! LIVE! LIVE! LIVE! LIVE! LIVE! LIVE! LIVE!

LIVE! LIVE! LIVE! LIVE! LIVE! LIVE! LIVE! LIVE! LIVE! LIVE! LIVE! LIVE! LIVE! LIVE! LIVE! LIVE! LIVE!!! LIVE!!! LIVE!!!

***

"Aaaaaaaaaah!" Kai screamed as he opened his eyes.

He jumped up as if stung but immediately fell back to the ground. Covered in a cold sweat, he was trembling. He couldn't stop screaming. It was a real nightmare. Infinite madness. Unthinkable torture.

All the fights, trials, loss, hardship, sorrow, and pain he had endured were nothing compared to the horror of real death — the death of the *Shell*. Kai was ready to face Kyle, the Puppeteer, and the entire House of Blood at once a hundred times, rather than feel like a *Spark* again even for a moment. What he felt wasn't at all like what he remembered feeling before occupying this body many years ago.

He was falling apart. A little more, and the feeling of being his own *Spark* would have killed him.

"Why?!" he wailed. "Why?!!!"

"Words can't describe it. I couldn't have warned you even if I wanted to. Not that you can mentally prepare for this, anyway," Green replied, observing him from a height.

After a few minutes, Kai finally calmed down. After about half an hour, he regained his senses.

"How long...?" he croaked, continuing to lie on the ground in the fetal position. "How long have I been gone?"

"A little more than a second."

"A second... It felt like an eternity... How can I remember all this...?"

"I haven't completely suppressed the connection between the *Shell* and the *Spark*. Otherwise, there would've been no point to all this."

"And… And now what?"

"Now you will have to repeat this at least a hundred times. Only then will you be able to try to learn how to control the *Will of the Spark*."

Kai shuddered.

"If you endure, you will be strong enough to take the next step. A crash course in hardening your soul, so to speak."

"I'm afraid I might break," Kai admitted.

"I understand. Get some rest now. For now, we will do this once a day. Don't worry, you'll get used to it."

"You… are insane…"

Green just chuckled, lowering himself on the ground next to him.

"When you come back to your senses, take out the *Tablets*. Between sessions, you will study advanced *Will* skills. They will slightly help on your road to perfect mastery."

Chapter 21
THE WILL OF THE SPARK

Stance... Sword... Blade... Sweep... Desire... Will... Obedience... Transfer...

A myriad of images swarmed through Kai's head, trying to assemble a coherent picture.

He opened his eyes.

Squeezing his hand shut, he felt soft sand seeping through his fingers. It was all that was left of the *Tablet*.

As promised, Green helped him, transforming the *Tablets* into artifacts. The information and pictures they held could be utilized not just once, but several times.

The meditation session was finally over. Slowly rising, Kai pulled *Deimos* out of its scabbard and admired the mesmerizing black blade for a moment before holding it out in front of himself. As he concentrated, the visions bestowed by the *Tablet* resurfaced before his eyes.

Touching the blade with his fingertips, he cut into his skin. A couple of crimson drops flowed down the blade, and Kai finally reached the deepest levels of understanding. His eyes opened wide, the seething *Will of Reason* filling his being. Focusing on a nearby boulder, he unleashed the full force of his desire at once.

A small crack appeared in the stone before it broke into two perfect halves.

Attention!

You have reached the minimum required level for learning an advanced Will skill.

You have unlocked the [Advanced Will of Sword].

Holding his breath, Kai slowly exhaled and smiled. He finally did it. He finally mastered all the advanced *Will* skills.

Closing his eyes, Kai looked inward. The installation of the *Advanced Will of Sword* into the *Shell* happened at lightning speed, allowing him to already feel the changes that had taken place.

When Kai opened his eyes, the cut boulder shattered into thousands of small, perfectly even cubes. The power of the mastered skill was amazing. He no longer needed to concentrate as much on the images and control every step. The skill operated on his behalf, drawing strength not only from the *Will of Reason* but also from the *Will of the Spark*.

The cubes rose into the air and merged under the most powerful force of attraction, turning into a huge sword, imbued with the *Advanced Will of Space*.

"Congratulations," Green said, emerging from meditation as well. "Are you ready to double the frequency of diving into your *Spark*?"

Just hearing the suggestion made Kai shudder. Despite the fact that he had already weakened the connection between his soul and body, he still struggled to endure that nightmare without screaming and trembling like a frightened child. More often than not, he found himself unable to move properly. Still, he was making progress. It was small, but it was still progress.

"Not now. In a couple of weeks," he said. "It's too soon."

"My, my, Kai, if I didn't know better, I'd think you were afraid."

***

The second month of training with Green was coming to an end, and Kai felt that he would soon connect with his desire to live, which meant that he would be able to start working on finding a way to communicate with the *Spark*. The moment of mastering the *Will of the Spark* was approaching.

All this time, Kai honed the advanced *Will* skills. He didn't have much free time on his hands, because every interaction with the *Spark* required a long period of recovery, but he spent every spare minute contemplating new elements. Having become *Adored by the Forces*, he was finally able to devote himself to the development of four new ones.

But first, he needed to choose them.

The basis of any cultivator's arsenal consisted of five types of techniques: combat, defense, enhancement, movement, and cover. And while Kai had two powerful combat techniques at his disposal that used six different elements, *Flame of Doom* on the basis of *Sword*, *Yin*, and *Heat Void*, and *Radiant Cold* that consisted of *Radiant Void*, *Yang*, and *Cold Void*, he lacked in movement skills the most. Only a couple of elements were compatible with them, and even then, they worked only in one of two ways: either by influencing the cultivator's body or their surroundings. Because of this, they were called either internal or external movement techniques.

Of all of them, I'm lacking internal movement techniques and reinforcement techniques. I still don't have a suitable element for the former. My bloodline is strong, but it comes with limitations... The Path of Body *is a good option, but I'm not sure if it's a good match for my bloodline. I need something else... Something more specific...*

After spending several days on research, he finally found the most suitable solution.

Path of Soul. *Finding a good teacher won't be easy, but it'll pay off. And while I could manage on my own, it'll be difficult to get far without knowing the* Shell's *structure. Hmm... Combined with the other three elements...* Kai nodded, satisfied. *It'll do just fine.*

***

Clenching his teeth and fists, Kai struggled to breathe.

"How... How much?" he barely squeezed out.

"Eighteen point two seconds," Green said. "Your personal record."

For the next ten minutes, Kai slowly came to his senses.

"I found it... My desire to live. I finally understand my *Spark*."

"Good." Green nodded. "It took you just three months. For now, keep resting. When you recover, we will move on to learning how to control your *Will of the Spark*."

"No need to wait. I'm ready," Kai answered with a wheeze. He had no time to waste.

"As you wish." Green shrugged. "In that case, start with attempts to communicate with the *Spark*. Now that you know and understand what it wants, you can try to find suitable images and use the *Will of Reason* to direct them to it."

"And how long will that take?"

"Nothing will come of it right away, but it will help you understand the essence of the process. Take your time. Experiment. I think three days will be enough for you."

"And then what?"

"Then we'll move on to training." Green chuckled, rising to his feet. "I'll be back soon. Come, Screamer."

Summoning a huge golden hawk, Green jumped on its back.

"Where are you going?"

"I need to get ready for training, too," Green answered, after which the giant bird soared into the air with a loud shriek.

Soon, its massive silhouette turned into a tiny dot on the horizon.

"Finally. I thought he would never leave," Viola muttered to herself.

"You dislike him so much? Odd, seeing how calm you are in his presence."

"He makes the blood river cold. He looks at me like he is about to devour me. For some reason, I feel like I cannot resist his call. His voice... It calls to me."

"You don't want to kill him?"

"Yes. But no. I wish to spill his blood, but I cannot lift my

blade against him."

"There is something odd about him, I admit. I'm surprised that you are afraid of him."

"I cannot explain it. The fear... It comes from somewhere in the depths of my being. I do not understand it. He is not like the others. He is not human. Humans are weak and vulnerable. Humans are born defenseless. But he... He is different. He wears the guise of a human. My soul trembles in his presence. I do not like it. "

Kai fell silent for a moment, pondering. Viola didn't lie or embellish things. If she was this afraid of Green, it meant that he was truly dangerous.

"If you want, I can transfer you to the *Storage* for a while."

"No. I will stay with you."

"As you wish. But if you change your mind, tell me."

"I shall. I wish to think. To explore."

"Just be careful. This is a dangerous anomaly. If anything happens, contact me immediately."

Materializing next to him, Viola looked around and stared somewhere in the direction of the center of the island, where lightning struck most often.

"I will be careful," she replied and rushed in the chosen direction, taking *Deimos* with her. Kai kept *Phobos* with him just in case.

Watching Viola disappear into the distance, he thought about his next steps.

Where should I start? What is the simplest way of communicating with the Spark?

Taking a pebble from the ground, Kai made it float over his palm. For a little while, he observed it spin and then he felt a sudden load on his soul.

A moment later, he turned off the *Field of Superiority* and tried keeping the pebble in the air using only the *Will of Reason*.

And now I need to ask Spark *to direct its* Will *to support this process. But, since it only wants to live, I need to convince it that this is vital for its survival...*

Closing his eyes, Kai began experimenting, going through the options as they crossed his mind. After a while, seeing that he was getting nowhere, he began to use more structured images from the *Tablets* as templates, adjusting them for himself. At first, this also didn't give any results, but after a while, he managed to figure something out. The newest image turned out to be much more successful, evoking a reaction from the previously unshakable *Spark*. Satisfied, he continued to experiment with this image, but he ended up getting nowhere.

Still, his desire to learn how to use the *Will of the Spark* didn't fade. On the contrary, it captured him so much that he stopped trying only when someone interfered.

"I see you're making progress." Green's *Will*-enhanced voice rang out in Kai's head. *"Maybe I should stay away and leave everything to you?"*

Waking up from meditation, Kai stared at Green, displeased with the interruption.

"Has it been three days already?"

"It's been four. You were so immersed in the process that I didn't have the heart to wake you up. Let me guess... You decided to use images from the *Tablets* and managed to get the *Spark* to react to them, albeit minimally. You've been going around in circles since."

"How did you know?"

"That's how it usually goes." Green shrugged. "So, are we going to continue our lesson or do you want to continue trying?"

"I don't have that kind of time."

"Time or patience?"

"As I understand it, Void and Abbadon don't have perfect mastery because of that?"

"Correct. They're both too young. Also, I didn't offer them my help. Although, Void had almost completed the process of getting to know his *Spark*, having spent almost two and a half thousand years on it."

Humbled, Kai could only nod in acknowledgment. If he hadn't had Green to help him, he would have never dared to weaken the connection between his body and soul.

"So... What now?"

"Let's start with something simple." With a wave of his hand, Green used *Earth* to create a stone table and two chairs. "Sit down and put your hand on the table."

Following the instructions, Kai felt a sudden grip on his forearm, accompanied by a flash of pain. A cut appeared on his wrist, and several drops of blood fell onto the table.

Kai's regeneration immediately began to take effect, but the wound didn't heal. Something invisible was actively interfering with his bloodline, blocking it in that exact place.

That's his Will's *doing*, Kai guessed, observing the blood pool on the stone.

"You can restore blood vessels and muscles, but not nerves," Green ordered, loosening his grip. "Don't resist. Weaken your *Will of Reason* as much as you can while concentrating on your *Spark*."

After a moment of hesitation, Kai nodded. He was already in too deep to give up now.

Returning the nod, Green unleashed his *Will* into Kai's body, steering it toward his soul. At first, it rushed like a fast-moving river, but the further it penetrated, the slower it became. Kai tried to ignore it and not interfere, but his *Will* resisted, feeling an alien presence permeating its abode.

Kai didn't understand what Green was planning, but he believed that nothing would come of it. Imagine his surprise when Green's *Will* suddenly accelerated, changing dramatically. In an instance, Kai's resistance dropped, and soon an invisible force reached his *Shell*, and then the *Spark*.

Concentrating on the latter, Kai saw dozens of images pouring into it.

The fingers of his right hand suddenly clenched into a fist.

The alien *Will* left his hand, and the pale Green wearily leaned back in his chair. He barely managed to hide the trembling in his hands.

"What did you do?" Kai gasped, staring in surprise at his unclenched fingers.

"I asked your *Spark* to direct the *Will* into the muscles of the forearm and contract them. Did you remember all the images? Use them and try again. Let's start with the simplest one: submission to one's flesh. Leave the nerves damaged to rule out false positives."

"But... how did you do it? How did you get to the *Spark*

and how did you know which images would work?"

"*Mimicry of Will*. I haven't used it for a long time. You can't even imagine how much strength it takes..." Green sighed, closing his eyes. "I was able to use it because I helped you leave your soul and body, which allowed me to study your *Spark*. When I got to it, I decided on the right images. I'm just very good at everything that concerns the *Will*. You could say that it's my forte."

"Like the *System*?"

"Ha!" Green let out a haughty laugh. "Each *Spark* is unique, but you can find similar aspects in all. The *System* has been connected to countless souls for billions of years. Its database contains vast information and it has access to countless souls and the *Sparks* that it can easily find suitable images for each and put them into the skill introduced into it. You just need to understand that these aren't perfect, which is why any systemic skills will always be inferior to the perfect mastery of *Will*. I, on the other hand, create these images from scratch, relying on the unique structure of the *Spark*, rather than just its general aspects."

"Are you saying you're better at this than the *System*?"

"I am saying that I'm not cutting back on resources helping you master the *Will of the Spark*," Green replied, dodging the question. "Enough talk. You have training to do. I'll rest for a while."

I can't let them notice my weakness. I'm almost at my limit, Green thought, immersing himself in a meditative state.

As soon as the conversation ended, Kai tried to recreate the images. The first try was a failure. As were the second and the third. For a while, he struggled with deciphering the images, but after the tenth try, he finally made some progress.

At first, his fingers only slightly twitched, but the more he practiced, the better the result was. After an hour, he could easily clench his entire fist.

"Good," Green said without opening his eyes. "Now use those images on other parts of your body. Only when you can control the entirety of it will I consider this lesson complete."

This turned out to be much more difficult. The images were suitable only for the hand, and Green didn't seem like he was planning to give him new ones anytime soon, leaving Kai to sort through various options and experiment with what he already had.

By the end of the sixth day, Kai had learned to move solely with the help of *Will*. It wasn't perfect, but he had made strides compared to the first day. Happy with his progress, he spent three more days refining his movement, and then he switched to more intricate mechanics of the flesh.

However, for this, he already needed Green's help.

The next phase of training was the subordination of the soul. Just as the flesh could move, heal, and breathe, the *Shell* could control *prana*, create *Force* particles, control techniques, and so on. Using an array of techniques, Green suppressed various parts of Kai's soul, after which he showed him how to control them through *Will*.

Before they started, Green collected several monsters from all over the anomaly for Kai to practice on.

The most difficult part was saved for last. The use of the *Will* outside one's own body was a complex task. It involved the usual manipulations of space, the impact on someone else's mind and the superficial short-term introduction of vibrations into the string, something called the *Will of the Elements*. All this took Kai twice as long as the previous two lessons combined.

Having spent about two and a half months on everything, Kai mastered the basics of the *Will of the Spark*.

"It will take months and years until these skills of yours reach the *Advanced* level, and then even more time to surpass it," Green told him. "I could teach you more, but I have already fulfilled my part of the bargain. My work here is done." He hesitated for a moment. "But there is one more thing I can give you. I taught you everything that can be done with *System* skills, but *Will's* abilities are much more extensive. Now that you know the basics, it's a matter of time before you come up with new ways of using the *Will*. I'm ready to teach you the feeling of intention. If you agree."

Kai frowned.

"And why wouldn't I?"

"It will hurt. A lot."

"More than it did with the *Spark*?"

Green's smile was unsettling.

"Much, much more."

"Well… I came this far… I'm in."

"Don't say I didn't warn you. It will be something like an exam and a lesson at the same time. You can't use techniques and cores. You can't ask the *System* for help either. Self-control only, it is the first step to perfect mastery of willpower. Focus on sharpening it. Your task is to focus on my *Will*, discern my intentions, and react accordingly. At first, I will actively emit my intentions, but then I will gradually begin to hide them. I will also use only my *Will*. There will be no breaks, and we'll be done when I say we're done."

"And that would be...?"

Green's smirk sent a shiver down Kai's spine, and he felt that he was in mortal danger.

Without hesitation, he distanced himself. As he stared at the motionless Green, he suddenly felt immense pain pierce his body and soul. Grabbing his stomach, he fell to his knees, gasping for air. The gaping hole in his abdomen had already healed, but the pain hadn't gone away. Feeling his body weakening, Kai stared at Green in a state of slight shock. Stretching out his hand and slowly opening his palm, Green showed Kai five multicolored spheres.

Only a moment before his death did he realize that these were his cores.

***

Kai suddenly became aware of himself standing next to Green. Alive and intact. What just happened seemed like nothing more than an illusion. A feverish dream.

"You're slow," Green said disapprovingly. "And I thought that one percent would be enough for you to resist."

The words seemed to come from afar. Kai felt his mind fading away.

Death. Resurrection. Pain...

By his fifth death, Kai realized that he was in some kind of *Master Stars Test*, where he was being reborn anew after each failed attempt. The only difference was that instead of nameless opponents, there was only Green.

What did he do? Is that why he chose this place? Is that why released that wave of Will at the very beginning of our training? Kai was confused. *No... No... I have to focus. I need to focus on surviving!*

***

"You are finally awake."

Wincing, Kai opened his eyes and stared at Green sitting next to him.

"Where I am?" he asked, seeing that he was lying on a bed and not on the ground.

"We're back at my mansion," Green replied, picking up a piece of fruit from a platter.

"Does that mean that we're done?" Touching his forehead, Kai sat up.

"We are. We fought twelve thousand four hundred and seventy-six times. Then I returned us to reality, where fatigue got to you and you fell unconscious."

"We fought?" Kai chuckled. "I didn't even touch you."

"Don't be so harsh on yourself." Green smiled. "You almost hit me once."

"Well… That's something…" Kai smiled tiredly, covering his face with his hand.

"I think your basic *Will* skills are good enough, as is your ability to read other people's intentions."

Green's hand blurred and halted in front of Kai's face. The tips of the chopsticks with which Green had been poking the fruit froze a hair's width from his eye — Kai caught the utensil just in time.

"Not bad," Green commented, returning to his fruit.

"How long did we stay there?" Kai asked, leaning back against the pillow.

"Three days."

"Twenty seconds per fight?" Kai grunted. The math was giving him a headache. "And now what?"

"I think it's time to tell you the secret of the eight-volume techniques."

Kai stared at him.

"But before that — a short history lesson. Have you ever wondered why the *Will of the Spark* is so strong?"

"Didn't you already answer this question by saying that there are a huge number of strings hidden in the *Spark*?" Kai asked, raising an eyebrow.

"Yes. But why does it become stronger during the so-called evolutions? Does it pick up even more strings? Have you ever experienced anything like that during a breakthrough?"

Kai gave it a thought.

"I don't remember," he admitted. "It seems more like the power pours out of the *Spark* itself, not like it comes from outside."

"That's right. However, any *Spark* has an unprecedented divine power, surpassing even that of the *Higher Ones*."

"I haven't noticed that in myself. Or others."

"Because that power is sealed. Getting into the World of the Dead, the *Spark* is cleansed and shackled. With seven layers of shackles. That is why even when a deity dies, their *Spark* returns as a mortal."

"So, when the *Spark* evolves, it throws off these shackles?"

"Correct. The *Soul Stage* removes a third of the first

layer of shackles, which allows them to attempt to manifest their *Will*. At the transition to the *Exorcist Stage*, the first layer is completely destroyed. Each next level weakens the following layers, and every stage breaks them. That is why the *Will of the Spark* grows so rapidly in comparison with the *Will of Reason*. When you start breaking through to the *Star Emperor Stage*, the fifth layer of shackles is at its weakest and there is a possibility of influencing the vibrations with the *Will of the Elements*, which is crucial for a successful breakthrough. With the fifth layer gone, the *Spark* not only grows stronger, but also acquires a primitive consciousness. Because of this, the deities can masterfully control their *Will*, as well as read Information."

"The fifth layer is removed at the *Star Emperor Stage*? The sixth at the *Limitless*, and the seventh upon becoming a *Higher One*?"

"Not quite. The breakthrough to the *Limitless Stage* doesn't remove the sixth layer, only weakens it. It collapses upon becoming a *Higher One*. Such power is extremely volatile, and the rare ones who obtain it are able to read vibrations of strings at an extremely deep level."

"I see. But what does this have to do with becoming a *Master of Eight Stars*?"

"Each layer of shackles is designed to accommodate up to seven small cracks. Each surface crack represents a *Star* of cultivator's willpower. The catch is that one can deepen them, and if these cracks reach somewhere around a third of the entire layer, that's *Seven Great Stars*. It's impossible to create more cracks, but there's a possibility to deepen them so much that the crack reaches the next shackle and leaves its mark upon it. If one does this, then their *Will of the Spark* will be more accessible. This is one of the steps to becoming a true *Master of Eight Stars* — an *Ascended* one, and this is what you need to do."

Kai narrowed his eyes.

"I can deepen only one crack?"

"That's the thing." Green smiled. "You can deepen all seven. But not beyond one third of the next layer. Thus, there is a gradation among the *Ascended*. Each deepened crack counts as one level."

"And what's Kyle's level?"

"One."

"What about Void?"

"Likewise."

"And you?"

Green's smile widened as he picked up another piece of fruit.

"Who knows?"

Chapter 22
THE MYSTERY OF THE EIGHT STARS

"I still have questions. Why doesn't the rating of the willpower change according to the stage after a breakthrough? When an entire layer of shackles collapses, don't the cracks disappear? So how come the *Stars* rating stays?"

"The nature of the shackles is more complicated that you imagine it to be. The removal of cracked shackles leads to the appearance of similar imperfections on the next layer. Therefore, the rating doesn't change."

Kai pondered Green's words for a moment.

"The *Will* grows stronger, but what about the rest of the parameters? Do they all have to be of *Eight Stars* for me to become an *Ascended*?"

"If you are talking about a *System* title, then yes. You must have *Eight Stars* in every parameter, except for secondary ones. However, it is not necessary to receive the *System's* recognition to become an *Ascended*. The willpower is the most important thing, and it will be enough to create at least one deep crack to embark on this path."

"But isn't it all about going beyond what's possible in every way?"

"It is, and that's why the crack needs to be deep. It will give you everything you need." Green set aside the fruit plate and leaned forward. "To do this, you need to understand the very essence of these cracks. There is an interesting oddity that can give you some food for thought. How come the cracks give much more than the destruction of the shackles?"

"Something doesn't add up," Kai drawled, thinking. "Now that you've mentioned it, it is odd..."

"There is indeed a catch. Removing the shackles does make the *Will* stronger than denting them does. After breakthroughs, the amount of soul energy and *ki* increases, forming new, more powerful layers, the *Shell* is hardened, and so on... However, all these processes require constant maintenance, so most of the *Will of the Spark* is spent on this, leaving little for free use. But when you create cracks, then no breakthrough occurs, and the *Will* doesn't need to seep into the body and soul. All its power remains under your control. However, things are different with deep cracks. With them, the *Spark* considers that another breakthrough has occurred, so it directs most of the *Will* into the body and soul. However, since no real breakthrough occurred, this *Will* has nothing to support. But since it's already there, you can use it to strengthen your body or increase your energy supply."

"So it's something like *Complete Submission*?"

"In a manner of speaking, yes. With it, you don't just subdue the strings within yourself — after all, they already belong to you, but manipulate them to move when you have no physical strength left. This goes beyond the capabilities of an average cultivator, because you are forcing your body to do things it wasn't meant to do."

"And the deep cracks?"

"In their case, the *Will* is forever embedded in the body and soul, so it doesn't need to be maintained. Not even subconsciously. Just like with *Complete Submission*. Furthermore, it's so deeply integrated into the strings that it can even amplify their vibrations, allowing you to tinker with both your body and soul."

"And how much power does a deep crack give?"

"It can raise your willpower up to two steps. If you had *Seven Great Stars*, you would be *Eight Average* ones. The *Will's* power that goes to your body can be equal up to about fourteen steps. And it's *you* who decide how to distribute them. For example, your body and energy reserves have already reached *Eight Stars*. You don't need to invest in them, so the extra power can be redirected to that part of the warrior's layer that is responsible for the *Forces*."

"Just like that?"

"There are only two restrictions: you can't use that *Will* for secondary parameters, and you can't put so much *Will* into one parameter that its power exceeds three *Steps*. In other words, you can't strengthen your bloodline or put everything into one parameter."

"And this is something anyone can do?"

"Not quite."

"How come?"

"The boundaries of what the soul, the body, and the *Spark* are capable of are clearly defined in the hyperstring of cultivation. However, the possibility of creating a deep crack isn't accounted for. This is the *Spark*'s loophole, so to say. *Sparks*, although to some extent subordinate to the universe, are, for the most part, independent existences with a unique nature. Therefore, the creation of a deep crack, as well as the power bestowed by it, is beyond the limits of what is possible for some."

Nodding, Kai slowly inched toward the edge of the bed and looked around the room. There seemed to be no one else besides Green and himself in the house.

"I think I get the basics. Now I just need to learn how to create a deep crack."

"This process consists of many steps, so becoming an *Ascended* will take a lot of time. I'd say about fifty or even seventy years."

Kai frowned in displeasure. He hadn't expected to become a *Master of Eight Stars* overnight, but he didn't think it would take that long. Five decades was nothing for a *Holy Lord* capable of living at least eight thousand years, only Kai's sister didn't have that much time. He needed to return to Saha before Julie's mortal life came to an end.

It's been fifteen years since. She should be thirty-nine now... I hope she's doing well. The elixir I gave her should keep her healthy but... I have to get there as soon as possible.

Before leaving, Kai made sure that Julie would have everything she could possibly need, including a roof over her head and enough money that she'd never have to work a day in her life. He also left her Jongo's sword, as well as a group of loyal and strong servants.

It's been so long... What if something happened to her? How would I even know? No. No. He shook his head. *Don't think about it. She's fine. She has to be.*

"Is there really no way to speed up the creation of a deep crack?"

Green pondered, looking up and stroking his chin.

"You seem awfully concerned about this... Going somewhere?"

"We can say that."

To return to Saha, Kai had to leave the Trial Worlds. But he couldn't do this without passing all the *Trials* and moving from world to world. Sooner or later, he would have to go to Bellum, where he would have to fight Kyle. And to defeat him, Kai had to become an *Ascended* as soon as possible.

"Theoretically, it's possible. But it depends completely on you. I can give you the technique I used to weaken the connection with the *Spark*, but that will entail communicating with it further. Are you ready for that?"

Kai flinched. The pain of non-existence was still fresh in his mind.

I have to do it. For Julie.

Gathering the courage, he firmly nodded.

"I am."

"Very well. There's only the matter of price."

"I was wondering when you'd get to that."

Green smiled.

"Void, Abaddon, Chag, and Qi. You will take two of them with you to the Ark. Let them serve the Temple until the end of our agreement."

"Why?"

"You need not concern yourself with that. You also don't have to worry about them hurting you or the Temple. I give you my word."

Kai frowned.

"Before I decide, tell me how much will this technique speed up the process."

"Again, it all depends on you. But I'd say at least two times."

Rising, Kai went to the window. For a few minutes, the room remained silent.

"I'll be watching them like a hawk," he finally said.

"It's your right to do so. Just don't discriminate. Let them do their part as your followers."

"I'll take Chag and Qi," Kai said, choosing who he believed were the weakest of the four. "But if they do anything to put the Temple in jeopardy, I will kill both of them."

"Don't worry, it won't come to that."

"I hope so."

"Now that that's settled, we can move on to the creation of the crack." Green took out a thick memory scroll from the sleeve of his robes. "You will need to undergo a false breakthrough to confuse the *Spark* and prepare it for removing its shackles. There are five steps to achieving this. First: you must be at the peak of your spiritual and physical capabilities. Second, you need to master all *Advanced System Will* skills, including at least one *Elemental Will* ability."

"I already have one of those."

"Correct. Third: you need to have perfect control of your body and soul. You have that as well. Fourth: the soul must be ready for a breakthrough. Fifth: your *Will of Reason* must be extremely strong. At least at the *Exorcist Stage* and, preferably, at the peak level."

"I assume I'll need your technique for that?"

"Indeed."

Having transferred the required technique into a scroll, Green handed it to Kai.

Peering into it, Kai was struck by the complexity of the knowledge bestowed upon him. He wouldn't be able to recreate the weaving, so he would have to either delegate this task to a group of clones or create an artifact based on the technique. He couldn't use the technique on himself, because he needed to reject his *Shell* when communicating with the *Spark*.

"The more often you plunge into that state, the faster your *Will of Reason* will reach the desired level. When you fulfill all these conditions, you can try to deepen the crack. You need to be under extreme pressure for a very long time to do that. You should be able to control the conditions through your *Will*. When you have no strength left to think let alone to move, that's when you need to start a breakthrough."

"It's a guaranteed death," Kai realized.

"Just what you need," Green replied with a menacing smile. "Someone so exhausted could never break through. Your concentrated desire to become stronger will reach the *Spark*, triggering a response. That's a false breakthrough. The *Spark* won't immediately understand what's going on, so you will have some time before it halts the process. At this time, the shackles will be much more pliable, allowing you to deepen the crack. To do this, the *Will of Reason* must reach the shackles at the moment of death. If there is enough strength and one of the cracks deepens enough, then the *Will* that spills out of it will help reconnect your body, *Shell*, and the *Spark*. If not, then you'll die."

If I involve the older clones in the process, with their Will of Reason *I won't even need this technique. But I don't think that it will work. I can't communicate with them if I'm one foot in the grave. This process would kill them, too. I'd have to order them to enter stasis before the false breakthrough occurs...*

"I still don't quite understand how the *Will of Reason* should do this. When the connection between the *Shell* and the body is severed, my mind will cease to function. Does it have anything to do with the conscious control of the *Will*?"

"Indeed it does." Green nodded. "Before you start a false breakthrough, you will have to subjugate the *Shell* with the *Will of the Spark* to keep the mental layer from turning off when the connection is broken."

"In other words, I need to leave behind a Shadow to use the *Will of Reason* and hit the shackles."

"Not really. Shadows are too unstable and unpredictable. It may not appear immediately, and when it does, it may have only a fragment of consciousness. Counting on it would be too risky. Instead, you can use the *Will of the Spark* to keep the mental layer active and hit the shackles."

"I take it this is all? Reach *Seven Great Stars*, raise the *Will of Reason* to the *Exorcist Stage*, deplete spirit and physical strength, make the *Shell* hit the shackles, and then start a breakthrough?"

"Yes."

"Strange..."

"What is?"

"If that's all, then why does the *System* say that there are only three *Masters of Eight Stars* in the Ecumene? Deities should be able to easily pull this off with their *Divine Will*."

"In theory, yes. But there are several issues. First of all, even if all the conditions are met, the chance of success is still low. Not everyone is willing to take this risk, and those who are often die in the process. Even a smallest mistake can be fatal. For the Gods, this isn't a problem, but for ordinary people… How many *Divine Stage* cultivators do you know who can control their *Spark*?"

"None. Only you. And one deity."

"The vast majority of deities didn't know how to control the *Will of the Spark* before breaking through to the *Star Emperor Stage*. Also, very few people in the Ecumene know the secret of becoming an *Ascended*, and they clearly don't intend to share it. And neither the *Star Emperors* nor most of the *Limitless* are capable of revealing it on their own. But the most important thing is that any *Master of Eight Stars* automatically becomes a contender for the Heavenly Throne."

"You're hiding, aren't you? Is that why neither you nor Void passed the *Master Stars Test*?"

"That's one of the reasons, yes."

***

The sun was slowly sinking toward the sea, painting the water's surface a beautiful burgundy. Looking at this enchanting sunset, Kai felt familiar auras. From the south, gliding across the water, three figures were rapidly approaching him. A few moments later, they were standing next to him on the sand.

"Buddy! How was your vacation, eh?" Shacks chuckled in greeting.

"Do you have any idea what happened while you were away?" Lilith grumbled, slightly annoyed. "The Temple's leader has been missing for almost half a year! Right after rumors about his crippled *Astral Body* began to spread! It would have been nice if you had at least told us where you went!"

The contents of the letter that Void had given her were for Kai's eyes only, so she never read it. No one but Kai knew where Green's mansion was. And since the latter would prefer it to stay that way, Kai was told to meet with his friends elsewhere.

"It's better this way," Kai replied, not taking his eyes off the setting sun. "You knew that I'd be leaving for a bit. Telling you more would have only complicated things, right Shaw? What does Sirius say?"

"Your disappearance has stirred up Insulaii's elite, prompting many to act. We are ready for anything."

"Great. When we get back, let Sirius start a retaliatory operation. Let's cleanse the empire of unwanted actors."

"What were you doing here anyway?" Shacks couldn't help but ask. "Did you really take a vacation?"

"He came to visit an old friend."

Startled, Lilith, Shaw, and Shacks turned around. Drawing their weapons, they stared at a group of warriors led by a tall, dark-haired man in blue robes. With his hands folded behind his back, he looked at Kai's comrades with his multi-colored eyes and a slight smile, causing bewilderment and confusion. Their intuition failed them, not allowing them to study the person in front of them. He seemed mysterious and completely ordinary at the same time.

Following him were three *Divine Stage* cultivators and one Heavenly Spirit, each of whom evoked only one thing in all of them — danger.

Lilith and Shaw immediately recognized the Emperor of Knolak and the Princes of the Abyss, but Shacks...

"Master Qi?" He was surprised to see the Spirit he met

in the Collisium. "And Chag? Wait... You're a *Divine Stage* cultivator?!"

"That's Lord Chag to you, peasant." Chag grinned. "By the way, I haven't forgotten you cheating in poker."

"I didn't forget how you tried to kill me. Your friend, too."

"I'm sure you noticed I only pretended to try to kill you to provoke Kai. As for Izao... I'll even help you kill him if we run into him."

"Is he in the Trial Worlds, too? And how did you end up here?"

"We can discuss that later." Intervening in the conversation, Kai looked first at Shacks, and then at Chag. "He and Qi will go with us to the Ark and join the Temple as Senior Acolytes."

"You sure know how to pick your followers… Although I'm grateful to Qi for helping me in a pinch, he threatened us and used us against you. I'm not sayin' anythin', but…"

"This isn't up for discussion," Kai told him curtly. "If you don't like it, you can be the one who will keep an eye on them. Also, Qi was a spy in the Collisium's ranks, so you can't blame him for what Yusa and the rest of the Guardians did."

"Fineeeeeee…"

"Actually, they will all join us. But only Chag and Qi will go to the Ark. It goes without saying that this information is confidential." He turned to Lilith. "Did you bring everything?"

Nodding, Lilith revealed five identical spiritual contracts.

Is the Emperor of Knolak about to join the Temple? What's

going on here? she wondered.

"It's standard procedure," Kai said as he took the scrolls and handed them to Green. "Once you sign them, your names will be entered into the list of Temple's members, and a tattoo will appear on your bodies."

"Very well."

"Also." Kai turned to Lilith and Shaw. "According to our agreement, from now on, the Knolak Empire will join us as an autonomous region."

"You're kidding, right?" Shaw asked, unable to believe his ears.

"Not at all."

"But that means…"

"…that the entire planet belongs to the Temple," Lilith finished the sentence for him.

"That's right. Therefore, as the head of the Administration Department and Ministry of Internal Affairs, this is now your job." Kai patted Shaw's shoulder. "You, Void and Abaddon will travel to Knolak today to figure out how to integrate the undersea part of Insulaii into the Empire. Your subordinates will join you later."

Shaw sighed.

"You're a tyrant, you know that? I've just finished dealing with three regions! Three! By myself! And what do I get in return?! More work! That's it! I quit!"

"Not according to your contract, my friend." Kai chuckled. "Until you find a successor, you're stuck doing paperwork."

"Stop whining, will you?" Lilith scoffed. "You have a bunch of assistants doing everything for you."

"My dear, if the assistants could do everything themselves, I'd be at a beach sipping cocktails and enjoying the summer breeze."

"How did you even become the head of the Cartel's Third Fleet?"

"Charm, my dear Lilith! Charm!"

Lilith sighed and rubbed the bridge of her nose.

"I swear by the Heavens…"

"Besides, I already have a successor!" Shaw turned to Kai. "Let Hiro do it. He's done great so far! I'm sure he can handle this, too!"

"He's an *Elementalist*, he needs to train."

"Damn it," Shaw hissed.

With no other options, Shaw was forced to comply. Having gotten acquainted with Void and Abaddon, he went with them to Knolak.

"Before I leave, I have one more thing to ask," Kai told Green. *Zhou Han Nam's granddaughter and Kuro were killed on Kronos during the attack of the Formless. The Unions thought that I was behind their deaths so they agreed to go to war against Avlaim. I checked Zhou Han Nam and Aash'Tsiron's souls and found that the girl and Kuro sent a message to their relatives before they were killed by someone who looked like me. Judging by those notes, this happened around the time when you and I were just heading into the Abyss. Given that Void was on Kronos at that moment, I can't help but wonder if you were the one who set me up."*

"It wasn't me."

"So, it wasn't Void?" Kai asked again, just in case.

"It wasn't."

"Then what was he doing there?"

In response, Green only grinned, indicating that he wouldn't say anything more. Still, Kai believed him.

With their meeting concluded, Kai transported himself and the others to the Ark.

***

During Kai's absence, his followers managed to deal with the issue of the empire's allies as well as extend his power over the territories under his control.

All sects, clans, families, orders, and other associations were reorganized according to the imperial legislation and turned into a single organization. Having become part of the empire, they acted like companies and corporations with their own military forces. All of them were included in a special register and paid taxes to the empire: both in money and resources and in talented warriors. To ensure peace, they were forbidden from fighting with each other. All conflicts were to be resolved in court, duels, or tournaments. Despite their right to establish an independent domestic policy, they were all ultimately overseen by the imperial chancellery.

Imperial representatives, chosen from the members of the Temple and led by clones, soon arrived in the cities to engage in the reorganization of local authority and distribution of land.

But the main development was the construction of the nine Warrior Temples and the completion of the special transportation arrays that allowed travel to other planets through the barrier surrounding Insulaii. Their exit points at Ferox and Bellum were also under imperial control.

There were only sixteen days left before the grand

opening of the Warrior Temples and the transfer arrays. Very soon, the news of Insulaii's unification would shake both Ferox and Bellum, prompting drastic changes in the Trial Worlds.

Having finished reading the reports, Kai leaned back in his chair and put his feet on the table. For several minutes, he stared at the ceiling, analyzing the events that took place during his absence and thinking about his next steps. Noticing a couple of oddities and inconsistencies, he frowned and activated *Ultimate Focus*.

"He will show up again soon," he said to himself. "The trap will close…"

The office around him disappeared, replaced by the boundless snow-white space of his personal dimension. Slowly, a meditation platform appeared under his feet, and a thick memory scroll materialized in his hands.

The artifact full of Green's memories held the secret of the eight-volume techniques, another gift that he shared with Kai. As it turned out, their idea was also strongly connected with the willpower and it wasn't about one separate technique, but a combining of a certain number of them into a super-weaving.

Connected, the techniques additionally strengthened and improved each other. It was impossible to fit everything into one technique, so eight-volume tomes were the perfect solution to this problem, a great tool of *Eight Stars* masters that allowed them to create the most diverse and multifunctional abilities.

Green not only explained the essence of the eight-volume techniques but also gave Kai instructions on how to apply them, as well as an example of a super-weaving. All of that was in the scroll Kai now had on him.

But Green didn't stop there. He gave him another gift.

Just before calling Lilith, Kai asked Green if he could somehow confirm that their souls would survive the punishment for violating the *System* oath. To his surprise, Green agreed and entered a temporary *Pact of Souls* with Kai. Having sworn that they would neither lie nor harm each other, Kai deliberately violated the oath.

But nothing happened.

"Satisfied?" Green had asked him.

"Very."

***

A few days later, Kai left Insulaii again to visit the Spirit Dimension. To do this, he once again had to move into the husk of an unknown sylph with the help of Sawan's artifact.

Just like before, Kai found himself in the middle of the large city of Rui. Grimacing at the unpleasant weakness caused by the lack of energy, he quickly got his bearings and headed to the bank.

On his way there, he noticed that the atmosphere in the city had changed. Outwardly, it remained the same, but its inhabitants seemed different. The Spirits and sylphs looked wary. Almost tense. There were more guards everywhere, and the city itself was much quieter and gloomier.

By the time he reached the bank, Kai had a vague idea of what was happening. As he had learned from overheard conversations, the war between neighboring principalities was halted after the ruling deities initiated negotiations. Their sudden truce came as a shock to the citizens. Throughout history, there had never been an instance of so many deities collaborating with each other at the same time.

Curious as this all was, it didn't concern Kai much. Minding his business, he went through the main entrance straight to the office and entered the Shakwir family treasury to collect some elemental threads. He needed them to replenish the *Paths* of *Sword* and *Space* and make new elements.

And the other thing he needed was Rune'Tan's help.

Almost a year and a half ago, Kai left him a message here in the hopes of finding something about himself. And now, having regained his memory, he wanted to meet his old friend and ask him for help regarding his *Soul Shell*.

To his pleasant surprise, Kai found a message from Rune'Tan in the treasury. Placing his hand on the artifact, he summoned a large projection.

"Are you in trouble again?" Rune'Tan chuckled. The sight of his cheerful face made Kai smile. "I leave you alone for a minute, and you're already losing your memory. Still, I hope you're doing well. I put everything I know into the scrolls. Check out the library. Unfortunately, I can't leave a longer message. We are dealing with some pressing matters here." Rune'Tan's face grew gloomy, "Something has happened. Don't worry. Everything is fine with me, with my father, and with Belteise, but… I won't be able to get in touch anymore. Not in the next century or two. I'm sorry I can't give you the details. Good luck, my friend! I hope our paths cross again!"

The projection faded, leaving Kai confused and lost in thought. This wasn't what he expected.

He sat there for the next half an hour, until he finally decided to leave the Spirit Dimension. Having contacted a bank employee through the terminal, Kai waited for the door to open.

He never would have thought that he'd be surrounded by a dozen Holy Spirits upon leaving the treasury.

Interlude
BEHIND THE SCENES

Startled, Qi halted his meditation and opened his eyes.

"Someone went to the Spirit Dimension?" he whispered in surprise, feeling the familiar vibrations rippling across the vast sea of space. "Is it Kai? A divine artifact and a body exchange… Interesting…"

For a moment, he pondered whether he should follow him. Deciding that his master would want to know where Kai was going, he plunged back into a meditative state. In theory, all spirits could go to the Spirit Dimension, but in practice, only a few of them were able to do this. Qi included. He wasn't only a Heavenly Spirit but also an entity born in the Spirit Dimension, one of the few that had managed to escape from this dungeon.

He's moving too fast. I won't be able to catch up…

Straining his meridians to the point of tearing, he accelerated the transfer. Alas, by the time he found himself at the border of Rui, he was already too late. Reaching out to the *Wood* and *Cold*, he felt an acute shortage of elemental threads in the air, the number of which continued to decrease.

All around him, crowds of spirits and sylphs were running away from the city center, making a terrible noise. Not looking at where they were going, several people even bumped into him in their hurry to leave.

What's going on here? Qi wondered as he stared in bewilderment at the huge column of smoke that rose to the heavens. Following it down, he saw scorched earth and a massive crater. *Wait... Where's the bank? What's going on here?*

Seven blurry figures fought near the ruins. Among them were the head of the bank, a couple of his subordinates, three senior officials, and Kai.

He's not alone, Qi realized as he headed toward them. *Has he merged with the Keeper of his weapon? But even so... How can he resist them without his real body? Did he absorb all those threads? Is this the power the Master warned me about?*

"In the name of the Principality of Ezart, I order everyone to stop fighting! I repeat: stop fighting immediately!" Qi shouted, releasing his power.

Mighty roots erupted from the ground, entangling the fighters, including Kai. Trapped in someone else's body, he couldn't use his powers to defend himself.

But before Qi had time to speak, a blazing figure suddenly appeared next to him, causing the temperature to rise rapidly. It was a tall, muscular creature, covered in fiery feathers and with the head of a Doberman.

Before them stood the ruler of the Principality of Ezart, the Fire God Graalt.

"How unusual... I rarely get to see these sorts of things nowadays. Almost never. A Spirit of the *Sword* and *Yin*... A *Holy Lord* in an *Exorcist's* body... How did you stand up to so many Heavenly Spirits and *Divine Stage* cultivators? Did you merge with a Spirit? Hmm, no… That wouldn't have been enough… *Divine Will*? No, such a weak *Spark* can't have it. Hmm… How peculiar," he thought aloud in a snarling voice and slowly turned to Qi. "And why did you intervene, my son?"

Spirits couldn't have children, and while Qi was only an adopted child, chosen among millions of other Spirits, he was Graalt's favorite.

"This sylph… That is, this human… He is…"

"*Connected with Him,*" Qi finished telepathically, showing his father Green's image. "*He asked me to keep an eye on this man.*"

Graalt tensed.

"*Then why isn't he carrying my symbol?*" he asked.

"*He is connected with Him but doesn't work for Him. He didn't give me the details, but I suspect that this man plays an important part in His plans. I didn't expect him to come here. Why did they fight? Did he do something?*"

Having given the situation some thought, Graalt briefly explained what happened and approached Kai.

"Since my son stood up for you, I will turn a blind eye to this incident," he told him. "And to prevent this from happening again, I will make you a guest of my principality." He opened his palm and held out a flaming feather that didn't emit any heat. "Take it with you next time you come to the Spirit Dimension."

Blinking in confusion, Kai bowed and accepted the gift.

"I'm really sorry for the inconvenience I have caused but I didn't know what else to do," he explained. "I still don't understand why the guards suddenly decided to arrest me.

When I refused to go with them, they attacked me without any explanation."

"Insolent child." Graalt grinned, patting Kai on the cheek. "But I like you more than Him... Qi will explain everything. Don't worry about the bank. I moved everyone out of it before you blew it up. I will, however, take this as compensation."

Graalt was talking about the weapon that the clones created together with Shacks, based on the technology he had discovered on Earth. When Kai engaged the guards, the bank's defense systems focused on him, so he had to use this weapon to break free.

Kai didn't reply. There was no point arguing with a deity. Graalt had been kind so far, but Kai suspected that his diplomatic behavior had more to do with Green than with Qi standing up for him. And nothing guaranteed that his patience would last.

"Why was I arrested?" Kai asked Qi, observing Graalt pick up the injured cultivators and disappear into thin air.

"The Principality's policies have become stricter. Earlier, you could come to Rui whenever you pleased, but now everyone is required to sign several contracts upon arrival," Qi replied with a sigh.

"That's it?" Kai was dumbfounded. "All this because of paperwork? Why didn't they just say so?"

"You're not a Spirit or a sylph. Outsiders are treated differently." He shrugged. "Officially, the Firsts' children are forbidden from coming here without Graalt's permission. But since the teleports work and anyone can try to get here, trespassers are arrested, interrogated, and imprisoned. No one is under any obligation to explain anything. I just found out about this myself. The law was introduced quite recently."

"What is behind the introduction of such laws? What about people's property in the bank? What about possible problems with Ecumene's deities?"

"I can't share that with you, but I will say that these are still considered mild restrictions. As for the bank and other Gods, you aren't the only honorable guest of the Spirit Dimension. If the trespasser has a divine patron, they will not be imprisoned but sent back to convey a message. If their patron can find a common language with my father, their faction will have the right to visit Rui. But only the bank. This also applies to you. The feather will automatically move you to your safe."

Kai frowned.

What is going on here? he thought. *Why did the Principality suddenly introduce these laws? Why did the local Gods stop fighting? And how big is Green's influence in all this? Why does Qi, an heir of an entire Principality, serve him?*

***

The nine Warrior Temples were about to open their doors to hundreds of thousands of mortals and Masters who wanted to test their strength in the entrance exam or go to another world. More than half a year after the installation of the barrier, Insulaii was finally ready to re-establish contact with Ferox and Bellum.

"Everyone in position?" a man asked, secretly watching a crowd of greedy merchants heading toward the teleportation Arches.

"Yes, sir. All nineteen groups are in place and waiting for further instructions."

"Roger that. We start exactly two minutes after the

activation of the Arches. We'll go with Plan B."

"Yes, sir."

Turning away from the window of his room and leaning against the wall, the man sighed softly. He slowly closed his eyes and smiled.

"You'll pay for everything, you dirty Avlaimians..."

Concentrating on spirit perception and gradually filling a couple of artifacts with energy, he waited with anticipation.

"I'm afraid to upset you, but your plans will have to be postponed," an unfamiliar voice said.

Startled, the man stared at the figure clad in the Temple's purple robes sitting in a chair four feet away from him.

"How?" he gasped. The signal array should have informed him of anyone's presence, but it never went off. "Who are you? I... This is my room! How dare you barge in on me?! Wait... Wait, wait... I remember you from the Grand Tournament... Haven't progressed much since then, have you?" He chuckled nervously. "You're as weak now as you were then..."

"Don't judge a book by its cover," the young man said, getting up.

Seeing the spears in the newcomer's hands, the man completed the weave inside the artifact he was saturating.

"DIE!"

Ryu froze, cocked his head, and smiled.

"Having trouble with it, are you?"

The man's eyes widened in confusion as his stomach

was pierced with lightning-imbued steel. But instead of crying out, he twisted his face into a fanatical grin. He stood no chance against a *Master of Seven Small Stars* that Ryu was now.

"That's not enough… Nothing can save…"

"What?" Ryu glared at him. Hundreds of years had passed for him, but the rage caused by the death of his friends was still fresh. "Nothing can save us? Heh…" He shook his head, leaned toward the man's ear. "Do you hear any explosions? I don't. Your accomplices are dead. As are those who sent you here. You wanted to capture the Temples and the Arches so badly that you didn't even realize that you had walked into a carefully prepared trap. We knew about your every move. Even about your Three Elders. And to think that High Elder Manhut is a Temple Official. Independence fighters?" Ryu chuckled, stepping back. "You are terrorists, unable to accept defeat."

Like poison, Ryu's *Will* penetrated deeper and deeper into the man's mind, sending him spiraling into panic. Grinning, Ryu pulled the spears out. The man bled out quickly, and Ryu transferred both his body and the spears into his *Storage*.

"You took a while," Kai's clone commented, appearing in the room.

"I'm sorry, I gave into my rage," Ryu lied without blinking, hiding the true reason for delaying his actions. "Are you done?"

The clone nodded.

"Seven Temples have been cleared out. We are finishing up in the last two. The attack on the Resistance has just begun. It's difficult to fight on foreign territory even with invisibility, especially when they're expecting you. Luring them out is proving difficult."

"Well, let's not keep them waiting then. We're heading out."

"Yes, sir."

***

Underneath the beautiful starry sky, surrounded by mountains and feeling a light breeze on his face, Kyle sighed and leaned back, relaxed. Exhaling a puff of steam, he sank deeper into the hot water of the springs filled with the healing power of many elements.

"What could be better than this?"

"A mortal battle with an equally powerful opponent?" the girl standing by the spring commented.

"Right as always, Hanna." Kyle smiled as he glanced at his apprentice. "What did you bring me this time?"

"There is some news from Insulaii and Ferox. I heard you passed another test. Congratulations."

"Oh, it's nothing." Kyle waved her away. "The second false breakthrough was only a matter of time."

"Nevertheless, it's a feat worth celebrating. I doubt that anyone else would have been able to withstand it all."

"Thank you. So, what's the news?"

"Communication with Insulaii has been re-established. Avlaim not only won the war against Tyr and Land but also captured them. After the unification, Kaiser founded the Eternal Path Empire. The Knolak Empire joined it shortly afterward as an autonomous region," Hanna reported shortly and without emotion.

"So, he has it all now?"

"Indeed. The barrier around Insulaii has been preserved. The only point of entry is the Arches, which are under the Eternal Path Empire's control."

Kyle broke into a smile, sincerely happy for Kai.

"He doesn't sit still. Which is awesome. I can't wait for our next meeting, Kai Arnhard," he muttered, looking at the stars. "And you, too, Green…"

Kyle closed his eyes, once again remembering his fights with Kai and Green. Especially the latter one.

It still stirred his blood.

The duel with Green had helped him understand himself more deeply and taught him how to use his powers better. Moreover, it motivated him to devote himself to training with renewed vigor and passion. He hadn't felt this alive since the beginning of his journey. Since then, his skills had greatly improved. He corrected many mistakes in his style and developed new techniques.

Such a quick and devastating defeat spurred him to become an *Ascended* of the second level. While training he also realized that nothing ends with the full formation of the *Shell's* layers. In fact, True Mastery had no limits. There was always room to grow. There was always something to improve. Kyle wanted to laugh at his stupidity. He should have realized this much, much sooner.

Opening his eyes, he took his hand out of the water and transferred three coal-black acorns and three nuts of the same color to his palm from his *Storage*.

"What is that?" Hanna asked, feeling the echoes of great power, but not seeing a *System* description.

"*Particles* of an *Elemental Soul* and an *Elemental Body*."

"Were you really a second-rank *Legend* in every world?" Hanna was surprised. "But how did you become one on Ferox and Bellum without reaching the *Divine Stage*?"

"It's not that hard to do if you have money and connections," Kyle replied with a shrug. "Promising to return the title, I negotiated with each of its holders. Having acquired it, I bought everything I needed at the *Altar*, fought him again, deliberately lost, and returned the title. Although this is really hard to pull this off on Bellum without good connections."

"Will the *Particles* give you anything, since you are already a Heavenly Miracle?"

"All of them together are actually useless, but one *Elemental Soul Particle* can still give me something."

"Then..."

"Then why didn't I use them?" Kyle grinned. "Isn't it obvious? Had I used them, I would have become stronger, and fighting would have become even more boring. But now... Now's the right time."

"I see..."

"Now, tell me..." Kyle leaned back. "What's happening with Ferox?"

***

Victor von Everstein sighed tiredly and put away the report regarding all the events that had transpired on Insulaii.

Hearing the rustling of papers, his wife turned to him.

"Are you done?" Yolana inquired.

"I am."

"Good. The guests will be here soon. Have you decided what you will say to them?"

Victor grimaced and took out a small vial from his *Storage*. Shaking his head, he closed his eyes for a few seconds.

"Do I have a choice? We have finally found a cure. You saw it yourself. As soon as you drank the elixir, the five-eyed mark faded away. If not this, then what else can save our children from pain and madness? What else will save us from extinction?"

"You're right. We have no choice," Yolana agreed with him. "But I shudder to think what they will demand in return."

***

The sounds of footsteps echoed down the dark corridor, bouncing off its damp walls. The once magnificent tunnel was now a miserable ruin filled with water, mud, bones, and anomalies.

Seeing that this underground city isn't on any maps, perhaps it truly does belong to the civilization that once ruled all of Ferox, Regis Glian Vinari pondered as he continued forward, not at all bothered by the impenetrable darkness that surrounded him. *Has no one found it yet? Or was it that well-hidden?*

The corridor opened up into a huge hall with dozens of converging tunnels. As he scanned his surroundings, Regis's eyes settled on the stranger sitting on the edge of a dilapidated wall.

"Did you summon me here?" he asked.

"Interesting…" The stranger chuckled. "I wanted to ask you the same. It turns out that we are both guests here."

"That you are," a third voice replied. The two turned around to see a handsome silver-haired elf emerge from the darkness of one of the corridors. "I'm the one who invited you both here."

The elf's aura was invisible, but the mere sight of him made a shiver run down Regis's spine.

A Master of Seven Great Stars? Regis tensed. *And the other one is a* Master of Seven Big Stars. *Both are* Divine Stage *cultivators. Just who are they?*

"I believe introductions are in order," the elf continued. "Regis, this is Ciel Eldivize, head of the Bright Moon Clan. Ciel, this is Regis Glian Vinari, the patriarch of the Vinari clan."

"And you are?" Ciel inquired. "Etiquette requires the host to introduce himself first."

"My name is irrelevant. You won't remember it anyway," the elf replied with a faint smile. "What's important is the reason for this meeting."

"And why is that?" Regis crossed his arms.

"Because of a mutual acquaintance. Kai Arnhard, better known in the Trial Worlds as Kaiser — the ruler of the Eternal Path Empire and the patriarch of the Eternal Path Temple. The unifier of Insulaii."

Unlike Regis, who learned about Kai's recent accomplishments as soon as Insulaii resumed contact with Firox and Bellum, Ciel was rather surprised by the news.

Is he truly the same Kai who won the Celestial Plateau Tournament? Ciel wondered. *I doubt it's a coincidence. But how? Weren't he and his friends supposed to be sacrificed to the Gates of Ecumene? Didn't they tell me that Kaiser is a* Holy Lord *now? But how could Kai become one in such a short time? Unless he also has the Accelerated Time-Space...? That would explain how Shacks appeared to be in the Trial Worlds...*

"But what does that have to do with us?" Regis asked.

The elf smiled.

"The people you seek are with him. Shacks, you beloved son," he told Ciel and then turned to Regis, "and your prized trophy."

Acilla is with him? But why? All the evidence pointed to the House of Blood. How did she end up with him again? Is he also working with the Cult?

"And you? What does he have that you want?"

"Oh, nothing in particular... Let's just say that I have some *complaints* about him."

"So? What do you propose? An alliance?"

"A temporary one."

"And why should we trust a stranger?"

"Because I am the only one who has the connections and resources necessary for this task. Or do you want to go against an entire empire on your own?"

"Can you confirm your words?" Ciel asked.

Instead of replying, the elf smiled and swore a long and detailed oath.

***

"I'm so sick of all of this!" a dorgan girl shouted and kicked the wet sand with all her might. "Don't do this, don't do that, don't fight with boys, don't train too hard, stay at home and help your mother! As if! Stupid father, stupid village, stupid island! Why did I have to be born here?!"

Venting her frustrations, she looked up at the sky. But the only answer she got was a few drops of rain that fell on her face.

"It's raining again... Day after day, fucking rain! This place is truly cursed!"

A sudden gust of wind swept over the beach as a bright flash lit up the sky, causing the girl to pause her rant and wince.

"Screw all of this!"

Turning around, her gaze fell on a strange object in the distance. Curious, she moved closer toward it. With each step she took, the outlines became clearer, until a giant turtle presented itself before her.

Feeling the faint echoes of the Titan's power, she stepped back and tripped on a stone sticking out of the sand. Startled, she curled up, afraid that the beast would gobble her up. But when nothing happened, she snuck a peek at the looming giant and realized with relief that it didn't seem to be moving.

"Is it dead...?" Slowly, fear gave way to joy. "It is! The Heavens must have heard me! Yes! Titan parts sell well on the market... I'll get rich and buy all the potions I need!" Equally quickly, joy gave way to gloom. "What if someone else finds it...? I should remove the big crystal... If I only knew what parts of its body are valuable..." She sighed. "And if only I knew how to properly obtain and store them..."

Having given it some thought, she walked around the carcass, trying to find a weak spot.

"I wonder how it died... I don't see any injuries... It's covered in bone-like growths... How do I open this? No, no, no... Oh, Heavens... I don't want to have to crawl in through its butt..."

Having made another lap around the Titan, she sighed

in relief.

"Even its ass is covered with plates! Through the mouth it is then."

Returning to the monster's head, the girl opened its mouth with difficulty and immediately jumped back, feeling the urge to vomit.

"Oof, what did you eat?" She grimaced. "C'mon, Layla… It's for your future… If you do this… You can move out… Live your dreams… Come on, you can do this…" she rallied herself.

Using her claws, she slowly made her way inside the monster. Deprived of a source of light, she navigated with the help of spirit perception. For it, the large crystal in the turtle's heart was like a small sun.

By evening, she had overcome only half of the neck. Growing tired, she left the beast's body, washed herself in the sea, and returned home. If she wasn't back by dinner time, her family would rush to look for her and then everybody would know about the turtle.

Ultimately, it took her three days of hard labor to reach the crystal. At first, she couldn't be happier, because this one pebble was worth more than their entire village, but then she quickly became wary.

"What is this?"

In the depths of the turtle's body was another odd object. It emitted a weak energy signal, but at the same time, it stirred her mind. Her intuition suggested that this was something very valuable. Even more valuable than the large crystal.

Layla couldn't make a decision for a long time. Leaving the turtle and hiding the crystal in a safe place, she took another day to contemplate her next move. On one hand, the path to the unknown object was longer than the one to the crystal, and she didn't know what she'd find there. It could be something valuable, something useless, or even something dangerous. But on the other hand, her intuition rarely let her down.

The following morning, she returned to the beach, where she spent another week digging around the rotting carcass, determined to uncover the secret within.

"What could it be?" she wondered as she grabbed an uneven elastic lump of flesh. "If I only had some light here... Guess I'll just have to take it out."

The task took her the entire day. By nightfall, she lay on the wet sand, exhausted, but finally out in the fresh air.

"I'm so tired... Shit! I'm late!"

Glancing at the massive lump of flesh, the girl carefully hid it and went home.

"Till tomorrow!"

As soon as the first rays of the sun illuminated the island, the girl was back to her find.

With a slight frown, she crouched by the lump and began to tear it. The valuable part had to be somewhere inside.

"It can't be..."

After cleaning the object in the water and carefully examining it, she realized that what she was holding was so much better than the giant crystal.

"I need a boat. But dad won't let me take it... I have to tell him about this... He'll want a share but it'll be worth it..."

She spent the rest of the next day thinking about how to explain this to her father. The conversation was long and hard, filled with shouting and threats of running away, but in the end, the old man agreed to help her. Her father was a grumpy bully who never let her do anything, but he wasn't a fool.

A day later, the two left Little Quelte — the westernmost island of Avlaim — and headed to Kaiser's Ark. If anyone would be able to appreciate their find, it would be the members of the Temple.

When they arrived three days later, they were taken to the Temple's hall and told to wait for one of the Hierarchs. Apparently, their case was so interesting that it was sent to the highest officials immediately.

The fishermen fidgeted nervously as they waited, unaccustomed to such luxury. Their anxiety wasn't relieved when the door finally opened to let in a Dorgan woman dressed in luxurious purple robes, who majestically entered the room. Seeing her, the guests jumped up from their seats and bowed their heads.

"Please, raise your heads," Nyako said. "Who found the item?"

"It… It was me." The girl uncertainly raised her hand. "A… A turtle washed up on the beach. I didn't know what it was until I pulled it out and saw the mark."

"Well done." Nyako smiled softly. "Each of you will receive a thousand *Azure Crystals* as a token of gratitude from the Temple. And you," she turned to the girl, "you can ask for anything you want. Take some time to think about it. When you decide, come to the city hall, and contact the mayor directly. Don't worry; they already know who you are and why you're coming."

"Um… Actually…"

"Yes?"

"I already know what I want."

"You do? And what is that?"

"I want to join the Emerald Warrior Temple."

"Are you sure?"

"I am."

"That can be arranged. You'll be enrolled as a special apprentice. You will be trained in combat, taught alchemy and history, and given resources. But if you can't keep up, you will be expelled. Do you agree? It's not too late to change your mind."

What she heard made the girl shudder. She took a moment to consider her options. In the end, she nodded with great enthusiasm.

"I agree!"

"Welcome to the Eternal Path Temple." Nyako smiled. "Do not leave the city, they will come for you. That's all."

Leaving the room, Nyako returned to the Ark through a network of portals.

So weak that even his Temple tattoo was erased, but still alive. Nyako smiled as she entered Ragnar's personal dimension, where he was already being healed by the *Complex's* arrays.

Chapter 23
PEACEFUL DAYS 1

Having completed the healing technique, Kai examined Ragnar's dried-up body and took a step back.

"How is he?" Lilith asked.

She also wanted to help him by using the Phoenix's healing power, but Kai didn't allow her to do so. She had already sacrificed too much of her life essence during the war. Also, there was nothing that she could do that the *Complex* hadn't already done on its own. Even Kai couldn't do more than carefully study Ragnar's body and soul without interfering with the healing process.

"I'm sure he will recover," he said to Nyako, "but it will take a long time. At least ten years."

"Shall we send him to the ATS?" Anatos suggested.

"Yes," Kai agreed. "We'll have to get everyone out, though. Ragnar is a *Divine Stage* cultivator, and helping him will take up a lot of its energy. It's not ideal but it's the only way we can help him."

"That's a week in real time. It'll pass in a heartbeat," Lilith said.

"Yes. However, even with our resources, healing him completely may still be beyond our reach. Plus, it might put a strain on his development."

"As long as he is alive." Nyako smiled.

"Lilith, you'll arrange for him to be transferred to ATS." Kai turned around. "In the meantime, we will leave him to rest."

With that, Lilith, Nyako, Shaw, Anatos, and Hiro left Ragnar's personal dimension. Kai went to the throne room. Previously bright and snow-white, it was now dark and gloomy. A stunning presentation of the night sky hung over a huge platform modeled like a mountaintop, dotted with myriads of stars. The blue moon cast a cold light on the endless snow-covered wastelands, lava rivers, and monsters below.

The columns were replaced by statues of the Temple's six founders along the edges of the platform. Each of them was imbued with the power to sacrifice themselves to protect the Eternal Throne.

At Kai's request, the Throne acquired a much simpler appearance, losing its former gloss and majesty, but it became even more powerful. Many modifications were added to it following its merge with the *Complex's* core. To make the throne room the last true bastion of the Temple, Kai merged it with his personal dimension, officially making it his private residence.

For a moment, he stood still in front of the Eternal Throne. Having admired it, he climbed the steps and sat down. As he did so, his consciousness expanded, covering almost the entire planet. Hundreds of tattoos, thousands of arrays, the Warrior Temples, the Ark, and the *Complex* united in a single giant system with the Eternal Throne in its center.

For a moment, Kai felt omnipotent. He saw everything, he knew everything, he could do anything...

Kai smiled. The Eternal Throne was the best place for cultivation on the planet, with the unfathomable potential even to the most developed of deities. And only he could use it.

Closing his eyes, Kai focused on the correct images: the Throne read his thoughts and stimulated his *Shell*, simplifying and improving the whole process. Kai had never experienced such deep concentration before. The subsequent absorption of the elemental threads brought from the Spirit Dimension went without a hitch.

Three days later, Kai completed his meditation and proceeded to study his *Shell*. More precisely, its *Manifestations*. He had restored his elemental layer a long time ago, but he couldn't find the time to train. He was a Heavenly Miracle after all, so in theory, he could master all the *Manifestations*. He just needed to open them within himself.

By the time Kai opened his eyes again, a week had already passed.

Attention!

[Soul Manifestation: Perfect Soul] has been obtained.

[Soul Manifestation: Forced Enlightenment] has been obtained.

[Soul Manifestation: Spirit Memory] has been obtained.

[Soul Manifestation: Cover Expansion] has been obtained.

[Soul Manifestation: Everything and Now] has been obtained.

[Soul Manifestation: Untamable Stream] has been obtained.

[Soul Manifestation: Renewal] has been obtained.

[Soul Manifestation: Strength Restoration] has been obtained.

[Soul Manifestation: Surveillance Zone] has been obtained.

[Soul Manifestation: Sudden Suppression] has been obtained.

As expected, Spirit Memory *is useless to me,* Kai thought as he read the detailed descriptions of all the abilities. *My memory is already perfect. But the rest of the* Manifestations *will come in handy.* Forced Enlightenment *will help me comprehend the elements better.* Cover Expansion, Surveillance Zone, *and* Sudden Suppression *will be a great addition to my arsenal.* Renewal *and* Strength Restoration *will make me even more resilient. And* Perfect Soul, Untamable Stream, *and* Everything and Now *will greatly enhance my ultimate attacks. It's a pity that all these abilities are only of the first level. I could've upgraded them while breaking through to the* Exorcist *and the* Holy Lord Stages. *But I've already missed that opportunity, so I'll have to wait until I become a deity. Then I'll be able to level-up all of them and make the manifestations merge and take on a new form. It's just that I can't become a deity in the Trial Worlds, and it's unlikely that I'll get out of here without bumping into Kyle.*

After pondering this problem for a while longer, Kai decided to devote some time to training. First, he tested the new abilities, and then he moved on to practical training, summoning the incarnation of one of the ancient warriors to fight against. He didn't rest until he got the hang of the

Manifestations. Only then did he leave the ancient warrior and return to the Throne to take care of another matter.

Extending his hand, he released several thin strands of flesh from his fingertips. Crawling to the bottom of the platform below, the pulsating tentacles grew and diverged to form humanoid shapes until they grew into Kai's clones.

Closing his eyes, Kai focused on duplicating his *Shell*. After his training with Green, he now had a better understanding of the soul's inner workings, which aided him in creating more perfect artificial souls. Previously, neither Kai nor the older clones could explain to each other how exactly they used their abilities, but from now on, his clones would have basic control of *Will* from the moment of their creation. They would only have to temper it in order to unleash its full potential. Also, now that he knew how they would be able to do this, he proceeded to infuse the artificial souls with more energy, thereby stimulating the process of acquiring strings with vibrations similar to his own.

Once the souls were formed, Kai made the clones come to life. For some time after the physical connection was severed, they simply lay on the floor. After a while, they clumsily scrambled to their feet and bowed their heads.

"Greetings, master," they said in unison.

Improved souls and bodies. Kai smiled. *I need to find time to upgrade the old clones. I wonder if I can create something like an* Astral Body… *Would that allow them to form* Spheres *and everything that comes with a proper* Soul Shell?

After clothing the clones and giving them the Eternal Path Temple marks, Kai took three of them under direct control with a parallel stream of consciousness so that he could continue making clones while simultaneously dealing with the Temple's and the empire's multiple affairs.

***

"As you can see, there is some effect, but it's not as strong as we'd like," one of the researchers of the technology center said. "On the other hand, the effect's duration is much longer when compared to the Formless, and the creation process requires very little resource."

Looking at the ring lying in front of him, Kai tried to use several different techniques on it. He changed weaves, elements, and the amount of invested *ki* and *Will*, but nothing worked. However, as soon as he tried to activate multiple techniques at once, he learned that the artifact blocked only the first three, completely ignoring the rest.

"So, using three techniques simultaneously over and over again will overload it. Interesting…"

"It would appear so. However, this isn't apparent, so I wouldn't call it a defect."

Kai nodded in agreement. Rare were those who used more than two techniques at once, so he didn't have to worry about being caught off guard.

Pondering, he returned his attention to the ring. The Formless' ability to sever the connection to the path of development around them was so fascinating that he couldn't help trying to find a way to utilize it. He handed this task over to a group from the technology center, along with samples of the angel flesh he had obtained in the House of Blood and the *Elixir of Formless Angels* Sirius had acquired from the Cartel.

It took a while, but the clones managed to incorporate this power into a Spiritual Plant that they grew for this purpose in the ATS. The tree not only successfully absorbed the angelic flesh, but also adopted some of its properties. By default, the ring made from the harvested bark didn't suppress anything, so the research team introduced *Yang* weaves based on the *Elixir's* structure. When activated, they caused the wood to gradually release its power.

"In theory, we can expand its area of influence, but this will probably not change its effect. To unleash an angel's full power, you need to combine its flesh with something very powerful. With something that won't yield to the soul. Basically, another soul."

"What about the Shadows?"

The researcher shook his head.

"Spirits won't do either. You need a soul with a *Spark*."

Angel flesh requires a living being's Spark? *Kai thought. Could it be because of the* Spark shackles' features? *Green said that they obey the* Higher Force of the Spark, *determining the life span depending on the number of shackles it has thrown off. Their strength must be incredible if they are able to hold back the Higher Spark.*

"Through many experiments, we managed to create a different version of the *Elixir*," the researcher continued in the meantime. "This version won't cause the subject to turn into a Formless nor will it change the *Shell*."

"That sounds like good progress."

"It is. However, the effect will be only temporary. Furthermore, the subject will be unable to use techniques while the *Elixir* remains in the system."

"Something tells me that it doesn't end there."

"It doesn't. The *Elixir* is still too unstable. Even the *Divine Stage* subjects died painfully within a few seconds after its consumption."

"Their *Shells* couldn't take the load?"

"I'm afraid not, sir."

"I see..." Kai thought, remembering his unique soul protection. "How many of these elixirs and rings can you create?"

"Three full doses and about five hundred rings."

"Have you found any other ways to counter the Formless' abilities?"

"Taking into account the information about the strings we received from you, we assume that the suppression zone is an oscillation that interacts with the hyperstring of the path of development and dampens the vibrations responsible for recognizing weaves. By using the waves found in the angelic flesh, it would be possible to create a vibration that would strengthen the necessary part of the hyperstring, thereby weakening the suppression. Unfortunately, since the natural sources of such fluctuations are unknown to us, we can't do anything without the power of a deity."

"I see."

"I would also like to inform you that my colleagues in the ATS have given your student one of the rings for testing under normal time flow conditions. We have received the report, but the ring is still with him."

"I know." Kai nodded. "He already told me. I let him keep the ring. You keep experimenting. Try to further strengthen the suppression zone and refine those *Elixirs*."

"Yes, sir."

***

Meanwhile, in another body, Kai was fighting.

"Faster!" he yelled, dodging one attack and blocking

another. "Show me some new moves! Improvise! Think!"

Picking up speed, Viola tried to attack from behind. Her blades were about to cut Kai in half when he arched back in a bone-crushing way, dodging her attack, and pierced her chest with his sword.

Taking advantage of the gap in his defense, Ryu attacked with both spears.

His right sword is in Viola's body. He won't be able to defend with only one blade!

As if reading his thoughts, Kai suddenly threw the sword right in Ryu's face. Letting go of the blade stuck in Viola's chest, he pushed off the ground.

Dodging the blade, Ryu found himself right under Kai who grabbed his spear with the speed of light and pulled it toward himself, flipping his position in the air.

In the next moment, Kai's heel hit the top of Ryu's head, pushing him to the ground. Kai's fists, elbows, and legs followed, not giving him even a chance to fight back.

The fight was finally over. Wounded and tired, Ryu and Viola fell to the ground.

"Not bad for the first time," Kai remarked. "But there is still a lot of work to be done. You have fifteen minutes to rest, and then we'll go again. Separately."

"This is a waste of time," Viola grumbled.

"On the contrary. The ability to use your body is one of the most important aspects of martial arts."

After several solo training sessions, Kai let Ryu and Viola rest while he used the Eternal Throne to analyze the fights and put his observations into memory scrolls, thus creating a detailed report.

During the first days of their training, Ryu and Viola were fully focused on learning how to control their bodies and weapons, but then Kai introduced a different training format, instructing them to fight exclusively with techniques and other spiritual abilities, highlighting a new aspect of Mastery.

"Only you can create techniques that are perfect for you. All I can do is teach you the basics, but you will have to complete the weaving yourself. Viola, you still have a long way to go. As for you, Ryu... With your talent for techniques and ATS, you'll be able to do this relatively quickly."

"But I have already created the necessary techniques for myself," Ryu said, confused.

"Yes. However, some of them can still be improved, and some should be replaced," Kai elaborated. "There are many things you don't know, and many more things you may not suspect at all. There's always room for improvement."

"Yes, sir..."

Five days went by in the blink of an eye. With the ability to split his consciousness across several clones, Kai didn't have to worry about time. They would run the Temple and the empire while he monitored Viola's and Ryu's progress. He wouldn't rest until he was certain that the two could cultivate properly on their own.

While Viola fought against one of the incarnations, Kai and Ryu worked inside the training artifact. Holding special pens, they poured the same amount of energy into the artifact, which resulted in two bright multi-colored dots inside a huge glass cube. By manipulating the infused power, they released threads from the clumps and directed them toward each other. The goal was to reach the other clump with a predetermined number of threads. The space was filled with extremely dense *Heavenly Water*, which made it very, very difficult to hold the threads and maneuver them. Each player could slow down, block, or even destroy the opponent's threads. The rather simple rules allowed for the implementation of a wide variety of tactics, which made Klart, as the game was called, an excellent way to practice energy control and learn strategy.

Nineteen rounds later, the number of threads on both sides was the same, but the red ones clearly overpowered the blue ones in strength. Finding a gap, several red threads separated from the mass and rushed toward the blue clump. The blue ones rushed to intercept, but they were too late.

"You handled yourself much better this time around. Your *ki* control has gotten better," Kai praised Ryu.

"There's still room for improvement." Ryu smiled sadly. "You're holding back, aren't you?"

"It would be unfair otherwise. This is a good exercise for me, too. This way, I'm learning to hold back. You shouldn't always attack with everything you have."

"Master…" Ryu said as they began the last round and formed the first threads. "Do you think this is really useful?"

"You think it's not?"

"I'm not sure," Ryu admitted. "I spent more than three hundred and thirty years in ATS after your return. All this time, I honed every aspect of my skill. But no matter what I did, every new step after reaching *Seven Small Stars* was incredibly difficult. And in recent decades, I didn't make any progress at all. I tried to force the layers to work more actively, but they didn't react to anything I did." Ryu spoke with notes of despair and humility. "I'm afraid I have reached the limit of my talent, and that you are only wasting your time on me…"

"We all feel like that at some point of our lives, but this isn't a reason to stop. True Mastery is the ability to perfectly use absolutely every tool in your arsenal, even those that seem useless at first glance," Kai explained, trying to remember where he heard these words. They seemed very familiar but he couldn't quite understand why. "Are layers really necessary for honing skills? I doubt it... Let's take a simple movement: sword swinging. Practicing it over and over again, you will eventually perfect it. But whose swing will be better, a mortal's or a True Master's?"

Ryu narrowed his eyes.

"Masters," he answered confidently.

"You're right." Kai nodded. "And why? Isn't the swing already perfect?"

"Everything is relative. What is perfect the way mortals understand it may be full of flaws in the eyes of a Master."

"Exactly. A mortal can practice the swing of the blade to perfection. And yet, a Master will still be able to detect the smallest fluctuations and irregularities in his movements. Mistakes so tiny that a mortal wouldn't ever be able to realize them. Practice makes perfect. To become better at anything, you need to practice."

"Are you saying that the implementation of the layers is just an enhancement and not a skill?"

"Exactly. By trying to do something we couldn't before, we push ourselves beyond our current capabilities. The layers don't make you better, but they enable you to become better. We mustn't mustn't overlook the importance of experience and practice. That is why even among the *Masters of Seven Great Stars,* there can be a considerable difference in skill. Even if you think you have reached your limit, you can still become stronger and more skillful. Understand?"

"Yes, sir." Ryu nodded with a smile.

"Show me your scorecard."

Giving Kai a confused look, Ryu found the *Master Stars Test* evaluation message and forwarded it to his mentor.

Master Star Challenge Scorecard

Master: Ryu Araki

Parameters of mastery relative to the Stage (extended version):

• (1) Mind (the ability to analyze and calculate your own and other people's actions in advance and make the most profitable decisions in a fight): Seven Small Stars (7.02)

• (1) Demonstration of spirit forces in a fight (quality of using personal techniques, unique skills, bloodline power, spirit power, and Divine Gift, if you have any): Seven Small Stars (7.23)

• (1) Demonstration of physical forces in a fight (quality of body and weapon use): Seven Small Stars (7.24)

• (2) Energy Control Level: Seven Small Stars (7.21)

• (2) Force Particle Control Level: Seven Small Stars (7.23)

Your Mastery Score: Seven Small Stars (7.17)

...

Parameters of strength relative to the Stage (extended version):

• (1) Willpower: Seven Small Stars (7.2)

• (2) Quality of Understanding of the Elements: Six Small Stars (6.24)

• (2) Power of Unique Skills (Ultimate Focus (level 3); Field of Superiority; Complete Submission; Average Heavenly Spirit of Spear; Average Heavenly Spirit of Space; Average Heavenly Spirit of Light; Average Heavenly Spirit of Wood): Seven Small Stars (7). (secondary parameter).

• (3) Technique Quality: Seven Big Stars (7.56)

• (3) Amount of ki: Seven Big Stars (7.75)

• (3) Physical Body Strength: Seven Big Stars (7.75)

• Power of the Divine Gift: None. (secondary parameter)

• Bloodline Strength: None. (secondary parameter)

Your Strength Score: Seven Small Stars (7.08)

You have been given the title of the Master of Seven Small Stars (7.12)

"As you can see, I hit the ceiling not only in the assessment of Mastery but also in the quality of knowledge of the *Forces*."

"I noticed." Kai nodded. "I can help you with that, too."

"Are you talking about *Elemental Soul Particles* and the *Favorite of the Forces* feature?"

"I am." Kai smiled. "And since you are my student, you shouldn't have any troubles obtaining them. With your strength and my authority, we will easily make you into a rank-two Legend on Insulaii. We'll pull it off on Ferox, too. We just need to make the *Exodus* first. Technically, this can be done without the *Exodus*, provided I make a deal with the Eversteins. After that, there's only Bellum left. That will be more difficult, but I think I have something to bribe the Order of Purity with so that they would let you fight their members and reach the required rating to buy the *Elemental Body* and *Soul Particles*."

Ryu stared at Kai dumbfounded.

"How many billions of *Runes* will I need for all this?"

"You don't need to worry about that. As your mentor, I'm willing to do whatever it takes to help you reach your potential, so stop doubting yourself. The *Particles* will help you with the elements, improve your energy control, and strengthen your body. I will assist you to further temper your *Will*, teach you to control it, and help you improve your techniques. All of this will improve and hone your skills that don't depend on the layers. You will also receive a bloodline and a *Divine Gift*. With all this, you will definitely become a *Master of Seven Big Stars*, and someday, if a suitable divine resource is found, of *Seven Great Stars*. You have my support and an unbending *Will* combined with an endless desire for self-improvement. And that, Ryu, is more important than any talent you could have been born with."

Chapter 24
PEACEFUL DAYS 2

Nearly a month later, Kai ended Ryu's training and took him to the *Altar*.

"Are we going to buy something?"

"You'll see."

In the golden hall, An'na, Renata, Nyako, Lily, and Malvur were already waiting for them.

"Have you already got your orders?" Kai asked as he approached the *Altar's* inverted pyramid.

"What's going on?" Ryu asked. Confused, he lagged behind the group.

"Here." Kai tossed a scroll to him. "Read it."

While Ryu was reading, Kai continued.

"As of today, Ryu Araki, Renata Vin'Thar, An'na Divide, Lily Wayat Stenshet, and Malvur di Santos No'Rhythm are officially appointed Templars of the Eternal Path Temple," he announced. "For this reason, you, as well as Nyakonalavius, are entitled to acquire the *Divine Gift*."

Having spent a significant amount of time training in

the ATS, Kai's friends reached the initial level of the *Divine Stage*. The only exception was Shacks, who, having reached the peak level of the *Holy Lord Stage*, got tired of hanging around in the confined space of the *Complex* and decided to postpone entering the ATS. With all the talent, skill, and not to mention the unique *Divine Gift* and experience that he possessed, he became a *Master of Seven Big Stars* in no time. Kai suspected that this wasn't his limit and that he would one day acquire *Seven Great Stars*.

"Bidding will end soon, so don't miss your chance," Kai said. "I gave you access to the Temple's treasury, so you have unlimited funds. Use this money wisely. I think you understand that there is no point in purchasing the most expensive *Gifts* if they don't suit you."

Nodding, they opened the desired section in anticipation.

Special:

• Higher Division (out of stock)

Divine Gift

Level 1

Full Description: Creates a clone equal in strength, allowing the user to instantly switch places with it. The number and duration of the clone's existence depends on the user's strength.

Seller: Heavenly Exaltation Pagoda

Initial cost: 250,000,000 Runes

Feature: Instant integration into the body of the buyer.

Limitation: Only for Commanders and above.

• **Supreme Weaponry (out of stock)**

Divine Gift

Level 1

Full description: Creates weapons and armor (or strengthens existing ones) that greatly enhance the user's attack power, defense, and speed. The power and duration of the Gift depend on the user's strength.

Seller: Heavenly Exaltation Pagoda

Initial cost: 250,000,000 Runes

Feature: Instant integration into the body of the buyer.

Limitation: Only for Commanders and above.

• **Thunder Stride (out of stock)**

Divine Gift

Level 2

Full description: When activated, unleashes a huge amount of Lightning in the form of an explosion, saturating the air around the user with it. The electrified space inflicts constant damage to any objects except the user. The first level of mastery allows the user to move with great speed using a Lightning Strike, which also inflicts a certain amount of damage.

Additional feature: Allows the user to quickly master the Path of Lightning.

Seller: Heavenly Exaltation Pagoda

Initial cost: 455,000,000 Runes

Feature: Instant integration into the body of the buyer.

Limitation: Only for Commanders (500 rating points) and above.

• **Advanced Alchemy**

Divine Gift

Level 3

Full description: When activated, significantly enhances the ability to see the internal structure of any potion, elixir, pill, or any other alchemical solution. The first level of mastery can lead up to stacking of their effects up to five times. The number of used alchemical solutions depends on the user's strength. The second level of mastery allows the user to create one portion of a special infusion once a year, which can permanently increase all their physical parameters. The infusion can be used repeatedly, as long as there is enough Will to sustain that much power. Only the owner of the Gift can consume the infusion.

Seller: Heavenly Exaltation Pagoda

Initial cost: 1,120,000,000 Runes

Current value: 2,715,000,000 Runes

Time remaining until the end of the auction: 12 minutes

Feature: Instant integration into the body of the buyer.

Limitation: Only for Commanders (1,000 rating points) and above.

• **Hunting in the Shadow**

Divine Gift

Level 3

Full description: While active, allows the user to merge with the shadows, completely hiding their presence, and teleport between them. The mark can be placed on any shadow, allowing easy tracking and teleporting, regardless of obstacles and distance. The first level of mastery improves the user's movement speed and control of the shadows, turning them into a separate one. The second level of mastery splits the user's shadow, creating Shadow Hunters, with abilities equal to the first two levels of mastery. The strength and number of Shadow Hunters depend on the user's strength, as well as the number of shadows around them, reaching their peak in pitch darkness.

Additional feature: The user can merge with the Shadow Hunters to increase their parameters.

Additional feature: Allows the user to quickly master the Path of Shadow.

Seller: Heavenly Exaltation Pagoda

Initial cost: 1,805,000,000 Runes

Current value: 3,150,000,000 Runes

Time remaining until the end of the auction: 12 minutes

Feature: Instant integration into the body of the buyer.

Limitation: Only for Commanders (1,000 rating points) and above.

- **Casket of Eternity**

Divine Gift

Level 4

Full description: Upon activation, creates a personal pocket dimension within the user's spiritual world. The Casket contains within itself a fully functional dimension of colossal size that remains inside the user forever. The strength of the Casket, the stability of the dimension, and its size depend on the user's strength. The first level of mastery allows the user to manipulate the dimension within the Casket however they please. The second level of mastery allows the user to summon the Casket into the physical world and open it, sucking everything around it into its dimension. Maintenance of the Casket relies on the user's power. Without the second level of mastery, items can only be moved into the Casket by touching them. The third level of mastery will destroy the Casket, turning it into a black hole, the power of which depends on the power of the Casket and its contents. After a year, the user will be able to create a new Casket. There can only be one Casket at a time.

Additional feature: Allows the user to master the Path of Space. If the Path of Space has already been mastered, the user gains a higher understanding of the element of Space.

Seller: Heavenly Exaltation Pagoda

Initial cost: 3,850,000,000 Runes

Current value: 4,470,000,000 Runes

Time remaining until the end of the auction: 12 minutes.

Feature: Instant integration into the body of the buyer.

Limitation: Only for Commanders (1,500 rating points) and above.

• Blood Staining (out of stock)

Divine Gift

Level 4

Full description: Possessing a part of the flesh (preferably blood), the user can perform a long ritual, putting a curse on the owner of the flesh and weakening their body and soul. The fresher the flesh, the higher the chance of the curse being imposed. The strength of the curse depends on the user's strength. The curse can be removed either by killing the user or by inflicting a force that is as strong as the Gift. If left unattended for a long period of time, the curse will wear off on its own. The first level of mastery allows the user to put up to three curses into one item. In total, the user can maintain up to ten inactive curses. The second level of mastery grants three additional curses: pain, confusion, and decay. The third level of mastery opens the possibility of creating a Wandering Curse from a living being. The Wandering Curse is incorporeal and pursues its target until it reaches it or is destroyed. The Wandering Curse is more powerful than a regular curse due to the sacrifice of a sentient being and encompasses all four types of curses. In addition, the user can sacrifice themselves to create the most powerful Wandering Curse. In this case, flesh is not required.

Seller: Heavenly Exaltation Pagoda

Initial cost: 3,850,000,000 Runes

Feature: Instant integration into the body of the buyer.

Limitation: Only for Commanders (1,500 rating points) and above.

• **Invincible Fortress**

Divine Gift

Level 4

Full description: [preview]

Seller: Heavenly Exaltation Pagoda

Initial cost: 4,050,000,000 Runes

Current value: 5,000,000,000 Runes

Time remaining until the end of the auction: 12 minutes

Feature: Instant integration into the body of the buyer.

Limitation: Only for Commanders (1,500 rating points) and above.

• **Breath of Ashes**

Divine Gift

Level 4

Full Description: By activating the Gift, the user can create

Ash, a unique combination of Fire and Death, and saturate their body and weapon techniques with it, enhancing their abilities. The Ash is very dangerous to other creatures on its own. The first level of mastery allows the user to create Ash Armor and Ash Bombs. The second level of mastery allows the user to use Ash Eruption, covering the surrounding area with concentrated Ash in just a few moments. The third level of mastery will turn the user into an Ash Avatar, granting them incredible strength and making their body immune to physical attacks. Anything the Avatar touches, including air, will turn into nothingness. Using his power, the Avatar is able to raise the dead, turning them into obedient puppets.

Additional feature: Allows the user to quickly master the Paths of Fire and Death. If one of the Paths has already been mastered, the user gains a higher understanding of one of the elements.

Seller: Heavenly Exaltation Pagoda

Initial cost: 4,140,000,000 Runes

Current value: 5,925,000,000 Runes

Time remaining until the end of the auction: 12 minutes.

Feature: Instant integration into the body of the buyer.

Limitation: Only for Commanders (1,900 rating points) and above.

• **Dreams Come True (out of stock)**

Divine Gift

Level 4

Full description: [Unavailable. Error]

Seller: Heavenly Exaltation Pagoda

Cost: 5,000,000,000 Runes

Feature: Instant integration into the body of the buyer.

Limitation: Only for Commanders (1,900 rating points) and above.

Kai reviewed the list, comparing it with the one he had seen at the *Great Altar*. The *Divine Gifts* here weren't even close to those sold in the Abyss, but they were still a highly sought commodity. The sale of *Divine Gifts* was rare, so only those with a lot of Runes could afford them.

In the Eternal Path Temple, everyone got what they deserved, so Kai was ready to invest in his followers. He had been tracking the section with *Divine Gifts* for a long time, patiently waiting for the auction.

Twelve minutes and just over thirty billion Runes later, the group left the *Altar* with their chosen *Divine Gifts*.

***

Their feet sank into the wet sand as the waves washed over the beach. A cool breeze played with the long hair of the two people strolling down the magnificent shore. Holding hands, Ivsim and Lily admired the star-filled sky. They didn't need to speak to understand each other's thoughts.

"You came," An'na greeted them, standing knee-deep in the azure water.

"Of course." Lily smiled. "After all, it was my idea."

"We are almost ready." An'na nodded behind her back. "Guts, Ailenx, Malvur, and Ragnar are waiting by the campfire."

"Eyo!" Ragnar waved them over with a grin. "I hope you don't mind me joining you? Everyone in the Temple has been so busy lately, so when I heard about this little get-together, I really wanted to join. I brought snacks!"

"We don't mind," Lily sat down on a log. "The more the merrier."

Ivsim nodded in agreement, dropping down beside her.

"It's a pity that Renata isn't here… Drinks anyone?"

"Wine. Good," Malvur said as he reached for a glass.

"Yes…" Ragnar drawled, pouring drinks. "After the war, we… There was a lot of stuff lying about. Like this wine. If I remember correctly, it came from Dragons' cellar."

"Smells amazing," Ivsim said as he brought his glass to his lips.

"So!" Ragnar raised his drink. "First of all, a toast to our newest members. Malvur. An'na. Lily." He saluted each of them in turn. "To your success! May the Heavens watch over you!"

"Congratulations!" everyone exclaimed and downed their wine.

The rest of the evening was full of tasty food, quality alcohol, and funny stories. At some point, a quarrel broke out, which culminated in an arm wrestling competition between Ailenx and Ragnar.

For more than a minute, the elf puffed and huffed, until Ragnar, eager to get some more wine, ended the match with a sharp movement. Ailenx's arm flew through the makeshift wooden table, showering them both with splinters.

"I demand a rematch!" Ailenx exclaimed, red in the face from both anger and alcohol.

"You're on!" Ragnar laughed. "Let me just… Find us another table…"

Three rounds later, the aesir was still undefeated.

"Anyone else wanna go?!"

"Again!" Ailenx shouted, slamming the empty glass on the table.

"You need a break, buddy." Ragnar slapped him on the shoulder, causing the already staggering Ailenx to almost fall. "What about you, Malvur? Wanna test your strength?"

The giant just shook his head as he continued to sip his wine. He enjoyed the evening but he didn't want to actively participate in it.

"What about me? I wanna test my strength!" An'na suddenly exclaimed.

"Oho? A new contestant?" Ragnar cracked his fingers. "Show me what you've got!"

Ragnar's large hand enveloped her small, delicate palm, and Ivsim's hand covered them both from above.

"Ready? Three, two, one!"

As Ivsim let go, Ragnar pushed with all his might in the opposite direction. Shock was written all over his face when he barely managed to stop his palm just a few inches from the table's surface.

"Something wrong?" An'na asked with an innocent smile.

"Did you pass the fourth transformation of the *Hydra Scale Flask*?" Ragnar hissed, pushing with all his might.

"I did." An'na continued to smile. "Just recently."

"I have... underestimated you..."

With a muffled growl, Ragnar began to slowly push An'na back. Everyone watched their struggle with interest.

The match dragged on for good fifteen minutes and ended in Ragnar's victory.

"Oh, well." An'na shrugged. "Once upon a time, even Kai couldn't defeat me."

"Those days are long gone." Lily smiled.

"Really?" Ragnar wondered as he finished his wine. "I thought he was born a muscular baby. Like, he could cultivate straight from the womb."

"He was good before, but not as strong," Lily recalled.

"It's a pity he isn't here," Ailenx muttered.

"He's always so busy with work," Ivsim mumbled.

"More wine?" Ragnar asked.

"Yes, please," An'na said.

There was silence for a while.

"Do you know what we need?" Lily suddenly said, catching everyone's attention. "Music! Guts is busy cooking, but we have Ivsim. He mastered many instruments, exploring the *Path of Sound*."

"...I might be blind, but I can feel you all staring at me."

"Come on, it'll be fun!"

"I don't mind." Ivsim smiled, turning to Lily. "But only if you play with me."

"Me?"

"I remember you telling me that you were taught how to play the lyre as a child. All aristocrats should know how to play at least one instrument, you said."

"That was ages ago!" Lily shook her head. "And I don't have a lyre!"

"Well, I just happen to have one. Please? I'm sure it'll all come back to you." Ivsim playfully nudged her in the side with his elbow. "Especially with the memory of a *Divine Stage* cultivator."

Lily pursed her lips and frowned. Everyone was waiting for an answer with interest.

"Okay." She sighed, defeated. "I'll try."

Ivsim gave her a lyre and took a transverse wooden flute for himself. Closing her eyes, Lily touched the strings. Remembering the distant past, she ran her fingers over them, enjoying the sound. After about a minute, she opened her eyes and nodded.

"Play what you know, and I will follow you," Ivsim said.

Lily stared at the instrument for a few seconds before finally touching the strings again. A quiet melody began its slow build-up. Soon, it was accompanied by the melodious song of the wooden flute, slightly amplified by Ivsim's *Sound* technique. After half a minute, Lily finally got into the rhythm, and the pleasant melody began to accelerate and change, becoming more dynamic, sublime, and somewhat dramatic. Pouring all of herself into the performance, Lily recalled her childhood and her hatred for the Clan, the clash with apostates and the death of her beloved grandfather, the Fallen Star Sect, the dungeons, the journey through half the Worlds to the Celestial Plateau, Ash's loyalty and self-sacrifice, the Earth, and much more.

The tempo rose and fell. Lily didn't notice when she began to improvise. But she did it beautifully. The splendor lasted for ten long minutes until the strings of the lyre finally calmed down. Only then did Lily feel the wetness in her eyes. The memories had awakened old and very strong emotions.

Brushing away her tears, she smiled.

"That was incredible!" An'na exclaimed.

"Amazing!" Ragnar applauded. "Let's drink! To good company and a great evening!"

"To a great evening!" the others cheered.

"The meat is ready."

"Took you long enough."

"Cooking is an art, and it doesn't tolerate haste," Guts replied.

The food was gone in a matter of seconds.

"I take it back. Such tender meat was worth the wait..." Ailenx drawled. "I had no idea that mortal food could be so tasty."

"You've been missing out," Ragnar said, stuffing his mouth with food.

"Told you!" Guts nodded. "Cooking helps clear my mind. And it gave me an idea..."

"Here we go..."

"Kai said that we would go to the Heavenly World, right? That he wants to return to his home on the periphery. But he won't drag the entire Temple with him there, will he? So I was thinking... If we settle in the Heavenly World, being a cook would be a great way to make money. There are many deities there and they like to indulge, yeah? So why not pursue the culinary arts?"

"And to think we've been fighting for our lives not so long ago..."

"Yeah..." Ailenx sighed. "Now we have a real home. We can finally do whatever we want."

"It's so much better here than in Cloud Abode and even

Belteise. I wonder what's happened with Rune'Tan's empire."

"Belteise?" Ragnar asked, reaching for a new plate of meat.

"A divine empire in the Middle Worlds of the Ecumene. We set off to the Trial Worlds from there," Ivsim explained.

"By the way, how did you meet Kai? I was sailing on the same ship with him when we flew into an anomaly. Turns out, the man I was with the entire time wasn't Kai, but Six. Kai swooped in at the end to save our asses."

An'na laughed.

"I've heard that one before. I met him at a tournament. We fought for our freedom so vigorously that he almost killed me that day. Then our paths diverged. I escaped slavery for a little while, but then I was imprisoned again. The Heavens must've been looking over me that day, since Kai happened to be nearby. He bailed me out. Malvur met him in the same place but before me."

"My story is much simpler," Guts said. "The two of us fulfilled a contract for a shady client, and then he invited me to join him as a mercenary. A strong Beast Master can come in handy everywhere, he said."

Ailenx chuckled.

"At least you have normal stories. Kai and Shacks fooled me and captured me, forcing me to do them a favor so that they could get to the qualifying exam in one elite academy with me. It worked in my favor, but still…"

"Speaking of him, where is Shacks?" Ragnar asked.

"Who knows?" An'na shrugged. "I told him about the party, but it looks like he decided not to show up. Maybe he's busy. I don't know. Besides, he has a bit of a difficult relationship with the group. He's on our side, but he's so…

so… He makes my blood boil sometimes!"

"I see. And what about you two?" Deciding not to go poking about the hornet's nest, Ragnar turned to Ivsim and Lily. "If I'm not mistaken, you've known him the longest."

"You're right." Ivsim nodded. "I met him back when he was at the *Body Stage* at a small regional tournament. I really thought he'd be among the first to drop out, so I was very surprised when he took the first place in the qualifying round. He suddenly disappeared right before the finals. It was a bittersweet victory, I have to admit. I was glad to have won, but it didn't feel quite right…"

"You wanted to fight him, didn't you?"

"Yes… We met again a few years later at an exam. That's it. Lily's story is more interesting."

"I wouldn't say that… I was on my way to the capital with family servants when our caravan was attacked by a pack of monsters. I couldn't use my powers to defend us, otherwise, my enemies would have tracked us down. The servants were dying one after another when a man came out of the forest in clothes so torn that he was practically naked. With one attack, he killed a *Mind-Stage* Berserker. Mind you, Kai was at the peak level of the *Body Stage* then. And butt-naked." She chuckled. "He joined the caravan as a guard since he was on his way to the capital, too. In return, I promised to help him find his sister. At some point, we were attacked by mercenaries. Shacks was actually one of them. We managed to escape, but we had to change our plans. Kai proposed a solution in exchange for my family's help. He met with our patriarch and even managed to convince him that he was right, enlisting his support. I still can't believe he did it… After that, we dealt with my family's enemies, joined the empire's biggest sect together, took part in a risky expedition, barely survived, and then went to join the planet's strongest sect. It was there that we met Ivsim." Smiling, Lily patted his cheek. "Shame that Shacks showed up there, too."

"Now I wanna hear Shacks's story even more!" Ragnar laughed. "Can't believe Kai was progressing so slowly."

"Apparently, he started quite late," Ivsim said.

"What a mysterious guy... Alright! Enough about the past. How about we open a new bottle of wine? Let's see... Hmm... Oh! Look at this! Five hundred thousand years old... You can't buy such a rarity even for a million Runes!"

The party continued deep into the night. Malvur was the first to leave, thanking everyone for a great time. A little later, Ragnar left as well, followed by the staggering Guts, and An'na, who helped them drag Ailenx home. Ragnar dropped the poor elf several times and even accidentally bumped into a couple of the trees along the way, but he didn't even notice.

In the end, only two remained.

Sitting down on Ivsim's knees, Lily put her arms around his neck.

"You know, I agree with Ailenx. Now we have a home. I think that's why I went after Kai. The Eternal Path Temple really looks like my final destination." She clung to his chest. "I'm happy here."

"Me too. It's kind of sad, though," Ivsim said thoughtfully. "There's no one else from Alkea here. Just us."

"That's not quite true," a voice suddenly came from nearby, making the couple flinch.

"Shacks? What are you doing sitting in a tree?" Lily gasped. "Why did you come now? The party's over."

"What are you talking about? I've been here this entire time. Not my problem none of you bothered to look up," he retorted with a grin.

"What do you mean 'not quite'?" Ivsim asked. "You're not from Alkea, are you?"

"Heavens forbid. But someone else is. You should know him." Shacks nodded at Lily. "A guy with very peculiar eyes."

Lily frowned even more.

"Greenrow?"

"Maaaaaybe."

"That's impossible! How can he be here?"

"Believe it or not, he is. Who do you think Kai's been hanging out with lately, hm? Though, this 'Greenrow' isn't like the pompous peacock you guys knew. He seems to have changed. For the worse, I'd say." Suddenly, he looked up. "Oh, dear me, look at the time! Well, I should go. Don't catch a cold!"

With a smile and a curtsy, he disappeared into the shadows.

Clenching her fists, Lily seethed with anger.

"You still haven't come to terms with what happened on Saha?" Ivsim put his arm around her shoulders. "Do you still want revenge?"

"Yes!"

"I hate to say this, but... you can't beat him."

"I know."

"Lily... Don't you think it's time to let go? Do you want to live like this all your life?"

"I don't, but..." Lily spoke through clenched teeth, lowering her gaze. "But this anger... It has already become a part of me. It's the flame that fuels my soul. It's so ingrained in me that I feel I'd be lost without it. But it seems that there is nothing to be done about it. I guess I just have to wait for him to die... I don't think there is another way."

"Let's just forget it. At least for tonight."

Taking a deep breath, Lily turned around and kissed him.

"You're right, I'm sorry," she replied with a smile, snuggling closer to him. "I love you, Ivsim."

"I love you, too, Lily."

***

Lightly shuddering, Kai slowly came to his senses. The *Eternal Throne* strengthened his mind, but couldn't help him completely alleviate the consequences of diving into the *Spark*. He still needed time to recover.

As planned, he created an artifact based on Green's technique, designed to weaken the connection between the flesh and the *Shell* as much as possible. Having introduced it into the Eternal Throne, he plunged into this state for the fifty-seventh time, finally achieving what he wanted: all the cracks on the shackles of his *Spark* reached their maximum depth. Now, his *Will* was equal to the strength of *Seven Great Stars*. The only thing left to do was to temper the *Will of Reason* so that he could someday create a deep crack and become an *Ascended*.

"Let's see..."

Parameters of mastery relative to the stage (extended

version):

• (1) Mind (the ability to analyze and calculate your own and other people's actions in advance and make the most profitable decisions in a fight): Seven Small Stars (7.23)

• (1) Demonstration of spirit forces in a fight (quality of using personal techniques, unique skills, bloodline power, spirit power, and Divine Gift, if you have any): Seven Big Stars (7.69)

• (1) Demonstration of physical forces in a fight (quality of body and weapon use): Seven Big Stars (7.7)

• (2) Energy Control Level: Seven Big Stars (7.75)

• (2) Force Particle Control Level: Seven Big Stars (7.75)

Your Mastery Score: Seven Big Stars (7.59).

...

Parameters of strength relative to the stage (extended version):

• (1) Willpower: Seven Big Stars (7.75)

• (1) Bloodline Strength: Seven Great Stars (7.75) (secondary parameter) (great connection)

• (2) Quality of understanding of the elements: Seven Big Stars (7.75)

• (2) Power of Unique Skills (Yin Yang Phantom Tattoo; Ultimate Focus (level 3); Supreme Simulation (level 2); Advanced Field of Superiority; Advanced Complete Submission; Advanced Desolation of the Weak; Advanced Will of Sword; Advanced Will of Space; completed bond with the Guardian of the Great Weapon; Cryde Technique; Manifestations of the Soul level 1 [preview]): Seven Big Stars (7.75) (secondary parameter)

• (3) Technique Quality: Seven Big Stars (7.75)

• (3) Amount of ki: Eight Stars (8)

• (3) Physical Body Strength: Eight Stars (8)

• Power of the Divine Gift: None. (secondary parameter)

Your Strength Score: Seven Big Stars (7.76)

You have been given the title of the Master of Seven Big Stars (7.66)

Having studied the logs, Kai began to train his *Will* control. Green had laid the groundwork, but he was still far from the heights of mastery.

Splitting his consciousness into an even greater number of parallel streams, Kai simultaneously trained, created clones, and controlled three more bodies.

The days flew by one after another, when suddenly...

There was a terrible explosion in the middle of the Kaiser's Ark.

Dropping everything that he was doing and returning to his main body, Kai teleported into the sky above the island. Discovering a huge conflagration in the southwest quarter of the outer city, he rushed there at full speed.

Luckily, this is a sparsely populated area, so there aren't many victims, Kai thought, moving the survivors to his *Storage* and applying a healing technique to them. *But these emanations...*

Ulu appeared nearby.

"What's the report?"

"The cause seems to have been a technique or an artifact. I do not know how they slipped by me. Forgive me, sir. I will bear the consequences of my failure." Ulu lowered her head. "Whoever it was, they knew how the island's tracking arrays worked."

"It's not your fault, Ulu. Besides, no artifact did this... No. Two extremely strong Masters clashed here. And both concealed their traces. We need to investigate the area thoroughly. Check every inch of the ground and the location of each mark. Every aura. I need answers," Kai ordered.

"At once, sir."

A state of emergency was declared on Kaiser's Ark following the explosion, and Sirius, Qi, and Chag were immediately placed under house arrest. Unfortunately, even the *Runes of Truth* didn't yield any useful information out of them.

The investigation was fruitless. The only shred of hope was a tattered letter, addressed personally to Kai. It hinted at a potential lead amidst the chaos.

I am very sorry that this happened, but I cannot reveal myself. Be warned that there is a traitor among your close associates. I wish I could tell you who they are, but I was ambushed just before I could make the discovery. My futile attempt to reveal their identity cost the lives of many innocent citizens.

Please, be careful.

A friend

Kai frowned, tapping his fingers on the armrest of the throne.

I was wondering when he'd make his next move, but I didn't even suspect that he was already here. And who is this "friend" of mine? Are they really trying to help me, or do they have an agenda of their own?

Chapter 25
INVESTIGATION AND ENLIGHTENMENT

The trail might have gotten cold but the search for the perpetrators didn't stop for a moment. The interrogation of Sirius, Qi, and Chag gave no results as all three of them were in a completely different place at the time of the explosion, under the clones' surveillance. Moreover, they hadn't interacted with anyone who had been in the area in the last twenty-four hours.

With such solid alibis, Kai could no longer keep them in custody, but he still had his doubts, so he restricted their movements. For now, they were forbidden to leave the central district of the city without permission.

After that, he returned to the contents of the mysterious letter.

A traitor among those close to me? he thought. *Who could it be?*

After thinking over the situation, he decided to use the last two *Runes of Truth* to get more answers. He had sensed something weird, tinkering with his mind, so it was time to use these unique artifacts. They could help find out things that even the speaker didn't know. Only "yes" or "no" questions, two per each *Rune*, but with the ability to divide his consciousness Kai didn't even need a counterparty. As a leader of the Temple, he had strong enough connection to this question to get answers.

"Is there a traitor among the members of the Eternal Path Temple?"

Trying to say yes, he couldn't even open his mouth.

"No."

"Are there people among my followers who have unknowingly or unwittingly cooperated with, obeyed, or were controlled by persons who wish to harm the Eternal Path Temple, me, or anyone else?"

An attempt to say "yes" didn't give anything. Much to his surprise, Kai found himself unable to say "no" either.

Is the answer so ambiguous? Or is something preventing the Rune of Truth *from giving an answer? I only have two attempts left so I should choose my questions carefully. I have already learned that there is no traitor in the Temple. So, the author of the message is either mistaken or he is lying...* Kai pondered for a moment. *Maybe I should learn more about them...*

"Does the author of the letter truly believe that they ran into one of my followers when the explosion happened?"

"Yes."

"Is the author of the letter one of my followers?"

"Yes."

As the *Zone of Truth* dissipated, Kai became lost in his thoughts once more.

There is no traitor, but it's apparent that one of my followers is under someone's control. Whoever is behind this is most likely under divine protection that hides them from the Runes. Closing his eyes, Kai rubbed his temple. *The author of the letter is also my follower, but they don't seem to have all the information.*

For a moment, Kai entertained the idea of making everyone swear an oath, but he immediately dismissed it. If the attacker found out that he was close to figuring out their identity, they might get scared and back away, and then he'd never catch them. No. It'd be best to continue pretending like he was unaware of any of this. Eventually, the attacker would make a mistake, and that was when he would get them.

Furthermore, the oath wouldn't guarantee anything. Even if it helped him uncover who was being controlled, it would kill the person in the process. And while this would rob his enemies of a pawn, it'd leave the Temple one member short. No contract, spirit or divine, would help either. If the controlled party really was under some sort of divine protection, then they'd null the contract without batting an eyelid.

"It's complicated… But I can't just sit here and do nothing. Ulu."

"Yes, sir?"

"Gather everyone in the throne room."

"At once, sir."

***

Less than half an hour later, Kai had gathered everyone, save for the clones, to fill them in on the investigation's results and the contents of the letter.

"I understand that this is sudden, but I have to ask all of you to allow the *Heavenly Development Complex* to check your memory of the last twenty-four hours," Kai said and nodded to the giant coffin-like object that appeared in the room.

"Dude, just admit you want to take a peep at my harem," Shacks said with a dramatic sigh. "You don't really have to put up a whole show…"

Lilith rolled her eyes and shook her head.

"Fool…"

"Is any of us a suspect?" Shaw asked.

"I just want to make sure I'm not mistaken."

Although revealing one's memories was somewhat unpleasant, it wasn't even close to being forced to take a *System* oath. Something most Masters didn't take very well, to put it mildly.

Sirius, Qi, and Chag had gone through a similar test earlier, but nothing suspicious was found. The same was the case with everyone else. Kai knew that memories could be tampered with, so he looked for any signs of interference in everyone's minds, but came up empty-handed.

"Thank you all for your cooperation. Shacks. Lilith, please stay. The rest of you are free to go."

As everyone made their way out, Shacks threw himself into the nearby chair and put his feet on the table.

"I know what you're thinking, but I'm not going to add Lilith to my harem."

Lilith shot him a glare.

"Traitor or not, the Temple would be a much quieter place without you around…"

"Settle down, you two. Shacks, I need you to be serious for a moment. We need to talk about current events."

"I take it this will also affect our little thing?" Shacks asked.

"What thing?" Lilith frowned. "What's going on here?"

Kai sighed and leaned back in his seat.

"I had a feeling that something bad would happen since a certain someone has been acting against us for a long time. Shacks suspected that there is a possible traitor among us. I thought it suspicious how the Vinaris always knew where we were. And then there was Diana von Everstein. The Dolls were behind her attack on us, but it's still unclear how they knew that I have the Hydra bloodline. Only the Eversteins and Rosen could have that information, but the former would rather never cultivate again than cooperate with the Cult, and the latter was with me in the Abyss and couldn't convey the message to his people so quickly. And then there is the fact that someone who looked and felt like me murdered Kuro and Zhou Han Nam's granddaughter. Were it not for this, I doubt that the Unions would have ventured into such a massive and risky invasion of Avlaim. And the last thing is Malvur. For as long as I have known him, he has displayed perfect control over himself and his emotions. Therefore, I find his outburst in the ice dimension rather hard to believe. He would never lose control so easily. He would never lay a finger on one of my clones and Igdrasil. I'm inclined to believe that someone tampered with his emotional layer."

Lilith frowned and tapped her chin in thought.

"There is a clear conspiracy against you. Not even against you, but against everyone important to you. There is strong hatred in this. Do you still think that one of us is being played like a puppet?"

"I do. In fact, there may be more than one of you."

"Do you have any idea who could be behind this?"

"Yes. Izao Livarius."

Shacks thought for a moment.

"If Chag is in the Trial Worlds, you think that Izao can also be here, as powerful as his buddy?"

"Yes."

"And who is this Izao?" Lilith asked.

"A talented *Master* of *Soul* and *Mind* from the Middle Worlds. He already did something similar once, manipulating Shacks and the rest to attack me, and then, when he failed to defeat me, he tried to make them commit suicide. If it wasn't for Rune'Tan, I wouldn't have been able to stop them."

"I still need to thank the old fart for that," Shacks mumbled to himself.

"I think that like Chag, he traveled to the Trial Worlds and quickly reached the pinnacle of True Mastery."

"ATS?" Shacks asked.

"Probably." Kai nodded. "To be honest, I think this is a little far-fetched, but there's one little detail that bothers me. At the very end of the expedition to Belteise, Izao suddenly disappeared along with the key to the gates of the Imperial Palace entrusted to him. Later, when I asked Sawan to investigate the matter, he said he found no trace of Izao. It was as if he evaporated just before leaving the Labyrinth. So, if he managed to hide from a *Star Emperor*, then there's a high probability that he could have a *Complex* with an ATS."

"Did you get anything from Chag?" Lilith asked.

"Nothing. He doesn't know if Izao is in the Trial Worlds and he refuses to talk about him. I also checked his memory, but there was nothing suspicious there. However, Chag has a rather strong *Divine Gift* that allows him to move into someone's body and control it. Izao may have a similar *Gift*, which fits the attacker's MO."

"That's an unsettling thought," Lilith said. "To be a mindless puppet…"

"The perpetrator doesn't necessarily have to be him; it could be one of his servants." Kai continued with a nod. "I doubt it's either of you two. Not only are you strong-willed, but both of you 'died' relatively recently. Your 'deaths' would have severed your connection with the puppeteer. That's why I trust you two the most now."

"Hmm, that makes sense…" Lilith nodded.

"The investigation will continue along with the state of emergency. Be careful. Keep an eye on everyone and report to me if you notice anything suspicious. Alfred, Ulu, this applies to you, too."

"As you wish, sir," Alfred replied.

"Yes, sir."

"And what about ATS?" Lilith asked. "If we are being controlled, wouldn't that be noticeable? The load inside it would be bigger, wouldn't it?"

"That's a good point." Kai thought about it for a moment. "Either they compensate for this with their own ATS, or our hypothesis is completely wrong. You, Hiro, and

Shaw have never been in the ATS before. I suggest you step inside for a few minutes. This won't be enough to affect your soul in any way, but it will help test our theory."

Lilith frowned, realizing that, in spite of everything, only Shacks was beyond suspicion.

"I'll do it." She nodded. "Shall I do it now?"

"If you don't mind."

"I'll show her to it," Shacks offered.

"Thank you."

With that, Shacks and Lilith left the throne room and Kai went back to his thoughts. Unfortunately, he couldn't tell them everything.

The less they know, the better. I have no choice but to risk everything...

***

"Look at you, all grown up!" Ragnar boomed.

"Pleased to finally meet you in person." Ryu bowed slightly, distracted from training. "Excuse my sloppy appearance, we've been hard at work."

"Not at all! I'm glad to see Kai got himself such a diligent student."

By this time, Ragnar's body and soul were healed, yet there were still invisible scars, forever limiting his development potential. Neither the Temple's divine artifacts nor even someone as powerful as the *Star Emperors* could heal such damage.

"It is him!" Viola exclaimed, turning her thoughts into sound with a special technique. "His flesh has been mended so that I could tear it asunder!"

"And you are...?" Ragnar asked, a little confused.

"This is Viola, the keeper of my swords."

"Y'know, where I come from, a duel to the death is equal to a marriage proposal," the aesir said with a grin.

"There must be many a widow in your village then. Come, dance the dance of death with me!"

"Viola," Kai warned. "Have you forgotten my order? What did I tell you?"

Grumbling, Viola faded away.

"Do not kill or harm anyone without permission or unless my life is in danger."

"What else?"

"All members of the Eternal Path Temple are my allies. And I have to respect them."

"Never forget that."

"The blade is getting rusty and my patience is growing thinner," she said before falling silent.

"So, why did you call me?" Ragnar asked Kai.

"How about a friendly spar?"

"I thought you'd never ask!" Ragnar exclaimed, rubbing his hands together. "Oh, I've been itching for a good fight. You have no idea how much I've been waiting for the opportunity to spar with you again! Wait..." He frowned, "That's not your real body. I'm not gonna fight one of your clones!"

"Oh, I wasn't going to propose you fight against me, but against them." Kai nodded at Ryu and Viola. "They're good, but they lack combat experience. I'd like to teach them to defend against as many styles and elements as possible."

"Are we going to shed blood?!" Viola exclaimed, appearing again and almost clapping her hands in excitement.

"As you wish..." Ragnar seemed slightly disappointed. "Both of them at the same time?"

"With all due respect," Ryu smiled, "but you will never be able to win against the two of us at once."

"First rule of fighting, boy: never underestimate your opponent."

"You'd be wise to follow your own advice, brother," Ryu replied with an even bigger smile.

"Oho! I like you, lad! Let's see what you can do!"

"I'll turn on the array. You two get ready. Viola, you'll go after."

Stepping outside the training area, Kai raised his hand.

"One. Two. Three!"

No sooner did the array's dome rise than the two clashed.

"Watch them carefully and learn," Kai told Viola. "Memorize and analyze every detail."

In the beginning, Ryu had the upper hand. Knowing his opponent's abilities gave him a considerable advantage, which he used to the fullest. But Ragnar's *Divine Gift* allowed him to withstand Ryu's onslaught and learn more about his style. At some point, it became difficult to determine who was stronger.

In the end, Ragnar won. His combat experience was significantly greater and he had fully mastered his *Invincible Fortress* while Ryu was still learning *Hunting in the Shadow* he had recently bought.

"That was good, boy. Very good." Sitting on the floor, Ragnar was catching his breath. "You were right; I wouldn't have managed the two of you at the same time. Ah, I'm getting old…" He let out a chuckle. "Soon, I'll be completely useless."

"You're far from it, my friend," Kai said as he cast a healing technique on Ragnar and Ryu. "Also, he can't hear you. He's unconscious."

"Really?" Ragnar looked at the boy. "I didn't notice. To be honest, for a moment there, I thought that I would actually lose. If he had fully mastered his *Divine Gift*, I'd be the one taking a nap right now. You've chosen yourself an excellent student."

"I know. Ready for round two? Viola is getting impatient."

Grinning wide, Ragnar nodded and stood up.

"Ready as I'll ever be."

"Rules are the same. Ready?"

"Ready!"

"Begin!"

Faced with such a resilient opponent for the first time, Viola was forced to adapt and find new ways to fight. Ragnar came out victorious once more, but after the second fight, he had to take a break to recuperate.

Ragnar spent two days with them, fighting twice with each of Kai's apprentices. Each spar was followed by an analysis of mistakes and work on their correction. For now, Kai didn't go into the details, highlighting only the main issues. At some point, he began inviting other Temple members to join the sparring sessions.

In almost a month of training, Ryu and Viola fought with the entire elite of the Temple. In addition to the usual crowd, there were even Ulu and Yor, a young draconoid that led Renata's squad during the war. Even Qi, Chag, and Sirius were invited to join and test their skills. There were also incarnations from the Hall of Fame, but training with a memory wasn't as beneficial for one's growth as fighting a living opponent.

"Ryu, you're ready for the next step," Kai announced after a week of analyzing Ryu's mistakes and explaining them to him.

"Next step?"

"The second stage of training. Now that you've gotten the hang of the basics, you are able to continue cultivating on your own. In these two months, I have collected enough information to put together a detailed training plan for you. You will spend five real days in the ATS, honing your skills under the clones' supervision. They will also give you an artifact that will help you temper your *Will*."

By that, Kai referred to *Spark* immersion that could help severe the connection of the *Spark* with the *Shell* and body. The copies of the super-weaving Green had given him had been implemented not only in the Eternal Throne but also in the ATS and the *Complex's* Training Hall.

Everyone, except for Lilith, Hiro, Ulu, Shacks and Green's acquaintances, had been entering the ATS to train and test their limit.

Since Lilith had the potential not only to become a deity but also to achieve a very high stage of mastering in her elements, Kai wasn't eager to send her to the ATS. To compensate, he devoted his time to help her detect mistakes in her style and fix them.

As for Ulu, her role as the island's guardian was too important for Kai to disable the Core's Central Array and leave the Ark undefended while she trained in the ATS.

Hiro, as always, stubbornly refused to train in the ATS. Even though he knew that he'd never get closer even to the *Divine Stage* if he continued like this, he didn't want to limit his soul in any shape or form.

Shacks's situation was both complicated and easy at the same time. He had simply reached the level at which Kai couldn't help him in terms of skill. After all, they were both *Masters of Seven Big Stars*. Also, Shacks had almost completely used up the protection of his *Divine Gift*, and now he needed to wait until it was restored.

The only thing that Kai could give him was resources and access to an artifact that weakened the connection with the *Spark* and helped with the tempering of one's *Will*. Shacks's ability to connect with an incredible number of his clan's ancestors was frightening, and it granted him almost limitless potential. Kai was certain that Shacks would master his *Will* even without the same images Green had given him. With the knowledge of how to create deep cracks, Shacks had a good chance of becoming an *Ascended*.

Lilith, Igdrasil, Viola, and Acilla also had this potential. If nothing stopped them, then they would become *Masters of Seven Great Stars*.

Never before had the Trial Worlds seen so many talented cultivators in one place.

***

The world slowly turned gray, and the details became blurrier. Looking down, I saw my body disappear.

"This is the end," said a woman holding a sword. My teacher. My mentor. The source of so much knowledge and experience, both eagerly shared with me.

"But why?" I didn't want anything to change.

"We gave you everything we could," the blurred image said in a masculine voice. "It's time to wake up."

"Wake up?" I was confused.

The gray world was abruptly swallowed up by darkness. My eyes finally opened to reveal a dimly-lit room. Under me were a soft mattress and clean sheets.

"Where I am? What is this place?"

As I sat up, I felt a familiar aura. Turning my head to the door, I saw a man leaning against the wall. He looked back at me with warmth and a smile. My eyes failed me, but the invisible bond connecting us reminded me of my debt.

"Kai?"

"Good morning, Acilla," he said softly.

"What's going on? Why are you here? Did... Did I lose to Regis?"

Kai crossed the room, sat down beside me on the bed, and told me how he suffered defeat in the fight with the Vinaris' patriarch, lost his memory, and was transferred to Insulaii.

"... a lot of time has passed since then. Magnus got my memories back. But before I made a deal with him, I met someone who helped me save you. The Pact of Souls helped me remember who you are."

"Losing to Regis should have made me his slave," I recalled. "How am I still here?"

Focusing, I tried to understand if my freedom really no

longer belonged to me. But my mind, soul, and Will were free of any bonds.

"Your divine heritage has freed you from the shackles of the Trial Worlds," Kai said with relief, having understood what I was thinking about.

"What divine heritage?"

"The person who helped me save you also helped me wake you up. You had been unconscious for a very long time. He said that the reason for that was that the mortal danger you had found yourself in caused your divine heritage to manifest itself. But since you were unconscious, you remained unaware of these changes and couldn't wake up on your own."

"And the divine heritage?"

"This is the power of your parents, bestowed upon you at the moment of conception. Apparently, your mother sealed it away to protect you. As a daughter of a Limitless, you were in grave danger."

"A Limitless?" I frowned. "But my mother was a peak Star Emperor."

"How could a peak Star Emperor put five high-quality hyperstrings into her child? Or maybe your father was the Limitless one? But then why did you stay with your mother, and not with him?"

Confused, I inspected my body. Each of my initial parameters now exceeded fifty thousand units. As the pieces clicked into place, I remembered the strange dream that kept looping in my head over and over again. The two armed warriors, the endless training, the complicated lessons…

Mom. Dad.

"Did she hide her power even from me?" I whispered, looking down. "But why?"

"Most likely, she was hiding from someone. That's probably why she sealed away your powers. To protect you."

"Perhaps." I smiled as I looked at Kai. "You have changed. I can barely recognize the kid I picked up in the Middle Worlds. Have you reached the Seven Stars?"

His lips stretched into a familiar smirk as an inscription appeared above his head.

[Master of Seven Big Stars]

"The student has surpassed the master. Well done," I said with a touch of sadness. I wasn't quite ready to stop being a mentor.

"Hardly," Kai replied with a chuckle. "After all, you have only just awakened your true talent and potential."

"I suppose you're right…" I fell silent, for a moment almost dreading the answer to the question I was about to ask. "How much time has passed? Usually, I can tell these things, but my biological clock seems to be off."

"A year and almost ten months."

Almost two years…

"Is everyone else alright?"

"In perfect health."

"And where are we? How far did you have to go to hide from the Vinaris?" I looked around the room. "This isn't your Storage mansion. Did someone take you in?"

Kai smiled again as if teasing me.

"This is the **Complex**."

"You had it fixed?"

"How are you feeling? Can you walk?"

"I think so."

"Come. I want to show you something," he said and held out his hand.

Surprised, I took his hand, and we moved to a huge platform, located beneath the starlit sky in the sea of misty, snow-capped mountains. Lines of statues stood frozen along the edges of the platform, stuffed with an incredible amount of divine artifacts, divine particles, Runes, and Azure Crystals. Ahead was a magical scarlet throne imbued with so much power that it made my soul vibrate in tune with it.

"What is this place?" I asked wearily, trying to see if there was someone else here. "Whose throne is this?"

Instead of replying, Kai smiled wider and held my hand tightly.

In the next moment, he was sitting on the throne, and I, on its armrest.

"It's mine," he said with a great deal of pride in his voice. "This is the Eternal Throne, and we are not hiding from anyone. We don't need to do that anymore."

With a wave of his hand, Kai changed our surroundings, and we found ourselves in the sky above a busy city, its streets filled with people going about their daily lives. In the center of this metropolis was a huge black tower, and suspended high above it was a gigantic azure sword.

"The blade is the Complex." Kai began to explain. "Directly below it is the tower of Earth Haven, the center of the former Belteise base at Insulaii. And all around it is the Kaiser's Ark, the capital of the island of the same name. All these are the *domains of the Eternal Path Temple, my organization."*

A moment later, the Eternal Throne soared skyward, flying over the countless islands and seas, until, finally, we were in space.

"And this is Insulaii, almost the entire territory of which now belongs to the Eternal Path Empire. That is, to me."

I wanted to ask him if he was trying to impress me, but the Pact confirmed that his words were true.

"We are safe, Acilla," he said, looking into my eyes. "For the time being, this is our new home. And I'd like nothing more if you stayed here with me."

***

Acilla spent the next three days training and practicing her new powers against the reincarnations from the Hall of Fame.

"You've made great progress. I think it's time for you to take the *Master Stars Test*," Kai suggested.

"It can wait," Acilla grunted. "I want to test you. To hold the first part of your final exam, so to speak."

"Really? You want a fight?"

"I want to see how much you've grown," she said with a wicked grin.

"In that case, I'd hate to disappoint you," Kai replied with an equally frightening smile, slowly unsheathing the *Blades of Nightmare*. "But before that, I want you to meet someone."

"Oh?"

A black and scarlet haze materialized in front of them, quickly taking on the appearance of a faceless woman.

"Meet Viola, the Guardian Spirit of my swords."

"Viola? I'm Acilla nor Adria, Kai's mentor. It's a pleasure."

"You smell of blood," the demoness said, observing the vampiress. "I like it."

"An odd compliment, but I will take it," Acilla replied with a smile.

"Shall we shed blood together?"

"Yes," Kai replied.

"Finally. The river… It calls," Viola whispered as she returned to the blades.

"Are you ready?" Kai looked at Acilla.

"Ready as I'll ever be." She pointed her sword at him. "Shall we begin?"

As soon as the barrier above them formed, Kai merged with Viola and enhanced all of his parameters.

In one jump, he was already behind Acilla's back.

Sensing his presence, she managed to get out of the surprise attack with just a cut on her side. A progenitor bloodline transformation changed her, turning her into a grotesque mixture of a human and a bat, covered with segmented gray armor. A pair of membranous wings sprouted from her back, and the nose and eyes disappeared from her face, leaving only a huge mouth with terrifying fangs.

Teleporting, Kai found himself unable more than three steps closer to Acilla. It was as if her aura repelled him. Rushing forward, he was about to pierce her heart, when Acilla turned around sharply, as if she had begun the motion even before Kai jumped.

Kai managed to shift to the side just in time to avoid her clawed hand. Driving *Phobos* into her clavicle, he strengthened the effect of the *Nightmare World*. But instead of falling to the ground in horror and agony, Acilla's body suddenly trembled and rippled.

Sensing danger, Kai bounced back and strengthened his defense just in time to shield himself from the strongest blow of the bloody explosion. He ended up with a few scratches on his hands and torso.

"Didn't I tell you never to let a vampire taste your blood in battle?" Acilla asked with a taunting smile, licking her bloody fingers.

The slight fatigue that had tormented Kai from the very first moment of Acilla's transformation intensified, weighing heavily on his shoulders.

"Never put your guard down," Acilla whispered into his ear, suddenly finding herself behind Kai.

Feeling immense danger and even fear, Kai activated a combination of core abilities. An *Ice Reflection* clone rushed to the side while the *Borrowing Flame* almost doubled Kai's current stats.

One wave and the bat-like body was gone.

Before Kai could even realize what he had done, his weakness suddenly intensified and his sense of danger warned him of a presence rushing at him from the side.

The fight lasted for six grueling minutes until Kai fell to the ground completely exhausted. Whatever technique Acilla was using on him lowered his strength to that of an average *Elementalist*. Nothing, not even his regeneration, seemed to work, leaving him unable to recuperate and heal.

Even Viola fell unconscious, having lost too much of her strength.

Having returned to her normal appearance, Acilla stood on the surface of the bloody pool that covered the entire arena. Unlike Kai, she looked energized and well-rested, her body and soul full of strength. Only her weakened *Will* testified that she had just completed a terribly exhausting battle.

With a pompous snap of her fingers, she sucked all the blood into her body.

"That was… That was…" Kai struggled to come up with something to say, but in the end, it all came down to one word: "terrifying. You are… the perfect counter for the Hydra bloodline… The power of the Elder Races' Ancestors is truly terrifying… You didn't even have to use your core abilities…"

"Honestly, I'm as surprised as you are. Though I feel like this isn't right. There's not a drop of my merit in this power." Acilla spoke with a tad of awe in her voice. "You have grown so much during this time, Kai. I'm pleasantly surprised by your progress. Soon enough, you'll no longer need me to mentor you."

Catching his breath, Kai stood up with an effort and gave her a smile.

"I wouldn't say that. You're yet to master your new powers. Who knows what you will learn along the way?"

"You're right. There's still so much to uncover and refine." She smiled back. "For now, we'll stick to what we know. The connection between our *Sparks* will make things easier. But before that…"

Acilla moved with lightning speed, pinning Kai against the shimmering wall of the dome.

"...we haven't discussed the subject of payment," she whispered. "My lessons aren't free."

"Same as before?"

"Same as before," she replied with a smile and sank her fangs into his neck.

She knew that she could have asked for anything and that Kai would have given it to her without second thought, but there was nothing more alluring and sweeter than a delicious meal. And the blood of the Heavenly Hydra was a delicacy few could boast of tasting.

***

The following day, Kai officially introduced Acilla to the Temple as a new Hierarch and head of the Medical Center.

In addition to Acilla's initiation and her passing the *Master Stars Test* as a *Master of Seven Big Stars*, Kai also finally finished modifying the old clones, sharing with them the enhanced elemental flesh and improved souls. Another significant event was Viola's attainment of the title of a *Master of Six Average Stars*. It was an amazing achievement in such a short time, which again spoke of her incredible talent.

But the surprises didn't end there.

Three days after Acilla's awakening, a delegation from the Everstein clan arrived in the Eternal City, led by the heads of the clan. The sylphs asked Kai to help them in a very dangerous but quite profitable expedition.

"An interesting proposal," Kai drawled. "What are we looking for?"

"A rare curiosity," Victor replied. "A Divine Berry."

Chapter 26
THE HEAVENLY TREE

By absorbing and accumulating spirit energy, a Spirit Plant would eventually form a Spirit Fruit, a physical manifestation of its collected excess power. Inside it was formed a complex weave of energy and particles — a super-weaving, which made such resources highly valuable. Spirit Fruits differed in quality, the complexity of the weave, the number of elements, characteristics, the presence of divine power, and so on. They could endow a mediocre cultivator with great talent, heal various soul wounds, and even save the dying, but their power still paled in comparison to that of the Spirit Berries.

If too much power accumulated in the Fruit, it would begin to compress, multiplying its super-weaving until a Spirit Berry formed. In essence, they were the purest form of spirit energy, which made them a very valuable and sought-after resource.

"After several weeks of searching, we have finally confirmed the presence of three Divine Berries. Unfortunately, we weren't able to proceed further, which is why we have come to you," Victor explained. "If you agree to help us, we will give you one of the three Berries."

"That's a rather generous offer, I must admit. Which makes me wonder what you need me for," Kai said. Today, he appeared in front of his guest wounded, but already almost recovered. It was all part of his plan.

"A special array guards the Berries."

"Special in what way?"

"The more force you use to defend yourself, the stronger it fights back. We have tried various techniques, core abilities, *Will* skills, *Divine Gifts*, and even divine artifacts, but nothing helped. The array is too powerful."

"Let me guess... To go past it, you mustn't use force, only pull through its initial attack."

"Indeed. And to do that, you need..."

"...insane regeneration."

"Precisely."

"It sounds very risky, even with my bloodline." Kai frowned, propping his head on his fist. "Are you sure I can make it through there?"

"I'm not. However, I can provide you with the results of all our tests and let you decide for yourself."

Victor held out his palm and teleported several memory scrolls onto the table. For a while, there was silence in the room while Kai went through all the records. After a couple of minutes, he opened his eyes and leaned back in his chair again.

"Very interesting," he murmured, observing Victor and Yolana. "However, I'll still require an oath."

"Why?"

"Just to make sure that you're not withholding information."

Victor and Yolana looked at each other without showing any emotions.

"Very well."

"There is also the matter of compensation."

"As my husband said," Yolana spoke up, "one of the Berries will be yours. We'll even let you choose which one. Furthermore, you can keep any resources you find during the expedition."

"A tempting offer, but still not enticing enough for me to take that kind of risk."

"How much do you want?" Victor asked. He was done beating around the bush.

"Thirty billion Runes."

"This is outrageous!" one of the sylphs from the entourage exploded in anger but Victor shut him up with a wave of his hand.

"But, sir, he is being—"

"Quiet."

Considering that Kai managed to collect about thirty-five billion Runes of indemnity from all over Tyr and the Land, he had more than enough resources. The fact that he was asking for more told the Eversteins that he had either made some poor financial decisions or that he was simply greedy.

"I would advise you to reconsider your conditions," Victor said coldly.

"You are in no position to advise anything. *You* need *me*. Not the other way around." Kai tilted his head. "If you want the ruler of all Insulaii to put himself in danger for your benefit, then you will pay thirty billion Runes. Now."

"Heavy is the head that wears the crown, they say." Yolana smiled. "But so inclined to falling off one's shoulders."

"I don't take kindly to being threatened in my own home, my lady."

"Oh, it's just a mere observation," she replied. "Still, your demands are far too high."

"Are they? Tell me: is either of you participating in the expedition?"

There was a short pause.

"No."

"Perhaps some of the leaders of the other big factions are participating? After all, it's not just the Eversteins who have gone to that place, right?"

"No, it's not just us. And no, we haven't heard of any major faction leaders participating."

"And why is that?" Kai's smile slightly widened as he continued his line of questioning. "Why do the most powerful members of the most powerful organizations almost never take an active part in important events?"

"Because their death could lead to the collapse of the entire said organization," Victor replied in a tone of a bored student being lectured by his teacher. "That's also why two leaders cannot engage in combat during negotiations, lest they risk starting a war."

"In that case, perhaps the Eversteins don't consider the Eternal Path Temple a powerful organization?"

Victor sighed. He had had enough.

"The amount is still too high. Especially considering that the cost of the Berry you will get exceeds twenty-five billion Runes."

"While that may be true, the risk exceeds the price of one Berry. Therefore, I don't intend to bargain. Thirty billion and I'll help you."

"Our clan can offer the Temple new exclusive goods and significant discounts, but we are not ready to pay that much."

"In that case..." Kai shrugged, rising from his chair. "It was a pleasure talking to you. Have a safe trip back."

With that, Kai descended the stairs that led to the throne and, followed by Lilith who has been standing next to his chair all this time, went to the door.

"Fine." Victor sighed. "Ten billion and additional benefits. But only after the expedition is over."

Kai glanced at him over his shoulder.

"I'm only interested in the money."

"Your persistence might have a negative effect on our alliance. While I understand the need for financial security, your insistence on such an absurd amount is ridiculous."

"It can't have a worse effect on our alliance than the Eighth Division's refusal to help the Temple in the war against the Unions."

"At that time, the Eighth Division had no mercenaries and the help of clan members wasn't included in our agreement. Derek couldn't take that risk."

"True, but my help is not included in our agreement

either."

"Fifteen billion," Victor hissed, now growing impatient.

"Thirty."

"Twenty."

"Thirty."

"Twenty-three."

"I've already told you that I don't intend to bargain. Thirty," Kai replied stubbornly.

"Twenty billion, plus the coordinates of the Ecumene Library. No one but the Eversteins and the Cult can access it," Victor almost growled.

Kai suddenly fell silent. After thinking for a few seconds, he smiled and returned to his seat.

"I accept your terms. Under one condition."

Victor took a deep breath, seemingly frustrated.

"That being?"

"That you give me the money and the coordinates now. The Berries might not even be there by the time I get to them."

Victor nodded, his face evidently gloomy.

After that, Kai and the Eversteins moved on to discussing the details and signing the contract. When the formalities were finally settled, Yolana handed Kai a scroll with the coordinates for the Ecumene Library, lost somewhere on Bellum.

"As agreed, we will deliver the money tomorrow," she said.

"And right after that, I will go with your people to Ferox." Kai nodded. "Now I would like to hear about the details of the expedition. Where exactly are we going? What can I expect to find there? What are the possible threats?"

"I don't know if you heard, but there was a cataclysm on Ferox," Yolana began to explain, making Kai shift uncomfortably in his seat. After all, he had been one of the causes of the said cataclysm. "Unfortunately, the Red Heavenly Tree was destroyed along with the anomaly surrounding it and the majority of the runic mist. The Spirits are gone, including the Tree Guardian."

"And now everyone has rushed to study the zone and look for treasures," Kai added.

"Precisely. However, we're not interested in this, but in the ancient city under the Tree. The fact that Spirit Plants as strong as the Heavenly Tree don't form Fruits, but Berries, has long been suspected. Even with the Spirits gone, few have been courageous enough to venture underground. Those who had gone before them never returned."

"But if the Tree was destroyed along with the anomaly and the Guardian, then where do the Berries come from? Did they survive? Why do you even assume they are there after all this time?"

"We don't assume; we are sure of it. When our people reached the ancient city, they couldn't only feel, but clearly see the Berries with the Eye of the Void." Yolana pointed to her forehead. "And these aren't just Spirit Berries, but berries imbued with divine power. However, even our bloodline couldn't help us overcome the last obstacle. The city's defense mechanisms, despite their age, remain as powerful and deadly as the day they were made. As for your first question, we believe that the Guardian managed to move these Berries to the city just moments before its death.

And since the roots penetrating the city survived, there is a considerable chance that these Berries will become powerful seeds for a new Heavenly Tree."

***

A flash illuminated the small hall, and three dark-skinned figures in dirty-gray cloaks materialized in its center. The trio quickly headed for the exit, passing the guards, who seemed not to notice anything at all.

Behind the doors, they were met by one of the Senior Servants of the Azure Warrior Temple, as well as a pair of sylphs.

"My lord," he greeted Kai with a respectful bow.

"Nice to finally meet you, Lord Kaiser." One of the sylphs smiled sweetly, although her eyes showed no joy. "My name is Viviette, and this," she pointed to the second sylph, "is Jeanne. Are you ready to go?"

"We are," answered a short, stocky man with a big nose and strong cheekbones, that is, Kai in disguise.

Due to Kai's recent endeavors and raise in popularity, he was no longer just another resident of the Trial Worlds, so he had to disguise himself. He changed his physical appearance without any problems, but things were somewhat more complicated with his aura.

Having learned the basics of *Will* control, including the introduction of elemental vibrations, he could much more effectively control individual strings, including those in the bundle that represented the aura. It wasn't even close to mimicking the *Will*, as Green had once demonstrated, but it allowed Kai to conceal and override the frequency of his aura with additional strings and false vibrations, fooling spirit perception until the moment he used his powers.

"And these are Lady Acilla and Master Shacks?" Viviette looked at the people accompanying Kai.

They also disguised themselves, only they hid their auras with masking artifacts.

"That's right," Kai confirmed.

This expedition was secret, so it was advised to take as few people as possible to avoid unnecessary attention. Just like the Temple, the Eversteins sent only three people. Viviette and Jeanne's companion was waiting for them in the ancient city.

"In that case, we can go. We will be transported directly to the remains of the Tree."

Kai nodded.

Following the Senior Servant, the group found themselves under the scorching desert sun. *Force* particles and elemental energies of the *Paths* of *Fire*, *Light*, and *Sand* were clearly felt in the air, making this place so hot and dry that even those with mastered *Paths* of *Water* and *Ice* would find it challenging to survive here.

The Akama Desert was located not far from the destroyed Tree. After Kyle's "visit," all the flora and fauna in the area died out, but the nearby trade routes forced the Masters of Ferox to repopulate the deserted city soon after. The Temple also managed to snatch a piece of land next to the former anomaly, making Adbol, a nearby district, a branch of the Azure Temple, connecting Ferox and Insulaii.

"Come closer," Viviette beckoned, opening the Eye of the Void and revealing an artifact. "Get ready. The transfer will take place in a few seconds. Don't resist."

In an instant, the space around them curved, contracted, and smoothed out. There were no flashes and shock waves. The whole group disappeared silently and imperceptibly.

Suddenly finding himself in the middle of an unfamiliar forest, Kai looked around in surprise.

"That wasn't a transfer," Kai realized, shocked. "It was teleportation."

Spatial transfer meant the construction of a tunnel of artificial space in the middle of nothingness that connected two points of three-dimensional reality. Inside this tunnel, there was a bubble that could travel at superluminal speed. So while moving from point A to point B was extremely fast, it still wasn't instantaneous.

Teleportation, on the other hand, implied an instant change of coordinates, overlaying two remote areas of space onto each other and "pushing" the object into the adjoining area. Teleportation required less preparation time and was less stable than a transfer, but it took much more effort. That was why it was used mostly used for combat, while the transfer was used for long-distance travel.

"I'm impressed," Kai said. "Your clan's ability to manipulate space is amazing, surpassing any array I had ever had a chance to see."

"It's less likely that someone will notice us this way," Viviette explained, straightening her hair and closing the Eye of the Void. "This way. Jeanne, hide us."

Nodding, the second sylph spread her arms wide and distorted the space around the group, enveloping them in a bubble-like barrier. Communication with the outside world was abruptly cut off as they were swallowed up by pitch darkness.

"Don't follow me closely and don't go outside the dome," Jeanne warned. "Light, sound, and spirit vibrations go around our bubble, and the radiation we emit can't leave it. For the sake of our mission, try to minimize your spirit activity."

Jeanne's ability made Kai think about his invisibility. Her technique was of higher quality, but it was also more complex and energy-intensive. Furthermore, it wasn't an obstacle for Kai's energy vision, which once again confirmed his suspicions that he saw not the energy, but something related to it.

So far, I could only guess, but now... he thought, continuing to follow the sylphs. *I'm sure that what I'm seeing is Information. That is, the picture of the world at a much deeper level. I see even when there isn't a drop of energy in the air. Isn't it because of the vibrations of strings? Each string interacts with hyperstrings, transmitting its vibration to them, and spreading in all directions, and my eyes are able to interpret it. Very interesting...*

Half an hour later, they reached their destination, and the exhausted Jeanne dispelled the bubble. The amount of noise and light that suddenly hit their senses momentarily stunned them.

The forest was replaced by uneven rocky terrain. The giant stump of the destroyed Heavenly Tree towered ahead, surrounded by thousands of semi-mechanical creatures. Some wandered aimlessly, some stood still, and some fought with groups of Masters who wanted to get into the underground city.

"Rune Ants are the main reason why there are only six of us here," Viviette explained. "We studied them well enough to understand that the larger and more competent the group, the more Ants will be sent to intercept it. That's why fighting them is undesirable. It's better to trap them and run away, rather than demonstrate our power. The second main problem is the blockage inside the underground city. The array blocks all *Paths*, preventing us from getting to the Berries. Fortunately, it has no effect on the Eye of the Void, so we were able to discover secret passages and shortcuts, which gives us a certain advantage."

"What's our next move?" Shacks asked.

"Now, we will rest," Viviette looked at Jeanne, "and wait for the right moment. Attacking them directly is too dangerous and unwise."

"What are these creatures anyway? City guards? Shouldn't they have been destroyed along with the Spirits?"

"They have a single hivemind. When the anomaly was destroyed, a huge number of Ants arrived from other Heavenly Trees via the root network that spreads through Ferox. Fortunately, after so much time, many of their mechanisms became inoperable, so it's still possible to get into the city. But under no circumstances should they be underestimated. In terms of combat power, each Ant is equal to a *Master of Five Big Stars*."

"Is it okay for us to just stand here like this?" Kai looked around.

"After the Guardian's death, they no longer stray away from the Tree. This is a safe zone. As for the others... Even if they dare to attack us, they will only provoke the guards. As long as we keep a low profile, the Ants won't even notice us."

The conversation ended there, and a prolonged wait began. The squad sat in place for almost three hours until Jeanne suddenly reported the presence of seven incoming auras.

"They are advancing toward one of the underground entrances on the other side of the Tree. It looks like they're members of the Mountain Sect Alliance."

"That's unexpected. I didn't anticipate their involvement, given their leader's death and the consequential redistribution of power. Hmm. This actually works for us. We'll use their arrival to get inside the city," Viviette said.

For a couple of minutes, she stood motionless with her eyes closed, until she abruptly jumped to her feet.

"It's time!" she exclaimed and turned to her companions. "As soon as we are in position, run after me at full speed. If the Ants attack, try to immobilize them. Do *not* kill them under any circumstance."

A few seconds later, they appeared several miles away from their original position, right at the remains of the Heavenly Tree. The stump was surrounded by Ants, and the group from the Mountain Sect Alliance was slowly moving forward through the shimmering sea of mandibles and antennae. The fact that they knew not to kill the guards, indicated this was clearly not their first attempt to get to the Tree.

As soon as Kai's feet touched the ground, he followed Viviette's order and rushed after the two sylphs toward the cave opening visible in the distance right under the stump.

Jumping past the motionless Ants, Kai felt a sticky sensation around him, as if the air had suddenly turned into glue. Viviette had moved them right to the very edge of the array's dome, which made the *Phantom Steps* difficult to use, and teleportation impossible.

Walking next to the dome's edge, they ran into several curious Ants that they quickly immobilized before moving on. Despite their best efforts, this attracted some attention from the rest of the guards, causing more than a hundred Ants to run after them.

"They're not very good pursuers, so just keep running. We'll get away easily," Viviette said.

The group finally descended into the underground complex of strange towering buildings and colossal anthills that lined the walls and ceiling like stalactites. In addition, dozens of massive roots penetrated the entire city, stretching far into the depths of the planet and forming a maze.

"I don't recommend touching anything unless you want to run again," Viviette warned.

"Is there anyone else here besides us?" Acilla asked.

"The city is divided into six underground levels. Many groups were able to get into the first and second, but only we, the cultists, and the Order, went further. Berries, of course, are located at the very bottom, guarded by many traps and other defense systems."

"Of course they are." Shacks sighed. "Why would anything be easy?"

"Don't worry, the Eye will detect them. Thanks to prior expeditions, we know the shortest path through the labyrinth to the fifth floor."

"Lead the way then." Kai nodded.

Motioning for them to follow and advising them to stay close, Viviette guided them through the ancient halls and hallways, occasionally telling them more about the architecture, the writings on the walls, and the statues erected in the city streets. Unlike her companion, Viviette wasn't only a fighter, but also a researcher. When Kai learned more about her project, he inquired further about the Tree, and Viviette kindly explained that Heavenly Trees were a grand-project of the ancient empire that ruled Ferox more than a billion years ago. The Trees were supposed to wrap their roots around the planet's ley lines in order to absorb the runic mist seeping out of Ferox's core along with energy. Thus, by controlling the plants, they intended to monopolize the Rune mining.

Surprisingly, they succeeded, which made the already powerful empire even stronger and wealthier. The appearance of the Heavenly Trees and the abundance of Runes allowed them to conquer Insulaii, as well as strengthen their influence on Bellum. They quickly became the dominant force in the Trial Worlds.

Peace and prosperity came to Insulaii after decades of chaos. All the martial arts, trade, and craftsman organizations joined the empire in order to use its resources to perfect their craft. A social order was established, the cost of resources decreased, more people took up cultivation and martial arts, clan wars became less frequent, and conflicts were no longer resolved on battlefields and in taverns but in courts and dueling arenas. The Trial Worlds flourished, ushered into the golden age of the development path, allowing the Masters to delve into the intricacies of other crafts.

"What went wrong?" Kai asked. "Greed and envy took over?"

"If only." Viviette sighed sadly. "Thirteen Guardian Spirits dwelling within Divine artifacts were at the head of the empire. Because of their special task here, they were in no hurry to leave the Trial Worlds to become Gods, but they quickly became Demigods. With such strength, they were practically invincible. And since they were Guardian Spirits, they lived exceptionally long lives. Every two hundred thousand years or so they entered a long sleep while their *Spark* evolved. While one of their kinsmen slept, the remaining twelve Spirits stood watch. According to records, they had an artifact that could show snippets of the future.

Nothing threatened their power, but they had no interest in taking over the empire. The problem was something else..." Viviette fell silent for a moment. "The will of the Trial Worlds."

"The will of the Trial Worlds?" Shacks asked, confused. "Do they really have a *Will*? Or is it a figure of speech?"

"Only partly. We believe that the Trial Worlds have a Heavenly Exaltation Pagoda that writes the Rules and manages the *Altars*. But there is something else... It seems that the Trial Worlds have an aversion to peace and order, which is what the ancient civilization brought. With this, they upset the balance, for which they paid in blood. The fall of the empire was linked to a being that the surviving records call 'Sazarek.' Roughly translated, it means 'he who brings death' in our language."

"Sazarek? The Cult leader?" Kai asked.

"No." Viviette shook her head. "The first mention of the Heavenly Exaltation Cult and its patriarch is quite recent. I think he calls himself that on purpose. He doesn't have the powers described in the records."

"I think we'd notice if he did."

"Yes." Viviette interrupted her story to give out a new set of orders. "There's a large group of Ants ahead. They're moving east. Wait here until they pass by. Jeanne, keep surveilling the area. I'll focus on the Ants."

***

"Will you tell us more about Sazarek and the empire?" Shacks asked some half an hour later when they continued their journey deep underground.

"Sazarek didn't waste time, destroying city after city, devastating entire continents, and killing everything and everyone on his path. The empire was strong, but none of its warriors managed to stop the Death Bringer. Only the Guardian Spirits with their artifacts managed to harm him. But then Sazarek retaliated and imposed an Insulaii restriction on them, turning them into *Elementalists*. As such, they no longer posed a threat. Two Demigods managed to retreat to Bellum with the empire's most important artifacts, but Sazarek found them there as well. Anomalies and runic fog were powerless to stop him. Based on recent findings, which include damaged memory scrolls among other things, there's a possibility that he could even control them."

"Sounds to me like he was some kind of deity," Shacks thought aloud.

"Is that why you think that was the Will of the Trial Worlds?" Kai asked.

"Yes. It's the only explanation for his sudden appearance and insane power." Viviette nodded. "But that's not all. Sazarek did something to the Heavenly Trees, which triggered the release of the accumulated fog from their trunks, thus creating anomalies filled with countless soul fragments. He annihilated all but the strongest Shadows that formed as the result of the massacre. He also killed the Spirits of each Tree, but kept their *Shells*, merging them with the surviving Shadows. Because of all this, the super-anomalies of the Heavenly Trees are the most dangerous places not only on Ferox but in all the Three Worlds."

At this, Viviette finished her history lesson, letting Jeanne explain their next steps.

"Third floor. Here and below are the strongest Ants. They can command the rest and summon them, and they also have very good sensors. Because of them, many groups have already died here, and others no longer risk descending.

We should switch to the spirit connection from now on. I'll hide us. "

The expedition continued in silence. From time to time, Viviette would warn them about the defensive arrays, as well as artifacts enveloped in the runic mist. Most of the time, they were trinkets, but sometimes, in the richest houses, they would find more valuable items. The sylphs picked up and categorized each find, since even the simplest artifact could contain a long-forgotten weaving that could expand the understanding of cultivation.

Three hours later, the group finally reached the fourth floor where the seventh member of their expedition awaited them — a large, gloomy man without hair, with the aura of a *Master of Seven Big Stars*.

"Overclay," he introduced himself and waved his hand, urging them to follow him. He was clearly not the talkative type.

Exchanging glances, the Temple trio followed the sylphs.

***

They had been wandering the fourth floor for a long time when suddenly Overclay reached back and halted them. Instead of using spirit connection, he glanced at Viviette, who explained everything.

"There are two groups ahead. Cultists and the Order. They are right in front of the passage to the fifth floor. They will notice us if we get closer. We can let them enter the floor first. We have already studied it, so we can go around without being noticed."

"What are they doing there?" Kai asked.

"It looks like they are sorting things out and deciding who will go first."

"Can you show us what's going on?" Shacks asked.

Viviette pondered for a moment before nodding. A memory scroll appeared in her hands, which she then offered to the trio. Guessing what she was up to, they touched the artifact and began to read the memories she was putting into it in real time.

The two tense groups were separated by about sixty feet of reinforced Rune Ants, pinned down so quickly that they didn't even have time to call for help. The Order had sent six *Masters* of *Seven Average Stars* and a couple of *Seven Big Stars*, led by the third Master of the Order — Deus Yen Talos.

Among the adepts, there were six Junior Pillars, all of which were *Masters of Seven Big Stars*. Kyle wasn't there. Due to preparations for the *Exodus* and unwillingness to take risks, the House of Passion refused to take participation in the expedition, and the House of Dolls sent only three of its members.

A whole crowd of young Cultists was obviously stronger, but the Order had the advantage in numbers and experience.

"I propose we solve this amicably," Deus said. "Let's toss a coin to determine who will go first. We have nothing to fight for."

"Are you afraid?" Blair, the Heiress of the House of Famine, teased him.

"Not at all," he replied with a shrug. "I have no doubts about the strength of my men. It's just that there's no point in fighting here and now. It would be a waste of energy. All the loot we have collected is insignificant. I'm sure you know that the most valuable things are down below." He pointed to his feet. "If we start a fight, we will only attract the Ants and waste our time, forcing us back a floor."

"Interesting." A dark-cloaked figure stepped forward, pulling back its hood. Kai immediately recognized Valor. A talented *Master of Seven Great Stars*, the second in power after Kyle in the House of Resistance.

Something's wrong. Kai frowned. *What is strange* Will? *Where is it coming from?*

"So, you suggest flipping a coin?" Valor inquired. "And then what? If we win, we actually lose. We'll go ahead of you and check for traps while you attack us from behind. And if we lose, you get ahead. It's a choice without a choice."

"You're right." Deus tilted his head. "We're on equal footing no matter who wins the coin toss. The simplest solution is for the loser to wait a little while the winner proceeds to the next floor. I suggest we sign a contract."

"Sounds reasonable." Valor nodded and threw off his cloak, revealing a muscular torso, six arms, and two pairs of horns on his head.

At the same moment, Kai realized that Valor could see them.

This is his Will *that I feel around us! Is he an heir with the same bloodline like Kyle, with abilities that increase their perception? But it's not* Clairvoyance, *it's much less powerful than that unique ability Kyle used against me. So, I guess he doesn't have a Progenitor bloodline, only racial abilities.*

Valor took a step forward, waves of the *Force* starting to swirl around his body.

"However, knowing you, I doubt that you will honor the deal. You are cunning as ever, Deus, always plotting," he said. "Do you think I didn't notice you control the Ants? Do you think I didn't notice the group that came after you? Do you think I can't sense them hiding nearby, ready to ambush us? The Alliance isn't here, and the Eversteins are ahead, so who are they?"

"I don't know what you're talking about." Deus frowned.

"Really? Let's check then. Come out!" Valor shouted loudly, turning his head and causing the nearest Ants to head toward the passage. "No?! Have it your way!"

One of his hands shot up sharply, and for a moment, a scarlet sphere shone in the center of his palm. The building next to Kai flew into the air.

"What are you doing?!" one of the Order members shouted in horror, realizing that now all the Ants on the floor know about their presence.

However, Valor didn't pay attention to his cry.

"You have five seconds before I gather all the Ants here!" Valor shouted. "Five! Four! Three!"

Deciding that escalating the situation further would be unwise, Viviette motioned for everyone to get out of hiding.

"Looks like I was wrong." Valor lowered his hand. "The Eversteins are here too. And who is this? Well, well... I'll be damned." He grinned nastily. "It's Kaiser himself, only he seems a little bit worse for wear. What a pity. Master Kyle told me a lot about you. To be honest, I expected more."

"And I expect an apology, Valor. As you can see, I'm not plotting anything. They're not with us."

"You're as sly as a fox, Deus. I still think you're plotting something."

"What are we going to do now?" Deus asked. "The Ants are on their way here. We can't stop that many, and if we engage in battle, we'll be up to our ears in trouble."

"The solution is simple." Valor smiled arrogantly. "I'll just kill everyone here."

He had barely finished speaking when he attacked. Without a word, four Adepts immediately rushed to his side. Together, they attacked with such might that they quickly wounded Overclay, after which they killed Shacks and Acilla. Having dealt with them, the Adepts easily dealt with the remaining three that tried to escape.

Each corpse emitted a barely perceptible bloody cloud, which the Pillars paid no attention to. They didn't find it strange that their enemies were so weak. They couldn't even remember who they fought. But this didn't bother them at all.

***

The group proceeded to the fifth floor under Jeanne's protective bubble, both baffled and relieved that their plan had worked. Their clones, woven from Acilla's bloodline, absorbed the attack while they walked past the gruesome carnage scene, their auras obscured by Shacks's *Divine Gift* even before Valor ordered them to show themselves.

"That guy's insane," Shack's muttered under his breath and looked at Kai. "Good thing you warned us in advance."

"We need to hurry," Viviette said. "The Ants on this floor will head toward the noise."

Picking up their pace, they hurried down the corridor until they were sure that they were safe. The chaos Valor had caused would buy them some time. Even if the Cult and the Order managed to escape, they wouldn't catch up with them any time soon.

Acting as quickly as possible, they attacked a large group of reinforced Ants near the passage to the sixth floor, managing to freeze, knock out, or incapacitate them before they could realize what was happening and send a signal for help.

Pressing forward, they found themselves before a living wall of countless swarming mechanical insects.

"Master Kaiser." Viviette turned to him. "Are you ready?"

"Just tell me what to do."

"These insects will attack anyone who isn't their master. And the more you resist, the more aggressive they become. They will notice even if you use your *Will*. You need to pass through their defense and find a room that belonged to the Tree Spirit. There will be amulets that can add a weaving to our auras, making the Ants perceive us as guests of honor. They'll still be on alert, but they won't be immediately hostile. After that, I'll make us a passage to the treasury. Fortunately, its defense systems are almost non-functional."

"Do you have the precise location of these amulets?"

"Here."

Accepting the offered scroll with a nod, Kai glanced at Shacks and Acilla and entered the wall of insects. Sensing the trespasser, the creatures turned their heads toward him and snapped their mandibles. In a heartbeat, Kai found himself torn asunder. He didn't resist being devoured, feeling that if he demonstrated even a hint of resistance, the onslaught would intensify.

Within seconds, he was stripped of his skin and sinew. He was very lucky that the Hydra bloodline adapted to the severity of its owner's injuries; otherwise, his body would have been picked clean. As it were, he was regenerating at the same rate as the insects were devouring his physical body.

For some reason, they didn't have an interest in the *Astral* one.

It took him more than three minutes to reach the opposite side of the "wall." Once he got there, he took a moment to recover. He was aching all over, and he needed to catch his breath.

Grimacing, he dug his fingers into his stomach and pulled out a few insects. After quickly examining these unusual artifacts, Kai froze them and moved them to his *Storage*. He'd study them later.

"Thank you for allowing me a moment to rest."

"There's no honor in attacking a worn-out and unarmed man," said Bjorn, the Junior Pillar of the House of Dolls, as he rose from the stone he had been sitting on. "And while I'd prefer to have you at peak strength, I am in a bit of a hurry."

Unlike Kai, he had passed through the wall of insects without a scratch. His augmented body, created from the flesh of strong Masters, possessed insane strength and durability.

"Don't worry," Kai replied with a smile and closed his eyes, releasing his true strength and enjoying the wave of power that washed over him. "You've given me more than enough time to recover. I can finally unwind. Though I may never see the end of this fight..."

***

Hiding far away from the entrance to the sixth floor to avoid detection, the rest of the group waited for Kai to return. The sylphs were observing their surroundings, the vampiress leaned against the wall, deep in thought, and the archer was playing with throwing knives, quickly and skillfully twisting them between his fingers with a slight smirk on his face.

"I've been wondering," Shacks drawled, observing Overclay, "what's the deal with your hair? A fashion statement or what?"

The Supreme Elder turned around and stared at Shacks with a frown. Though, without eyebrows, it was a bit hard to tell if he was angry or surprised by the question.

"What? C'mon, man, I'm just trying to make small-talk."

"Did they not teach you manners at that Temple of yours?" Viviette hissed.

Overclay was about to open his mouth to respond when Shacks's figure blurred and disappeared. Turning around with lightning speed, the archer cut off Viviette's head with one swift movement. A throwing knife materialized in the air and, with a deafening whistle, pierced Jeanne's *Shell*.

At the same time, Acilla rushed toward Overclay. Swinging her sword, she split his body in two. A moment before the death of his physical shell, he opened the Eye of the Void, which then exploded in a cloud of blood mist. The sacrificed organ broke through the blockage of space for a second, taking Shacks and Acilla with it.

Finding himself in semi-darkness, ankle-deep in water, the surprised archer slowly turned around and spotted a figure.

"Fancy meeting you here, old man," he sneered. "Are you visiting or just passing by?"

***

Swinging a finisher, Acilla suddenly found herself in a completely different place. Overclay, Shacks, the corpses of Viviette and Jeanne — everything was gone. The strange spherical room was almost completely dotted with large holes leading into the unknown.

"One of the hives?" she guessed.

"There you are, my dear," Regis said cheerfully, his face turning serious in a blink of an eye. "I order you: on your knees!"

Horror appeared on Acilla's face, and her legs buckled.

"That's more like it."

***

"This is everyone who is left on the island," Ulu reported.

Lilith nodded and looked around at the crowd of Masters who had arrived at the Tower.

"Let's move," she ordered. "Ulu, transfer everyone to the Teleportation Hall."

In an instant, they found themselves in the *Complex*, their faces worried and gloomy upon finding out that someone had breached the planetary barrier and attacked the empire. To weed out the intruders, Lilith gathered all the combat-ready members of the Temple that were on the Ark and ordered the Masters outside of it to go to the Purple Temple. Simultaneously, she issued a command to mobilize all the Temple forces without delay.

After finishing setting up the terminal on the transfer platform, Lilith activated the array and took a step back. A moment later, a bright flash covered the small army of just a little over ten thousand fighters. But as soon as it went out, those present were surprised to realize that they had remained in place.

"Lady Lilith, the security system detected something on the other side of the dimensional tunnel as soon as it formed. If you had been inside it when it collapsed, you would have fallen into oblivion. Therefore, I took the liberty of stopping the transfer," Alfred said.

"Can the *Complex* create a tunnel that won't be destroyed?" Lilith asked, surprised.

"I fear that it cannot. The power of the jamming artifact is too great."

"Is that so…?" Lilith whispered, tucking a strand of hair behind her ear.

A few moments later, a nightmarish earthquake began on the Ark. It was so strong that it was felt even in the protected *Complex*. When Alfred and Ulu peeked outside, they realized that the tremor wasn't an earthquake at all, but a terribly strong blow.

The protective barrier above the island was collapsing, revealing a giant black sphere — a *Limitless Heavenly Complex*. Before Alfred had time to inform Lilith about this, the Ark was subjected to massive shelling. The city barrier fell quickly, after which the *Divine* attacks released by the mysterious *Complex* claimed the lives of thousands of Masters and mortals. Following this, a large-scale invasion began. Together, the Mountain Sect Alliance, the Mercenary Guild, and the Vinari clan launched a massive attack on the city, deploying both artillery and defense arrays.

There were only three *Divine Stage* cultivators leading the attack, a pair of *Seven Big Star Masters*, and one *Seven Great Stars Master*. But all of them possessed a perfectly formed central core and a *Manticore Heart*.

Interlude
SIX-THREE-NINE-NINE

Many years ago...

A group of children stood lined up in a row in a spacious white room. They all wore identical white uniforms, which differed only by the embroidered four-digit number on their chests. The children were silent, afraid to move without permission, while a masked figure paced back and forth in front of them. Clad in black baggy clothes and sporting long hair, it was impossible to discern whether it was a man or a woman. The children knew only one thing: they must obey any orders.

The person halted and nodded, concluding the morning inspection.

"Six-Three-Eight-Zero," they said in a mechanical voice.

A girl took a step forward.

"Hand these out."

Carefully taking the offered pouch, the girl gave the

rest of the children one bottle of elixir each and returned the empty bag to the warden.

"Drink."

The children obediently unscrewed the corks and drank the elixirs. Just a few seconds later, many of them grimaced in pain, but no one dared to utter a sound. All but one poor soul, who, unable to stand it, collapsed to the floor. Screaming in agony, he curled up, trembling, and pulled his knees to his chest.

Under the horrified looks of her classmates, one of the girls burst into tears and sat down, pressing her hand to her mouth to stifle her cries. Only one of the twenty remained unperturbed. Six-Three-Nine-Nine was in as much pain as the others, but he didn't let it show.

A few seconds later, another warden in a black uniform entered the room. Approaching the screaming boy, he crouched down and jerked his head to the side with a slight movement. There was a crunch, and the child went limp, his neck broken.

After that, the warden looked at the crying girl. By now, she was already back on her feet, biting her bottom lip until it bled and shuddering, trying her best not to make a sound.

The warden observed her for a while, then silently left, dragging the murdered boy behind him. The door closed automatically, obscuring any hint of a passage ever being there.

For the next few minutes, the children continued to stand still in silence as the spiritual pain that had gripped their minds slowly subsided. Five minutes later, the motionless warden finally spoke.

"Thirty laps."

The children turned around and ran, throwing the empty vials into a special hole in the floor along the way. Their training had begun. After running, they moved on to other physical exercises, and then they split into pairs to practice martial arts. As the group got smaller, Six-Three-Nine-Nine decided to stay alone and shadowbox. The warden soon joined him, wishing to test the boy. Six-Three-Nine-Nine, having shown what he was capable of, even earned the highest praise from the warden — a slight nod.

After the training session, the children were told to meditate. After a few hours of contemplation, it was time to study. One of the compartments hidden in the wall opened, revealing books and writing utensils. Taking what they needed, the children sat on the floor, and the warden began to teach them writing, reading, mathematics, history, geography, and much more. Each lesson lasted no more than half an hour. There were no breaks, and at the end, the students had to take a difficult test on all the material covered today. Those who failed to score a certain amount of points were disposed of.

As usual, Six-Three-Nine-Nine scored the highest. He glanced around at the others and could tell from their expressions that no one had failed.

Then they finally got some food. Dinner was the first and only meal of the day. The rest of the nutrients were provided by the morning elixir, which not only affected their souls but also made them stronger and smarter, simultaneously boosting regeneration and giving them energy.

Dinner was the children's favorite time of the day because they were left alone and the day's activities ended. Shelves of books and toys would open, leaving them four precious hours to have fun until bedtime. Also, they were finally allowed to speak to each other. Usually, they started talking as soon as the door closed behind the departing warden, but today no one was in a hurry to say anything. Eight-Six's death hit the group hard.

"They'll kill me tomorrow, I know it…" The girl who could hardly restrain her screams in the morning burst into tears again. "I can't stand another elixir… I don't want to die… I don't want to…"

The threat of death loomed over them every morning, as no one knew what kind of elixir they'd be given that day. Only a few of them had figured out that its composition constantly changed, due to which at times the pain could be weaker or stronger and no one could develop immunity to the elixir's effects.

"We have to run away," one of the boys muttered. "And get revenge!"

"And how do you imagine we do that?" another boy asked skeptically. "We don't even know what's outside of this room. We've been living here since we were taken from the nursery. For all we know, there might be nothing behind these walls."

"Doesn't mean we shouldn't try!"

"Try what? To die before our time?"

A quarrel broke out, dividing the group into those who were willing to do something and those who resigned themselves to the hopelessness of their situation.

"And what about you? You can't always be silent," one of the girls said, noticing Six-Three-Nine-Nine's indifference.

"Me?" He smiled faintly in response and shrugged. "I'd just like to play while we still can."

His answer elicited an immediate reaction. Some of the

children shouted at him furiously, some insulted him, and some even laughed at his words. But he just continued to smile. Noticing all sorts of details, he studied his classmates, trying not just to understand their way of thinking, but their personalities, too. For him, "reading" a person was as easy as two plus two. He easily noticed the smallest details in other people's behavior and speech, analyzed them, compiled a holistic image, and came up with ways to exploit this knowledge to his advantage.

It even worked with the wardens. Even though they wore masks, concealed their emotions, and kept their body language in check, Six-Three-Nine-Nine still noticed things.

The steps he was taking were tiny, but they'd eventually lead him to his goal.

Days passed. The children continued to train and drink the elixirs. As the months passed by, the group was becoming smaller and smaller, and two years later, they were finally released from the white room and allowed to join the general group. Constant trials, harsh living conditions, and brutal training hardened their spirit and taught them unquestioning obedience and numerous lessons, especially history, instilled loyalty toward the clan into their brains.

The group consisted of hundreds of students between the ages of seven and sixteen, who were kept on a large isolated island. Everyone was given a separate room, provided with quality alchemy, and taught more advanced skills and techniques. They also got new clothes: instead of white, they now wore gray uniforms.

However, they still weren't granted any privacy. They were closely monitored, but in comparison with the white room, life on the island, while more difficult, was better. They were given more free time and greater liberty. They continued to be called by numbers, and it didn't look like they'd be allowed to have their own names anytime soon. Or ever.

The next day, the children were informed about what awaited them on the island. All their training and education had been for the sake of feeling and controlling energy — for the sake of awakening their warrior layer. As it turned out, this had to be achieved before they turned sixteen. Those who failed would be sent to a special zone and given an infusion that would affect their *Shell*, forcing the process to begin. This was a dangerous procedure, but thanks to it, a third of the children eventually passed through the zone and the infusion gave them the boost they needed to embark on the path of cultivation. Those who still failed after all this were eliminated if the infusion's effect didn't kill them already.

In a way, it was just a bigger version of the white room, only instead of the walls there was a sea, and instead of twenty victims, there were hundreds to choose from.

But the children persisted, living the best they could in such dire circumstances.

Six months have passed.

"Hello," Six-Three-Nine-Nine said, sitting down next to a fellow classmate.

Taking his eyes off the book, the boy stared coldly at the uninvited guest.

"You're new, aren't you?" Six-Three-Nine-Nine asked. "You're Six-Five-Zero-One. Zero-One... And I'm Six-Three-Nine-Nine. Together, we make a hundred!"

"Can't you see I am reading? Go away."

"Don't be like that. I thought we could be friends."

Sighing heavily, Six-Five-Zero-One put the book down.

"Have you forgotten what we were taught? No names. No emotions. We can't have personalities, let alone friends," he said coldly. "We're not even clan servants, but pawns. We are candidates for Numbers. You could get in trouble by behaving like this."

"That sounds boring…" Six-Three-Nine-Nine drawled, continuing to smile. "What are you reading?"

With a flick of the wrist too quick to follow, he snagged Six-Five-Zero-One's book. The disgruntled boy reached out to retrieve it, but Six-Three-Nine-Nine grabbed his wrist. Getting annoyed, Six-Five-Zero-One reached out with his other hand, but Six-Three-Nine-Nine leaned back and raised the book above his head.

"Let me go! And give me back my book!" Six-Five-Zero-One said, jumping up and down.

"Say we're friends first!"

"Give it back! Or else—"

"Or else what?"

"Or else I'll beat the shit out of you!"

"Do I hear a challenge?" Six-Three-Nine-Nine chuckled. "I accept!"

"You asked for it!" Six-Five-Zero-One stood up, escaping from the grip, and straightened his uniform. "I demand a duel!" he shouted loudly, attracting the attention of the library's warden.

With a gust of wind, the warden appeared next to their table.

"I approve," they replied in a mechanical voice.

After that, the warden disappeared, and Six-Five-Zero-

One stomped toward the door. Six-Three-Nine-Nine followed suit, waddling behind him like a duck.

"Choose your weapon," Six-Five-Zero-One said once they reached the training ground.

"You first," Six-Three-Nine-Nine replied with a smile.

Six-Five-Zero-One turned toward the weapon racks and picked out a pair of small and light blades. Turning around, he stared at his opponent.

"How long do you intend to wait?"

"I'm waiting for you."

"What? Choose your weapon!"

"I don't need it."

Angrily muttering something, Six-Five-Zero-One rushed at him. He had no doubts about victory. He not only surpassed his peers in physique and strength, but he was also a very talented fighter.

Approaching Six-Three-Nine-Nine, he charged at him and…

…landed onto the sand with a painful yelp.

Six-Five-Zero-One was the best in his former group, but Six-Three-Nine-Nine was in a league of his own.

"So, are we friends now?" Six-Three-Nine-Nine asked as he crouched down near his defeated opponent.

"Fine. We'll be friends."

After that, Six-Five-Zero-One couldn't get rid of the annoying Six-Three-Nine-Nine. With time, however, he got used to his company. And by the time they were done with their first year of training, they genuinely became friends.

Once a year was up, the children started being sent on

perilous missions inland, from which only seven out of ten usually returned. They were also forced to fight one another, often resulting in someone's death.

***

"Left flank!" shouted a ten-year-old boy.

Breaking through the trees, a huge bison dashed into the depths of the forest, its body littered with makeshift wooden spears that tried but failed to stop it. The children desperately tried to catch up with the beast, but the distance between them only widened.

Suddenly, something flashed from above, and one of the children found itself on the monster's back. The bison tried to shake him off, but the boy controlled his body so well that he managed to keep his balance and not fall off. A few moments later, a long, thin knife entered the beast's eye socket, reaching all the way to the brain. Six-Three-Nine-Nine jumped off the bison's shuddering back, avoiding the thick tree that the carcass had crashed into at the last second.

"What? No praise?!" Six-Three-Nine-Nine exclaimed as he rose from the ground.

"Good job," Six-Five-Zero-One grunted, shaking his head.

The rest of the team just smiled. For the vast majority, such an expression of emotion was nonsense, given the trials they had gone through. However, the children around Six-Three-Nine-Nine were slightly different from the others. They were a little more alive and free, and a little less of mindless robots.

In the past, Six-Three-Nine-Nine thought he was great at reading people, but now he knew that he was only at the beginning of this journey. The new group and experience allowed him to hone his skills. He learned not only to look into souls but also to manipulate them, creating personalities he needed.

But that wasn't all. With his abilities, he could play any role. Even his current personality was only a mask to hide a ruthless, cold, and calculating mind. With it, he resisted years of incessant propaganda and brainwashing aimed at turning him and the others into obedient servants, but at the same time, he didn't allow the wardens to doubt his loyalty even for a moment.

"Bow!" the older students shouted as soon as the wardens entered the forest.

The children lined up in a perfect rectangle and bent sharply at a ninety-degree angle. After standing like this for a few seconds, they returned to their previous position and froze, staring straight ahead with their hands folded behind their backs. They didn't move while the wardens walked between the rows, meticulously scrutinizing each child.

Suddenly, one of them stopped. Staring at the boy in front of him, he looked down at him for a couple of seconds and then put his hand on his shoulder.

"Do you feel this?"

The boy nodded.

"What exactly do you feel?"

"A tap on the shoulder."

The warden removed his hand and took a step back. To the other children, he looked unperturbed, but the small movements of his hands and head betrayed his surprise.

"Six-Three-Nine-Nine," a mechanical voice said. "Follow me."

Several wardens took the boy away, after which

numerous checks and tests began. When the evaluations were concluded, he was locked in a room with a single window that overlooked a huge flying ship that docked at the island that evening. After a while, the door opened to let in a tall young man with long hair, dressed in expensive clothes.

Six-Three-Nine-Nine bowed his head.

"Do you know who I am?" the man asked.

His voice was calm, but Six-Three-Nine-Nine felt a shiver run down his spine.

"Yes. You are Ciel Eldivize, the patriarch of our great clan."

"How can you be so sure?"

Six-Three-Nine-Nine thought for a moment before answering.

"Intuition."

"Raise your head," the man said. "You are right. But I'm not only the patriarch. I'm also your father. Father of all the children on this island."

Nine-Nine wasn't particularly surprised; he had suspected something like this for a long time. He couldn't help noticing his resemblance to other children. They had to have at least one parent in common.

"Do you have any idea why I came to see you?"

Six-Three-Nine-Nine nodded.

"My energy control woke up very early."

"That's right. You're eleven. This hasn't happened since Jiang Dao of the Seven Blades Clan. In addition, your test results indicate that you have tremendous potential. It has been worth the effort over decades. Are you ready to be my heir?"

"I will obey your every order. If you wish it, I will become your heir."

"Excellent."

Ciel was about to leave the room when he noticed that Six-Three-Nine-Nine was still bowing.

"Is there something wrong?"

"I'd like to ask you something, if it would be all right with you."

"Ask."

"How come you don't have an actual heir? Why did the choice fall on a simple student?"

"Why do you think?"

"I'd assume that it'd be too risky to invest everything into a single child. There are many geniuses born in the world, but only a few achieve something worthwhile."

"Correct. Still, this doesn't mean that you should consider yourself special. Before you, there were dozens of others. Some stronger, some weaker, but all equally worthy of my time and resources. Unfortunately, they all failed to meet my expectations in the end. I hope a different fate awaits you."

Six-Three-Nine-Nine nodded. Ciel's brief explanation was in line with many of his initial assumptions. There were still things that didn't add up, but he couldn't ask about those right now. It would be too suspicious. He had already pushed it too far.

"Is that all?"

"Can I take one of my brothers with me?"

"And why should I allow that?"

"He is talented. I believe that it would be more profitable for the clan to make him into a warrior rather than just another faceless warden."

"Would it, now?"

"I estimate he will awaken his warrior layer by the age of thirteen."

"Thirteen? You are indeed my children, but I have not put more than a fraction of my power into your seed. So where does such confidence come from? Can you see the future? Or is it just a hunch again?"

"Intuition."

"And if he doesn't live up to my expectations?"

"If my prediction comes true, I'd like him to join me."

"Very well. But when you want something, you must be willing to give something in return. If your brother doesn't awaken his warrior layer before the age of thirteen, you will have to kill him yourself."

Nine-Nine winced and clenched his fists. His face slightly darkened.

"As you wish."

"His number?"

"Six-Five-Zero-One."

"Would that be all?"

"There's one more thing, if I may be so bold."

"I'll end up spoiling you, boy." Ciel smiled. "Very well. I appreciate your audacious spirit, so I'll allow it."

"Can I have a name?"

"What a... human thing to ask. What would you like to be called?"

"Shacks."

Ciel nodded.

"It's time for us to go, Shacks."

This was the end of Shacks's stay on the nameless island. In the end, no one ever found out that Six-Three-Nine-Nine manipulated not only the students but even the wardens. No one ever found out that all this time he received more potions than the rest, studied what he should have not, and even postponed the awakening of his warrior layer to gain more influence on the wardens.

No one ever realized what kind of monster joined the Bright Moon Clan and how far-reaching his plans were.

Chapter 27
FATHER AND SON

"You don't look surprised," Ciel noted, folding his hands behind his back.

"I'm not. We suspected from the start that this was a trap. Our suspicions were confirmed as soon as the contract scroll with Eversteins began to fade." Shacks shrugged. "We were a little bit slow with killing the last sylph, but hey... Or are you talking about the fact that you're here? That's not a surprise for me either. If you knew that I was in the Trial Worlds, then I knew you were here, too. After all, we share the *Divine Gift*. The Bright Moon Altar gave me a hint."

Ciel nodded.

"You have become stronger."

"You, too." Shacks grinned. "So? Did you come to take me back? Have you come to reprimand me for taking the *Gift* from Ai and ruining your plans? However..." Shacks paused for a moment. "No. You know who I work for. You don't have the resources for such a thing. You wouldn't dare risk it."

"I've come to talk. Rather, I've come here to ask you to fulfill your duty. You must lead the Bright Moon Clan."

"Oh?" Shacks raised an eyebrow. "You're retiring?"

"My *Spark* is damaged. A few more years and my *Shell* won't be able to hold it. I'm dying, Shacks," Ciel looked his son straight in the eyes. "You must take my place and lead the clan on."

"I dunno... I quite like being a vagabond." Yawning, Shacks stretched and clasped his hands behind his head. His father's words didn't seem to make any impression on him. "Have you forgotten that you sent me to my death? Where's Ai, anyway? Shouldn't she be the heir after my death?"

"Ai is dead," Ciel replied grimly. "She was ripped apart by Tyrants while she was on an expedition in the far reaches of the Waste Lands. She wanted to put herself in a life-or-death situation and become stronger, but she overestimated her abilities. The sad fate of most geniuses..."

"What about her guards? I doubt she ventured out alone."

"Dead as well. You know that one should never rely on others to protect them, lest they risk making no progress at all. Ai told them to stand back while she fought, and they arrived too late. And even if they had interfered, they wouldn't have been strong enough to stop three Tyrants at once."

"A shame." Shacks sighed. "But that doesn't change anything. You should find someone else to take care of the clan. I have other things to do."

"The Bright Moon Clan is ready to join the Temple and become part of the Eternal Path Empire."

"A wise choice." Shacks nodded and turned around. "But you can do that without me. Good luck finding a new heir!"

"Shacks!" Ciel shouted as his son began to disappear into the shadows.

The world around them changed in an instant. Ciel and Shacks were transported from the dark sewers to a cave with a small pond in its center, filled with luminous blue water. Above it was a small golden bridge with a pedestal holding a silver bowl.

"Our Altar?" Turning around, Shacks tilted his head. "Interesting... How did you summon my mind here?"

"If you give me a chance to speak, you will find out," Ciel answered, approaching the bowl. "Right now, you are the only one who is qualified to be the new head of the clan. And you can't just refuse it. The fate of the entire Ecumene depends on the fate of the Bright Moon Clan, so it needs a strong leader. You—"

"Hold on, hold on!" Chuckling, Shacks waved his hands. "Do you hear yourself? The fate of the Ecumene? Depending on our little clan? I don't know what you've been smoking, but I want some of it."

"You should know that the creator of the clan's power was a Higher One. Our founder was a Higher One!"

"So what? That was ages ago! Now we're just a bunch of nobodies."

"Time doesn't matter when it comes to power," Ciel said angrily. "You know who she was. But what you don't know is that she was the main contender for the Heavenly Throne. She was the Destroyer!"

"Something doesn't add up..." Shacks frowned. "The destroyer was Or'drok Okka Yashnir. A man."

"Do you think he was the only one with that title?" Ciel chuckled. "I'm talking about events much older than the massacre of Atrazoth's disciples. This is the thirteenth Age. The previous Ruler of the Ecumene and teacher of Yashnir, Atrazoth, was born at the beginning of the eleventh, and our Lady of the Bright Moon in the ninth."

"Fine, but what does this change?" Shacks folded his arms across his chest. "How are our clan and the fate of Ecumene connected?"

Instead of replying, Ciel picked up the bowl from the pedestal.

"The reason is the legacy our Lady left behind," Ciel continued as soon as the vessel was filled with a scarlet liquid. "Before our clan was almost destroyed, our elders managed to find a way to open the Bright Moon Tomb, which is tied to the power of our *Divine Gift*. We didn't have time to enter it, but we were able to find out what was in it. If this falls into the wrong hands, the Ecumene will be engulfed in chaos again. It is our clan's duty to preserve and hide the Lady's heritage from the rest of the world. Unless the Eternal Path Temple intends to stay in the Trial Worlds forever, then this will affect it as well. That's why I'm asking you to take charge of the clan. It will benefit both you and Kai." He turned to Shacks. "I have poured some of my knowledge into this bowl with the help of the *Supreme Order*. Consume it and you will know everything about the Tomb and the clan that the oath forbids me to pass on in any other way."

Approaching Shacks, Ciel handed him the bowl. Looking at the scarlet liquid, similar to the *Divine Gift* his father once gave him, Shacks raised the bowl to his face and sniffed. There was no point in doing it since this place existed only in their minds, but he still wanted to know.

It smelled like flowers.

"By the way, I forgot to ask." Moving the bowl away from his face, Shacks looked up at Ciel. "How did you even end up in the Trial Worlds?"

"Very little was saved by our ancestors when they fled to Saha, but they were able to protect and take the interstellar transfer array with them. It can reach even the Middle Worlds. From there, one can reach the Heavenly World."

"Is the Tomb there?"

"No, but we can get to the right world through it."

Nodding, Shacks raised the bowl again, but then suddenly pushed it away again.

"Wait a second... That's why you've been collecting stones and energy crystals all these years. For the array!" he remembered. "But what's with all the lies about the Gates of Ecumene? Why did you push the Seven Blades to discover them?"

"Are you going to drink that or not?" Ciel asked gloomily, nodding at the bowl.

"Just answer the question."

"Because of the Old Man, his accomplices, and, of course, Jiang Dao. They were too strong and dangerous. I needed to get rid of them. One left and the rest died. After that, no one could prevent us from taking the Plateau and the rest of the planet, which only accelerated the extraction of stones and energy crystals. Also, we needed the Gates to open. Without the divine power, the interstellar transfer array could only work through the System Tower. It's so powerful that it needed not energy, but divine particles to function. The Gates required energy to connect with the array."

"I see... And how did you get the Contenders? One *Master of Six Stars* is needed for every nineteen weaker souls in order for the group to pass into the Trial Worlds. How many such *Masters* does the clan have?"

"Enough. We brought along many people, including elders and even patriarchs."

"There's no way the clan had so many *Masters of Six Stars*. Not on Saha." Shacks frowned. "Dark arts?"

"There was no choice."

"And you're suggesting that I take over the reins of a clan full of dark art adepts?" Shacks arched an eyebrow.

"That was a sacrifice we had to make for the sake of the future. We are not adepts, but simply people who sacrificed their honor and pride for a greater good. We no longer practice the dark arts. It is forbidden."

"Still, you bear the marks, so according to the laws of the Eternal Path Empire, you are criminals. We cannot have such a clan in our ranks."

"I have read the laws of your empire," Ciel replied. "And they state that if the mark was forced upon an individual, they can be pardoned. That's precisely what happened to our clan. But if our noble sacrifice isn't enough for you, then feel free to wash away the shame with blood!" Ciel spoke angrily. "Kill anyone with the mark if you think that's the punishment they deserve for using the opportunity to lead their families and clan to prosperity."

"Calm down, old man. I don't want you to pop a vessel."

Smiling, Shacks finally brought the bowl to his mouth. As the crimson liquid touched his lips, he suddenly stopped again. Ciel's left eyelid seemed to twitch.

"Do you really have an ATS?"

"Oh, for Heavens' sake, Shacks…" Ciel groaned. "Drink that, and you will find out everything. What are these questions for, if all the answers are already in your hands?"

"I'm just curious. What if some of the answers aren't in here?" he replied with a shrug. "Well?"

"Yes, the clan has a small ATS. And no, we couldn't get the divine particles out of it."

"See? That wasn't so hard, was it?" Shacks grinned. "Bottoms up!"

Shacks raised the bowl to his face and let the odorous crimson liquid pour into his mouth...

...and then he spat it all right into Ciel's face with a ringing laugh.

"Did you honestly think that I would fall for such a stupid trick?" he asked as he tossed away the bowl, which automatically teleported back to the pedestal. "Seriously?"

In a moment, they were back in the dark sewers of the ancient capital. Having found a way out, Shacks no longer wanted to linger at the Bright Moon Altar. Ciel left immediately after his son.

"If you don't want to do it, I'll have to make you," Ciel hissed, concentrating on his *Storage*.

A man suddenly appeared right in front of him, bellowing and shuddering in terrible pain. Ciel's dagger sank into his back, piercing the *Astral Body*, the tip resting on his *Shell*. With his other hand, he grabbed the man by the neck.

"Don't you recognize him?" Ciel asked. "Your beloved little brother... Did you miss him? Thought I wouldn't notice your closeness?"

"Don't you dare! Knox!" Shacks shouted furiously as a pair of crossbows appeared in his hands, his face contorted in a grimace of hatred and pain. "Let him go!"

"His life is in your hands now, my dear son," Ciel replied and summoned a suppression collar. He kicked it toward Shacks. "Whether you like it or not, you will become the head of the clan. Put on the collar or Knox's *Shell* will feel the sharpness of my dagger."

"Wait! I—"

"Shut up! No more questions! The longer you stall, the sooner he'll die! Don't even try to pull off one of your tricks!"

Shacks gritted his teeth, then slowly bent down and picked up the artifact, examining it with spirit perception as he did so. For someone with his abilities, this was enough to understand how complex the item's structure was. Filled with intricate weaves, the collar was a real work of art, designed to deprive high-ranked Masters of freedom. It was far superior to the items he had seen in the clan's treasury before. Compared to this, they were just trinkets scavenged from Saha's ruins. Most likely, the collar was from the Trial Worlds. He wondered what did Ciel have to give for it?

Straightening up, Shacks stared at his father.

"Swear you'll let him go and spare his life when I put the collar on."

"Aaaaaaaaaah!" Knox cried out as Ciel's hand moved slightly forward, his eyes red and knees buckling.

At the sight of his brother's suffering, Shacks took a step forward but quickly stopped when he saw his father's menacing look.

"Do you think I'm bluffing?" Ciel growled. "Put on the collar!"

"Not until you swear an oath!"

"Ignorant brat!" Ciel cried out in frustration. "You want

an oath? I'll give you an oath..."

Ciel swore an oath, adding to it the condition that it would cease to be valid if Shacks removed the collar or was able to resist its effects. The oath would take effect the moment the collar was put on.

"A deal is a deal," Ciel said, nodding at the steel hoop in Shacks's hands.

"I'm sorry," Shacks whispered, casting one last glance at his brother.

As the metal was about to touch his neck, he suddenly grinned, and opened his eyes. There was no trace of rage, despair, or sadness on his face. Just a slight smirk and an arrogant look.

There was a click.

Staggering, Ciel looked at his chest. A hole the size of a fist gaped in his torso, as well as in Knox's. Their *Astral Bodies* were also pierced.

Screaming in pain and rage, he cut Knox in two with a single swing, destroying his soul. Shacks didn't so much as blink at the sight of his brother's death. A moment later, he vanished. Ciel immediately followed him, and they engaged in battle invisible to the naked eye. They both relied on extremely stealthy and pinpoint fighting styles, trading physical strength for precision and agility.

They used the *Divine Gift*, but since they shared the same one, it was of little use. They couldn't hide from each other in the fog or use clones to lure their opponent out in the open. Even the *Supreme Order* was useless, since their *Wills* were equally powerful.

But Shacks had the advantage of youth and a strong physical and *Astral* bodies, which eventually tipped the scales in his favor.

Wounded and exhausted, Ciel fell to his knees before his son. Grabbing his father by the hair, Shacks pressed one of the crossbows against his head.

"I feel kinda bad, fighting a sick man," Shacks said, tilting his head. "Actually, no, I don't. After all you've done, this will be an act of mercy. I can't think of torture horrible enough to make you repent for everything you've done, but no matter… Getting rid of you will do just fine."

"Just get it over with, boy." Ciel coughed.

Shacks laughed.

"You wound me, you know? I stand before you as a *Master of Seven Average Stars* and not once did you bother to ask how come I became so strong. Or better yet, how come your reports have been so wrong. They told you I have only six, didn't they?" He chuckled. "Your data is outdated, old man. Ah… You should have seen your face when I fired. Priceless. I bet you thought that I was desperate, that I surrendered. You did, didn't you? Ha! Thought that all your plans worked out? Ha-ha! Oh, it gives me great pleasure to see all your hopes and dreams shatter in an instant…"

Ciel chuckled and shook his head.

"You killed your own brother… For what? Just to spite me? You are truly deranged, boy."

"Ah, yes… Poor little Knox…" Shacks's face twisted in a grin. "That was a trap. Ah, but you knew that, didn't you? You taught me this tactic after all. If you want to lure the enemy into your net, let them use your weakness. But if you don't want to lose anything…"

"…then create a weakness," Ciel finished for him. "You never cared about Knox, did you?"

"Not even for a bit."

"By the Heavens... I've created a monster..." Ciel sighed. "Ah, Shacks... You would have been perfect... It's a shame that you turned out to be such a disappointment."

"Oh, don't be like that. I bet you feel at least a tad proud. You just don't want to admit it." Shacks chuckled. "I've been a patient little boy, waiting all this time to surprise you... I didn't know where and when, but I was sure that we'd meet again."

"It's a shame..."

"...that I'm such a disappointment. I know!" Shacks nodded, hitting Ciel in the face with the butt of the crossbow. "Just once, I'd like it if you didn't give me that condescending look... Just once!"

"Ha..."

"I spent years planning it all out... I was preparing even before I had a name, while we were still on that godforsaken island. Oh, but you knew... You knew and you hoped you could change it, that you could break me, mold me into the perfect little puppet. Your ego was your undoing, old man. It has always been your biggest weakness. Even now." He hit him again. "Or else, why did you come here alone, huh? Thought you didn't need help to handle me? Why isn't there a single *Divine Stage* cultivator in the clan besides you, if you had the ATS, time, and resources to train them?! I'll tell you why! Because you're a paranoid megalomaniac! You didn't share those resources with anyone, did you?! You didn't let anyone into the ATS for a long time! Why?!"

"Traitors..."

"Ah, yes... Traitors... Everyone's favorite pawn." He grinned. "How many failed coups, attempted assassinations, conspiracies, and betrayals has the clan survived during all this time? Dozens? Hundreds? How many of your loyal men had to be killed? Many, I'm sure."

"That... All of that was your doing... Wasn't it?"

"It was." Shacks continued to smile. "Do you think Knox was my only 'dear friend'? Do you know into how many ears I've whispered over the years? How many I gently nudged in the right direction? How many promises I had given and threats made? It's so easy to put things into people's heads. One by one, I lured them over to my side. When I departed, I left behind those who were supposed to bring you to ruin. I didn't want to get rid of you too quickly. No. That wouldn't have been interesting... So I orchestrated this whole little play just for the two of us. They say intelligent people are easy to manipulate. I thought this wouldn't apply to Masters since we're built differently from mortals, but I was wrong. All that it took was a little worm of doubt. Over the years, it dug quite a hole in your brain, making my job all that much easier..."

"I should have known..."

"You should have. Perhaps deep down, you did. Perhaps you just didn't want to admit that the great Ciel Eldivize was fooled by a snotty brat. That's why you came here underprepared. That's why you underestimated me until the fight began. Because how could a child, and that was what I always was in your eyes, defeat a Master like you?"

Ciel closed his eyes and sighed heavily. He hated to admit it, but Shacks had a point.

"There's one thing I'm curious about, though," Shacks said, jerking him by the hair. "Hey! Are you listening? Don't give up on me now!"

"You talk too much, boy," Ciel grumbled. "What is it?"

"This isn't your *Shell*, is it? You were incomplete before, but now you seem almost empty. Are you a puppet? A thoughtless pawn with a soul? Do you have a consciousness at all?"

"That's more than one question..."

"Shut up!" Shacks shook him again. "What the hell did you give me at the Altar? You wanted to turn me into a doll, too, didn't you? Actually, no. Don't answer. I'll find out myself."

With that, he kicked Ciel in the stomach. The surging power of the blow hit the *Shell*, knocking the man unconscious.

"Sweet dreams, old man."

With a grin, he shackled Ciel with artifacts and alchemy and transferred him to his pocket dimension where he'd be safe until they returned to the Temple.

"Now... Where the fuck is the exit?"

Chapter 28
THE TRAP

"I order you to obey."

"I—"

"Shut up. Don't move."

Seeing that the vampiress froze, Regis nodded contentedly and relaxed.

"We didn't think he'd take you with him to Ferox," he said. "We planned to participate in the invasion, but his little stunt forced me to change my plans. However, this turned out to be even better. You practically walked into my arms. Get up," he ordered. "Take off your clothes."

With a soft rustle of discarded fabric, Acilla stood naked before Regis. Smiling wide, he admired the work of art he considered her perfect form.

"I've been waiting for this for so long… Soon, you will become a vessel for my strength." He slid his hand across Acilla's stomach. "It will ripen inside you… Ah, the power you will give me…"

With that, he grabbed the vampiress by the hand and jerked her toward himself.

"Don't resist," he whispered into her ear and pressed his lips against hers.

The kiss lasted for several seconds when Regis began to notice that Acilla's tongue was penetrating deeper and deeper into his mouth. As he opened his eyes, he felt something soft slide down his throat. Startled and disgusted, he pushed Acilla away and reinforced his mental defenses.

Standing before him now was no longer a beautiful woman but a terrible humanoid creature with gray skin and blood-red eyes. It had no hair or ears, and its bloodless lips hid shark-like teeth. Dancing in the depths of its gaping maw was a thick, fleshy tongue with spikes.

Almost gagging at the realization that he had allowed such a foul beast to touch him, Regis released a sickle of scarlet energy with a wave of his hand, cutting the monster in half. Spitting in disgust, he turned at the sudden sound of sonorous laughter only to find Acilla fully clothed, observing him from across the room.

"Ah, if only you could have seen the look on your face," she sneered, mimicking his horrified expression. "I should have let her play with you a little longer."

"You bitch!" Regis shouted and lunged at her.

As he crossed the distance separating them, something hit him with incredible force and speed, throwing him a dozen feet away. Gasping for air and struggling to his feet, he saw the imprint of Acilla's shoe on his chest.

"How?!" He coughed. "Where did such power come from? Since when are you a master of the *Path of Mind*? Why aren't you following my orders?"

"I have you to thank for that. Your little... experiments awakened the dormant power in my blood." Acilla smiled.

"You should know that vampires are natural users of the *Path of Absorption*, capable of temporarily taking away almost any power. I borrowed the *Path of Mind* from one of the Temple followers, so to speak."

Acilla kept silent about the fact that only those with the ancestral bloodline could do this. Ordinary vampires could only take away physical and spiritual strength, but not specific abilities.

Ending the lesson on her kind's powers there, Acilla extended her hand and activated the *Will of Blood*. The walls of the hive around them began to ooze scarlet liquid, and the air was filled with the same scarlet haze.

Sensing danger, Regis concentrated on healing techniques, potions, and items to heal his damaged *Astral Body*.

The Ring... *Why isn't it working?!*

"Performance anxiety?" Acilla sneered, enjoying his struggle.

"What did you do?!"

"Borrowed a little bit of Overclay's blood and power. The Eversteins are something else, aren't they? I'd hate for our little reunion to be ruined by some trinket."

Cutting her palm with her fingernail, Acilla released an unnaturally large amount of blood from the wound. Pooling under her feet, it mixed with the scarlet mist and liquid to form a miniature army of Blood Servants.

"He's all yours."

With a shrill scream, the Servants rushed to Regis, who tore through their ranks like through paper and, fueled with burning hatred, threw himself at Acilla. He no longer held back, increasing his strength with Runes to unleash his most powerful attack. Thousands of blinding lightning bolts branched out from his palm, destroying most of the hive.

But the Queen Bee was no longer there.

Suddenly falling to his knees, Regis howled in pain. Blood gushed from his right shoulder, and his *Astral Body* in that place was torn. Acilla appeared behind him with a menacing smile and a severed limb in her hand. A progenitor bloodline transformation gave her powers even without changing her appearance, and her *Blood Aura* tormented Regis, draining his *Astral* and physical body with every second. The same way as it did in the fight against Kai.

"You don't seem to understand the rules of the game. I'm not your opponent," she said, stepping back. "They are."

The Blood Servants charged at Regis again, but he tore through them once more. When he tried to escape the horde's grip, Acilla foiled his plans.

"What are you planning?" he asked as he slaughtered another wave of creatures.

The vampiress only smiled.

Regis was becoming more desperate by the second, barely holding his ground, missing more and more attacks.

"How does it feel to be toyed with, Regis?" She smiled. "Doesn't feel as fun when you're on the receiving end, does it?"

Regis's eyes widened in horror as he was violently knocked to the ground. The number of creatures suddenly decreased, their power equally distributed among a dozen individuals that began to tear him apart like a pack of hungry dogs. With a sickening crunch, his limbs were torn one by one.

"Stop! Enough! Agh!" he squealed, trembling madly and

trying to escape, but all of his attempts were futile. By taking his blood, Acilla had blocked his ability to numb his senses or escape into the soul world. "NO!"

Dismissing the Servants, Acilla approached Regis and gave him a mocking and contemptuous smile. He answered her with insane fury in his eyes. Someone like him, tempered in the flames of war and trials, couldn't be broken so easily. A couple of hours of mental rest and he'd be as good as new.

However, he didn't have a few hours. Acilla now had complete control over him. He couldn't even blink without her permission.

"I won't kill you," she said, bending over him with a terrible smile. "You can still be of use."

Outstretching her hand, she plunged it into Regis's deformed stomach and wrapped her fingers around his soul. Tightening her grip, she poured out all the absorbed power, covering his *Shell* with invisible fetters. All this was done to activate the unique ability of the vampire progenitor bloodline.

"Rise, my *Blood Puppet*," she whispered as she pulled out her hand and stepped back. "And dance to my tune."

Guided by her *Will*, Regis rose obediently.

"From today on, you're my slave."

"Yes, mistress."

***

Another explosion shook the area. The barriers flickered but remained stable.

The battle for the Ark continued. The enemy troops made camps in the northern and western parts of the city, deploying their combat arrays there. They were actively bombarding all other areas, while their detachments moved inland, killing everyone in their path.

Those who didn't manage to evacuate in time perished in the first moments of the attack, while others ended up trapped in the suppression zone that covered the Ark sometime later. The city systems and the *Complex* tried to deactivate it but failed since the barrier's source was the enemy *Heavenly Complex*.

Together with the rest of the Technology Center, Nyako tirelessly worked on maintaining the defensive arrays. Operated by Temple members and Artificial Spirits, it became the first line of defense, deflecting the bulk of enemy attacks and saving many lives by directing to numerous shelters those who didn't have tattoos and lived in the outer city.

"Malvur, it's coming your way! Now!" Nyako warned.

A moment later, the sky over the center of the Ark flashed. There was a powerful explosion, but Malvur activated *Invincible Fortress* and covered the refugees. It wasn't for nothing that he got his *Divine Gift* and spent years mastering it in ATS. Not to mention that Kai turned this whole arena into one of the key defensive points along with the Earth and Heaven Havens.

"What is Heaven Haven doing?! Shouldn't they be helping us?!" Ragnar shouted in frustration as he positioned himself at the other entrance to aid Malvur in protecting the evacuees.

"Look at the sky! I— Shit!" Nyako suddenly cursed.

"Is it bad?" Malvur asked.

"They're breaking through our formation. Crap... They'll be here soon."

"What about the clones?" Ragnar asked. "Shouldn't they be able to stop them now? Didn't Kai give them a boost or something?"

"There are too few of them!"

Before Nyako had time to warn anyone about the incoming danger, a wave of fire covered the southern arena entrance, killing all but a handful of people closest to Ragnar.

"You—" Ragnar gasped at the sight of so many burned bodies. "I'll kill them all myself!"

"*Ragnar, no!*" Nyako shouted after him, but it was too late.

Cursing, she turned around.

"*We're moving out*", she told the silent shadows behind her.

The darkness stirred, responding with a nod, and headed straight to Ragnar who engaged in a fight with an approaching enemy squad. The aesir was in rage with blinding fury despite his injuries and the fact that most of his group had long been rendered unable to assist him, cut down or burned to a crisp.

Sending her bodyguards clones to aid her friend, Nyako took a moment to study their enemy. Judging by the insignia, they were members of the O'Crime family. One, like her, stood idly by and observed, and the other under the support of his family guards toyed with Ragnar by throwing fireballs at him. Nyako didn't have to tear them open to know that they were Heavenly Manticores; she could smell their wretched bloodline even from here. Luckily, they didn't have the *Hearts*, but they did undergo the second evolution, which meant that they had *Partial Transformation*, perfect cores, and much more. And judging by the stench, they used dark alchemy and Runes.

"How about you give me a hand here?!" Ragnar shouted.

Nodding, Nyako summoned a small multi-colored box and threw open the lid. The arrays covered the district with a dense barrier that hindered movement through space.

The idle figure turned its head to look at her. He must've figured out her plan because he gave a mental command to his partner to back away from Ragnar.

"Like that'll help you," Nyako muttered to herself as she fully activated her *Divine Gift* and the opened *Casket of Eternity* began to suck in everything in front of it with incredible force.

The force of attraction was so great that the nearby buildings were pulled in along with the foundation. Debris and entire boulders flew up to Nyako, compressed, and disappeared into the endless depths of the box along with the Manticores' guards.

The two surviving enemies were about to close in on Nyako when they were stopped by a stunning roar and then thrown back by Ragnar who, like a charging bull, crashed into them. Tumbling, the trio was carried to the *Casket*, unable to cling onto anything for support. As he passed by her, Nyako placed a mark on Ragnar, forcing him to the ground, but the strongest Manticore didn't let him get away, dragging him along.

"Get off!" the aesir shouted, kicking the dangling Manticore in his face.

The man groaned in pain and let go, disappearing into the abyss with his companion.

Ragnar fell to the ground with a groan, lifting up a huge

cloud of dust.

"Oof... I'm getting too old for this."

Nyako helped him up and dusted him off.

"Come on."

Together, they moved inside the *Casket*. Nyako and her team had worked forty-three long ATS years on its contents, producing a monstrous structure of thousands of arrays with only one goal — the total annihilation of any enemy.

As a master of arrays without equal, Nyako chose the *Casket of Eternity* as her *Divine Gift* for its size and ease of access. With its ability to hold all of her creations in one place, the *Casket* made it possible to move her enemies to the most dangerous place for them — right into the belly of the mechanical beast. For Nyako, the *Casket* was her kingdom, and for her enemies, it was a deadly labyrinth without an exit.

Like rats, the O'Crimes scurried about, trying to survive the numerous traps. The clones made quick work of the guards, killing one of their masters and injuring the other when he, in a desperate struggle, used the ability of his central core, simultaneously activating that of his fallen comrade. *Fire* and *Water*, the main elements of the two Manticores, met in a clash that shook the entire dimension. It trembled as it began to collapse in the cell with the Fire Master.

"Feisty little buggers, ain't they?" Ragnar commented.

"Shame I have to kill them."

The force of the explosion destroyed the area around the struggling Master. In order to prevent it from escaping from the *Casket*, Nyako rearranged the rooms, placing them into one another, like a nesting doll. The force of the impact collapsed several cells, irrevocably destroying some of the expensive equipment, but the explosion was contained.

To Nyako's surprise, the man continued to stand for a little while before collapsing from exhaustion. His *Spark* lingered for a bit before it died out.

It took the life of one clone, Ragnar's bravery to act as a decoy, a near-suicidal idea, over forty ATS years of preparation, and hundreds of millions of Runes, but they won. It was an expensive victory, but one well-worth all the resources.

Shame that I never found a way to replace the artillery array operators with Artificial Spirits and Shadows... Nyako grimaced, biting her nails. *We could have avoided unnecessary destruction and simply shot them... If I had known about the attack... If I had at least had time to gather additional array operators... I should find someone to stay in the* Casket, *but who in their right mind would agree to lock themselves in a prison and throw away the key? If I survive this attack, I'll figure out how to replace everything with Shadows and Artificial Spirits.*

Chapter 29
THE TRAP 2

"I give up! Stop, please!"

Ryu's foot came, crashing down on the man's head. Shaking off the blood and brain matter from his boot, he looked around. Decimated, the members of the Mountain Sect Alliance lay strewn around him. There were no survivors. No one had managed to escape his wrath.

"Clear," Renata said.

Ryu nodded.

"Let's move on."

The group took off, continuing its journey eastward. While most of the Temple's combat-ready members were providing cover and support for the evacuating populace, the most capable ones were advancing toward the enemy formation along with the clones. Ryu, Renata, and An'na were one of those groups.

Ryu's face was darker than a cloud. The image of his sister haunted him all the time. He should have had her transferred to the Temple ages ago, but he never got around to it. And now, because of his carelessness, she was... He shook his head, feeling his heart break anew. He couldn't take it anymore. The pain was becoming unbearable.

"Ahead of us! A group of survivors!" Ulu, who coordinated the defense, brought him out of his thoughts. *"Two enemy units are approaching from the northeast.* Masters of Four Stars."

"I'll take care of the survivors, you intercept the Alliance troops," Ryu said to An'na and Renata.

The girls didn't answer, only nodded as Ryu accelerated and disappeared.

Inside the ruined building, he found a whole group of heavily injured people. The relief on their faces when they recognized his robes was almost palpable.

Giving them a reassuring smile, Ryu focused on identifying the most serious injuries and mending them with healing techniques and potions.

By the time he finished patching them up and returned, An'na and Renata had destroyed several enemy units.

Suddenly, a column of smoke shot up into the air a dozen miles ahead and the ground shook as a sonic wave swept over their heads.

"Another cluster of artillery arrays has been destroyed," Ulu informed. *"Keep fighting! Victory will surely be ours!"*

Ryu continued to stare at the pillar of unceasing flame. Six and his brothers were their main weapons in this battle, fighting on the front lines and pushing back the main enemy forces. Ryu would give anything to join them, but Lilith's order was crystal clear: "No one is to get in their way." And so, Ryu could only keep his distance, intercepting the enemy units that broke into the depths of the city and saving the surviving residents.

"Found ya..." he heard a voice.

A powerful sweep passed through Ryu's after-mirage of fading light specks, hitting Renata and An'na instead. The former repelled the blow with one saber and counterattacked with another, and the latter deflected the sweep and released a *Fire* technique from her free hand.

As they put some distance between themselves and the opponent, Ryu recognized Tina, one of Rosen's "main gals." Despite the strong retaliatory attack, she had skillfully defended herself and dodged without a scratch.

"Ah, you must be Kaiser's favorite lapdog? The faithful follower of a killer of defenseless and innocent children," she sneered, her voice full of pain and venom. "I wonder how he will feel when he finds out you're dead... Will he be sad? Will he suffer? Oh, I hope he suffers."

Before Tina had time to finish speaking, Renata and An'na activated their *Divine Gift* and transformed into *Ash Avatars*, while Ryu gave himself a power boost. Determined to gain the initiative, the trio attacked in unison.

Infusing her blade with incredible power and squeezing the four *Spheres* around her weapon, Tina saturated it with *Yang* and attacked. Using *Everything and Now* and all the soul energy she had available, she put a significant part of her strength into this swing. But as soon as her blade reached the peak point of its movement, it disappeared, crumbled into dust.

The trio approached through the settling curtain of ash, attacking from both sides at once. Just as their blades closed in on her, a bunch of wide metal stripes filled with the same power as her shattered blade burst out of the ground and Tina's body.

Fighting against the three *Masters of Seven Average Stars* at once required the power of her perfectly compressed core — *Metal Multiplication*, infusing each replica with the power of the original sword. These copies could be made on any surface unless the air was saturated with energy and *Will* higher than hers.

An'na flew back with a cry of pain and clutched her wounded leg. The *Avatar* form protected her from physical but not spiritual attacks.

Ryu was about to turn into a cluster of light particles again when one of the metal stripes, surrounded by a spatial distortion that restrained the movement of *Light*, pierced his stomach. The attack broke through his flesh and *Astral Body* and released a powerful charge of electricity, almost rendering him unconscious. His strong *Will* helped him endure the pain and complete the process of disintegration.

"Ha! Don't think you can pull that trick on me!" Tina shouted triumphantly.

The only one who managed to defend herself was Renata, deflecting several stripes with her sabers, and covering Ryu as he finally completed his transformation and disappeared.

Gathering her strength, An'na spread the *Will of Sword* and used one of her strongest techniques to keep Tina at bay. But her opponent swiftly evaded the affected area, sensing danger. But before she knew it, the *Lost Swing* bolted after her like a hunting dog, claiming her right hand, despite the stripes protecting it. Both her physical and *Astral Bodies* were damaged.

An'na swayed, exhausted, while Renata and Ryu went after Tina, with the former finally completing the technique necessary to raise the nearby dead.

"You're mine!" Ryu shouted, emerging from the cluster of light behind Tina.

"Not on your life!" she growled as dozens of stripes burst out of her.

Like a snake, the shimmering metal slithered toward both the living and the undead and tore apart what turned out to be one of Ryu's *Light Clones*.

As the real Ryu manifested behind Tina, he pulled out a crackling spear and threw it at his opponent with great force before he disappeared again. Left without enough material on her head and torso as well as time to form more stripes, she had to direct those that covered her legs to intercept the flying spear.

Renata jumped in. Managing to repel the attack that had flown at her and An'na and absorbing some of its strength, she launched a retaliatory blow, forming a legless skeleton woven from *Ash* in front of Tina.

In an attempt to defend herself, Tina was forced to use what little power she had left after activating the core. A huge ball of lightning covered her, absorbing both Ryu's technique and Renata's huge skeleton.

Tina remained unharmed, but she was breathing heavily, having already spent a lot of strength. Her opponents were formidable and they worked well as a team.

Seeing his chance, Ryu finally activated the *Ephemeral Star Rays*, the unique ability he learned thanks to his perfectly compressed Central Core that he managed to achieve during his meditations. His big achievement unleashed beams of artificial light from his body in various directions. Moving at an alarming speed, they passed through buildings and the ground, changing trajectories. Tina prepared to defend herself when she realized that the rays didn't pose any threat, so she let them fly by.

"You're wasting your time!"

Another cluster of metal stripes rushed toward the trio and the walking corpses. Renata and An'na had to dodge and defend themselves, but they were becoming less and less successful with each attempt. Even when working together, they were forced to spend a huge amount of strength. More and more wounds appeared on their *Astral Bodies*.

Ryu disappeared as soon as the stripes approached him, reappearing at the end of one of the rays that passed right next to Tina.

Two spears hurtled toward her head and stomach but she managed to beat off one with a stripe and evade the second. Ryu moved directly above her and almost knocked her off her feet with a powerful kick to the back of her head. The spear that fell on her neck painfully shook her *Astral Body*.

Light Clones began to form around her while Ryu continued to use the *Ephemeral Star Rays*, moving and attacking her from all directions. He managed to pull this off eight times until Tina finally figured out the pattern and caught him when he appeared behind her. Several metal stripes pierced his head, chest, and soul with great force. Tina grinned, pleased, when another *Beam* activated and another Ryu suddenly appeared in front of her.

The last of her stripes rushed toward him, but he sank into the ground, partially emerging a moment later right from under Tina's feet, and rammed his spear through her chest, piercing her soul. The two stripes that stood in his way couldn't stop the reinforced blow.

Tina fell, disappearing into the shimmering mist of disintegrating stripes. Convinced that she was dead, Ryu returned to his original form and teleported to Renata and An'na.

The girls played a huge role in his victory, distracting Tina, but they sustained serious injuries in the process. An'na suffered many severe injuries to her *Astral Body* and lost both of her arms. Renata's soul was damaged by the excessive load, leaving her on the verge of dying. She could still be cured, but it needed to be done as quickly as possible.

Ryu took the girls and hurried to Earth Haven — the only place they could receive the urgent care they needed.

***

Six and his brothers froze in amazement. Approaching the enemy squad, they didn't expect that all the work would be done for them. The ground was covered in blood and desiccated corpses, and the artillery arrays were deactivated. In the center of it all stood a single figure in a dark gray cloak. Its face was hidden by a hood, spilling strands of long, blond hair. Behind the veil of darkness, there were two glowing scarlet eyes. In its right hand was a sword woven from blood, and in the left, an identical one was just beginning to form, reeking the stench of forbidden magic.

Six felt the presence of a defective Temple mark on the figure, but couldn't identify it, since it was constantly changing and distorting. Experiencing an overwhelming sense of danger, comparable only to the threat posed by their creator, they didn't dare to attack. Despite their invisibility, they were certain that the figure could see them.

It moved slowly, but each step carried it hundreds of feet. In a matter of seconds, it left the clones' area of perception, at the same time disappearing from their memory as well. There was not so much as a wisp of its nightmarish presence left behind.

***

While the Mountain Sect Alliance, the Eversteins, and the Vinaris defended the artillery arrays, systematically moving deeper into the city, Varimas, Luberg, and Gotrid O'Crime lead an army of family servants toward the very heart of Kaiser's Ark — Earth Haven.

Hindering their advance were almost a hundred and fifty clones, Lilith, as well as Qi and Chag. Alas, even with such power and the support of the tower arrays, they could hardly hold off the strengthened Manticores.

Unleashing the power of her blade and transforming into the Golden Phoenix, Lilith desperately poured torrents of fire on Varimas. Despite being in his human form, his high parameters and resistance to *Fire* made him virtually untouchable.

The Manticores wanted revenge so badly that they didn't hesitate to cooperate even with the cultists. Namely, the House of Blood. In exchange for their flesh imbued with power and willingness to become lab rats, the O'Crimes received forbidden bloodline-enhancing drugs, as well as three special infusions made from *Heart Blood*. Thanks to them, the three brothers — the only owners of the *Manticore Hearts* among the attackers — not only strengthened their *Full Transformations* but also made it so that they could maintain their human form through *Complete Submission* without losing the *Transformation* bonuses or abilities.

If it weren't for the advantage in numbers, as well as Chag and Qi, the defenders would have lost long ago. Despite their insane regeneration and Lilith's healing flame, there were fewer and fewer clones on the battlefield with each passing moment.

Unlike Chag, enhanced by the *Divine Gift*, Lilith had

to keep her distance. Even as a Phoenix, she didn't have such high parameters. Struggling to support her allies with ranged attacks and healing, she frantically thought about what else she could do.

The evacuation is still ongoing. Shelling the city isn't an option yet, she pondered, receiving data from Ulu and the island's arrays. *At this rate, the Manticores will slaughter us before we can launch a large-scale attack. I have to hold back or I will incinerate a significant part of the island. Phoenix powers aren't suitable for precise attacks...*

Lilith had decided to order the clones to retreat to Earth Haven when she was overwhelmed by a powerful sense of danger. She barely had time to cover herself with a healing flame and shift to the side when one of her wings was cut off, damaging the *Astral Body* as well. The wound was immediately covered with the ice of the *Cold Void*, and she, frozen to the bones, plummeted to the ground at a great speed.

Hitting the ground, Lilith tried to heal her wing, but she needed more time than she had on her hands. The powerful Concept, enhanced by the Manticore bloodline, actively resisted the power of the Phoenix Progenitor.

"You thought you could just kill my sister and get away with it?" Varimas asked in an icy tone, looking straight at Lilith, and used more drops of *Heart Blood*. "I'll show you, you bitch..."

"Lilith!"

Several clones jumped at him in an attempt to protect Lilith, but Varimas eliminated them, simultaneously deflecting Qi's attack.

"You're not so fearless when Kaiser isn't around, are you?" he continued, kicking Chag back toward his brother.

"The Temple isn't worth shit without him around. We've done well, luring him away… Honestly, I expected more from Rosen's murderers."

I should have known that they were behind this… Lilith's face darkened. She decided to entertain his ego for a while. Hopefully, she'd buy herself enough time to heal her wing. "The Eversteins helped you break through the planetary barrier, didn't they? Why aren't they here?"

"They did their part. We can handle you on our own. We'll kill every member of the Temple. And even if Kaiser comes back alive, all he'll see will be scorched earth, ruins, your heads on stakes, and us, ready to tear him apart. And don't even think for a second that I don't understand why you're stalling. Your wing won't help you."

Varimas disappeared with a sneer, and Lilith, bursting into flames, felt terrible pain. It seemed to her that she would die when it all stopped as suddenly as it began. Her perception suggested that Chag and Qi intervened, having managed to save her from death and rebirth in the last *Phoenix Egg*.

Varimas was about to finish what he started when Ulu reported that ninety-nine percent of the arrays had been shut down, the barrier around the tower weakened, and the amount of power around it drastically decreased. A moment later, two beams of monstrous power erupted from the *Complex*. One hit the enemy's *Complex*, severely damaging it, while the second passed along the northern and eastern parts of the inner city, where the main enemy forces and artillery arrays were located. The entire city shook.

The battle near the tower practically stopped. The explosion caught everyone's attention but only Lilith understood what had happened. The only person capable of unleashing such devastation was the owner of the Eternal

Throne.

"Preparing and gathering forces took a little longer than expected, but I finished just in time. Sorry to have kept you waiting," a voice rang out from above them.

"You..." Varimas looked up. "We didn't expect you this soon. The journey back should have taken you much longer..."

"The journey back?" Kai grinned. "Why, I have been here the entire time."

Chapter 30
THE ENDGAME

Luberg was about to say something to Kai, but the sense of danger that flooded his mind made him lose his train of thought and jump aside. In an instant, three servants were killed, and Luberg and Gotrid almost lost their heads.

At the same time, a dozen Manticores attacked Kai with multiple techniques. Suddenly frozen in place, he activated the *Cover Expansion*, turning his armor into a protective dome, one much stronger than an ordinary *Cover*. At the same time, he was enveloped in the golden light of the *Radiant Void*.

The attack failed to break through, forcing the trio to try to push back Kai with *Spheres* and *Will*, all of which fell apart upon coming into contact with his *Advanced Field of Superiority*.

Growing increasingly frustrated, the brothers activated their central core abilities. A dense stream of sand escaped from Luberg's body, parting into several streams to envelop Gotrid as he turned into a shimmering figure and disappeared within the golden wave.

An eerie grin flared across his face when he appeared

next to Kai and lowered his blade.

"Quick. But not quick enough," Kai said, dodging the blow with incredible speed and fighting back with one of his blades.

His actions were a trick. He allowed Gotrid to believe that he'd hit him so that he could catch him by surprise and attack with *Deimos*.

But then Gotrid's hand was suddenly covered with crystalline armor, blocking the attack of the cursed blade and shattering under the power of *Advanced Sword Will*. Carried by momentum, *Deimos* continued forward through the shower of crystal dust, cutting off Gotrid's forearm.

Gotrid didn't despair, however, believing in Luberg's abilities. Even though the armor stopped the blade for just a moment, it was enough for Gotrid to not only protect his *Astral Body* but also plan and prepare his retreat.

Kai tried to follow his opponent, but found himself shackled by crystals. Growing rapidly, the crystals spread all over his body, trying to penetrate deep into his flesh, *Astral Body*, and soul.

Thanks to the sand particles scattered in the air, Luberg's *Three-Stage Crystallization* could now turn almost everything it touched into durable crystals. With its power, the *Crystallization* could protect Luberg and his allies or shackle his enemies, quickly turning them into statues.

In just a matter of moments, Kai was brought to a halt and forced to focus on fighting the *Forces* that had infiltrated his body and soul. Taking advantage of this, the trio unleashed even more techniques on their opponent, including a destructive wave of compressed energy.

"Hold him tight, Luberg," Varimas instructed. "We'll deal with him."

"Just be quick about it."

Kai was well aware that the attack-wave would kill him if he didn't do something. He couldn't activate *Cover Expansion* again so soon. Not that it would have worked, anyway, since a large part of him already turned into crystal. And yet, a light smile danced on his lips.

One moment and the whole world seemed to freeze. *Ultimate Focus* could grant him maximum perception for only a matter of moments, but that should provide him with more than enough time to activate a new *Path of Blood* technique that increased the power of his bloodline, as well as the abilities it granted, *Six Body Gates* and *Partial Transformation*.

This way, he didn't have to cut off the crystallized skin, since the enhanced regeneration, together with the *Radiant Void*, overpowered the effect of Luberg's ability, leaving his *Astral Body* unharmed.

Meanwhile, the first enemy attacks destroyed the crystal's outer layers. But instead of hitting him, they simply passed through Kai. His eyes flashed a deep violet hue of horror, and his opponents, their bodies heavy as lead, began to lose control of their energy as Kai activated his *Will* and filled the space around with aura. *Advanced Look of the Lord*, one of the rarest *Will* control abilities, struck the Manticores, while the *Advanced Desolation of the Weak* started to steal their energy. Cursed blades launched the *Nightmare World*, and Kai activated *Sudden Suppression*, a *Soul Manifestation* that emitted a surge of his aura that immobilized and prevented Manticores from using their spirit powers.

A moment later, Kai disappeared, having used the *Advanced Will of Space* to introduce the necessary vibrations into the air and his energy cover and even his body. This simplified the process of manipulating the surrounding space, making his movement faster and defense even stronger. Now only spatial attacks and blows imbued with a strong *Will* could hurt him.

By making the space more pliable, using two movement techniques at once, Kai moved so fast that he seemed to be in several different places at the same time. Luberg's and Gotrid's *Wills* were stronger than his, so he couldn't get too close, but Kai was so all over the place that they didn't have time to react.

In a matter of seconds, more than twelve Manticores and both O'Crimes were killed. A few of the family guards attempted to resurrect using the Manticore Bloodline powers, but failed due to the pressure of Kai's *Will* and scattered techniques.

Meanwhile, Varimas, busy fighting Chag and Lilith, shuddered with fury when he felt the death of his brothers. He had believed that they would tire out Kai, and even if they didn't win, they would at least detain him.

Their deaths aren't meaningless, he repeated to himself over and over again. *They forced him to reveal his trump cards, giving me time to study his fighting style and find a way to counter it.*

Varimas could no longer increase his parameters using conventional methods. Right now, his abilities were at their peak, and spending drops of *Heart Blood* could only help him adapt to new attacks, but not strengthen his defense against the old ones.

Realizing that there was no way out, Varimas strengthened himself with a huge number of Runes, killing Lilith and wounding Chag with the *Perfect Sword Core ability*.

"That attack..." Kai whispered. "It's..."

"*The Eight Blades Incarnation!*"

The same ability that Rosen used in his fight against Kai. The *Sword Core* gave the Manticores the ability to manifest their blade and their bodies at any point they could see or feel. They could attack at the speed of thought, unbothered by the restrictions of flesh and movement techniques. As long as they saw or felt the desired point in space, no obstacles could stop them.

One of the swords pierced Kai's body, cutting through his soul. Or rather, so it seemed to Varimas.

The blade actually ended up a foot away from its target. Varimas's mind was deceived, forcing him to strengthen his mind to prevent such a trick from happening again and spend many drops of *Heart Blood* to adapt to the *Path of Mind*.

But none of this prevented Kai from keeping up with him and blocking the incoming attacks. Somehow, despite all of Varimas's efforts, their parameters remained equal.

How?! Varimas wondered, shocked. *He was much weaker just a moment ago!*

With a snarl, he increased the pressure of his *Will* and unleashed multiple blows, hoping to overwhelm his opponent, but nothing came of it as Kai used *Borrowing Flame*. The core ability was slowly burning his body, granting the strength he needed just to be on equal terms with the Manticore. No more no less.

As soon as the preparations were complete, Varimas used the *Second* and *Third Blade Incarnation*, appearing behind Kai. But his swords once again failed to pierce his opponent's body. However, this time, his mind was clear.

Kai made an assumption during the battle with Rosen that Varimas's *First Blade* finally confirmed. The *Eight Blades Incarnation* split the wielder into strings, after which it recreated them in another place. Only the *Spark* remained unchanged, moving along with the vibrations. A new body was formed from the free strings closest to the activation point, but if there were none, then the hyperstrings separated the necessary amount of material from themselves. This was what Kai did.

Sensing Varimas's intention, he compressed the *Spheres* where the swords were supposed to appear, stopping them a few inches away from his skin. Shocked, Varimas pushed the blades forward but failed to break through the reinforced protection. Grinning, Kai kicked him in retaliation, sending him flying.

Varimas had barely landed when a devastating attack struck him from above, forcing him to raise his blades over his head just in time to block another blow.

The ground trembled under the colossal power, and Varimas fell to one knee, feeling his insides and *Astral Body* shudder. Blood gushed from his nose and ears, and the bones in his hands painfully cracked. If it weren't for the *Heart Blood*, he would have lost consciousness.

Kai's *Borrowed Flames* intensified, and in the next moment, he deprived Varimas of his arm along with part of the *Astral Body*. The regeneration spurred on by the *Manticore Heart* immediately set to work, but it required time. Furthermore, Kai's energy that remained in the wound was actively interfering with Varimas's recovery.

Desperate, Varimas resorted to the power of Runes to such an extent that they began to harm his soul and body. He needed to buy just a little more time, only Kai had already read his intentions and didn't give him even the slightest opportunity to regain his strength.

Suddenly, the center of the city was lit up by a flash followed by a loud cry.

"YOUNG MASTER!"

Exploding with power, an old man, who was a Varimas's personal servant, pushed a crowd of clones and Qi away from him and rushed straight to his master. Strengthened by a *Lightning Core* and so many Runes that his soul literally disintegrated on the fly, he became almost unstoppable for a while.

Kai was about to give himself another boost when a spear suddenly appeared in the servant's hands and was hurled at him, turning into a streak of divine light.

Alas, he was late. Kai pierced Varimas's *Shell*, tearing his body apart, and took off at great speed. The spear followed but failed to reach its target as Kai established his connection with the Eternal Throne. The attack simply crashed into the barrier created by the *Complex*.

At the same time, the old man approached his master's remains and moved them to the *Storage*, activating another artifact and triggering a terrible explosion that shook the city's central square.

Maintaining his connection with the *Complex*, Kai watched as the enemy *Complex* began to retreat. Unlike his brothers, Varimas had still had his *Second Chance*. The ability of the Manticore True Descendants would let him resurrect even with his soul destroyed. He used his chance and now it was gone for the next few thousand years. Protecting him, the old man bought his master enough time to resurrect and moved him to the *Complex*, sacrificing his life to distract the defenders.

Closing his eyes, Kai deactivated all the techniques.

He won't make it far... The plan worked, that's the only thing that matters.

"The plan worked?" an angry voice inquired. *"Is that how you see it? Did you know about the attack? You did, didn't you? Why didn't you say anything? Why didn't you order us to prepare? Why did you allow thousands of people to die?"*

Opening his eyes and lowering his gaze, Kai saw Lilith's artificial copy, in the spatial pocket of which was her last Phoenix Egg.

"I knew about it, yes," he replied, monitoring the situation on the island. "Well, that's not entirely true. To some extent, I was the one who organized this attack."

Chapter 31
NECESSARY EVIL

For several seconds, there was silence, allowing the newly discovered facts to sink in.

"Tell me you're joking!" Lilith exclaimed in disbelief. "By the Heavens... You aren't..."

Kai stared at her in silence for a moment. He made his way to the Throne and slowly sat on it.

"But why?" She looked up. "I don't understand. Why all this? Why so many victims?"

"For our future. We had to destroy the Manticores. They would never back down after what we did. The war was inevitable."

"And you decided it was necessary to put the entire island at risk?!"

"Yes. That was the best option. I knew the O'Crimes would want revenge, so I decided to meet them on Bellum."

"So that's why you made your *Astral Body* look so damaged. To lure them out..." It had suddenly dawned upon her.

"Precisely. I paid a huge amount of money for a temporary truce, deliberately not reinforcing it with an oath. They saw what I could do in the ice dimension on Bellum so I needed to make them lower their guard and convince them that I'm not as big of a threat after the war. Fortunately, their thirst for revenge was strong enough to blind them. Still, I had to be careful not to give them a reason to be suspicious of me."

"Do you know how many of your followers almost died? How many lives were lost? How many homes and families were destroyed?"

Kai was silent for a moment.

"There's no victory without sacrifice," he said quietly.

"Do you hear yourself?! You're no better than them with such a way of thinking!"

"You of all people should know the price of peace, Lilith."

"You should have told me! Had I known about this, I would've been able to save them!"

"I should have, yes... But I couldn't. Not while there was a traitor in our midst. Whoever's controlling them wants to take away everything dear to me. You said it yourself. And this someone has enough resources to operate in many places and at different levels. I'm sure they'll take advantage of our conflict with the Manticores. We would have given ourselves away."

"You said you trusted me."

"I do trust you. But what would you have done with this information? It was too risky to tell you. The traitor could have noticed that something was off. I'm sorry for not telling you, but I couldn't risk it."

Lilith was at a loss for words. On one hand, she didn't like being kept in the dark, but on the other, she understood that sometimes certain information had to be kept a secret.

"Was the deal with the Eversteins part of your plan as well?"

"Yes. I knew from the very beginning that they would betray us, since they were solely interested in finding a cure that only the O'Crimes could offer. Without the Eversteins' help, the Manticores would have been unable to find the Ark, let alone break through the barrier. They needed each other."

"Is that why you demanded such an exorbitant amount of money? To test how far they were willing to go to lure you out?"

Kai nodded.

"There was a slim chance it was a mistake and that they weren't collaborating with the O'Crimes. I had to make sure." Propping his head on his fist, Kai leaned back in his seat. "Then it was just a matter of letting them 'abduct' me from Insulaii. By that time, the truce had already lasted for more than six months, and the Manticores weren't making any moves. At first, I wanted to leave Insulaii on my own and leak this information, to provoke them into action. But I realized that they might sense something was wrong, so I invited all the important members of the Temple to Ryu's training to show how strong the clones and I were. Then I paid for the *Divine Gifts* and brought back Acilla. All of this was supposed to tell the traitor that the Temple was growing. This probably made them convince the Manticores to keep me away from the Temple, so as not to jeopardize their entire plan."

"Doesn't this contradict your idea of portraying yourself as weak?"

"In a way, this was to urge them into action. To show them that time was running out…"

"But why were you so sure that the traitor would convince the Manticores to lure you away?"

"Thanks to Shacks. He's very good at profiling people, so he concluded that Izao was the most likely culprit. He's so hellbent on making me experience true despair that he would not risk killing me ahead of time. Killing me would make you guys suffer, but killing all of you and destroying my empire…"

"…would have left you devastated."

"Exactly. Also, he needed a reason to convince the O'Crimes to agree to his plan. I had to be very careful."

"So you told Shacks but not me? That sounds like you don't trust me."

"I didn't tell him. Like I've said, he's good at profiling people. He figured it out himself."

"Sure."

"In the end, everything went according to plan."

"If that's what you call this massacre…"

"Lilith…"

"So, you didn't actually go to Ferox?" she continued, ignoring him. *"How did you fool the Eversteins? Did you use clones? But they don't have* Astral Bodies *and auras that the* Eye of the Void *can detect."*

"The plan was to use the *Path of Mind* and a divine artifact to deceive them, but then Acilla helped me with her *Blood Twins*. Even I see *Sparks* inside them that aren't really there. My double was led into the trap, followed by Acilla and Shacks. The technique is too complex to be maintained from such a great distance, so she had to be there. Shacks was kind enough to offer to keep an eye on her."

"So you never left Insulaii... But why did you join the battle so late?"

"There was just too much to do. The Throne, the barrier, the observation posts... It takes both time and effort. I also had to maintain control over the clone hiding inside the *Twin*."

"And the clones? Why couldn't your clones defeat the Manticores?"

"I ordered them to hold back and not reveal all their abilities. I couldn't let the O'Crimes adapt to my new powers or run away before I arrived."

"But how many of them died because of this? Do you have any pity for your own creations?"

"None."

"What?!"

"They don't really die. I implanted a mechanism in their souls that shrinks the mental layer into an invulnerable structure when their bodies or souls suffer critical damage. It's very taxing on the *Spark* but it's difficult to detect. Their deaths are temporary, so to speak."

"*And that makes it okay?!*" Lilith was seething. "*How many people could your clones have saved if they hadn't held back?! Or is this an acceptable loss, too?!*"

"I don't deny my guilt in their deaths, but I couldn't find a better option."

"Couldn't or didn't want to bother?"

"Lilith..."

"Don't."

"The Temple can't rely on my clones all the time.

What would you do if I died? Consider this a rite of passage. Without such trials, the Temple can't survive in the Ecumene."

"That still doesn't justify it…" Lilith grumbled. "I just don't understand why you had to play this game with the Manticores. You let Varimas escape. Why didn't you kill them right away? Why did your clones start fighting at full strength only after he left?"

"I was waiting for the Eversteins or the traitor to make their move. If we had unleashed our full strength right away, we could have scared them off if they were watching. I'm sorry you wasted another Egg because of this, but we had to take them all out at once. As for Varimas, rest assured, he won't get far. Don't worry about him."

"So what was all of this for? Why did you have to destroy the Manticores if you could just scare them away? Did you really have to be this radical? Wouldn't it have been better to avoid this bloodshed? To focus on defense and the development of the Temple? Are the O'Crimes really that big of a threat that you had to make all these sacrifices? You couldn't wait?"

"I wish it could have been avoided. I really do…" Kai sighed, shaking his head. "We only have eighteen years left."

"Eighteen years? To do what?"

"The Manticores have only recently appeared in the Trial Worlds and they could have only passed one Trial at most. There are nine of them in total, and each subsequent trial can be completed only a year after the previous one. There is also the Final Trial, necessary for the Exodus from the Three Worlds. It can only be completed ten years after the last regular Trial. Thus, we have no more than eighteen years before the O'Crimes can leave the Trial Worlds."

"Are you afraid of their main clan? But they're not even

in the Near Worlds. The Heavenly Manticores reside far in the depths of the Ecumene, to avoid the risk of exposing themselves to La'Gert's servants."

"There's more. I didn't tell you, but I had a contract-reinforced conversation with Rosen before we fought in the Abyss. According to him, Or'Drok has been reborn."

"The Destroyer?"

"I highly doubt it, but the bottom line is that this Yashnir is gathering the New Army of Truth, which already has many deities. They are moving toward the center of the Ecumene. In fifteen years, they will be in the Heavenly World. If the Manticores tell them about the Temple and about me, who bears the bloodline of the Hydra and has the mark of the real Or'Drok," clenching his fist in front of him, Kai showed the black and snow-white patterns, "then we are doomed. There is no way we can resist such a force. What happened today was a necessary evil. I had to sacrifice some of us now to ensure our future. It wasn't an easy decision, but it had to be done."

"What's to stop them from hiring someone who has already passed all the Trials and has been in these Worlds long enough? Are you so sure that the O'Crimes haven't sent out a message about us yet?"

"To some extent. I preserved and studied their *Shells*, particularly those of Mia, Rosen, and his daughter, but even the *Complex's* strongest arrays couldn't find anything in their memory. There are seals on their souls that seem to have been placed by a very strong *Limitless* or even a *Higher One*, which will instantly destroy the *Shell* if anyone tries to remove it. All this suggests that the deity who sent them to the Trial Worlds is very concerned about keeping all important information secret. And a trip to the Trial Worlds is precisely such information. I'm more than certain that the

System, La'Gert, and his servants are already aware of the New Army of Truth, so such precautionary measures make sense."

"So you think that no one but the O'Crimes can be sent as messengers with information because only they have the seals that can keep it secret from the enemies of the New Army?"

"That's right. Now, there are only three of them left: Varimas, who has very little time left to live, their mother, and one of her children. We killed Varimas's servants, Gotrid, Luberg, and Rosen, and the servant of one of the daughters, who died along with her mistress in the ice dimension. As for the twins' servants, they died even before the Manticores arrived in the Trial Worlds. In addition, we have eliminated all the clan members who came with the O'Crimes, and we will soon deal with the main forces of the Mountain Sect Alliance, rendering them unable of providing adequate protection for the remaining two Manticores. Unfortunately, I couldn't find out anything about the matriarch of the O'Crime family and her other child, except for the fact that they are together around the clock. That's probably why the child didn't take part in the attack. In any case, it will be much easier to find and kill them in the next eighteen years. The remnants of the Alliance will no longer protect them, and the Eversteins don't pose a big threat. To us, at least. With me, Acilla, Shacks, and you, we will finish this hunt."

"All this is just speculation. Highly probable, but still just speculation. What if they are wrong? What if you are wrong? What if we deal with the Manticores and still die at the hands of the New Army of Truth?"

"You are right. There is no guarantee." Kai agreed, rising from the Eternal Throne. "If I'm wrong, then it's the end for us. But I can't stay idle. It's better to try to save ourselves than to do nothing at all and die for sure."

Lilith lowered her head.

"There is an alternative. We don't have to leave the Trial Worlds. We are strong here. There are no deities here. In a few decades, with the ATS and your clones, even the Cultists will not be able to resist us. So why leave?"

Descending from the Throne, Kai looked at her in surprise.

"Why? The Temple's philosophy. A true warrior never abandons his path. Trial Worlds are limited; this is a golden cage. We can't become deities here. If we leave, then the Temple really risks being destroyed, but if we stay, then it will definitely disappear. To a certain extent, that's even worse than death."

Lilith fell silent, unsure of what to say. Kai walked slowly toward her.

"I understand your feelings. You should rest, Lilith. This has all been rather taxing on you." Kai extended his hand, partially revealing two *Spheres*. "I hope you will keep everything you've just heard a secret."

"*Wait*—"

But Lilith never got to say what was on her mind, put to sleep by a technique based on the *Paths* of *Soul* and *Mind*.

"It's time to put an end to all this," Kai whispered and disappeared.

Chapter 32
THE PUPPET

Kai couldn't and didn't intend to hide the truth from his followers. But he also used the time during his conversation with Lilith to restore the strength spent in the battle with the Manticores, prepare a new attack on the enemy *Complex* through the Eternal Throne, and track down Varimas.

The battle was drawing to a close. Following Varimas's departure, the Alliance, the Vinaris, and the mercenaries lost the support of his *Complex*, causing the power of the flying fortress to fall on the heads of those who were lucky enough to survive its first attack.

The jammers also powered down, allowing the last of the city's inhabitants to evacuate and the defenders to fight at full force. And although they were outnumbered, their offensive power was unmatched. Fighting on their territory, with the support of the *Complex* and the clones, made them invincible.

By the time Kai arrived, the last of the attackers were either fleeing or being sent to meet their ancestors. But they didn't get far. Fugitives were relentlessly pursued, and anyone who survived the onslaught was brought to the underground dungeon for further questioning.

Seeing that his help was no longer needed, Kai left the island. Communication with the Purple Temple had been lost during the initial stages of the invasion, and since the communication arrays had not been restored since, he was worried that something had gone wrong. No doubt the Manticores wanted to distract them with this attack and kill anyone who came to the aid of the Purple Temple during the transfer. Perhaps they would have succeeded in this endeavor if not for the safety systems and Alfred.

Cutting through the clouds, Kai peeked into his *Storage*. The *Manticore Hearts* were where he had left them, except for Varimas's, which turned into a useless scarlet goo. After he resurrected, all the power and all the Information stored inside the old *Heart* was transferred to the new one, destroying the former.

Shame... he thought, feeling slightly annoyed.

The island finally appeared on the horizon. As he descended, Kai noticed that the battle at the Purple Temple was still ongoing. To make matters worse, the attackers weren't the same people who attacked the main Temple.

A loud whistle suddenly covered the central square.

Kai landed among a crowd of enemies, killing dozens with a single shockwave. The dust that rose into the air quickly settled, revealing many familiar faces.

Every single one of them was twisted in a grimace of fear and horror.

Seeing Kai, some of them began to shout furiously. Several attacks were launched in his direction, only he was no longer in the same place. The massive explosion caused by the collision of multiple techniques showered the square with a rain of multicolored sparks, hurting several bystanders.

Pulling *Deimos* from its sheath, Kai activated its skill for the first time. Black slime poured out of the blade onto the ground, forming three *Awakened Nightmares*. At the same time, he transferred the five clones he had taken with him from the *Storage*.

"Take care of the rest," he instructed, thrusting *Deimos* into the ground.

"*With pleasure,*" Viola rejoiced as she formed next to him.

Picking up her weapon, she threw herself into the fray.

After the recent purge, Kai believed that there were no large and active groups of rebels left on Insulaii. Sirius had done his job well, detecting and exterminating all the conspirators, but this group somehow managed to slip under his radar. If it weren't for the fact that everyone here reeked of the dark arts, Kai would have suspected that Sirius had done this on purpose for the sake of pursuing his own agenda.

So the Manticores got mixed up with the Cult for revenge? Or is this one of His tricks?

While Viola was having fun taking care of enemies, Kai turned to the dilapidated Purple Temple, the main giant fortification of the island, observing its protective dome with his spiritual perception. Having located the most vulnerable parts of the barrier, he sighed grimly and rose into the air.

The protective dome still contained a huge amount of power, but it took Kai only a few seconds to appear on the other side. The moment he did so, a few shells tried to pierce his body, but they dissipated before they hit his cover. Without wasting any more time, Kai appeared next to the defenders of the Temple.

"Good shot," he said and patted Shaw on the shoulder.

"Kai?" Shaw blinked in surprise. "Stand down!"

The men next to Shaw lowered their weapons. They had no idea what was going on outside, so they fired as soon as they noticed a hole in the dome.

"Sorry about that." Shaw smiled apologetically. "We're a bit jumpy."

"No need to apologize. It was the right decision," Kai replied as he studied the area inside the dome. Noticing Hiro covered in blood, he frowned. "Are you all right?"

"Compared to everyone else, I'm as good as new."

There were many people in and around the palace, both injured and dead. Ailenx was cursing and tending to his severed leg, watching over the unconscious Guts and Ivsim. The three of them, along with Hiro and Shaw, were outside the Ark during the attack so they flew toward the Purple Temple as soon as they received Lilith's message.

Unfortunately, the Purple Temple wasn't prepared for an attack from within. Too many of its members turned out to be under the enemy's control, with their memory blocked until today.

In an instant, Kai's *Spheres* opened up and a small scarlet star formed in his hands. Taking off, it painted the sky menacing red, unnerving the already nervous Temple members even more. However, instead of smiting them, the star filled their bodies with strength and healed their injuries, buying the mortally wounded enough time until the healers got to them.

Kai's gaze fell on the group standing near one of the few surviving artillery arrays.

"Shaw. I see your *Astral Body* is damaged."

"Ah, it's not that bad."

"I'll be the judge of that."

Kai activated the improved version of the *Inevitable Healing Technique*, and then he repeated the process with the rest of the group, injecting them with exactly the amount of energy needed to heal their wounds. Fortunately, no one's *Astral Body* was seriously damaged.

He moved as quickly as possible, analyzing each patient and adapting the technique to their injuries, but he never got to Ailenx, Ivsim, and Guts. Sensing impending danger, he suddenly disappeared.

Someone had broken through the weakened barrier and released five large-scale techniques. Currents of air filled with wind blades rushed in all directions toward the defenseless bystanders.

Slightly exhausted, Kai increased his *Ultimate Focus*, forming dozens of weaves while simultaneously calculating the speed of enemy attacks and their exact trajectory.

I won't let you get away with this!

Huge ice walls appeared in multiple places, reinforced by *Yang* and the *Cold Void*. Shaw and Hiro rushed toward the attacker at the same time, but Kai, empowered by the *Borrowing Flame*, beat them to it.

Crashing into the enemy at full speed, Kai tried to pierce their soul with *Phobos*, but his opponent deflected the blow with their blade, simultaneously blocking Kai's *Spheres*, *Will*, and several abilities. Kai couldn't see the attacker's face, as it was covered with a closed gray helmet that matched their armor.

Seven Great Stars? Or not? I don't understand... Kai frowned, trying to determine the attacker's strength. They, too, were an adept of the dark arts.

Wanting to deal with them as soon as possible, Kai unleashed all of his power and lowered his sword. An attack of this magnitude should have cut through the armor like through butter, only his opponent reacted unexpectedly quickly. Every part of their body began to move, shifting and changing at an insane speed until their body was three times its original size and equally as powerful.

And yet, that wasn't enough.

The multi-layered barrier that flashed above the Cultist shattered and Kai's blade collided with their sword. The stranger's weapon and limb were covered with hundreds of cracks, and their body was sent plummeting toward the ground.

Kai followed suit, descending like a comet. But when he landed, his opponent had already teleported away and continued to transform and strengthen their abilities. Their soul vibrated strangely as various forbidden potions and pills entered their system, altering their energy flow and body structure.

Wind, Body, and Sword Spheres, teleportation, and Blood healing, Kai concluded. *These aren't their powers. Their whole body is modified, like Bjorn's and Diana's. But they're not a doll. They have a Spark and their soul looks like it's woven from several pieces, unnaturally bloated from all that power. House of Famine? And the potions... It looks like the work of the House of Blood. Are they a creation of the three Houses? I didn't know they worked so closely...*

As he pondered, a huge wave of black flame erupted from *Phobos* and rushed at the Cultist at incredible speed.

They prepared to defend themselves when Kai appeared behind their back, using the *Advanced Will of Space*.

Reacting too slowly, the Cultist lost the hand holding the blade. Still, they managed to catch Kai off-guard, almost hitting him with the sword that suddenly materialized in their other hand. And while the blade bounced off Kai's defense, it left a dent in it, prompting Kai to become even more diligent.

As the fight progressed, Kai finally figured out what was going on. His opponent possessed the *Divine Gift* of *Advanced Alchemy*, which let them consume more potions and alchemical preparations than was normally allowed, stacking their effects, and allowed them to make an infusion that permanently increased all their initial parameters as long as their *Will* was strong enough to sustain such power. This could be done only once per year, but having in mind the average lifespan of a cultivator, this could lead to acquiring insane amounts of power even without retorting to forbidden techniques and alchemy.

Looks like I need to step up my game.

The power of the *Borrowing Flame* reached its maximum as *Phobos's* tip sunk into the enemy's flesh.

The combined power of Kai's compressed energy, *Advanced Complete Submission*, and *Will* burst out of the steel as a roaring stream of the *Flames of Doom*, burning off the Cultist's lower torso, legs, and other arm. What remained of the body plummeted to the ground, devoid of a soul. Energy vision suggested that his opponent didn't have any traps prepared, so Kai powered down. The day was long, so he needed to preserve his strength and energy.

As he moved his hand to touch the scabbard and return his sword to its place, his legs buckled. His head seemed to explode from pain, and his soul experienced a strong hit, leaving it shaken but intact.

A horrible noise filled his mind, like millions of nails scraping against a blackboard, but he found the strength to resist and even deployed his *Spheres* of *Mind* and *Soul*. Everyone inside the barrier seemed to be experiencing the same excruciating pain. The massive psychic-spirit attack lasted only a few seconds, but that was enough to reduce the number of survivors.

As the noise died down, Kai shambled to his feet and looked at his opponent's remains, once again making sure that they weren't the source of the attack.

Where's it coming from then? he wondered as he looked around.

As his gaze passed over the Temple members, he froze. A figure began to rise from the pile of unconscious people with an ease that suggested that there wasn't a single scratch on him.

"How nice, you covered even me with your *Spheres*," Ivsim said in a strange voice. "You honestly surprised me. I didn't expect that you would master the *Paths* of *Mind* and *Soul* so soon. But no matter. It won't ruin my plans."

"You—"

Tilting his head, Ivsim smiled.

"Me."

Wasting no time, Kai dashed toward the elf and pierced him with his sword.

Chapter 33
PAYBACK TIME

"I advise you not to move, Izao."

"Or what?" he asked, holding out his hand to the blade. "Oh? Ah, how clever," he mused, observing as his whole body, save for the head, was covered in ice.

"Don't think I won't hurt a friend," Kai hissed.

"Oh, I know you wouldn't hesitate to cut off his hand." He grinned. "You wouldn't hesitate to kill him either. After all, they're all just pawns in your game, aren't they?"

"That's not true," Kai growled, pushing the blade further. "I'll encase you in frost like a fossil."

"Will you now? And deprive your precious friend of freedom?"

"It's a small price to pay for his safety. You can't control him forever."

"Or can I?" He chuckled. "You don't know what I'm capable of, Kai."

"It doesn't matter, because it will all end here."

"Are you sure? It's your friend you're holding hostage,

not me. You did a good job outsmarting the O'Crimes, but don't think you can play these games with me. Unlike them, I suspected from the start that you might have stayed on Kaiser's Ark, so I prepared for it. I was three steps ahead of you all the time. To be honest, I was hoping it would come to this."

"You could have continued to hide, using your position to harm the Temple and me. I don't know what exactly you're up to, but this seems like a mistake."

Izao laughed.

"Oh, Kai, Kai, Kai... It's like you're the blind one here." He snickered. "You'll see the bigger picture soon."

"So what happens now?"

"Now I'll tell you why I hate you so much."

"Because you blame me for Bane's death? I'm sorry that your cousin died like that." *Who knew that actions of that fool would lead to that? He went after us to the Ishar Desert, with thirst for revenge, pockets full of powerful artifacts, and he ended up losing his life... Shacks cut off his head and ended the story of Bane Livarius, the descendant of one of the seven great elven families in Nikrim.*

"Hah! I don't give a shit about that scum. But, you *are* one of the main reasons for my whole family's downfall."

"You're delusional. I didn't do anything to your family."

"Several branches of the Livarius family were killed when Kyros attacked Tael."

"Why am I responsible for Kyros's act of revenge? Niagala and Nikrim had a very long history of conflict."

"Did you ever wonder why no one but the Livariuses died? Because that bastard Uriel didn't allow our family to sit next to him during the parade, where we were originally supposed to be. That is, in the safest place in the city. Can you guess why?"

"Because of the elder Lorius who picked on me at the banquet and demanded a duel? But that's idiotic. How is that my fault? If you follow this logic, everyone who was there is responsible."

"That is exactly what it is," Izao grinned, "for each of you is worthy of revenge. Alas, Kyros and Bane, who started all this, died before I could get to them. But Lorius wasn't that lucky. He survived in the dungeons only to meet his end at my hand. The members of Tael's Secret Police who put Lorius on the guest list so that he would notice you weren't spared either. So now it's down to Uriel, Shacks, and you. At that time, I couldn't get to the former, just as I couldn't stay on Nikrim. But I left gifts for his children. By now, they probably went insane and killed themselves. Shacks probably has already lost something very valuable. And you… You'll be the cherry on top."

"I knew you were insane, I just didn't think you were this deranged." Kai laughed weakly. "Why not you just kill everyone then? By your logic, we are all connected to your family's death."

"Not a bad idea," Izao sneered. "I'll think about it when I'm done with you. And now, I have a little proposition for you. I will leave Ivsim's body if you fulfill two small requests."

"And why would you do that?"

"Because it's no fun killing you like this."

"State your conditions."

"We'll go outside the dome, it's too cramped here. Also, you'll let me get to my real body."

"I have studied your *Divine Gift* so I know that it destroys your 'vessel's' *Spark* when the connection is broken. As soon as you get out of Ivsim, he will die."

"This is true only if the 'vessel,' as you've put it, doesn't possess a *Gift*. He will be alive and well. I assure you."

"You will swear an oath."

"I'll swear as many of them as you want."

"Fine. It's a deal."

Izao stared at him for a moment before bursting into laughter.

"Don't even think about it, Kai. Don't even think about it. I know you can break *System* oaths with little to no consequence. Oh, no... You will swear the most ordinary oath."

"Just that?"

"Surely, you wouldn't go against your Temple's philosophy and values, would you? That would be a bad example for your followers and students."

"And that's it?" Kai couldn't believe it. "You will just leave Ivsim's body and leave?"

"That's it. I will just leave."

"Do you think I'm stupid or something? You wouldn't reveal yourself if you just wanted to leave. Why even come here to simply leave empty handed?"

"Who knows? You yourself called me crazy. Hurry now. If you don't make a decision soon, I'll kill your friend."

It can't be this easy. It can't. What's he planning? Can he break System oaths, too? But even so, do I have a choice? If this deal will save Ivsim...

Sighing, Kai agreed to Izao's terms, adding only that their deal would be nullified if Izao did anything else other than get out of Ivism's body in the next ten minutes.

Accepting these conditions, Izao swore his oath.

When all the formalities were finally observed, Kai unfroze Ivsim's body.

"Ivsim is awake," Izao informed him. "He hears and feels everything, he just can't do anything. But before I go, there's one more thing I'd like you to do."

"We've already made a deal."

"It won't take a minute of your time, I assure you. It's not a trap either."

"...what do you want?"

"Unmask the adept you killed and take a look at their face."

Narrowing his eyes in suspicion, Kai looked over at the discarded body. Thousands of different thoughts flashed through his head as he slowly approached the corpse. A storm of emotions raged in his chest, making it difficult for him to retain the aura of indifference.

Kneeling down, he carefully removed the mask and felt his heart sink to his feet.

It was her. Pale, with harsher features, and a face twisted due to alchemy, but it was her.

"Lily..."

"And scene! What a performance!" Izao exclaimed happily. "A splendid spectacle!"

"This... This is a puppet..."

"Fear not, my friend! It's her, body and soul! Ha-ha! Ah,

I wish I could be there when you tell your friend that you killed his unborn child, too."

Kai gently ran his fingers along Lily's face. He couldn't imagine the things she must have gone through to become this.

I'll make this right, Lily. I promise.

Slowly getting up and throwing the mask aside, Kai turned around and stared at Izao. Laughing, he stood next to Ivsim's unconscious body in a spectral form.

"What did you do to him?"

"Nothing," Izao replied once he calmed down. "It'll take a bit for his body to recover, but he'll be back on his feet in no time."

"He better. Otherwise…"

"What? Hm?" Izao smiled. "Now do you understand why I revealed myself? Do you still think my plan is stupid? Look, here I am. All you need to do is take a step and reach for my soul. Don't you want to get revenge? No? They said you are as cold as ice, but I thought they were only joking."

"Stop trying to provoke me. It's not going to work."

"Shame. Would've been fun…"

"And you? Won't you go get your body? The clock is ticking. Ten minutes won't be enough for me to recuperate. I'll be easy prey. Was that your plan?"

Izao scoffed.

"Do I look like an idiot to you? You think I don't know how strong you really are? Do you think I don't know how much of a threat you will become in the future? I never planned and do not plan to fight you."

"But you said—"

"I said I wanted revenge, yes. I want to see you suffer. And suffering doesn't always need to be physical. Well, my time is up. I wish you all the worst, Kai Arnhard," he said, waving goodbye, and disappeared far beyond the island.

Kai continued to stand in the same place, staring into nothingness, and tried to understand where he had gone wrong. How could he have missed this? What could he have done to prevent it?

At some point, he heard a wheeze. Looking down, he saw Ivsim stretching out a trembling hand to Lily, his eyes filled with despair.

Falling to his knees, he embraced the twisted corpse. For several seconds, he knelt motionless, and then a pair of blades suddenly appeared in his hands.

"Ivsim, no!"

Kai teleported, reacting before his friend could end his life. The blades struck uselessly against his back as he held him. Feeling the paralyzing cold on his hands, Ivsim tried to destroy his own soul but failed. Kai wouldn't let him do that either.

Helpless, Ivsim let out a heart-wrenching scream.

Chapter 34
RESPITE

Having put Ivsim to sleep with a *Path of Soul* technique, Kai tried to harmonize his emotional layer, but his lack of familiarity with the *Shell's* structure hindered him. He was new on this *Path*, so he couldn't use these techniques as efficiently as trained Soul Masters could.

The road to recovery would be long, but Kai would make sure to give Ivsim whatever he needed.

08:54:48

Having moved Ivsim to the *Storage*, Kai turned to Lily. For a moment, he entertained the idea of harvesting her brain so that he could explore her memories in the future when he became better acquainted with the *Path of Mind*, only that would be too cruel. Also, someone as experienced as Izao wouldn't be foolish enough to leave information about himself lying around like that.

For the time being, Kai put away her remains into his *Storage*. They'd bid her a proper farewell later.

Exhausted, Kai cast a glance at Hiro, Shaw, and the rest of the Masters, sat down on the ground, and closed his eyes. After a short rest and several mind-enhancing potions, he began to meditate.

08:19:02

For beginning practitioners, only three things influenced their personality: the subconscious, the physiology of the body, and the external environment. These were strong but simple and relatively stable factors.

However, the situation was much more complicated for Masters. Already after the *Mind Stage*, the body's influence was gradually replaced by the influence of the emotional layer, which intensified with each new stage and level. This allowed them to absorb more complex information, but it also made them more sensitive to influences, forcing them to pay more attention to their emotional state. In addition, the influence of their power was much more unpredictable.

Thus, to avoid losing control over themselves, a Master had to know how to balance all these factors. *Willpower* was a great tool for achieving harmony, but it alone couldn't do more than fuel one's desire to live. And the stronger one's soul, the greater the support it required, making those with weaker *Shells* and minds more prone to losing themselves and slipping into insanity.

Staying true to oneself was crucial for avoiding the tainting and weakening of *Willpower* and soul and thus accelerating the process of degradation. For humans, lying wasn't all that big of an issue, but for Masters, it could often lead to corruption from within.

And yet Kai reproached himself for staying true to his word and letting Izao go instead of killing him.

Now is not the time, he remained himself and Kai activated *Ultimate Focus* and *Supreme Simulation* with the support of the *Paths* of *Mind* and *Soul*.

08:18:01

For the sake of the experiment, his consciousness was divided into hundreds of parallel streams. All of them, except the main one, temporarily lost access to memories and were cleared of any extraneous thoughts, launching several accelerated simulations in which Kai broke his promise and killed Izao.

All the scenarios in which he didn't erase the memories of everyone who witnessed what happened were discarded. The problem wasn't only that they led to a much worse outcome, but also that he didn't have enough information to accurately model the actions of so many individuals.

07:20:55

Concentrating on himself, Kai modeled various hypothetical events of the next few thousand years, paying close attention to his own behavior. By carefully controlling all the simulations and analyzing the information received from his copies, he made adjustments and repeated the process. Soon, he got the first results.

06:59:17

As expected, in each of the simulations, he initially tried not to go against his word. In nine percent of the cases, he managed to resist the temptation. In the remaining ninety-one percent, however, he succumbed and continued to break his promises. Numerous difficulties forced him to compromise his principles again and again for the common good, slowly eroding the foundation of his personality.

After that, there were only five possible scenarios left.

In the first, Kai remained true to himself, albeit with some difficulty and possibility of relapse.

05:12:08

In the second, he abandoned cultivation and give up his power. This happened in about eleven simulations out of a hundred in which he violated his principles again.

04:52:41

In the third, in six percent of cases, he resorted to altering memories. In these scenarios, his enhanced memory became like a curse. Erasing this information, stored not only in his mind and *Shell* but also in his artificial *Spark*, was impossible. Kai could only seal the memories from the moment of Izao's murder to insure the stability of his mind.

Deleting or blocking memories from the *Shell* wasn't easy to fix. Therefore, in only twenty percent of these simulations, Kai became himself again.

But blocking memories made no sense, since they would inevitably resurface and lead to even worse consequences.

04:00:20

In the fourth scenario, Kai changed. He never managed to fully recover, so he replaced one principle with another in the hopes of staying sane. In these versions, he began to use falsehood as a weapon, gradually turning into a manipulative liar. He broke his promise to Jongo and decided not to return to Saha to Julie. Many of his close associates turned away from him, and the Temple turned into a regular sect, abandoning its teachings and philosophy.

03:33:54

And in the, fifth, Kai's attempts to remain true to himself failed, and he went on a rampage. Over the course of decades, he abandoned not only the principle of loyalty but also everything else. He no longer had friends, but pawns. He no longer kept his distance from those he considered the biggest violators of the heavenly principles but began to mingle with them. And, worst of all, he turned to the dark arts. His personality slowly eroded, and Kai lost himself, turning many against him. The Temple fell soon after. In a matter of years, Kai spiraled into madness and met his demise.

02:42:56

Of course, all these simulations and assumptions were far from the actual future. Kai didn't have the necessary data and computing power for accurate predictions, and therefore they couldn't dispel his doubts about the correctness of his actions.

And yet, it gave him a piece of mind, as well as helped him make an important decision. He wouldn't go back on his promise, but he would no longer restrain himself or count on anyone's morality and compassion.

01:51:43

After everything he had been through, the simulations finally exhausted him. But he wasn't going to take a break. By activating *Renewal*, he restored the entire supply of his spirit stamina.

00:00:00

The promised ten minutes were up.

Opening his eyes, Kai was ready to act again.

***

"I just can't believe it," Victor said irritably, pacing around the room. "The element of surprise, a small army, a *Limitless Complex*, dozens of *Seven Star Masters*, and even one *Master of Seven Great Stars* with a *Manticore Heart*! How?! How the hell could one person singlehandedly defeat such a force?!"

"You underestimated him, although I warned you a long time ago," Izao replied, looking out the window at the fantastic view of the icy wasteland. "Had you helped us, our chances would've been greater. But you were cowards."

They were in the Eversteins' secret shelter, built in the icy ocean at the very edge of the south pole, in the depths of Insulaii's largest anomaly. Without the Eye of the Void, it was almost impossible to find it.

"Shut up! Do you hear me?! Shut up!" Victor growled. "Just because I let you into this place doesn't mean you can speak to me like that! Our task was to create an entrance and an exit, which we did! And you... You didn't do a damn thing! You ran away when he came to reclaim the Purple Temple!"

Izao was silent.

"We shouldn't have used the *Complex* to break through the barrier," Varimas said wearily. "It entered the battle with only half the energy reserve, while theirs was full. Not to mention that they have generator crystals."

"As if that alone could lead to such an outcome!" Victor snorted. "How did he defeat you and your brothers?"

Varimas pursed his lips, and then said in a low voice:

"There is a possibility that he is a deity reincarnated with the help of an artifact of the First Ones."

Looking out the window, Izao stayed silent. Victor froze in his tracks.

"Are you serious? But how? Who?"

"One of the leaders of the old Destroyer's army."

Suddenly, the door opened and Yolana entered the room.

"What's the prognosis?" Victor asked, his voice softening at the sight of his wife.

"Their eyes haven't yet fully recovered after breaking through the planetary barrier. We'll need another thirty minutes or so to prepare for another strike."

"Very well."

Having stopped pacing, Victor sat on the sofa and thought. Yolana sat down next to him but didn't distract him. Minutes passed, and no one was in a hurry to break the silence until both sylphs suddenly jumped up with their Eyes half open.

Before anyone realized that the blackness of a dimensional rift had opened up in the middle of the room, Varimas had already been cut in half. It was his bloodline that Kai was guided by, using energy vision, the Eternal Throne, and the obtained *Manticore Hearts*.

Ignoring everyone, Kai leaped at Izao. He was about to kill him, when the space flooded with a bright white light and he lost the sensations in his entire body. His eyes beheld a vast darkness dotted with myriads of stars.

The Eversteins had prepared for a possible attack. Thirty Eyes of the Void and the core of Varimas's *Complex* was the price they had to pay to move anything and anyone into space in an instant.

Kai unexpectedly lost contact with the Eternal Throne and found himself surrounded by many *Masters of Seven Stars*, who were no longer affected by Insulaii's restrictions.

He had fallen into a trap.

"Don't think this'll stop me," came his cold voice.

Chapter 35
COMPLETELY DIFFERENT LEAGUES

My body burns with pain. But it's a pleasant, sweet pain. The pain of power.

Memories flashed before my mind's eye: two familiar purple eyes, two eyes of mismatched colors, a white mask, and a white-blue eye without a pupil. Kyle, Green, Nomen, Magnus — you are all nothing compared to them. Unions, Rosen, Izao, O'Crimes, and Eversteins are just stepping stones on my path.

It's even funny. Here they are, surrounding me. No restrictions. They're watching me. They think they got me. That their trap worked. How naive...

But they can't stop me now.

***

Before anyone had time to realize anything, Kai was next to Izao. After merging with Viola and maxing out the *Borrowing Flame*, he burned up all of himself and brought the brunt of this power upon his opponent. Grinning at his attempt, Izao materialized a spear and blocked the blow.

The blades collided in a shower of sparks when Kai felt something try to invade his mind and soul. Aware that he couldn't handle such an amount of pressure in his current state, he summoned several large crystals from his pocket. Made out of energy crystalized at a high pressure, they acted like miniature bombs.

The explosion was supposed to destroy everything within a radius of hundreds of miles, only it didn't go that far. Opening the Eyes, Victor and Yolana expanded the space around Kai and Izao, cutting them off with an artificial horizon and sealing all of them in a spatial labyrinth.

A moment later, everyone among the Eversteins felt a growing threat. Reacting quickly, they activated their best defensive techniques and artifacts, but they couldn't see or feel anyone even with the Eyes.

And then Kai appeared before them from another time stream of *Ice Reflection*, his eyes flashing brightly as all the *prana* around them disappeared. Clad in a milky white crystalline armor of runic mist, he radiated a growing aura of overwhelming power. But he didn't attack. Instead, he continued to hang motionless in the void.

The dumbfounded Eversteins unleashed their techniques, not daring to approach, but their attacks disappeared as soon as they got close enough.

Ignoring the pressure of the *Will* and *Spheres* surrounding him, Kai disappeared, turning almost a dozen Eversteins closest to him into bloody lumps.

Their sacrifice bought their brothers and sisters enough time to open their Eyes and prepare a massive attack that threw Kai to the side before he could reach their leaders. Turning mid-flight, he tried to change his trajectory, but failed. With the power of their bloodline, the Eversteins distorted and tangled the space so much that Kai couldn't break through to them.

Kai was rushing from side to side until he was surrounded by a group of nine *Masters of Seven Big Stars*. Deprived of the weaves, they were going to use the only power available to them besides the raw elemental energy. Their cores opened and unleashed the power of their most powerful abilities. Kai's eyes glowed, and instead of him dying, two *Masters* vanished in a blink of an eye.

Advanced?! Victor was shocked. *Bastard! How come Varimas and Izao failed to recognize the* Advanced Will of Space?! *Or have they missed it? Where did he get it from anyway? Can he really be a reincarnated deity...?*

"This is not going well. I'm going all in."

"No. It's too risky," Yolana objected, concentrating on supporting her clan mates and distorting the space around Kai.

"I have no choice. Without energy, we won't get far. We don't know how long he can last, and we can't hold on forever. Cover me."

Yolana clenched her teeth and nodded.

Giving her a reassuring smile, Victor dashed forward, entered the labyrinth and appeared behind Kai. Sensing him, Kai turned around and defended himself from the *Chaos Strikes*. Without even touching Kai, Victor's fist released a monstrous gravitational wave. Focusing all its power in a single spot, he aimed to destroy the armor but only managed to create a small crack in it.

Kai's blades sliced through space, but Victor was no longer there. He constantly flickered around his target with incredible speed, inflicting more and more damage. He had spent almost half of his available core power when he realized that he was only able to break through the first layer of Kai's armor. And that was with the support of the other seven *Masters*.

"One more attack! Aim for the torso! You need to hurt his soul!" Victor ordered.

He almost unleashed another *Chaos Strike* when Kai's aura began to emit even greater power. His body was aflame, burning up before Victor's very eyes. The *Touch of Nothingness* obliterated everyone in Kai's immediate surroundings. Victor remained standing only thanks to his worn-out, but resilient and high-quality divine armor.

Kai exploded into hundreds of false *Holy Punishments,* destroying the spatial labyrinth. Despite the loses, there were many Eversteins who managed to survive his suicidal attack. For a moment, they thought they were safe, but then they noticed that the overwhelming sense of danger hadn't gone away.

Having distracted his opponents and hid in another time stream, Kai finally escaped from the constantly distorting spatial labyrinth. Before anyone could figure out where he had gone, his sword hit Yolana's armor with frightening force.

Quick on her feet, Yolana reacted before the blade reached her soul. She teleported, but still couldn't get away from Kai even in the space they created themselves. His grip tightened on Yolana's helmet, after which the milky white crystal began to coat her armor and connect their bodies.

"I can't… Too… Too much energy. I can't… break free," she gasped, trying to teleport and break away.

Kai's blade continued to press against her armor.

Succumbing to the pressure and exhaustion, Yolana eventually stopped trying to escape. Instead, she moved closer to her husband.

As soon as Victor saw her, he rushed at Kai and began to beat him furiously, putting maximum strength into each blow. The rest of the sylphs joined him, but Kai paid no heed to their attacks. He continued to pierce Yolana's armor. At the moment, she was his biggest threat. Owning the best control of the Eye of the Void, she was keeping the other Eversteins out of danger, moving them away whenever he got too close to them. He needed to eliminate her as soon as possible if he wanted to wrap this up before he ran out of energy.

The first cracks began to appear in Yolana's helmet and armor. Putting all of himself into the blows, Victor furiously hit Kai's blade, trying to keep him away from his wife. But the sword had already penetrated the many layers of the crystal that had merged with Yolana's body.

"No, no, no!"

Victor watched with horror as the broken pieces of the armor turned into runic mist and returned to Kai.

Not sparing energy, Kai intensified the power of the *Borrowing Flame*, and activated three soul manifestations at once. The *Untamable Stream* released almost ninety percent of his soul's energy that he shot out of himself with *Everything and Now*. At the same time, he used the *Perfect Soul* to drain his *Shell* in exchange for even more strength.

The *Tattoo* was activated, too. *Primal Flash* strengthened his body and armor with compressed power of the *Yang* as the multiple *Touches of Nothingness* focused at the tip of the blade continued to destroy Yolana's armor. He topped it all off with another particle of the *Trophy*, which allowed him to use even more energy.

The armor began to crack as Kai's blades, enhanced by *Advanced Sword Will* and energy, slowly sank deeper and deeper into the crystal. Victor almost went mad at the sight. Screaming, he desperately hit Kai.

"Let her go!!!" he shouted, his voice hoarse. "Let her go, you bastard!!!"

"It's... no use," Yolana whispered softly. "Victor... I'm sorry..."

"No!"

With the expression of true horror on his face, Victor reached out to his wife. But he never got a hold of her. Disappearing, he reappeared thousands of miles away. Yolana's Eye burst and closed, but she had no regrets.

Closing her eyes, she contacted the remaining Eversteins. After a few seconds of manipulating space, many of them began to fly away.

Kai's sword finally broke through the armor, piercing Yolana's *Shell* as well. But he was too late. Aware of her demise, Yolana had already sacrificed her soul. If she was to die, she was determined to take Kai with her.

The space around the two of them began to distort into a rapidly growing black dot. Kai's armor crackled as he tried in vain to break free. The dying Yolana firmly held his sword and his hand, freezing the space around them. Kai briefly entertained the idea of cutting off a limb to escape but dismissed it. He wasn't going to leave Viola behind.

Having reached a critical size, the miniature black hole began to devour the two. Most of Kai's body had been swallowed when he powered up again, unleashing bolts of energy in all directions, but the attack was immediately pulled back. In the end, there was nothing left. The *Masters*, pale from exhaustion, stopped maintaining the spatial distortion.

A black hole hung in Insulaii's orbit, absorbing the remnants of the explosion as it shrank.

The remaining Eversteins looked at their creation in disbelief when one of them extended his hand in horror, pointing at a piece of flesh that materialized out of thin air.

Kai was alive. Barely, but he was alive. More than seventy percent of his *Astral* body was damaged, he had exhausted his bloodline, lost almost all of the armor, and used a *Renewal Rune* to activate another *Ice Reflection*, but he was alive.

The exhausted Eversteins were quick, but not enough to prevent Kai from rebuilding himself from a lump of flesh and begin healing his *Astral Body* by introducing artificial energy into his *Spark*.

Dodging their attacks, Kai decapitated a dozen sylphs. Not having enough strength to distort the space around him, the remaining Eversteins began to run.

Having finished with the most stubborn ones, Kai looked toward the distant Ferox. After thinking for a while, he decided to not go after the fugitives. He had almost no strength left.

The victory was costly, but it was his. He was two *Trophy* particles and almost a billion Runes short, having used them on the armor. Three *Runes of Renewal* out of the seven that appeared in Insulaii *Altars* were spent to save his life, as well as one of the three elixirs developed from the angel's flesh. Also, for the first time, he completely merged with Viola. Normally, due to the difference in development, this threatened to destroy his body, soul, and *Spark*, but the increase in *Willpower* gained from the *Trophy* allowed him to withstand such a load. Lastly, he merged with Zero — a completely new clone, which consisted of the bodies and souls of four ordinary clones.

It was Zero who went with Shacks to Ferox, under Acilla's disguise technique. Having dealt with Bjorn, he found the *Altar* on the top floor of the ancient city and returned to Insulaii, where he restored the spent energy in the ATS.

Only after that did Kai go after his enemies.

Unfortunately, a huge amount of effort, time, and resources had to be expended on the creation of Zero, so he existed in a single copy until Kai sacrificed him to escape from the black hole.

And yet, Kai didn't regret it. After all, not only was Zero many times stronger than his brothers, but he also had the ability to merge with his creator, transferring his strength, *Force* particles, and *Will* to him. It was thanks to the *Trophy*, Zero, and Viola that the pressure of the Eversteins' *Willpower* had little effect on him.

Throughout the battle, he was faster, stronger, and sturdier than most of his opponents. And this was without taking into account his armor, *Advanced Will of Space*, and other abilities.

Varimas was the only one who could oppose him without Insulaii's restrictions. Fortunately, Kai managed to eliminate him at the very beginning and claim his *Manticore Heart*.

As for Izao...

The bastard had fled.

"You won't get far."

Closing his eyes, Kai concentrated on spirit perception.

He'd sniff him out like a bloodhound if he had to.

Sensing a trail, he immediately took off in pursuit.

Izao wouldn't escape.

Not this time.

Chapter 36
ANOTHER WAY

The blue-green vortex of the large portal twisted in a spiral and shrank, hanging nearby as Kai contemplated the situation. Izao's tracks led to the dimensional passage, but continuing further was risky in his current situation. Viola was resting, his *Astral Body* was recovering, and his soul energy and bloodline reserves were nearly depleted. Not to mention that he was feeling weak and that his *Shell* had almost dried up after everything he had been through today.

Another issue was the portal itself. The fact that it was open reeked of a setup. Kai could send a clone over or pull a similar trick to check whatever was on the other side. Then again, knowing Izao, he probably counted exactly on that.

Let's see how smart you are. I'm ready to play your game. You won't run away this time!

Having created a clone from the surviving parts of Zero's soul, Kai sent him to the other side.

Due to fatigue, Kai couldn't control the clone or see through his eyes, but he didn't need to. All the souls used to make Zero had strong *Will* and techniques, so Two-Hundred-And-Ninety, whose soul broke through this time, returned rather quickly. After the fight, he was also weak but had enough strength to maintain invisibility. Flying up to Kai, he shared with him what he saw.

Kai learned that there were many dead cultists on the other side. There were no detectable auras or traps either. By the looks of it, there was no ambush. After slight hesitation, Kai decided to send the clone back in, just in case.

Kai waited for about a minute before going after him. The Trial Worlds immediately requested the activation of the *Pass* and informed him that he had arrived on Ferox.

Two-Hundred-And-Ninety's report was correct. The other side was littered with corpses. And judging by their robes, they were representatives of the House of Dolls. How and why they ended up in the center of some underground base at the bottom of the ocean he had no clue.

Grimacing at the stench of death and decay that permeated both the physical air and the energy streams, Kai continued to explore. He sensed three functioning auras somewhere deep within the complex. The weakest of them seemed to belong to Izao. He was slowly dying.

Turning to the portal, Kai pondered. Did whoever killed these people leave the passage open for him so that he'd witness Izao's demise? But why?

He wouldn't have purposefully fled to a base that was under attack. No. Someone must've followed after him. Which means I was being watched... Kai frowned. *But who was watching?*

There was only one way to find out.

Using *Phantom Steps*, Kai headed toward the auras. He came to a stop in front of a pair of massive, but destroyed gates that lead to a network of underground caves.

"Sir." Two-Hundred-And-Ninety turned around at the sight of him and nodded.

"Follow me."

As they reached the center cave, Kai slowly stepped toward the only living beings in this place.

Nailed to the cave wall with his own spear, Izao was bleeding heavily. He was missing an eye and several limbs, but the cause of his pain wasn't physical, but spiritual. Something terrible had happened to his *Shell*, and it could no longer maintain its integrity.

Next to him, on one of the stones sat a man with a familiar aura, his head hanging low. Nearby stood a cloaked figure, with thin strands of blond hair spilling from under its hood. Darkness obscured the figure's face in an unnatural manner, leaving only two flaming dots. Grasped in their hands was a pair of smoky swords. It was the same cultivator the clones had encountered on the Ark and were forced to forget.

"You came," muttered the sitting man. His face was obscured by long black hair. "I didn't know whether to reveal the truth or keep it a secret. In the end, I decided to leave it to fate."

With a sigh, he stood up.

He was tall, dressed in simple dark robes. His eyes were now scarlet, matching the asymmetrical symbol carved into his forehead and bridge of his nose.

Kai knew that grim face well.

It was the face of the strongest *Exorcist* on Insulaii.

The face of Ryu Araki.

"What's the meaning of this?" Kai asked. For the first

time in a long while, he didn't know what to think.

"Are you talking about me or Izao?"

"About everything."

"Then it's better to start from the end." Ryu sat back on the stone. "I did this to him. Unfortunately, after going through his memory, I realized that this isn't the real Izao."

"He managed to run away then?"

"No, not really. This one," Ryu nodded at the dying elf next to him, "was inside Ivsim. However, it's only a copy. A fake. The real one forced his personality upon one of the High Apostles of the House of Dolls. As for Ivsim, he was his puppet since the Belteise Labyrinth and he was watching you since your first months in the Trial Worlds."

"So soon? But then..."

Kai realized that if he had broken his promise and killed Izao, it wouldn't have changed anything. There was no right choice. Of all the things to take into account, Izao didn't take just one — Ryu.

All this time, it was Izao hidden in Ivsim's body, passing information to the Vinaris and giving away their hiding position. Connected to the original, the fake observed. Kai had no idea how the two communicated, but whatever method they employed, it was so discreet that even Shacks remained unaware of their little scheme. Kai hated to admit it, but Izao was clever. Not once did he take the bait when Shacks gave them incorrect data about their route in hopes of uncovering the traitor.

"But how?" Kai pondered aloud. "How did he remain undetected in the *Complex* and in the ATS?"

"Izao had a *Complex*, made by the Higher One. It disguised the fake's thoughts and reimbursed all the energy for an extra soul in your ATS. When the Manticores attacked, he seized full control of Ivsim and traveled outside the Ark, taking Lily with him. He then placed her in his *Complex*, and sent it to Bellum. Seems the planetary barrier didn't react to it. Lily returned already different. I imagine his *Complex's* ATS is faster than ours since Lily aged a lot in just two and a half days."

"The attack of Diana's doll, Malvur's weird behavior, as well as the deaths of Zhou Han Nam's granddaughter and Kuro… Was he behind all this?"

"Yes." Ryu nodded. "Sometimes it was Izao himself, and sometimes, his copy helped."

Kai pondered for a moment.

"But how could the copy know all these details? Did he plan to erase everything from the copy's memory in case it was captured?"

"Yes. But his specialty is control, not memory manipulation. Therefore, the power of his *Spheres* was insufficient to erase everything. I not only managed to stop his technique, but I also restored the previously deleted memories."

"But why Ivsim? And for how long has this been going on?"

"I don't know. Though, I assume it has something to do with him being a deranged lunatic. Ivsim and Lily love each other, so he could hurt one by hurting the other. As for the second question… Izao had been manipulating Ivsim since the divine Labyrinth on Belteise. But thanks to the *Complex* and the absence of any activity on Izao's part, even Sawan was unable to notice him."

"What about the child? Did he lie about that, too?"

"I'm sorry, but no. During Lily's stay in the ATS, Izao found a way to halt the child's development, resuming it when she returned to the outside world."

"Do you know who he worked for? Who gave him a *Complex*? And why? I still find it hard to believe that this is just about revenge."

"Izao did a particularly good job of erasing memories related to his goal. His own included. It's the only thing I haven't been able to recover. Even he doesn't know the answer to the first question. All I know is that it's a woman, since they referred to their employer as a 'lady who appears in a dream.' Izao speculates that it might be Tel'Naal, who mysteriously disappeared after the battle for the Heavenly Throne."

"I see..." Kai sighed, remembering many the other oddities related to the last contenders for the Heavenly Throne.

The *Tattoo*, the *Azure Cube*, Yashnir's sword in the destroyed Spirit Temple, and the Manticores, announcing the rebirth of the Destroyer. Eva, Eria, the Sinams, and the Eversteins. They all had La'Gert's five-eyed marks. Izao and Chag, who were probably working for Tel'Naal. And, finally, Belteise — an empire born from the "seeds" of the Heavenly Night. Was it a coincidence that he kept running into things linked to the three beings that once ruled the Ecumene? He doubted it.

"Izao woke up in Ivsim only in the Trial Worlds," Ryu continued. "Before the collision with the Vinaris, no one suspected that there was a traitor. In these six months, he contacted the Cult, became the Puppeteer's apprentice, and acquired knowledge pertaining to the heritages of the Houses of Blood and Famine in exchange for the right to use his *Complex*. But not the ATS. It was then that he created his copy and planted it in Ivsim."

"And who is this?" Kai nodded at the hooded figure. "Also, what happened to your appearance and soul? Actually, why are you here at all?"

"My appearance?" Ryu touched his face in surprise and felt the symbol on his forehead. "I sometimes forget about that... It must be the *Duelist's Mark*. Let me tell you my story, my ex-teacher. I hope you'll find it interesting enough. After completing the Road, I received a technique scroll made by the creator of the Trial Worlds. But this scroll wasn't real, tangible. I couldn't open it and I couldn't tell anyone about it. Until the war... Then the scroll opened, modifying my soul multiple times. The *Heavenly Mortal Style* became its basis, *Soul Concealment* made me invisible in the eyes of the *System* and anyone I wished, and the *Duelist's Mark* let me embark on the *One Path* and use its techniques. So far, I mastered only one of the five, but it's quite interesting — it's called *Infinite Potential*. At first, I didn't understand exactly how it worked as it was all rather intuitive. But after a while it became pretty clear..."

Ryu turned to the hooded figure.

"...It is based on the dark arts."

"Really? The Worlds' creator dabbled in those?"

"It would seem so." Ryu nodded. "For a while, I wasn't sure what to do. The technique would give me strength that I so desperately needed but I didn't want to violate the Temple's philosophy. In the end, I gave it up. I needed time to think it over. Then I ran into one of the rebel informants during the purge, that hadn't yet been contacted by Sirius and your clones. This old man had long since retired. Most thought he was dead. But he stubbornly clung to life when we fought against each other, and I couldn't but admire that. He agreed to become my right hand after he lost to me in the

Contender's Duel. Since then I wasn't sure that I want to use those powers, I shared them with him through a *Soul Particle*. We have a strange bond, so I gave him *Soul Concealment* and the *Duelist's Mark* so that he would use them to protect the empire. It was he who sensed that an adept of the dark arts was inside Ivsim. He didn't know who it was, though."

Standing up, Ryu looked Kai straight in the eyes.

"In the end, however... I realized that this wasn't enough, that acting through another man I can't achieve my goals. That my decision not to accept that power is wrong. I could no longer tolerate my weakness, so I took back the *Duelist's Mark*."

"Do you think it's the right choice? And what does it do exactly?"

"I think it is. It allows you to establish a connection with another soul. As the name implies, during a duel. In case of victory, it gives you power over it. What you do with it depends on your techniques..."

"And with *Infinite Potential*..."

"...I can acquire other people's knowledge, experience, and talent. And since the old man served in all five Houses during his lifetime, I received a lot of information about them. I learned many secrets of the dark arts, but don't worry, that's not really my future road. I don't intend to become a Cultist and use their tools. My path is to acquire the talent of those I managed to defeat in a fair fight."

"And if you give in to temptation? If you decide that you want even more?"

"A man should be driven by his desire to improve, not his thirst for power," Ryu said. "That's exactly what I plan to do. Cultists strive for power. At any cost. They don't care about development. You can't cheat your way to greatness."

"But the Temple's teachings…"

"The *Temple's* teachings, yes." Ryu nodded. "*Your* teachings. *Your* philosophy. Based on *your* worldview and experience. What about those without such vast experience? What about all those who have already reached their peak? What about those who have nothing else to improve?"

Ryu took a short pause so that Kai could think about his questions, and then continued.

"Master Six said that we use *Spirit Fruits* and alchemy because we can only do so much on our own. At some point, we hit a wall. I've been trying to tear mine down for a while now. And now what? How should I cultivate further if I have come to the end of my path?"

"You can always find new ways to improve," Kai told him. "We've already talked about this. You will need a lot of rare resources, but this isn't the end of the world. You can become a *Master of Seven Big Stars* someday, and maybe even the *Master of Seven Great Stars*."

"That's funny, coming from someone whose path stretches into infinity. *Seven Big Stars*? Maybe, with a lot of work and expensive resources. *Seven Great Stars*? Not in a million years. Not without a miracle. And even if I manage, then what? There will always be someone stronger. And while I don't care about the power difference, I'm torn apart by the fact that I can never do anything about it. I can't keep getting better."

"So, you're just going to give up?"

"No. That would be the easy way out, wouldn't it?" Ryu chuckled. "To give up and keel over. I might as well just die. No. If I want to continue my journey, then I must do whatever will allow me to continue to improve. Before, I had *Fruits* and alchemy. Now, I have the dark arts."

"Once again I must ask — what if you give in to temptation?"

"I won't," Ryu replied firmly. "I crave power, but my desire to become better is higher than mere greed. It's at the core of my being. Stealing their strength, their parameters and mastery would be easy, but I'm not going to do that. I'll only borrow their knowledge and talent, so that I could use it to improve further."

There was silence. Kai didn't know what to say. Ryu had already made a decision. There was no talking him out of it.

"You will probably never understand this, but that's fine." Ryu lowered his head. "I'm sorry. I appreciate all you did for me, I truly do. There's no longer a place for me in the Temple, but I don't want to leave it. I have embarked on this path to be able to protect what is precious to me." Ryu smiled grimly. "Just as we were taught. So, I will continue to serve the Temple in my own way. I will become its shadow, which it sometimes needs so much. I will become its darkness, destroying its enemies. I understand why you did it. Why you put the Ark in jeopardy, forcing the Manticores to attack. And yet… I hope I'll never have a reason to consider you a threat to the Temple. Thank you for everything, and goodbye."

Epilogue

There wasn't an *Altar* at the House of Doll's underground base, so Kai had to reason to stick around. Having exhausted the remnants of the already activated *Trophy's* power on destroying this place and covering his traces, he flew to the nearest branch of one of the Temples, from where he moved to Insulaii.

He didn't see the point in even trying to go after Ryu. The boy was too far gone.

Kai and Two-Hundred-and-Ninety, whose memories of Ryu and Kai's conversation were erased, returned to the Ark. The battle had ended with the Temple's victory.

Resting on the Throne, Kai requested a full report from Ulu.

"...out of more than one hundred and twenty thousand enemy troops, about twenty-four thousand survived," Ulu concluded the briefing. *"Most of them are mercenaries, but there are also low-ranking members of the Mountain Sect Alliance and the Vinari Clan who weren't bound by strict contracts and who surrendered after the death of their leaders. Unfortunately, there isn't a single high-class* Master *among them, as they all refused to surrender, choosing to die in battle instead. All the prisoners have been taken to the dungeon, where*

they remain under increased surveillance. We need to decide what to do with them."

Kai sat silent for a few seconds.

"Release from spiritual contracts all craftsmen and artisans among them. They will take an oath of service, given tools and resources, and be sent to a desert island. Let them work for the good of the Temple and pay compensation for their wrongdoings through their craft."

"For how long?"

"Five thousand years."

"Why not forever?"

"No one would ever agree to eternal slavery."

"Very well."

"The only exceptions will be those who are too heavily burdened with oaths and promises. They, as well as for the rest of the prisoners, will also serve for the benefit of the Temple in another way, in a new training dungeon, becoming its new resource."

"Resource?"

"They will be used for education and training of our members, as well as for experiments, should they misbehave. Nyako mentioned that she needs many people. Also, they can be used to aid in construction."

"Will this not lead to an uprising? These people hoped for a better outcome when they surrendered."

"Don't worry about that. I will swear by the System that those of them who survive a hundred years of imprisonment will be released. It will give them hope and reduce the chances of an uprising."

The decision was cruel and reminiscent of the dark arts, but… They were the enemy. In the future, Kai knew well that he'd face even more of those who would go against him. He was obliged to strike fear into the hearts of anyone who might try to follow in their footsteps, Kai couldn't allow himself to show even a sliver of mercy. This world was cruel, and it'd be best if they all came to terms with that. It was his decision and he was ready to take responsibility for that. None had ever said to him that the road to the Heavens would be easy.

Having discussed the details and sent Ulu on her way, Kai meditated for a while before going to the *Altar*. Entering the coordinates of another *Altar* on Ferox, he disappeared. Normally, the transfer to another world would be interrupted, but the Arches and the Ark's *Altar* were connected to the array interacting with the planetary barrier.

In the blink of an eye, Kai found himself in the ancient city under the Heavenly Tree. After defeating Bjorn, Zero found the amulets that operated the mechanisms and changed their settings. The Ants wouldn't bother them anymore, and the Temple now had a direct connection with the ancient city.

Using the "master" amulet, Kai found Shacks and Acilla, who had lost their way without their guides.

Returning with them to the sixth floor at the *Altar*, Kai informed them about what had happened.

"Man, you were having all the fun while we were stuck here…" Shacks sighed. "How does this keep happening?"

"I think this will be the perfect place for the Ferox branch of the Temple. Perhaps we could make it our main city after the Exodus from Insulaii," Kai said, looking around.

"There is a lot of work to be done, but..."

"What about the *Berries*?" Shacks asked. "Was it all a lie?"

The corners of Kai's mouth twitched, indicating a barely perceptible smile.

"There." He extended his hand toward the largest beehive on the top floor. "Even with these amulets, we can't get there, but I saw these three blazing dots. They are definitely there, and it's only a matter of time before we get to them."

But even with the Eyes of the Void he had obtained during his fight with the Eversteins, it wouldn't be possible to do this anytime soon.

The *Berries* would have to wait.

***

Dangling his feet over the edge of the building, Shacks observed the horizon.

"Ah, there you are... The man of the hour."

"I wouldn't say that." Kai sat down next to him. "I think I'll lay low for this one."

In front of them, a sea of people stirred, itching for battle. They meditated, checked their equipment, and prepared artillery and defensive arrays, waiting for the moment when the clones would finish setting up the transfer array in the center of enemy territory. With it, they'd have a shot at a surprise attack.

The Temple's base was the area near the abandoned *Altar* in the destroyed town of Bellum. Their target was the Mountain Sect Alliance. Weakened after the fights in the ice dimension and on the Ark, they would be easy prey. It was time to pay them in kind.

"With any luck, we'll draw out the remaining four Manticores," Shacks sneered.

"Don't underestimate them. Especially here on Bellum."

"You worry too much. We have enough people and firepower. Acilla is a force to be reckoned with. I wouldn't like to be on her bad side!" Grinning, he slapped Kai on the shoulder. "Lilith and I aren't bad either. Push comes to shove, we'll manage to survive until your arrival, and then they won't stand a chance. Right now, we should worry about whether we will have time to capture the key areas and gain a foothold before the Order and the Cult catch wind of this. After all, this is only the beginning..."

In addition to the Mountain Sect Alliance, the Temple needed to deal with the Vinaris and the Eversteins. Kai had special plans for the former since their patriarch became Acilla's puppet, but he considered attacking the latter to be dangerous. Their main forces didn't participate in the attack on the Ark, so they remained strong. Especially on their own territory.

His revenge would have to wait.

"What about the Bright Moon Clan?"

"I took everything that could be taken, including the ATS. I'll send you what little craftsmen we have left. The Bright Moon Clan is officially disbanded."

"You refused to become the patriarch?"

"When did I ever comply with my father's wishes? Honestly, it's like you don't know me."

"Speaking of him... What happened between you two?"

"Ciel turned out to be just a toy in the hands of a more important player. When the Bright Moon Clan — the original one, not what remained of it on Saha — lost the war, its last deity hid. Dying in despair and helplessness, they went mad. They influenced the Bright Moon Altar and left in it not only their experience and knowledge, as it usually happened, but their entire personality. After that, they forced all the surviving carriers of the *Divine Gift* to accept it. The deity died after helping them escape to the depths of the Ecumene. Along with the knowledge, the carriers were given fragments of the deity's personality and one goal — to get to the founder's tomb. Their plan could have worked out, but the more the alien personality was in someone's body, the less of it remained, as it constantly struggled against the *Shell* of the vessel it was inhabiting. Following the will of the deity, the previous patriarch killed himself and passed his memories to the heir — Ciel. He wanted to do the same to me, fill my head with the memories of my predecessors and make me the vessel for our divine's personality."

"Interesting... Does this mean that there are other surviving members of the Bright Moon Clan?"

"Yeah."

"What do you think about all that? Sooner or later, we'll get to the Heavenly world, from where we can get to the Bright Moon Tomb. Was your ancestor really the Destroyer before Yashnir?"

"I don't know. And, I don't want to think about it until we make a complete Exodus."

Kai nodded.

"Seems it's about to start."

"Take care, Shacks."

"You, too, buddy."

As Shacks left after the army, Kai continued to sit alone for a while, watching the portal. After some time, he teleported to the *Altar*. He'd let the Temple deal with this on its own. After all, he couldn't keep an eye on it forever.

Also, he had something else on his mind.

Having chosen the Cursed Continent as the transfer point — the largest super-anomaly on Bellum and all the Trial Worlds — Kai was attacked by the space itself as soon as he appeared there. If it weren't for *Partial Transformation*, he would have been seriously injured. Having subjugated the *prana* in his surroundings and dispelled most of the anomalies around him, Kai soared into the heavens. With a specific location in mind, he rushed south at great speed, destroying all anomalies and disturbing local Spirits in his path.

Within three hours, he reached the edge of the sunken peninsula. Entering the water at full speed, he fought his way through the anomalies all the way to the Ecumene Library.

***

The top of one of the highest mountains on Bellum was covered in blood. Deus Yen Talos looked at the burning ruins of a temple in disbelief. Kagan, his elder brother, the first Master, and the main contender for the post of Supreme Master, lay lifeless on the ground, surrounded by the corpses of dozens of cultists and Formless. The body of Kagan's best friend, the second Master, was lying nearby.

"Satisfied?" Rihanna asked, licking the blood from her hands. "Your main competitors have been eliminated. I have fulfilled my part of the deal."

Deus looked up at her. Rihanna had come here on his

invitation, along with the both Masters. He had dreamed of the day when he would deal with his brother and become the ruler of the Order, but there wasn't a drop of joy in Deus's eyes now.

"Why?" he gritted through his teeth. "Why was it necessary to kill the old man?!"

Turning around, Rihanna looked at the ruins. Deus's mentor, the Supreme Master of the Order, had been conducting a breakthrough to the *Star Emperor Stage* in one of the halls before her arrival.

"It was the best way to get them all in one spot," she replied with a shrug. "They flocked to protect him."

"That wasn't a part of the deal!" Deus growled in rage. "You shouldn't have killed him!"

"You can't make an omelet without cracking a few eggs, as they say," Rihanna said indifferently as she watched the transfer array activate. "I thought you didn't care about this place if you decided to set a trap right here."

But Deus was done listening. Unleashing his energy, he rushed at Rihanna. Her followers jumped in to protect her, taking the brunt of Deus's techniques. To his surprise, his *Path of Mind* seemed to have no effect on anyone.

"Did you really think I'd come unprepared?" she sneered as she stepped onto the array platform. "Finish him off."

"Yes, mistress!" they shouted in unison and threw themselves at their opponent.

Deus roared furiously, killing one adept after another, while Rihanna and her son were swallowed up by a bright flash.

***

"You have put quite a show, mother."

Stepping off the platform, Rihanna gave her son a smile and laughed heartily.

"Things have turned out better than I expected," she said, patting his head. "Come, boy. The real work is yet to begin."

A long time ago, Rihanna offered to help Deus become the Supreme Elder in exchange for several favors. One of these was the assassination of the House of Resistance's Junior Apostle candidates, who remained behind to defend the Wandering Islands on Insulaii. This allowed Rihanna to push her idea of a retaliatory attack on the Council of Houses.

Both events sowed the seeds of war within both the Order and the Cult. And today, those seeds had finally sprouted. A full-blown war between the strongest organizations of the Trial Worlds became inevitable.

Real chaos was approaching. Just as she wanted.

***

"How are things going?" Illarion Yen Talos asked the old man that just entered the room.

"It has reached the boiling point. Now that your father is gone, there is no one to prevent the Order from going into war with the Cult. People are demanding to launch a retaliatory attack. Refusal to do so has been subjected to harsh criticism at best, and threats of murder at worse. Deus is trying to usurp power. He ordered all the *Runes of Truth* purchased at full price to be handed over to him, and gathered those who have the right to buy them at a discount."

Illarion nodded. He also had several *Runes of Truth*.

"I'm not surprised. He doesn't want anyone to know

about his involvement in the deaths of the Supreme Master and his brother."

"If only we could get the truth out to the others instead of hiding here…" The man sighed. "Alas…"

"I'm afraid no one will give us a chance to explain," Illarion agreed gloomily.

"Sir, they are looking for you!" a young man reported, bursting into the room. "They will be here soon!"

Someone cursed.

"Is everyone here?" Illarion got up, examining the gathered crowd that consisted of members of his faction and all those who remained loyal to his father. "In that case, we'll break through. There aren't many of us, but Deus can't act openly yet. Let's use this opportunity to break through to the *Altar*."

"What will we do once we get there, sir?"

"You are still young. The Trials of Bellum haven't left their marks on you, so you can move to another world. As for the others… I managed to visit the treasury before Deus caught on with my plans. All the *Second Pass Runes* are now in my hands."

"Where will we go? Is there a place where he won't be able to reach us?"

"There is." Illarion nodded firmly. "A place called the Eternal Path Temple, located on Insulaii."

***

A huge crowd of people had gathered in the northern part of Kaiser's Ark to say goodbye and pay tribute to their fallen comrades. After the Manticore attack, only ruins remained of the once thriving city. Through the joined effort of both the Temple members and the civilians, the ruins were turned into a beautiful park with a giant sword and shield in the very center, engraved with the names of all those who fell in battle. Among them, near Lily Wayat Stenshet, was Ryu Araki, the truth about whom Kai shared only with his followers. Officially, the boy died defending the island.

"Didn't expect to see you here," Kai told Shacks as they took part in a moment of silence. *"You don't strike me as a mournful man."*

"Likewise," Shacks replied. *"I'm really sorry that she is no longer with us. Even though she hated me with all her heart, the feeling wasn't mutual."*

"Do you wish you could have parted on better terms?"

"Yes. But it can't be helped, can it? Some people are just made to hate each other no matter what. Her hatred fueled her desire for excellence. I don't think she would have made it this far without it. So, in a way, I helped her become better. Ironic, isn't it? I did try my best not to push her too far, though. I did tease her a lot, but I always tried to be there in case she needed something. I wanted her to get better, but not at the cost of her sanity."

"I didn't know you were such a softie."

"I like to keep you on your toes." Shacks chuckled. *"I just wished I could have seen her become a* Master of Seven Small Stars.*"*

"Why?"

"So that I could fight her, of course! I'd challenge her to an epic duel and fake my death. Hopefully, that would have ended her crazy race for power." Shacks sighed. *"Perhaps I should have done it on Belteise. Perhaps she would have stayed with Ivsim there..."*

"You can't blame yourself for such things. You couldn't

have known how things would turn up."

They were silent for a few seconds, when Shacks spoke up again.

"He is here."

"I know."

Once the service was over, they left together with the rest of Temple's highest members. Only they didn't go back inside. Instead, they went east, where they found themselves on top of a high flowering hill.

Sitting on a nearby stone was Ivsim. The grief seemed to have aged him, and his glassy eyes looked emptier than ever before.

"I'm leaving," he said and slowly got up.

Despite the pain Ivsim's confession brought him, Kai kept a straight face, the expression of which had hardly changed since Lily's death.

"I hate to see you go," Kai finally said, "but it's your right. I know this won't mean much to you given the circumstances, but we are always here for you and there will always be a place in the Temple for you to come back to. I am grateful to have met you, Ivsim, and I hope we meet again."

Remembering a scene from a long time ago, Kai extended his hand.

He was sitting on the grass with a stack of special tokens next to him. The Caltea tournament had just started, and he had already passed the qualifiers. Suddenly, a boy with silver hair approached him, armed with a pair of blades.

"Ivsim," he said without any malicious intent and held out his hand for acquaintance. "The second in the rankings, right after you."

"Ushan." Kai answered the handshake, rising to his feet.

Blinking, Kai returned to reality.

Ivsim held out his hand but didn't shake Kai's. Instead, he presented to him a pair of sheathed blades and his Temple robes. Taking the *Spatial Ring* off his finger, he threw the bundle right at Kai's feet.

"I am leaving," he repeated in a tone that implied that he was leaving not only the Temple but the world of cultivation, too.

Kai's hand remained outstretched as Ivsim turned around and walked away.

"Shacks..."

"I wasn't going to do anything. Honestly, I had no intention of messing with his feelings. He has made his choice. Who am I to stand in my friend's way?"

***

Clouds of gas, chunks of ice, biting cold, and the bright radiance of a lone star, nestled in the center of an old star system in which life had never originated. Suddenly, the space near the orbit of the fifth planet distorted, letting through a tall white-haired man with light blue eyes without pupils.

For a moment, he took in the vast emptiness, and then he descended on the surface of the rocky planet. A Mining Station, sparkling with a myriad of lights, appeared in his field of vision, resembling a three-axis gyroscope.

The main task of this superstructure was to search for lifeless, energy-rich planets and extract their spiritual materials. Such Mining Stations were often found in the Near and Middle Worlds. For centuries, they had been enriching thousands of deities from the Central and Heavenly Worlds who owned the largest corporation in the Ecumene — Otrey.

The visitor was about to move toward the station when the space nearby rippled and seemed to freeze. The air became viscous, and the ground underfoot crystalized.

There were thousands of *Star Emperors* lurking in the extra layers of space, but only a small group of *Limitless* and *Higher Ones* dared to approach him. Among them were the most respected and venerated members of the Empire of Night: the supreme elders and patriarchs of the Death Tamers, Nine-Headed Heavenly Hydra, Eye of the Void, Time Lords, and the Sinam clans. As well as the major generals of the Army of Truth, including Ulrich himself. At the head of this small army were Atrazoth's three students: Tel'Naal, La'Gert, and Or'drok Okka Yashnir, in the company of the *Administrators*.

The most powerful beings of Ecumene came here against a single man.

"Hiding under our very noses... How very brave of you," La'Gert said. "You hid your tracks well, creating a whole dimension between the Universal Energy Flows. But that's what got you in trouble. Unable to absorb *prana*, you were forced to buy an incredible amount of *Crystals* every once in a while. Such a big purchase didn't go unnoticed."

"You are a poor liar," the man said. "It was the *System*, wasn't it? It noticed my attempts to understand the *Higher Force of the Spark*."

"You've always been too smart for your own good." La'Gert laughed. "I propose we settle this peacefully. Surrender and do what you should have done a long time ago."

"Surrender? And why would I do that?"

"Because you can't beat us. And you can't escape."

"Is that what you think?" The man chuckled. "Have you forgotten who I am?"

The air around him began to tremble as soon as he said that. The *Limitless* even retreated a couple of steps. Only the *Higher Ones* withstood the pressure, but even they were forced to grit their teeth.

"Answer the question. Do you know who you came for?"

The influence of his *Will* was so strong that it was easier for La'Gert to obey than to resist.

"You… You are the Progenitor of Dragons, the first among them. The strongest creation of the First. A disciple of the Creator himself. The first Lord of the Ecumene, who refused to go beyond the Edge after his masters. The first who walked the *Path of Absorption*. The sole reason for the prohibition of the dark arts in the Ecumene. You are the one who disturbs the world balance and threatens the *System* itself. You are too strong for our universe, Or'drok Okka Magnus, and therefore you must either leave or perish!" he exclaimed.

"Now!" Yashnir shouted.

Until now, they had been stalling for time, waiting for the battle arrays to complete their preparations.

The space around Magnus crystalized, shackling him, and a blinding beam of power descended from the heavens as the *Emperors* and their entourage threw themselves at him.

Suddenly, the light went out, and the deities stared in horror at the unharmed Magnus standing in a pool of magma. Tiny scales framed his eyes, a crown of horns adorned his head, and long claws grew on his hands. Behind him, a tail slashed the air like a whip. It looked like *Partial Transformation*, but it was actually a *Full* one. In their true form, dragons never stopped growing, although their growth slowed down over time. And so, Magnus, who had lived for more than ten billion years, would have been the size of a small star in his true form.

"And that's it?" Magnus tilted his head, condescendingly looking at the shocked deities, and waved his hand.

The reinforced reality cracked, and the entire planet was destroyed.

The *Emperors* died instantly, most of the *Limitless* were critically injured, and only three *Higher Ones* and their closest associates remained almost unharmed, having defended themselves with their powers and weapons to the best of their abilities. In an instant, Magnus was bombarded with attacks capable of tearing a hole through space and time and slaying deities, but he dodged them with ease. It looked almost as if he was playing with them.

"Enough of this."

Extending his hand and releasing his *Will*, Magnus froze his opponents, subjecting them to nightmarish pain that began to break down the shackles around their *Sparks*.

"You know how I said I tried to comprehend the *Higher Force of the Spark*?" he sneered. "I mastered it."

Yashnir shouted furiously and rushed forward. He was told not to use his main ability unless absolutely necessary, but he couldn't think of a better moment than this one to demonstrate his powers of Creation and Destruction.

His sword flared with Light and Darkness, and for the first time in the fight, surprise appeared on Magnus's face, and he was forced to fight back.

A weapon appeared in the dragon's clawed hands — a milky-white crystalline hammer rich with adamantite. Surpassing Yashnir in both strength and skill, Magnus repelled his attack and pinned him to the surface of the collapsing planet with his tail. Yashnir desperately resisted and tried to break free, but he couldn't do anything to resist Magnus's overwhelming power.

Soon, everyone's *Sparks* would go to the World of the Dead. The fight was almost over.

So, another Or'drok, another potential Destroyer... Magnus pondered as he read Yashnir's information field. *No... You're already the one. Interesting. So, that makes, what, five? Why did you even get involved in this?*

Raising the hammer above his head, he was about to end Yashnir, when his body became completely paralyzed for a moment.

At the same time, a figure of a creature with three faces appeared nearby.

"You," Magnus hissed.

Three-Faced, the strongest guardian, and the main defender of the *System*, produced a spear out of his forehead and launched it at the dragon, piercing through his head and the central part of the *Shell*. Behind Magnus, the figure of Atrazoth formed, seated on the Heavenly Throne.

Only the current Lord of the Ecumene could threaten the former.

A moment later, Atrazoth was swept away and Three-Faced was disembodied. The dragon fled, but he was slowly dying.

***

The memory ended, and Magnus opened his eyes — the fusion with the Eye he had recently acquired in the ice dimension was finally completed.

"What a nostalgic fool I am," he said to himself and sighed. "I almost had it all…"

The appearance of Atrazoth and his attack had come as a surprise. Having once sat on the Heavenly Throne, the *Higher One* could no longer leave it, only go beyond the Edge. The Lord of the Ecumene and the Heavenly Throne became one, slowly accumulating strength to go to the Firsts.

And yet Magnus refused such a fate. Breaking the usually unbreakable bond, he left the Heavenly Throne. This shocked the *System* so much that it imposed a ban on the dark arts that gave the dragon such power, and then decided to eliminate the offender.

For billions of years, Magnus hid. He was aware that he would eventually be found, but he never would have guessed that the *System* would allow Atrazoth not only to temporarily break the connection with the Heavenly Throne but even create its projection so that he could continue to power himself. These were such risky and atypical actions for the *System* that because of them, everyone in the Ecumene lost contact with it for several hours. Consequentially, Atrazoth couldn't go beyond the Edge, so he succumbed to his wounds, leaving his disciples wanting revenge.

And they got it, in a way.

Magnus was on the verge of death, but he wasn't ready to part with this world just yet. His Hammer of Souls was yet to be finished, and he'd be damned if he left before he completed his life-long project.

Using the knowledge of the *Cycle of Life*, Magnus came up with a way to be reborn. He knew that he wouldn't be able to restore his *Divine Shell* in all details, but he could try to partially cleanse it and bind it to a new vessel. To do that, he created the Trial Worlds, leaving the Heavenly Exaltation Pagoda, a *Complex* presented to him by the Creator, to take care of everything. The Hammer of Souls, saturated with the power of the strongest *Higher One* the Ecumene has ever seen, was ground into dust and turned into runic fog: the main resource and the main means of defense of the Trial Worlds from the *System*.

Just before his death, Magnus sealed his *Spark* in the Pagoda, preventing it from slipping into the World of the Dead, and from the remains of his body and the *Divine Shell*, he created a powerful Shadow, so that it would finalize the revival of the Dragon Progenitor when the Hammer of Souls was completed.

And this would happen very soon.

Before the beginning of the Harvest drew near.

END OF BOOK 11

Thank you for reading!

Hi everyone!

I hope you enjoyed 11th book of Kai's adventures. I'm glad to share with you that I'm already working hard on book 12.

It will be coming with extra cultivation, more plot twists and epic fights with truly dangerous opponents, the best of the best in all Trial Worlds! The big war is coming, and all the big players are ready to make their move! Forgotten Masters emerge from the shadows and begin their final game!

Let me know in the reviews what you enjoyed the most in this book and the whole series! I read them all and I really appreciate your feedback and support.

Your support means a lot to me. Your ratings and reviews promote the series and help other people to learn about the *Heavenly Throne* universe.

Book 12 should be already available for pre-order. Check it out!

Don't forget to follow me on Amazon, so you don't miss the release of my future books.

For all the latest info, feel free to follow my team who translate the *Throne* on their social networks, or if you have any questions send me an email.

Facebook: Litrpg, GameLit, Wuxia, and Xianxia
Email: yuri.ajinwuxia@gmail.com

Made in United States
Troutdale, OR
08/27/2023

12393971R10332